Born in Adelaide to German immigrants, Kyra Geddes spent her infancy in the South Australian opal fields before moving to Sydney. Following a successful career in marketing, Kyra returned to university to study English and pursue her life-long dream of writing, publishing two short stories and earning the Vice-Chancellor's Award for Academic Excellence. *The Story Thief* is her debut novel, and the culmination of almost a decade of research and writing. When not at her desk, Kyra can often be found visiting one of Sydney's many art galleries or daydreaming about future travel with her husband and two children.

To connect with Kyra please visit:

kyrageddes.com
Instagram: @kyrageddes
Facebook: kyrageddesauthor

Kyra Geddes deftly weaves literature, history and the possibility of truth to give the Drover's Wife a name. In doing so, she invites us to imagine the lives of other women whose stories have been told by men.

Pip Williams

Brimming with evocative, authentic detail, *The Story Thief* brings a fresh, feminist perspective to Australian literature and art. Australian historical fiction at its finest.

Liane Moriarty

A richly textured and immersive novel filled with defining moments, minute detail and compelling insights into the meaning of loss, love and family.

Nicole Alexander

Nuanced and richly layered. A sweeping tale of heartbreak, loss, love, the search for truth and redemption. Poignant, immediate and real.

Tania Blanchard

Raising questions about the telling and ownership of stories, *The Story Thief* is a fascinating meditation on the formative narratives we encounter.

Melissa Ashley

Kyra Geddes might be a debut author, but she is an accomplished writer. With an intriguing premise, crystal-clear prose and an unfaltering sense of pacing, the reader is drawn into the story and held spellbound. *The Story Thief* is wonderful from beginning to end.

BELINDA ALEXANDRA

Richly told and moving, with a beautiful sense of place, *The Story Thief* is a novel to savour.

DIANNE YARWOOD

Vividly drawn – a delightful book.

WENDY SHARPE

The Story Thief is a finely wrought historical novel about those who have been seen, but not seen, in Australian literature and in life.

RYAN O'NEILL

Kyra Geddes artfully weaves literature and history into an epic Australian novel.

DAVID HUNT

The Story Thief

KYRA GEDDES

Kyra Geddes

affirm press

affirm press

First published by Affirm Press in 2024
Bunurong/Boon Wurrung Country
28 Thistlethwaite Street
South Melbourne, VIC 3205
affirmpress.com.au

Affirm Press is located on the unceded land of the Bunurong/Boon Wurrung peoples of the Kulin Nation. Affirm Press pays respect to their Elders past and present.

10 9 8 7 6 5 4 3 2 1

NATIONAL LIBRARY OF AUSTRALIA
A catalogue record for this book is available from the National Library of Australia

ISBN: 9781922992277 (paperback)

Cover design by Andy Warren © Affirm Press
Author photo © über photography
Internal cover image of *The drover's wife* c.1945, oil on canvas, 51.5 x 61.5 cm. National Gallery of Australia, Canberra © Estate of Russell Drysdale and reproduced with permission
Typeset in Garamond Premier Pro by J&M Typesetting
Proudly printed and bound in Australia by the Opus Group

FSC www.fsc.org MIX Paper | Supporting responsible forestry FSC® C001695

Dedicated to my mother, with love,
and to my earliest memories of this country's opal-hearted red interior

No Australian who has wrestled with the ardours and subtleties of resolving this continent in terms of literature will discount Henry Lawson.

MILES FRANKLIN (1942)

Women have a different history. Someone ought to write it down. We're not sheep or shadows, or silly saints the way Mr Lawson would have. There is more to us. More to me than any of them have written, if it comes to that.

BARBARA JEFFERIS, 'THE DROVER'S WIFE' (1980)

Prologue

January 1900

On the morning after my eighth birthday, I awoke to the smell of smoke.

I had been dreaming about yesterday's johnnycakes spread generously with golden syrup and was disappointed when I opened my eyes. The square curtain tacked over the window above my bed had not yet been tied back but already there was enough light to see the whole room. My brothers' shared bed lay empty, but Esther was still fast asleep beside me, her head pressed moistly against my shoulder and, as always, taking up too much of the pillow.

I put my free hand to the ground and as my fingers closed around my birthday gift – a thick book of fairytales in almost perfection condition – they tingled with anticipation; it was not often I had the chance to read before morning chores. Yet the sight of my brothers' unmade bed and the unmistakable stench in the air had set off a sick feeling in my tummy, as though I'd drunk milk left in the sun for too long.

I wriggled out of the bedclothes, taking care not to wake my sister, and peered into Mother and Father's room. Empty. When I reached the large bark kitchen, my footsteps silent on the earthen floor, I found the hearth cold and none of the usual breakfast preparations underway. A cockroach scurried out from behind the dresser, then disappeared into one of the large cracks beneath the kitchen table.

I hurried out to the verandah and circled our small timber house, screwing up my face as the smell of smoke intensified. A glance at the thermometer, hanging crookedly on its rusty hook, showed the mercury nudging its way towards one hundred. Another scorcher on the way.

I stepped off the verandah and ran towards the paddock, looking for Mother or the boys. Father was away, droving. The hot breath of the wind made me run faster and, as I arched my back, I could feel the sweat-damp cotton of my nightdress already beginning to dry. Finally, I caught sight of Mother in the distance, Baby Eadie on her hip.

'Mummy!' I ran towards the lopsided figure in the mulga-dotted landscape. 'What is it?'

'There's fire coming,' she said, clutching the baby to her chest and pointing to the horizon. Our old dog sat beside her, panting softly.

My throat was suddenly hurting, as if I had swallowed a large stone. 'How fast?'

'Don't know.' Mother's nostrils flared as she lifted her face and sniffed at the air. 'Depends on the wind.' She wiped her nose with the edge of her apron, leaving a faint smear of red dust above her lip.

'Where are the boys?' I asked.

'Filling buckets from the soak. I sent them down at first light.' She paused. 'I should've known. I saw it in the colour of the sun last night. Like a picture, it was.'

'The fire might not come this way.' I was pleading. 'You said it came close that last time, when Father was back, but then it turned.'

'Depends on the wind, child. This westerly seems real set in.' She grimaced then kissed my baby sister's head, an instinctive gesture that I had witnessed countless times each day and which left me feeling faintly jealous. 'No more questions, Lillian.' Her voice took on a sharp steel edge.

'Enough time's been wasted already. Where's Esther?'

'Still asleep.' Despite my mounting sense of dread, I was pleased to have woken before my sister. Though barely two years older than me, ten-year-old Esther had always been our mother's chosen helper, and I the baby of the family – up until last year, when Edith was born. Baby Eadie, as we all still called her. As for Tommy and Jacky, they ignored us girls most of the time, begrudgingly completing the chores expected of them and bragging of a different future. At seventeen, Tommy was almost a man now and had gone droving with Father last winter. Soon he would be leaving us for good.

'Why didn't you wake her? Go on and do it now.' She shook her head and grunted. 'After that, you'll ride to your uncle's place and get help. You know the way.'

I gasped. Panic robbed me of the ability to speak as my lungs fought against the smoky air. A flock of black cockatoos passed overhead, their raucous screeching momentarily drowning out the roar of the wind. Despite the warning suggested by their wild cries, they flew slowly, seemingly confident in their ability to outpace any danger.

'Go on now, Lillian. Just do it,' Mother said, her voice as firm and unflinching as her hand when raised in discipline against any of us kids. 'I need Esther to take the baby and see to the house while I get everything else sorted with the boys until your uncle gets here.'

I clenched my fists but said nothing. With spiralling fear, I listened as she began muttering a plan: shift the animals, wet the woollen blankets, cover the wood heap, move any alcohol and lard far from the house.

I had not moved, and Mother abruptly turned to me. 'What's the matter, child? We've no time for any bosh.'

'It's just the smoke. It stings.' I brushed away my tears with the heel of my hand.

She looked into my eyes, her features softening briefly, then gazed back at the smoke-filled horizon. 'All right, my girl,' she said. 'I'll send

Tommy instead. He'll get there the fastest of any of us. You can ride with him to your uncle's place and stay there, out of harm's way. Just do as you're told. Uncle Bill will sound the alarm and ride back here on his own horse. We'll need all the help we can get.'

Relief made me brave. 'Don't worry, Mother. We won't let that fire get within cooee of this place, you'll see.' I took Baby Eadie from her arms.

'Go get Esther and get yourself dressed. I'll send Tommy up with the horse.' Already walking back to the house, she swung around to issue one last instruction. 'Hurry now, my girl, I'm counting on you.'

~

It was Old Mary who told me the news.

'They're all gone, girlie. Gone into the fire.'

I doubled over as if punched in the stomach.

Mary kept talking, and though her voice was soothing and her dark eyes pooled with kindness, I could take in nothing more of what the Aboriginal woman said.

I turned towards the doorway of my uncle's crudely built house where his new girl-wife stood watching me. 'I – I want to go home,' I hiccupped. 'I want to see my mother. I shouldn't have stayed here. I'm needed at home.'

'Home? Don't talk to me no more about home, you stupid little wretch,' my so-called aunt hissed. 'I've got me own troubles to worry about, thanks to you. Your lot have made me into a widow – and here's me not even twenty years old. What in God's name am I s'posed to do now?' She glared at me and spat at the ground, her pregnant belly swollen and protruding, like an accusation.

I opened my mouth to speak but the words wrapped themselves around my dry tongue and turned to dust. I turned and ran, without looking back, without stopping, running even as my breath became one long ragged cough and my legs cried out in pain. For all I knew I was running into the arms of the fire itself. Running to my mother. I could almost hear Baby Eadie, who would be crying and hungry by now, ready for a feed.

I ran until the tears, now tasting of smoke, dried on my cheeks and my legs gave out. I fell to the ground, watching rather than feeling the flakes of ash land on my skin, waiting and hoping for someone to come and get me. After an hour, or perhaps two, it finally dawned on me that no one was coming. That none of them would ever come for me again. Slowly I made my way back to my uncle's lonely shack.

PART ONE

1908–1916

As a girl, she built the usual castles in the air;
but all her girlish hopes and aspirations have long been dead.

Henry Lawson, 'The Drover's Wife' (1892)

Chapter 1

Parlour Day

I awoke to the smell of smoke.

I leaped from my dormitory bed. I must have cried out because the other girls were all sitting up and looking at me with alarm.

'Fire,' I breathed. 'Hurry!'

'Another one?' asked Dora, darting to the window and flinging back the curtain. 'I can't see anything.'

Hilda, though slower to rise, was the first to perceive my mistake. 'Don't open it, Dora. You'll only let more smoke in. It must still be from yesterday.'

Fragments of the prior afternoon started to pierce through my confusion.

'It's all right, Lill. It's just smoke in the air.' Hilda guided me to the large dormer window so I could see for myself. 'The wind must've blown it back our way.'

I rubbed my eyes with both hands, willing them into focus. I was sure I'd heard someone calling out for help. The wail of an infant?

'It's all right, Lill,' repeated Hilda. 'Come on, I'll open the window for you – but just for a few seconds. You'll see.'

The shrill thrum of cicadas entered the room. Though their song of summer was both loud and comforting, my nostrils continued to twitch. Sensing the danger that no one else could perceive, I forced myself to breathe in the smoke-filled air and peered down through the weak blue light of dawn, looking not only at the grounds outside the convent's main school building but also at the Rose Bay bushland encircling it. The scene was just as it should be for this time of morning. Sister Harris was carrying a bucket of kitchen scraps towards the henhouse, Mrs Spicer was watering her geraniums, her husband was carting firewood across the yard, and the sun was just coming up over two steamers crossing paths on the grey-blue harbour below.

I turned to my best friend and sighed pitifully.

Hilda eased the window shut and gently led me back to bed. 'Close your eyes a few more minutes, Lill. It's nearly time for morning prayers anyway.'

The other girls groaned, pulling their sheets over their heads in protest.

I lay in my bed, ashamed and still trembling, while Hilda stilled any further complaints. The dormitory became quiet once more. Now the window had been opened, the air was even more acrid than before, and shutting my eyes only made it worse.

I blinked a few times and tried to think. There *had* been a bushfire yesterday. It was not just another one of my bad dreams, not this time. Nor was it the first fire I had experienced in my eight years living at Sacred Heart. This one – thankfully – was only small. The fire must have started somewhere nearby, but before it could spread anywhere near the school buildings, Mr Spicer and the other men had succeeded in driving it down to the water's edge, where it put itself out, leaving only a narrow line of blackened bush in its trail and a pervasive smell in the air. My breathing began to slow down as my mind finally accepted that the danger had passed. Though modest in size, our resident fire brigade was well-practised and prided itself on the efficiency with which these occasional small summer fires could be extinguished.

According to school folklore, however, it was God Himself who had kept the convent safe right from the start. We had all heard the story of how Reverend-Mother Salmon and the others had miraculously fought off the great fire of 1888 using the power of their devotional garments, a bizarre claim meant to be proven by the fact of Mother Moran's perfectly intact scapular being found among the ashes. Quite how they had stopped the flames was unclear. Nevertheless, when I was younger, I too had faithfully accepted this account, taking comfort from the idea that nothing could harm me here. Inevitably though, as the years passed and my reasoning matured, I came to ask myself why God had not intervened to keep my own family safe during our time of need. Perhaps God's protection could only be earned through unwavering faith. But then what of my baby sister? Surely no one could blame Baby Eadie for lacking faith.

It wasn't only smoke that triggered memories of my past. Sometimes it was the familiar rumbling of possums on the roof at night, reminding me of the hiding my brothers would get for cursing them when they should have been asleep. Other times it was the sight of a young wallaby chewing methodically on tender new leaves and eyeing me from a distance, or the piercing echo of a flock of cockatoos, stark white forms wheeling in a sapphire sky. From there, my thoughts would lead to other half-remembered glimpses from my past: the howl of a wild dog as dusk turned to night; emu tracks, pointed like arrows in the dirt; passing mobs of kangaroos or the occasional lone male; a string of camels outlined against the sunset or a swarm of grasshoppers that filled the air with sound; and the spine-tingling sight of a great big goanna as it scuttled past on all fours, long claws raking the earth. What had happened to all those creatures after the fire? Where were they now if not just in my dreams?

~

If I timed it just right and if the clouds kept their distance that day, the sunlight would hit the chapel's stained-glass windows and cast a rainbow at my feet. Squinting and tilting my head to one side, then the other, it was easy to imagine myself disappearing into that rainbow.

Since Father's death from a sudden fever, barely two years after I had been sent to Sacred Heart, I had all but given up on prayer. But even after that second devastating loss, which had officially left me an orphan, I still drew comfort from being in our school's new chapel, especially during those rare moments, like now, when I could claim this space for myself.

In the beginning, long before Hilda came, I had yearned for more attention, craving touch and something else I could not articulate. But eventually I had come to see my solitude as a kind of blessing, one that allowed me to keep a safe distance between my heart and anyone, or anything, that might come close to it.

Nevertheless, these precious interludes in the chapel did not come often. Most hours of the day were taken up with a strict timetable of lessons, prayer and religious instruction, relieved only partially by the surprisingly delicious meals cooked for us by the French nuns, while our few short periods of scheduled recreation were usually monopolised by communal games such as rounders and *cache-cache*, the French equivalent of hide and seek.

I owed my place here at Sacred Heart in Sydney's eastern suburbs to Mr O'Loughlin, a wealthy Scottish grazier for whom my father had worked. From the moment we met, when he came to rescue me from my uncle's shanty and from his spiteful girl-wife who had barely looked at me during those few weeks I'd had to live with her, I'd been struck by the elderly man's gentle spirit.

'Your father's always been a good worker, Lillian. Honest. Loyal, too.' His pale eyes had glistened. 'That's why, when this evil fire came and took your family – while your da was away droving my sheep, I don't forget that fact – I said to myself, I have a duty to this man.' And then, as I now knew was his habit, Mr O'Loughlin had crossed his chest with a fast and fluid motion, as if whipping cream for a cake.

At the time of my arrival, Mother Scroope had instructed the other girls not to ask questions about my family or why I would not be going home for the holidays. Bull-nosed Ivy had persisted the longest, demanding to know – with her crooked teeth and mean eyes – why my father never came to see me.

'He's a drover, ain't he?' I'd retort, fighting the urge to pinch Ivy's skinny arm and tell her to shut up and mind her own business. 'Father's too busy finding feed for Mr O'Loughlin's sheep over the border. He can't just come whenever he likes, you know.'

My chest tightened in memory of my flimsy excuses. *It's too far for him to come*, I had told myself then. *Surely, he would come if he could.* But another voice, from deep inside, had always known why Father stayed away, and why he had never replied to my letters. For I alone had survived when the others had not.

Kneeling before the altar, I breathed in the calm air of the chapel and sighed as the bitter feeling slowly receded. Despite the heat and lingering smoke outside, the chapel was light and airy, its marble floor remaining cool to the touch. All along its length, softly hued stone walls rose sheer from the floor, arching towards each other to meet at their highest point. I returned my gaze to the five lancet windows above the altar. One for each of them. The large central window was for Mother while the smaller arched windows on either side, graduating downwards in height, lay claim to my brothers, Tommy and Jacky, and to my sisters, hardworking Esther and dear little Baby Eadie.

I took another deep breath and looked up just as morning sunshine flooded in through the stained glass, jewel tones kaleidoscoping before me. As always, the sight of the rainbow filled me with awe, causing the tears, which I had managed to hold in until now, to spill down my hot cheeks like wax from a candle.

A bell rang out in the distance. I rose from my knees with a sigh, brushing away my tears. Convent life was governed by all manner of rules and restrictions, leaving me as tightly bound as the stitched hem of my school uniform, with its coarse holland cloth. And although the feel of hard pavements and floorboards no longer felt strange beneath my feet, there were still days when I longed to remove my black stockings and stiff leather boots and run barefoot into the bush.

~

Later that day, once all traces of smoke had blown away, we were allowed back outside. Being a Saturday, and thus Parlour Day, some of the girls were expecting visitors; Hilda and myself were among them.

'Mr Quong Tart's Tea Rooms!' Hilda sang the words like an anthem, while linking her arm through mine and dancing me around the lawn. 'At the Queen Victoria Building!'

Hilda's mother would soon be here to collect us in the family's newest carriage. Outings between vacations were strictly limited, and we had required a special dispensation, presumably granted in recognition of all that the Fitzwilliam name represented. I adjusted my gloves and allowed a quick squeal of my own to burst out.

Tall, slim and fashionably dressed, Lady Fitzwilliam had a voice like butter and round gliding vowels that confirmed her aristocratic origins. At two o'clock sharp, she stepped down from the carriage to greet us both. Although Hilda had introduced me to her mother on several occasions, I had never been invited to join them on an excursion before today. Having already started bobbing, I wisely reassessed the situation and instead made the full Sacred Heart curtsy: one, two, three, down … four, five, six, up.

Triumphing over the afternoon heat with a palm-leaf fan, Lady

Fitzwilliam stretched languidly on her seat as we rolled out of the school grounds.

'Hilda, darling, why aren't you waving back?' Hilda's mother smiled at the trio of animated faces waving madly from a second-storey window.

'Not to them.' Hilda dismissed them with a nonchalant sweep of her hand. 'Why should I?'

'Please speak nicely of your classmates, Hilda. They look perfectly charming. Such pretty girls, too.'

'And don't they know it!' Hilda rolled her eyes. 'Not one of them would normally give me the time of day. I bet they were just trying to make themselves look good in front of you.'

Torn between loyalty and politeness, I avoided Hilda's knowing glance.

'It's true, Mother. That's how Lillian and I came to be such good friends – wasn't it, Lill?' She turned to me for corroboration.

I nodded reassuringly.

'She was the only one to stick up for me when I first came to Sacred Heart. Those other girls teased me and said I was fatter than a prize-winning cow, and Lill was the only one who defended me.' Hilda gave an audible huff. 'And then another time, when we overheard them saying that even my name was ugly, Lill convinced me they were wrong. She said lots of girls have names like flowers or jewels – like Pearl, Daphne, Ruby or Violet – but that there's more to life than just being a pretty decoration with nothing of value to say.'

Conscious of Lady Fitzwilliam now appraising me with fresh eyes, I almost wished I'd brought a book to hide behind, however ungrateful it might have made me appear. Instead, as the carriage wound its way down New South Head Road towards town, I leaned back in my seat and gazed politely into the distance while Hilda and her mother discussed family matters – talk of the new baby soon to be expected by Hilda's older sister, imminent plans for redecorating, recurring troubles with the servants.

My best friend had often complained to me about her mother, claiming they had nothing in common. Yet as I listened to them talk, stealing quick glances as Lady Fitzwilliam gave a small laugh or stroked Hilda's arm, a painful twinge of jealousy shot through my chest. Hilda didn't know how lucky she was. No matter how hard I tried, Mother's image was slipping ever further from my memory, more of a shape or outline now, than rendered flesh and feature. Sometimes the sound of her reading voice would come to me, or the calloused touch of her hand, but these evocations were always fragile and the moment I tried to grasp hold of them they would elude me like the eye of a needle in a dimly lit room.

The carriage gave a sharp jerk and I flinched, ricocheted back in time to my first carriage ride during my 1500-mile long journey to the convent. Chaperoned by Mr O'Loughlin, we'd travelled all the way from my uncle's shanty to Sydney, the legendary metropolis I knew only from Mother's bedtime stories. If I closed my eyes, I could still hear the crack of the whip from the Cobb & Co. coach and see the clouds of white steam gushing forth from the incoming train at Bourke.

Even harder to forget was the smell of stale beer and the sickening sound of bareknuckle fist fighting outside the Great Western Hotel. Shaking his head with disapproval, Mr O'Loughlin had given the men a wide berth as we entered, shielding me from view, then looked back with concern as their jeering suddenly grew louder. Beside the huddle of shearers, I saw a Chinaman, no older than Tommy. Though he showed no sign of having been amongst the fighting, he stood cowering in fear.

'Poor wretch,' muttered Mr O'Loughlin. 'They mean for him to fight the winner.'

He pushed me further inside the building with strict instructions not to come out. I watched him approach the shearers and whisper something into the ear of the man who'd grabbed hold of the Chinaman's collar, then press something into his hand. Tobacco juice ran down the shearer's jaw as he opened his mouth and bestowed an ugly toothless smile on Mr

O'Loughlin, before letting the Chinaman go free.

'Funny how money always talks,' Mr O'Loughlin had said as he joined me inside and asked the hotelkeeper to show us to our rooms. 'Especially for those who are otherwise hard of hearing.'

Back then, I hadn't understood what he'd meant, but over the years I had seen how he found ways to use his wealth to help those in need, not least of all me. That afternoon in Bourke, Mr O'Loughlin had also given me another piece of advice.

'One mustn't judge a book by its binding, lass. Just because a man has yellow skin, or even black skin, and ours is white, that doesn't make him any less worthy in God's eyes. Lord knows I faced enough discrimination as a Catholic in my younger years, I'm not about to do the same thing to someone else.'

Bleary-eyed and weak the next morning, my window seat on the train had revealed nothing but dusty plains, littered with dead or dying livestock, proof enough that the drought existed in places other than my own forlorn backyard. Then came the unexpected sensation of climbing upwards into the mountains, where the brown landscape gave way to alien grey-green hues, followed by the excitement in the carriage as the train passed through the famous Lithgow Zig Zag on its way to Sydney Terminal.

I think I slept through most of the relatively short onward journey to the school at Rose Bay, riding in the omnibus pulled by the four greys who laboured valiantly up the hill three times each day, forced to repeat their climb over and over like that king from Greek mythology. Finally, I remembered waking up to the spectacular sight of Sydney Harbour, shimmering in the haze of early autumn and dotted with little steamers and pleasure boats. This was immediately followed by my first glimpse of the nuns dressed in their black habits, small faces framed with white goffered coifs, and encountering the peculiar nasal accents – I soon knew as French – with which some of them spoke. My new home could not have been any more different to the one I'd left behind. Most painful of all was the realisation that I was expected to address each of these women as *Mother* or *Sister*, this latter title being reserved for those without teaching responsibilities.

'Do you play the pianoforte, Lillian?' asked Lady Fitzwilliam, abruptly shattering my daydream.

'Unfortunately, no, Lady Fitzwilliam. I've never taken lessons.' I blushed, knowing the additional cost of piano tuition was not something that would naturally occur to her.

'I was hoping you might encourage my daughter to practise more diligently.' Lady Fitzwilliam cast a resigned look at Hilda. 'Her sister sings and plays beautifully, and I'm quite convinced Hilda would be equally accomplished, if only she made more of an effort.'

Hilda frowned, while I felt another stab of envy.

'Drawing then?'

I shook my head again, trying desperately to think of something interesting to say to divert the attention from myself. For the first time, I felt grateful that the nuns had succeeded in removing all traces of my once broad Australian accent.

A diversion came of its own accord as we neared the end of William Street. Hyde Park loomed before us, its cool green perimeter formally signalling the city's importance.

'Mother, can you have the carriage take us down past the harbour before we go on to the tea rooms? It'll give Lillian a chance to see more of town.' Hilda tilted her head to one side and batted her eyelashes. 'Pretty please.'

Lady Fitzwilliam extended a long, graceful arm, glancing down at the delicate diamond watch circling her wrist, then nodded graciously and instructed her driver.

With the city now laid out before us, Lady Fitzwilliam asked no further questions and joined Hilda in pointing out the sights as our carriage turned right onto College Street. Though I shyly returned each of the smiles Lady Fitzwilliam bestowed, I felt awkward in her presence, and wondered how much she had been told about my situation. As the grand society doyenne Hilda had described, she probably spent her days presiding over gala charity events and raising hundreds of pounds in subscriptions for orphanages and the like. Perhaps I was just another poor soul to be pitied? Even so, her smiles appeared genuine and beneath her finely bejewelled exterior I sensed the same kindness of spirit as Hilda possessed.

'Look, that's St Mary's Cathedral,' said Hilda, elbowing me in her eagerness to ensure nothing went unseen. 'I went there years ago with Mother and Father for the opening by Cardinal Moran. You've heard the nuns talk about St Mary's, haven't you, Lill?'

The carriage continued down Macquarie Street, flanked by grand sandstone buildings and elegant townhouses, offering tantalising glimpses of the Botanic Gardens. Obediently, I looked from left to right as Lady Fitzwilliam was called upon to confirm the name of numerous imposing structures – Burdekin House, the hospital, the Royal Mint and too many others to remember. Despite our bird's eye view from the convent, I'd had little idea that all this existed. The world was so much bigger than I had imagined.

The traffic grew heavy. We were forced to a temporary standstill beside a rank of hansom cabs, and I couldn't help but gape at the cabbies in their three-piece suits and flashing gold watch chains. Like a collection of prize roosters they stood in line, chests expanded with self-importance as they puffed on their pipes and stared back at me from under jauntily set bowler hats. Nearby on the pavement, a man was kneeling beside a display of watercolour pictures, his crumpled clothes in stark contrast to most of the passers-by. One lady, covered head to toe in black mourning attire, smiled and dropped a few coins into the artist's upturned hat before continuing her promenade. One day, I vowed, I would come back here and buy a painting myself.

The road steepened as Sydney Harbour came into view, familiar yet different from this vantage point. I counted a dozen or more steamships in port, some docked and others blowing plumes of dark smoke into the air, unwelcome blemishes on an otherwise blue sky. Scattered along Circular Quay, ferry terminals promised passage to various seaside destinations – Manly, Milsons Point and Watsons Bay, home to many of the poor day students who came to Sacred Heart.

'Wharfies,' said Hilda, indicating the men loitering in small groups at the harbour's edge.

My breath quickened at the sight of one man's bearded profile. Something about the way he was leaning against the heavy iron gates, eyes to the ground and back to the water while he chewed his tobacco, reminded me of Father. But this time, on top of my usual reaction – a bilious mixture of guilt, hurt and anger that he'd cast me aside so cruelly after the fire, and even that he had died and left me an orphan – a new feeling came to me: sympathy. I had never once bothered to consider whether he might have been lonely throughout his long months droving, whether he'd had enough to eat or a soft bed in which to sleep. My only thought, then until now, had been of his work keeping him from home. It suddenly occurred to me that Father's premature death might have been caused by despair just as much as by that fever from which he had never recovered.

Elsewhere by the quay, heavily laden draught horses waited patiently or enjoyed a feed from their nosebags. Hilda, uncharacteristically proud, explained how her father's wool was stored and auctioned here from Mort's wool store, before being loaded onto the clipper ships bound for London.

'So, what do you think?' she asked, flinging her arms wide like a priest at his pulpit.

I nodded vigorously. Hilda had been right. Town was jolly exciting.

Detour complete, our driver steered the horses up busy George Street towards the tea rooms at last. Competing with cabs, buggies, electrified trams, brewery wagons, bicycles and all manner of vehicles, our progress was slow and, at times – owing to the frequent presence of potholes – dangerous. Just then, I spotted a group of flannel-shirted navvies hard at work on road repairs. While Lady Fitzwilliam raised a lace-edged handkerchief to her face to cover the smell of hot pitch bubbling from the tar boiler, one of the men looked at me and winked, licking his lips in a way that made me shrink into my seat, suddenly conscious that I was approaching womanhood. Nobody had ever looked at me like that before.

By now, I was beginning to tire of buildings and instead turned my attention to the flower stalls in the middle of an open thoroughfare known as Martin Place, delighted by the huge wicker baskets full of colourful blooms. An elderly couple, both leaning heavily on canes, stopped before one of the umbrella-shaded stalls. The man pointed to a pastel pink posy and looked to his wife for approval. As the flower vendor wrapped the purchase, I grinned to see the wife plant a passionate kiss squarely on her husband's lips. Such romance, even at their age! I wondered if Father had ever bought flowers for Mother here in Sydney when they first met, or whether anyone would ever buy flowers for me?

I thought of last month's *Rentrée*, the official start of the school year. Amidst the rustle of brown paper-wrapped parcels filling the hallway and the clatter of pigskin valises being dragged up the stairs had been the usual talk of picnics and pantomimes, merry-go-rounds and matinees. This year, I'd been caught off guard by a surprising new kind of chatter, although thankfully not yet from Hilda. More than a few of our fellow fifth-formers came back talking of French fizz and flirtations, and wearing dreamy expressions, moderated only by the discomfort of their also recently adopted corsets. Several courtships had apparently progressed to dizzying new heights, and Esme Porter was reported to have received a firm offer of marriage. It was all quite unsettling, and I wasn't sure whether I felt envy or relief that nothing like this was happening to me.

Finally, we approached the Queen Victoria Building. Even from a distance, it was easy to identify from its many copper domes. As the carriage pulled closer, I gasped as the building's full length was revealed. Built on the scale of a grand cathedral, it appeared almost double the size of St Mary's.

'I said you'd be impressed, didn't I?' Hilda laughed.

I could only nod in return as I gawped at the elaborately decorated sandstone exterior.

'Romanesque, I believe,' murmured Lady Fitzwilliam as we alighted one by one.

'It's so hot, I'm positively sweating.' Hilda tugged at her dress.

Lady Fitzwilliam looked at her serenely, eyebrows arched, and shook her head ever so slightly. 'Stand straight, please, Hilda. A young lady's posture speaks volumes.'

I quickly pulled back my own shoulders and lifted my chest, thinking of the chest expanders and other calisthenics equipment newly installed on the lower south verandah, which we girls had dubbed 'The Chamber of Horrors'.

'At night, the whole place is lit up,' said Hilda, waving her arms around in a grand theatrical gesture. 'Not just with gas burners, you know, but real electric light. Lots of the other buildings around here, too.' She gave a loud pant. 'I'm so thirsty, Mother. I could faint.'

Hilda continued her moaning right up to the main entrance. Peering up just in time to glimpse a huddle of marble figures overhead, I found myself in the most ornamental space I could ever imagine. A myriad of colours, textures and shapes vied for my attention – shining balustrades, trachyte stone stairways, stained-glass windows and an intricately tiled mosaic floor that reminded me of a geometry pattern I had once copied out during class. As golden sunshine poured in from the skylights and lit up the abundant riches surrounding us, I felt giddy and disoriented.

Following closely behind Lady Fitzwilliam, we glided through a spacious and elegant room on the ground floor, before ascending a plushly carpeted staircase which led directly to Quong Tart's Elite Hall. Instantly, I felt myself transported to another realm. Surrounded by ferns, fountains and fans, it was as if we had sailed into the mystical Orient. Despite its immense size and exotic decoration, the hall itself was inviting and intimate. Adorning the room were treasures galore: mirrors hand-painted in Japan, according to Lady Fitzwilliam; massive wood-carvings from China; and marble reservoirs in which golden carp swam. The effect was one of exquisite coolness and the heat of the day was washed away, receding into mere memory.

I took my place at the table, holding my breath as the waiter eased my chair into position. A menu was placed into my trembling hands, offering endless choices of soup, fish, entrees, joints and cold joints, poultry, vegetables, salads, entremets, jellies, ices, fruit salads and creams. My eyes began to swim like the fish in the pond. I turned to Hilda, who fortunately had the situation well in hand.

'A large plate of oysters with bread and butter,' she pronounced with confidence, suggesting I have the same. Seeing my horrified reaction, Lady Fitzwilliam tactfully recommended the corned beef and carrots instead.

When the waiter returned, Lady Fitzwilliam ordered our meals and Hilda seized the opportunity to ask which iced fountain drink flavours were on offer that day. 'Wait till you try yours, Lillian. I promise you'll love it. It's the latest thing.'

Before I could reply, Hilda leaned in.

'It was ever so sad when Mr Quong Tart died,' Hilda spoke in a stage whisper. 'You must remember the girls talking about it a few years ago? Murdered right here in his office – bashed with an iron bar and robbed. Can you believe it?'

'Please don't be melodramatic, Hilda. He was not murdered.' Lady Fitzwilliam had also lowered her voice. 'He was attacked, as you said, and then the poor chap never recovered and died a year later. It really was a dreadful business.'

'Everybody loved him. And everybody went to his funeral.' Hilda spoke almost as if she had been there herself. 'Afterwards, lots of people named their racehorses in his honour. Remember, Lill – like Marion's father?'

I did remember hearing such stories. I also recalled wondering how a Chinese immigrant had managed to achieve such success in his business ventures and – even more impressive – how he had risen to such heights within Sydney high society. Maybe anything was possible here in the big city?

A moment later, a tall glass was placed before me with a flourish. I took my first sip of the ruby-coloured soda and reared back in surprise. Bubbles danced up my nose, making my eyes water, but Hilda had been right again – it was sweet and delicious.

When our meals arrived, I could hardly eat for excitement. I observed the effortless ease with which Lady Fitzwilliam navigated clear oxtail soup and curry of chicken and tried to replicate her elegant manners.

'I hope you're not watching your figure, Lillian Taylor,' Hilda waggled her finger in warning. 'With your tiny waist, all the boys will be making sheep's eyes at you before long!'

I blushed, trying to catch Hilda's eye to make her stop teasing, then noticed Lady Fitzwilliam's despairing glance towards my friend's significantly more cuddly form.

'I know, I know,' said Hilda, hiccupping loudly thanks to the soda and ignoring her mother's dismayed expression. 'You're not going to get married. You're going to be a teacher and live happily ever after – all on your own!'

'Is that what you have in mind, Lillian?' Lady Fitzwilliam turned to me.

I felt my blush travelling further down my neck and nodded. 'I would like to become a governess, or even a qualified teacher, if I could, Lady Fitzwilliam. It will depend on how I go with my studies during the next couple of years and on ...' My voice trailed off uncertainly.

Though my heart was set on going to Sydney University, I was trying to keep my expectations in check. During his last visit in winter, Mr O'Loughlin had already indicated his willingness to pay my university fees and even the cost of residing at The Women's College. Provided I could pass the public entrance exam, I might just achieve my goal. Living life as a university-educated teacher offered the kind of social status and independence afforded to very few women, even more so than being a private governess. It was an ambitious thought for someone like me.

'Lillian's clever as a whip, Mother. Even in Latin. Last year, she topped the class almost every month for the *Compétition*.'

'And how were your latest test results, Hilda?' asked Lady Fitzwilliam. 'Reverend-Mother Salmon tells me your French is still very passable – we can be grateful for that Parisian governess your father hired when you were younger – but that you could apply yourself more to some of the *arts d'agrément* ... your singing, dancing and the pianoforte, as we've already discussed.' She looked meaningfully at her daughter.

Hilda pouted, and I finally began to feel a little sorry for her. Music and dancing aside, neither of us could match the artistic flair of some of the French nuns, exemplified by their exquisite lettering and illumination work, or even by the floral arrangements and *tableaux vivants* they created for feasts and receptions.

The waiter approached bearing a large silver tray.

'Just in the nick of time! Here's your rhubarb pie, Mother. And your rice custard, Lill. You must try the scones next time, they're famous.' Hilda wiped her chin with the back of her hand as hot butter dripped from her lips.

As Lady Fitzwilliam's eyebrows arched yet again, I hid my smile behind my spoon.

~

Back in the carriage, sleepy and satisfied after our indulgent meal, Hilda half-heartedly pointed out a few more buildings along George Street. Here was the Town Hall, with its grand staircase and ornate decoration. There was St Andrew's Anglican Cathedral – smaller than St Mary's, but soaring in height. I glanced back at the Queen Victoria Building and caught sight of the immense central dome in all its glory, its copper roof already weathered to a silvery-green colour that reminded me of lichen. Crowning this great dome was the cupola, together resembling one of Queen Victoria's own magnificent crowns, or – as Hilda suggested – a multi-layered cream cake with a cherry on top.

As we retraced our path back to Sacred Heart, I felt a marked change from a few hours earlier – beyond the cool breeze that had developed while we were inside the tea rooms and which had thankfully broken the heaviness of the air. I felt different ... more hopeful somehow, and more grown up, if this could be possible after such a short time. Like the twists and turns of one of the daringly paced novels Mrs Spicer occasionally let me read during the holidays, the world outside the convent had revealed itself to be full of exciting possibilities.

Chapter 2
'The Drover's Wife'

Humidity hung over the room, typical of a February afternoon in Sydney, and reminded me of the heavy Roehampton blankets which covered my bed each winter. Together with the drone of cicadas outside and the pleasant sensation of a full belly, the heat was making me drowsy. The quiet voice of Mother McKenna, softened further by its lilting Irish accent, was warm and soothing. Perhaps no one would notice if I closed my eyes for a moment or two.

'Today, girls,' Mother McKenna began, making an effort to speak loudly, 'we are going to read something different, a wonderful story about an Australian bush heroine.'

I felt myself begin to sway in my chair and tried to set my posture in an upright position.

'It was written by Mr Henry Lawson in 1892,' our teacher continued, 'the same year that some of you were born, in fact.'

As one of those girls, my eyes opened briefly before again drifting shut. My own sixteenth birthday had passed by unnoticed the previous month while the other girls were all home with their families for the summer vacation. Only Hilda had thought to send me a card, along with a huge tin of biscuits, eager for my opinion on Arnott's new Iced VoVo, a delicious pink and white concoction suggestive of a lamington cake.

'Today's story – this sketch, I should say – is called 'The Drover's Wife' and we will be reading from Mr Lawson's celebrated collection of Australian stories, *While the Billy Boils*.'

My eyes opened involuntarily at the word *drover* then closed, deliberately this time, blocking out the room. I took a deep breath and forced my expression to remain impassive.

'We're going to take turns reading aloud from the story,' murmured Mother McKenna, as she thumbed through the pages of a small green book. 'Dora, we will begin with you.' She placed the open book into the hands of one of the weaker readers of our class and smiled encouragingly.

'The two-roomed house is built of round timber, slabs, and stringy bark, and floored with split slabs,' Dora intoned, tripping over the last two words. 'A big bark kitchen standing at one end is larger than the house itself, verandah included,' she continued. 'Bush all round – bush with no horizon, for the country is flat.'

I felt a tug of recognition, for a world far removed from the convent – a place that did not exist anymore, or at least not for my family. As Dora read on, I found myself nodding in agreement with the details of the bush setting. Still on the first page, a snake appeared in the story, and while some of the others gasped in horror – feigned or otherwise – my own nodding simply became more pronounced. A snake was nothing out of the ordinary where I'd come from.

'"Tommy, come here, or you'll be bit. Come here at once when I tell you, you little wretch!"' read Dora, trying to command the authority and speech of the drover's wife.

I started, not at the coarseness of the language, which had some of the girls raising their eyebrows in mock indignation, but at the name of the eldest boy. *Tommy*. My own brother, Tommy, had been almost eighteen when he died. He would have been twenty-five or twenty-six by now, most likely married and with a family of his own. I felt ashamed that I couldn't remember his actual birthday, especially now, when there was no way for me to ever find out. My last memories of my brother were of clinging onto his strong wiry frame as we raced towards our uncle's shanty, and of his curt wave goodbye as he rode straight back home to meet the fire. I think I'd felt glad to get away from the pungent smell of his sweat-soaked shirt and from the sea of red dust kicked up by the horses' hooves as he and Uncle Bill galloped into the distance.

Janet took over from Dora, and I felt myself succumb to the story's grip. Nightfall was coming and the drover's wife needed to keep the children safe while she and the dog kept vigil, watching and waiting for the snake's reappearance. I pictured the family scene that was so like my own – two older boys, two younger girls, a father away droving, and a mother capable of knocking down anything that crossed her path. Only the writer's description of an impending thunderstorm, followed by rain that came down in torrents, jarred with the images forming in my mind.

As the reading continued in Janet's far more capable hands, I started again in recognition, this time over the mention of the *Young Ladies' Journal*. Mother used to read that journal, along with whatever else she could lay her hands on. She would take turns reading aloud with my sister and me, encouraging us to sound out the longer words and not simply look at the illustrations, as Esther was prone to do.

I smiled as Janet narrated the humorous exchange between the two brothers bickering at bedtime, and did not immediately register the name of the younger brother, *Jacky*. But when I did, I sat up straight, as shocked as if I had seen a ghost.

Seated beside me, Hilda felt my movement and raised her eyebrows in question.

'Same as my brother,' I whispered. 'Both of them.'

Hilda nodded sympathetically, patting my leg under the desk.

I heard a knock on the classroom door, and looked up guiltily, as if I'd been caught talking in class and was now to be punished. But it was only Mere De Konig, our animal-loving German portress, with a message. Mother McKenna rose from her desk and raised her palm in the air, calling a temporary halt to the reading.

'Sorry, Lill,' whispered Hilda, taking the chance to continue our conversation. 'I know you still miss them.'

'It's like he's talking about my family,' I breathed. 'And even our house.'

Behind us, I sensed Ivy trying to listen in.

'Thank you, Janet. Your turn now, Ivy,' instructed Mother McKenna, closing the door behind her.

'Thank you, Mother,' said my old arch nemesis in her sickly-sweet voice. 'But I think Lillian wants to ask you something about the story first.'

'Lillian?' Mother McKenna prompted.

'It's nothing,' I mumbled, wishing I could turn around and kick Ivy in the shins as she deserved.

'Something about her brothers, I think,' Ivy added, cunningly assuming a helpful expression.

'What is it you wanted to ask, Lillian?' Mother McKenna had always encouraged my love of literature.

'I'm sorry, Mother,' I said, wrangling with myself. 'I do have a question.'

'Go ahead.'

'Do you think ... I wondered if ... Does Mr Lawson base his stories on real life?' I lifted my eyes to meet those of my teacher while avoiding Hilda's quizzical expression.

'I expect he does,' said Mother McKenna. 'He is well known for his true-to-life accounts of the bush and those who live there. Carry on now, please, Ivy.'

'I'm sorry, Mother.' I bit down on my lip, feeling utterly exposed yet determined to finish what I had now started. 'It's just that I think Mr

Lawson may have written this story about my family.'

Mother McKenna smiled benignly while some of the girls appeared curious and others, like Ivy, stifled a giggle. 'Come now, Lillian. I'm sure he's met all sorts of people who have inspired his stories. It's natural that country folk or those hailing from the outback, like yourself, should identify with his yarns, might even see themselves in certain characters, but the likelihood of this story being based on your own blessed family is very slim, my dear girl. Why don't you read for us next instead?' She took the book from Ivy, who was now grinning with delight, and handed it to me.

I took a deep breath and prepared to begin reading but found I could not. 'My oldest brother was called Tommy, just like this in the story. And my other brother was called Jacky, just like this one. And the house sounds like ours. And we used to read the *Young Ladies' Journal*. And—'

'I do understand, Lillian,' Mother McKenna cut me off, 'but I'm quite certain these are all simply coincidences, and you must know those boys' names are very common.' She pulled the book from my trembling hands and thrust it towards Hilda, who was looking at me anxiously. 'Now, let's continue.'

A deep blush rose from my chest and throat, spreading to my cheeks, which blazed an uncomfortable crimson. The other girls took their cue from Mother McKenna's clear-cut pronouncement so that my claim no longer seemed intriguing but ridiculous. Fresh giggles erupted, with no effort to stifle them this time, and while Hilda shot daggers at the ringleaders, Mother McKenna merely raised her hand until order was restored to the room. Hilda began reading.

I shrank down into my seat, my heart thumping so loudly I was sure everyone could hear it. At first, I was too embarrassed to concentrate on the unfolding story of the drover's wife, but – as my best friend's soothing tone gradually penetrated my defences – I began to listen with determination, cataloguing each additional 'coincidence' with the exacting skill of a librarian. Possums, yes. An uncle living nearby, yes. His 'little son' bitten by a snake, no – that part he must have made up. But the uncle bringing provisions, yes. I still remembered Uncle Bill riding up every few weeks when Father was away, his saddlebags full. My job was to help Esther make the tea and fix up dinner while he sat under the verandah to yarn with Mother or took a nap inside.

The *Young Ladies' Journal*, yes, the fashion plates, oh yes. My father's occasional talk about moving us to town when he next came home, yes, I remembered that too. Afterwards, Mother would say it was all very well for Father to keep building up our hopes like that, but that we might as well accept the life we'd been given and make the best of it. I nodded now at the wisdom of this advice.

I nodded even more emphatically at the description of the last two children being born in the bush – for yes, I had been one of them. And I, too, had been told the story of how Old Mary, whom Mr Lawson was calling Black Mary, had made much better work of attending to Esther's birth than that useless old quack of a doctor, whom Mother had not even bothered to call in for my own birth.

In contrast to these familiar family anecdotes, some of which I had all but forgotten over the years, I listened with horror at the untold secret of a dead child and the thought of my mother riding out alone for assistance. I shivered instinctively, despite our hot classroom. Poor, brave Mother. Had that really happened?

To Hilda's left, the next reader began and now Mr Lawson's story took an exciting turn as the drover's wife faced challenge after challenge: fighting a grass fire – yes, it was not the first or the last our family had seen; a flood and the washing away of the dam – that must have been before I was born because I had no memory of anything like that; cattle disease, a mad bullock, crows, eagles, swagmen and sundowners – was there nothing Mother could not do?

My chest, still flushed with humiliation, now swelled with pride.

Though I was desperate to speak out once more, I could not fail to notice Ivy and the other girls still exchanging scornful glances. Fear of further judgement kept me silent.

As the final reader took her turn, the story came to its dramatic climax, both terrifying and exhilarating in its inevitability. In the grotesque image of the faithful dog shaking the snake between its gnashing jaws and in the imagined thud-thud-thud of the mother's club as she broke the snake's back, the truth came to me – unassailable and absolute. It was almost funny, I conceded. It was the dog that proved what I had known all along. I hadn't picked up on it earlier – its name, Alligator. A good name for a dog, no denying it, but didn't Mr Lawson know there were no alligators in Australia? That, I thought with grim satisfaction, was why our own dog had been called Crocodile.

Chapter 3
My Brilliant Idea

After class, I kept my head down as Hilda fell into stride with me. 'You never usually want to talk about your family, Lillian. I don't even think I knew your brothers' names before today.'

I brought my index finger to my lips and indicated the two nuns ahead of us in the corridor.

Hilda lowered her voice. 'But wouldn't it be incredible if Mr Lawson really had called in on your house and if that's what gave him the idea for his story?'

My breath caught but I shook my head. 'It was all just a coincidence,' I whispered. 'Just like Mother McKenna said.'

'Are you sure?' Hilda looked doubtful.

I gave a decisive nod. 'I let myself be carried away by my imagination, that's all.'

~

Later that day, despite these outward assurances, and despite the consequences if I were to be discovered, I seized upon my first opportunity to return to the classroom alone. I found the small volume of stories, with its distinctive green binding and gilt lettering, on Mother McKenna's desk and slipped it into the pocket of my ulster. Then, after pleading a headache at supper, I was excused for the night and went to my room. In the thick yellow light of evening, I lay on my narrow iron bed, leafing through the book until I found the story. I read it through once, then a second time, using my neatest handwriting to record every possible reference to my family in my notebook.

By now, there was no doubt at all in my mind. It all fit together. My brothers' names. The ages of the children, the two boys, the two girls, even the dog. I must have been that baby that the drover's wife had quickly snatched up from the ground when the snake first appeared. Comforted by the image of little Lillian resting safely on Mother's hip, my heart fluttered and soared like a kite in the breeze.

Yet, even as I took comfort in these vivid new images of my family and home, something about the way Mr Lawson had presented them was bothering me. All afternoon I'd felt it eating away at me, penetrating my usual defences, like a worm boring its rotten trail through an apple to reach its core. By now thoroughly vexed, I pored over the twelve typeset pages, searching for the underlying cause of my distress. Mr Lawson's unkind descriptions of my brothers and sisters as 'ragged' and 'dried up' were hard to ignore – although if he had looked more closely, he would have seen that Mother made us wash our hands and faces every morning and night, regardless of the effort required to bring water up from the soak. But no, it wasn't that. I kept looking.

There was also the full-page illustration at the end of the story. Against a rustic kitchen backdrop was a boy – presumably meant to be Tommy – dressed in his nightshirt, arms wrapped around his mother's neck, with a caption: 'Mother, I won't never go drovin'; blarst me if I do!' To my ears, this promise to stay and help our mother sounded more like something

Esther would have said than Tommy, who couldn't wait to leave home and join Father. But no, it wasn't that either.

Then it fell into place.

It was the names themselves that were troubling me. Mr Lawson had chosen to name both my brothers in the story, Tommy and Jacky – that was what had first alerted my attention in class. I was so happy to see their names there in print. Even our old dog had been allowed to keep his own name, or something very close to it. But where was Esther's name? Where was my name? Where was my mother's name? Surely Mother would have introduced the whole family to Mr Lawson, as with any other guest welcomed into our home. Here was a story about all of us, a surviving piece of my family, and yet even here we had been half-erased. It felt like someone was squeezing my heart and I started to tremble.

True, my father's name was not included either. He was simply *the drover*. But that made better sense to me. He would have been away when the writer paid his visit. Mother might not even have mentioned his name. And anyway, thinking about how little time Father had even spent with us at home, Mr Lawson's honorary title lent my father a kind of authority I wasn't sure he deserved.

But my mother, my brave and capable mother – the heroine herself, for goodness' sake – she was just 'the drover's wife'. Never mind that she was the subject of the whole story, to Henry Lawson, and everyone else who read this tale – her tale – she would never be anything more than a drover's *wife*. As if that said it all.

The longer I thought about it the more furious I became. To have been seen but not seen. To have been featured in a story read by thousands of people, probably hundreds of thousands, but not to be acknowledged. It was not right. This should have been our story too, mine and Esther's and Mother's – it *was* our story – but without our names in it for all to read, no one would ever believe that to be true.

~

As the weeks passed, my anger towards Henry Lawson intensified, growing darker and gathering momentum like a Sydney summer storm. After my humiliation that day in class, I had vowed never to reveal my suspicions again. At least, not until I had the evidence to prove them. By the time the school term ended, and Hilda and the other girls had gone home for the winter break, I had the beginnings of a plan. I had also settled upon an unwitting accomplice for my fact-finding mission.

'Mrs Spicer,' I began, as I worked beside her over the steaming copper pots, helping her wash sheets in the tiny boiler room, 'Hilda and I are doing a school project next term about a famous Australian and we've picked Henry Lawson.'

'The writer?' She looked surprised. 'Are you sure Hilda's parents would approve of your choice? I suppose he's famous enough, but I doubt Lady Fitzwilliam would care for his republican views.'

'Oh yes, they think it's wonderful. Hilda's father just adores bush poetry.' I couldn't believe the lies coming from my mouth.

Mrs Spicer looked at me strangely as she positioned the first dripping wet bedsheet between the mangle's two rollers, ready for me to start the wringing.

'We just have a few questions we'd like him to answer for our project. Do you think you could find out his address so I could send him a letter?'

Mrs Spicer's eyes narrowed further. 'I'm not sure that's a good idea.'

'Why not?'

'Let's just say Mr Lawson has had a lot of bother in his personal life ever since he returned from London some years back. He might not have the time to answer your questions.'

'What kind of bother?' I was like a dog with a bone. Or, better still, like the dog in Lawson's story with the snake locked between his jaws.

Mrs Spicer looked around to make certain none of the nuns were within earshot. 'I gather his marriage ended badly and that he ... has trouble staying away from alcohol. I don't approve of idle gossip, as you'd know, but seeing as this was in the newspaper and all, I guess there's no harm telling you.'

Although still speaking in a low voice, she now appeared to be enjoying her role. 'Well, as it happens, he was even sent to gaol one time – in fact, I've heard it was more than once – for not giving his wife and children the money he was supposed to, for their upkeep and so forth. They're divorced, you see.' She shook her head disapprovingly, then gave an involuntary shudder, as if these mortal sins had been hers. 'There was also that "fall" he took from a cliff in Manly and various "hospital" stays – if you get my meaning. It might be best, dear, if you and Hilda chose a more suitable Australian for your project.'

My mind whirred furiously, churning through Mrs Spicer's revelations faster than my hands could turn the crank. A drinking problem ... divorce ... neglecting his children, mysterious falls, hospitalisations and even gaol. When I compared such scandalous behaviour to Mr Lawson's austere writing style and the message of heroism in his stories, it made no sense. And although I was shocked to think of how far his fortunes had fallen and how unhappy his life must be, I was also felt a certain satisfaction. Why should he profit from my family's story?

'But Mrs Spicer, it's too late to change now, we've already made a start. Isn't there anything you can give me to help?'

'My, my, you are a persistent so-and-so today, aren't you? I suppose I could pass on whatever I come across in the paper about him. And I can look through some of our old *Bulletin* magazines – there's always one of his poems or stories in there. But mind you keep them to yourself. I don't want anyone saying I'm giving you funny ideas.' She raised her reddened fingers to her lips and winked, as she often did when slipping reading material my way.

'Thank you, Mrs Spicer. You know I'm always grateful for whatever you can give me.'

Although I missed Hilda during the two vacations each year, and was still expected to help with chores, the holidays were my only chance to read fiction, rather than just the heavy factual books read aloud to us each day and designed to improve our minds. In contrast to this dreary torrent of information which usually went in one of my ears and out the other, a well-written novel could set my imagination on fire. Best of all, I could almost always rely on a novel's happy ending – something sorely lacking in my own life.

~

True to her word, Mrs Spicer presented me with a handful of *Bulletin* magazines the following morning, along with a book.

'*My Brilliant Career* by Miles Franklin,' I read aloud. 'Thank you, I've been dying to read it.' Quite a few of the girls had talked about this novel and I knew its contents were in some way controversial.

'It was written by a young woman from the bush, when she was not much older than you. But don't go getting any funny ideas, you hear? And remember, you didn't get this from me.'

'Thanks a lot, Mrs Spicer,' I grinned, surrendering myself wholeheartedly to both my mission and this thrill of the illicit.

I spent the rest of the day, in between chores, looking through the magazines, but was disappointed by every single one of Henry Lawson's stories and poems printed within. Not because they were badly written – far from it, I had to admit – but because I could find no further mentions of my family, direct or otherwise.

The following day, I took a break from my research task and instead read Miss Franklin's novel, devouring the whole book in a matter of hours. Her story of Sybylla Melvyn was laced with uncensored judgements about country society and the expectations on girls and young women to conform (girls like me!). It wasn't hard to see why it had caused such a sensation when it was published six or seven years earlier. Part of me wished Sybylla had taken the easy option and married wealthy young Harold Beecham when she'd had the chance, but I understood why she felt she could not. I said a silent prayer that my own future pupils would be nothing like the unruly charges with whom she'd had to contend as an indentured governess to the dreadful M'Swat family. If only I had Miss Franklin's talent for writing, as well as her boldness, perhaps I too might carve out my own 'brilliant career'.

Aside from the story itself, which left me wondering which parts were fact and which parts fiction, I was intrigued by the warm preface from Henry Lawson at the start. Perhaps this was the real reason Mrs Spicer had thought to lend it to me?

The preface was marked 'England, April 1901', and hence, I presumed, before Mr Lawson's life had taken a downward slide. In it, he described how he had received a letter from the author – whom he'd quickly discerned to be an authoress, despite the ambiguity of her name – asking him to read her manuscript and to advise on its publishing. Mr Lawson went on from there to discuss the book and praise its quality of truth and Australianness.

What should I make of this? On the one hand, I found it patronising that Mr Lawson called such a talented writer 'a little bush girl', and I thought again of my nameless mother and sister. On the other hand, he had undoubtedly gone out of his way to assist Miss Franklin in her goal. Like honey dripping over my morning porridge, a sweet trickle of hope now ran through my veins. Perhaps, if I couched my enquiry in just the right manner, Henry Lawson might be willing to answer my questions after all?

~

At the end of the week, Mrs Spicer had another pile of magazines waiting for me in the boiler room. 'Some of them are very old, I know, but they're still worth a read.' She leaned over and winked conspiratorially. 'Mr Spicer never approved of my subscription because he said it filled my head with grand notions, but I make it a rule never to listen to him when he's talking rubbish.'

'*The Dawn: a journal for Australian women*,' I recited, rubbing the thick paper stock between my fingers, and trying not to look shocked at what Mrs Spicer had said about her husband.

'You know who published that, don't you?'

I glanced down. 'Edited by Dora Falconer.'

'No, no, don't pay any attention to that. That was just her pen name. See here,' she said, thrusting another cover at me. 'Mrs Louisa Lawson.'

I had first heard mention of Louisa Lawson a few years earlier when the Suffrage Act had been passed by Parliament, giving women of New South Wales the right to vote. 'Henry Lawson's mother?' I ventured, feeling a trifle foolish that I had not made the connection myself. 'Don't they call her the Mother of Suffrage?'

'Exactly! And when it comes to politics or business, or writing, for that matter, Mrs Lawson is as good as any man. Better than most, in fact. Do you know she was the first woman editress in this country? And everyone she had working for her was a woman too. Right from the beginning, the men tried to bully her out of business, but she wasn't having any of it. That's a good lesson for you right there, Lillian. Don't ever let a man tell you what to do, not even your own husband.'

'Yes, Mrs Spicer,' I promised, wondering what it might take for me to keep this promise for life.

'Listen to this, for starters,' Mrs Spicer said, adopting an unexpectedly melodramatic tone as she began reading. 'Bound, padded, compressed and laced, the modern woman is a highly artificial product, made not after God's image but as near as possible to a fashion plate; and if any inhabitant of another planet were curious to see what a real natural woman was like, we should have to take him to some of the few women who are not afraid to use dress for purposes of health and comfort only, and beg him to overlook those who, by corsets, high heels, and a score of other inventions, have succeeded in constructing in themselves, a new variety of woman.'

I giggled. 'A new variety of woman – she makes it sound funny. I should show it to some of the girls in our form who've started wearing stays this year.'

'She wrote that in 1889, nearly twenty years ago, before you were born. It was good advice then, and it's good advice now, but not much has changed for the better. Lord knows men have a lot to answer for, but women can be just as stupid all on their own too.'

I grinned, silently adding corsets and high heels to the list of things I must not do.

'My point is this, Lillian: Mrs Lawson stopped putting out *The Dawn* a few years ago, and I'm not exactly sure what she's up to now, but don't you think she'd make a much better famous Australian for your project than her son?'

'Oh,' I mumbled, temporarily deflated. I'd been hoping these journals might somehow hold the key to my quest about 'The Drover's Wife'. I forced myself to smile and nod. 'Thanks Mrs Spicer. I'll be sure to talk to Hilda about it when she comes back.'

~

Having previously read the popular Australian detective novel *The Mystery of a Hansom Cab*, and more than a few of Conan Doyle's stories, I was beginning to think of myself as something of a Sherlock Holmes. And just when I'd given up on getting any new clues from Mrs Spicer, inspiration for the next chapter in my investigation came from an unexpected source.

I'd been polishing the silver and was laying the knives, forks and spoons in neat rows across the pile of old newspapers retained for this purpose. The sheets laid out were from *The Freeman's Journal*, a Catholic publication whose masthead proclaimed it as the oldest weekly newspaper in the Australasian colonies, and as I was setting down a spoon I spotted Henry Lawson's name. It was in the Personal columns, beneath a photograph of an American actress touring Australia and above an advertisement for Maitland Brewing Company. I quickly began reading, wondering whether his drinking problems had landed him in gaol or hospital once again. Instead of any details about his present living circumstances, this mention concerned the writer's childhood.

> Henry Lawson's early days seem to have been the rugged lot of the child on new diggings. He tells of his life in *The Lone Hand*, and his first memories are of Pipe Clay, Mudgee, Gulgong, and other scenes of early rushes for gold. Those early years form a tale of hardship, poverty, squalor, and misery, but the poet found many bright and happy memories of his younger years.

Still holding a knife in one hand, I considered this description. But even though I was poised and ready to find fault with his character at the first opportunity, I was instead reminded of my own childhood beginnings. As I continued reading, I was surprised to discover other similarities between his experiences and mine. Although not a Catholic, he had apparently attended a Catholic school in Mudgee for some months. *Try living in a convent for eight years*, I imagined saying to him, *and you'd soon discover just how many prayers can be crammed into a single school week*. I read on.

'He writes that he doesn't know why he was sent there, but guessed it was because his mother had got disgusted with their own churchmen of the time.' My eyes widened at this picture of Louisa Lawson's defiance, though given the tone of her writing in *The Dawn*, I should not have been so shocked. Lawson's grandfather was described as 'a swarth "man of Kent" whose people were supposed to be gypsies', while his father was a Norwegian who left his ship in search of Australian gold. *A gold-digger*, I mused, and wondered whether Lawson's father had been away from home as much as mine. Finally, Lawson wrote affectionately about a Father O'Donovan who had spoken kindly and drawn him out of himself, talking of poetry and of Edgar Allen Poe, whose book of poems Lawson's mother had allowed him to read. Like me, it seemed he had been a reader from a young age, and shy.

I now wondered what other useful nuggets of information might be hiding amongst the rest of Henry Lawson's youthful recollections. What if these memories extended to describing his travels into the far north-west of New South Wales, where my family had lived? I considered asking Mrs Spicer whether she could procure me a copy of this *Lone Hand* newspaper but, in the end, I figured it would be safer not to ask.

Although no closer than before to having Henry Lawson's mailing address, a new idea suddenly occurred to me. I would follow the example of another enterprising young lady from the bush, the now famous Miss Miles Franklin, who had written to him care of the *Bulletin* newspaper to ask his advice about getting her novel published. As one of their most regular contributors, surely someone there would be able to pass on my letter to the man himself.

Now that was a 'brilliant' idea.

~

More than a week passed before I had the opportunity to write my letter and give it to Mr Spicer (and not Mrs Spicer) to post on my behalf. It had taken a few drafts for me to be satisfied with its wording. Although my hand trembled with both anger and longing as I held my pen, I was careful not to let my emotions show on the page. I had to be polite and not put him on his guard, else he would never give me the answers I needed. I made certain to include my return address at the convent and even enclosed another envelope and stamp for his reply.

Mr Henry Lawson (the writer)

c/ The Bulletin Newspaper

214 George street North

Sydney, N. S. Wales

Australia

11 July 1908

Dear Mr Lawson,

I hope this letter finds you in good health. Although you don't know me (or at least not to recognise me as I look today), I hope you will remember meeting my mother during your previous inland travels.

My family lived in the middle of the bush, somewhere in the far north-west of our colony, in a small two-roomed house with a large bark kitchen at one end. My father was a drover and was often away with sheep for long periods. In his absence, my mother took charge of us children, my two older brothers, Tommy and Jacky, along with my older sister who was called Esther. (There was also my baby sister, Eadie, but that was not until after your visit.)

By now, I trust you will have guessed the identity of my family since you portrayed us so accurately in your celebrated story of 'The Drover's Wife', which you wrote the same year I was born.

I am sure you will be very sorry to hear that my mother, along with my brothers and sisters, died in a bushfire in 1900. Since then, I've been a boarder at Sacred Heart, where I am presently in my penultimate year of studies. My father is also dead.

Please be assured that I am not writing this letter to cause any trouble. I understand that as a writer you must meet all kinds of people and hear all kinds of stories. I expect it's only natural to want to share some of them with a wider audience, a bit like a journalist reporting on the news.

Perhaps one day, once I have finished school, we could meet? You could tell me more about your memories of the time you spent with my family and anything else you noticed about my mother, or that she might have talked to you about, but which you did not have time to mention in your story.

In the meantime, I have a small favour to ask: the next time our story comes to be reprinted, would you ever consider including the rest of my family's names too?

Yours faithfully,

Miss Lillian Taylor

Chapter 4

A Clear View

The rest of the year, along with some of the next, passed by like any other, except that I was still waiting on a reply to my letter from Mr Lawson. What had begun as sweet honeylike anticipation was now a heavy lump in my gut which I could do little to shift on my own.

One rainy afternoon in needlework class, during which we were required to converse entirely in French, there was a knock at the door. The room fell quiet, save for the constant drone of the rain, while Mother Chevreux went to see who was there.

Beside me, at the arched window, water cascaded down the glass like rivulets of silver. '*Il pleut*,' I pronounced inaudibly, relishing the way the verb made my lips pop outwards, like a raindrop bursting open as it hit the ground. '*Il pleut beaucoup*,' I added for good measure, practising my French with uncustomary zeal.

Before coming to Sydney, I never knew it could rain like this. Home for me had meant scorching summers and fiery hot winds, producing whirlies and dangerous dust storms that sent everyone running for cover; short sharp winters with cooler nights but little respite from the daytime sun; the occasional mocking clap of dry thunder; and, above all else, the ever-present red dust leaching its way into every corner of our house and into the very fabric of my skin. Despite Mother's wistful descriptions of the way the earth would spring to life in the wet, it was hard to imagine that same earth giving life to anything other than sparse mulga bush and the occasional straggling gum.

'Mother Hughes would like to see you, Lillian,' Mother Chevreux announced, speaking in English as she held the door open for me. 'You may be excused.'

What had I done? What could I possibly have done? I packed away my needlework and hurried out of the classroom, taking care not to be seen running. I stopped short when I reached the doorway at the end of the corridor. The sweet aroma of beeswax emanated from its dark timber frame.

The only other time I'd been summoned to see the Mistress General had been when I was just ten years old, when Mr O'Loughlin came unannounced to deliver the news about Father's death. When he'd begun by stammering an apology, and Mother Scroope started talking about heaven, I'd foolishly leaped to the conclusion he couldn't afford to pay my school fees any longer and that it was time for me to leave Sacred Heart and join my father. Droving. Or rather *drovin'*, as Father had always pronounced it. The very word had given me a thrill of nervous energy. Adventure. Freedom. Father's forgiveness.

Poor Mr O'Loughlin. My childish delusions that day had made his task so much harder. I squared my shoulders and opened the door.

~

This time, it was about Mr O'Loughlin himself. I fought back tears as Mother Hughes told me he had died in his sleep a few days earlier. Having long surpassed the three score and ten years which the Psalms lead us to expect, my benefactor's passing should not have been a surprise. A true

Christian to the end, he had taken the time to put his affairs in order. Mother Hughes was quick to reassure me that my boarding and tuition fees had all been paid to the end of the following year, so I would be able to graduate from Sacred Heart as planned.

That much I might have anticipated. What astounded me, though, was that Mr O'Loughlin had not forgotten his intention for me to go on to university. To make this possible, he had left a generous bequest to provide for me until I completed my teaching studies, together with a letter of recommendation that he fervently hoped would persuade Sydney University to grant my entry, despite our school not meeting certain requirements for the public examination.

Unable to hold them any longer, tears trickled from my eyes as I walked stiffly back down the corridor. Alone again. It was almost a relief. Despite the letters I had sent Mr O'Loughlin each term under strict instruction from the Reverend-Mother – short, formal communications, designed to demonstrate my educational advancements and my gratitude, without presuming to trouble him with any questions of my own – we had met in person on only a handful of occasions, and I had deliberately tried to hold myself back from becoming close to him. And although Mr O'Loughlin had had little personal contact with my father during the years of his employment and had never met my mother or anyone else in our family, his death also meant there was no one left to remember them but me. Other than Henry Lawson, that was.

When I shared the news with Hilda, I bowed my head in shame.

'What's the matter?' she asked, immediately perceiving I felt something more than sadness for his loss.

'It's not right,' I finally admitted. 'A gift like this is something that should only be given within a family.'

Hilda puffed up her cheeks in indignation. 'Codswallop. You've earned it, working hard all these years. I bet he was proud to have helped you on your way.'

'I'm not sure I agree with you, but I'll do my best not to let him down. Do you think it would be enough if I could become a good teacher and help other young children as he has helped me?'

Hilda nodded emphatically and gave me a tight hug.

~

Seated alone in the garden at dusk, the rich perfume of jasmine filled the air. Spring was in full bloom and my final year of school was almost over. I gazed past the greenery and down to the water, luxuriating in the golden evening light. Set high on the hill of Rose Bay, our grounds presented a sweeping vista of Sydney's Eastern Harbour. Closing one eye, I stretched out my finger to trace the familiar outline of the shore and distant city horizon, lingering over its curves and craggy edges like a child straining to keep within the lines of a colouring book. Yet I was no longer a child.

In place of my once plump and ruddy cheeks, like those of Baby Eadie, were defined cheekbones and a 'milk and roses complexion', as the magazines described such skin. And though my eyes were still the same deep shade of amber as before, my hair had grown darker, and my plait thicker. Thanks to the kindly discipline of the Sisters of Sacred Heart, I now dressed differently, behaved differently and even spoke differently. If Mother were alive today, would she still recognise the young woman I had become?

Beside me, a magpie sailed down onto the grass, its black and white feathers contrasting against the emerald blades as it raised its head and trilled. It was soon joined by two more, one of them still bearing the soft brown feathers that revealed its youth. The young one followed its mother around the garden, squawking and pecking hopefully at the ground at regular intervals until, sooner than one might expect, a pale worm was pulled up from the fertile soil.

‘Well done,’ I whispered, grinning with vicarious delight before my thoughts circled back to the past.

Nearly ten years had passed since the fire; since that terrible day which had set the course for the rest of my life. Looking back, it was almost funny to think that I had come to the convent during the all-important year of Federation. To think that while the nation was carving out its new identity, mine had been taken. Ironic, no less, to consider the many great debates taking place all over the country in the year preceding, all those votes to be cast and counted, as six separate colonies finally came together to form their own kind of family – the Commonwealth of Australia – when all the while a great fire had been coming for mine.

From the comparative wisdom of my present self, I thought back to that little eight-year-old girl who had arrived here all alone, without a single possession from home – no photographs, no toys, no books, nothing but the clothes she was wearing – and who thought everything had been taken from her, until a day came when yet one more thing was taken. How had I not fallen to pieces at the news of Father’s death? Instead, I’d told myself that if I alone had been spared, I owed it to the rest of my family to hold onto whatever part of them was not lost. To carry on.

I now had Lawson’s story too, which was mine to keep, even if no one else knew it to be so. And even if the writer himself was never going to admit it.

Neither Henry Lawson nor anyone else from the *Bulletin* office had replied to my letter. I considered writing a second letter, just in case the first had not reached him, but what would I ask this time? *What colour were my mother’s eyes? Did I seem like a happy baby? How long was your visit?* All I wanted was to know more about my family and where I came from, but would he even remember? A man like that probably took what he needed for the sake of a good yarn and then forgot all about it. Why should he be considered the caretaker of my family story when he had treated it so poorly?

Startled by the sound of footsteps, I stood and curtsied towards Sister Farraher walking towards the chaplain's cottage. I turned back to face the harbour, resuming my seat just as the *Golden Rose* ferry came into view for its final journey of the day.

All around me, the world was changing, for better or worse, while within the walls of the convent, everything stayed the same. Like the nuns, I felt as if I too had been part of an enclosed order these past years at Sacred Heart, unable to venture outside even if I had wanted to. I was ready to break free of these safe confines and find my own way forward. The real question was what kind of future did I want for myself?

If anything, the world was changing even faster for women. This time last year, Victoria had become the last Australian state to grant women's suffrage, a change long overdue, especially given most Australian women had been allowed to vote in federal elections since 1902.

On the day when Mrs Spicer had first shown me *The Dawn*, I had been more concerned with finding out a way to contact Henry Lawson. But in the following weeks, as I had started to read Mrs Spicer's back-issues of the magazine, my interest in the women's movement had grown rapidly. Hours spent reading the words written and commissioned by Henry's fearsome mother, Louisa Lawson, had fuelled in me a curiosity for what it meant to be a woman. Or rather, what it might mean in the future, since my present rights as a seventeen-year-old orphaned schoolgirl living in a convent were by necessity limited.

When I'd heard that the Victorian suffrage bill had finally passed, I had instantly thought of Louisa Lawson again. I was glad to think of how much had changed in the years since her magazine had ceased and felt grateful for all that she and other women like her had sacrificed to make these changes possible. But even as I celebrated that latest victory, I had asked myself (admittedly not out loud), whether it was enough. Achieving franchise was one thing. But what I had learned from *The Dawn* and my conversations with Mrs Spicer was that the road to female equality was only just beginning and so many freedoms remained out of reach. Although a bird might sing prettily in its cage each day, perhaps that was only because the door had never been opened.

I slid my hand down my lap, feeling the hard edges of the little green and gilt book I had tucked into the pocket of my ulster earlier in the day. It was Lawson's book of stories, the one I had stolen from Mother McKenna's desk on the day I first read 'The Drover's Wife'. Normally I kept it hidden at the bottom of my bedside drawer, under all my birthday cards from Hilda.

The faraway sound of a bell signalled the commencement of supper. I rose slowly from my bench, casting one last glance at the horizon. Stumbling across Lawson's story in the classroom that first day had been like a double-edged sword, I reflected, as I made my way back through the garden. On one side, there had been joy in that first moment of recognition – here was my family, together once more! But then on the other side, when their namelessness had left me unable to claim them, it was like they had been taken away from me all over again, and I still felt the sharp pain of this second withdrawal just as if it had been a blade. My teacher's reaction, along with that of the rest of the class, had convinced me there was nothing to be gained by speaking up and demanding acknowledgement – not even from Hilda, who would have given it willingly. Yet even now, despite my chosen vow of silence, I felt wronged, as if something had been taken from me and could never be returned.

Admittedly there were moments when I suffered doubt and asked myself whether Henry Lawson really had met my family or whether, as Mother McKenna had said, it was all just a series of coincidences. But other than during these rare lapses, my anger towards the famous writer burned hotter than ever. Not only for telling my family's story but for telling it better than I might have done myself.

One thing remained certain: it was not his story to tell.

Chapter 5

Together Yet Alone

University life was proving to be everything I had hoped. And, in many ways, more than I was ready for. Mr O'Loughlin's letter had succeeded in gaining the sympathy of Miss Louisa Macdonald, principal of The Women's College since its inception in 1892, which was also, whether by coincidence or fate, the year of my birth and of Lawson's story.

After a nerve-wracking interview, to which I had come armed with my school reports and all manner of persuasive (but ultimately unnecessary) arguments, this refined and wholly impressive Scotchwoman had allowed me to become a resident at her college with the understanding that I would work for my matriculation during my first year before formally entering university the next. Under the supervision of my appointed tutor, my studies were progressing well, and I was excited about the prospect of commencing my Bachelor of Arts in a few months' time. During my one and only visit back to Sacred Heart, some of my former teachers, and even Mrs Spicer, told me they were proud of how far I had come, assuring me that Mr O'Loughlin would have felt the same way. Hilda was equally proud of my achievements, notwithstanding that she herself had spent the better part of the year making her debut and accompanying her mother to social events.

After ten years of convent living, I was understandably more comfortable around other girls and women than the opposite sex. To my great relief, The Women's College had immediately lived up to its reputation as a unique feminine sanctuary within the predominantly masculine environment of the university, and of society in general. For many, the college was like a home away from home, while for me, it represented a safe resting place on my way to an unknown future.

Miss Macdonald was always telling us how fortunate we were, not only to be granted access to a university education, but to be awarded a degree afterwards, unlike women in many other parts of the Empire. In this regard, at least, Australia could hold its head high and not feel the usual colonial sting of perceived inferiority.

Some of my fellow residents still had to contend with opposing family opinions or lack of finances. But others seemed to accept their privileged pioneering status as a matter of course, and – without completely neglecting their studies – directed their daily energies towards less serious matters. University life offered endless opportunities to socialise, from tennis tournaments and the University Women's Boat Club to regular dances and performances of the Dramatic Society. Off-campus entertainment options were in equal abundance: concerts, garden parties, cycling expeditions, matinees at the Crystal Palace or Roxy Theatre and shopping trips to Mark Foy's, Anthony Hordern's or one of the arcades in town.

Though I sometimes joined in bush picnics or fine weather excursions on the harbour, my allowance under Mr O'Loughlin's bequest only went so far. In any case, I preferred to spend my free hours reading, either in my room or at the Fisher Library, or taking long rambles on the university grounds, as was my intention this morning.

I exited our simple but dignified brick building with a spring in my step and headed towards the long row of oak trees.

'You're coming, aren't you, Lillian?'

I felt a hand on my shoulder and turned around to face Miss Evelyn Dickinson. Dick, as the girls usually called her, but which didn't sit quite right with me, was what was commonly known as a 'New Woman'. She wore tailored suits and starched collars, kept her hair short and spoke in a rather gruff voice, possibly due to the cigars she was rumoured to smoke in private. Originally from Dublin, Miss Dickinson was our principal's secretary and had been here from the start. Although she and Miss Macdonald appeared to have little in common on the surface, everyone knew they had been friends since their early days together at the progressive University of London's College Hall and had remained inseparable ever since.

'Coming where, Miss Dickinson?' I asked. 'I was just going out for a walk.'

'The men are playing rugby. Most of the other girls are there already.'

'... Yes, of course,' I agreed after a moment's hesitation, hoping no one would notice if I walked around the oval during the match instead.

'That's the spirit. So, you haven't anyone in particular to be cheering on, then?'

I blushed. 'I thought we weren't meant to choose sides.'

'Right you are, Lillian.' Miss Dickinson grinned mischievously.

Despite the university's non-denominational stance, its three men's colleges were unequivocally religious: Catholic, Anglican and Presbyterian. However, for reasons of practicality, ours was officially secular. Thus, when the men competed in their sporting fixtures on the oval or boat races on the river, we girls could maintain neutrality, diplomatically wearing the colours of every team and crew, regardless of any personal attachments.

'And how do you feel you're settling in? It's Arts you'll be studying, isn't it?'

I nodded. 'Very well, thank you. I'm very grateful to be here. And yes, I plan to major in English with a minor in French.'

'*Oui, oui*, that seems sensible. Quite a few of the nuns over at Sacred Heart are French, aren't they?'

I nodded again. 'Some of them only came to Australia after the religious expulsion in France. It must have been very hard for them to leave their homes and start again, but they greatly enhanced our school culture.' I looked at Miss Dickinson and saw she understood my meaning, as both an immigrant and, like me, an orphan.

'Have you joined any of the university societies or the women's clubs around town?'

'Not yet. I thought I'd wait until I've started my degree. Or maybe even once I have my first teaching position and know where I'll be living. In some ways, it feels as if I'm in a women's club here at college anyway.'

Miss Dickinson laughed. 'I expect it's not too different here from the convent in that regard.'

I laughed too. 'Only without quite the same vows.'

'Or as many rules?'

'It's certainly a great deal more freedom than I'm accustomed to having,' I admitted. 'I have to stop myself from doing the full Sacred Heart curtsy half a dozen times a day.'

It was a requirement that we attend morning prayers and mealtimes, and if we wanted to stay out past 9.30pm we had to apply for leave, but otherwise there were remarkably few formal rules at college. It was a complete reversal of what I had experienced as a child coming to the convent. And even though I had resented many of the restrictions at the convent and had thought I was ready to go out into the world, it was taking some time for me to adjust.

'So you're a reader then, I presume? Who do you like to read?'

'Anyone and everyone, to be honest. I'm still getting used to having access to all these books.'

‘Well, I hope you’ll start with the women authors first. Unlike you girls, who have your own desks and study-bedrooms, not to mention access to tertiary education, some of them had to write under pathetic conditions – scraps of paper balanced on their laps while they sat with their mothers and sisters in the family parlour all day, fending off judgement, constant interruptions and proposals from ugly old men.’

I nodded vigorously. ‘I will.’

Miss Dickinson was a prolific writer herself. Entertaining and outspoken, she somehow managed to churn out a steady stream of articles, reviews and even successful novels (prompting threats of legal action from certain members of Sydney society, who may have recognised themselves and not liked what they saw). She was fearless and downright intimidating. Today’s conversation was by far the longest we had ever had, and I was relieved to have come through unscathed.

By now, we had arrived at the oval. Having reluctantly concluded I would have to stay put and at least pretend to watch, I dutifully stood beside Miss Dickinson on the sidelines. The match appeared to be in full swing, although I had little idea of the rules or even the objective of the game. All those men running around, bumping into each other, grunting and shouting while chasing a ball from left to right – I couldn’t see the point. But the crowd of spectators was cheering wildly, among them many of my fellow residents.

Then, emerging from within the centre of the fracas, I saw Freddy Parker limp off the field with the assistance of one of his teammates. Or possibly one of his opponents, it was hard for me to tell.

‘This way, young man,’ called Miss Dickinson. ‘Let me take a look.’

Given all her other talents, I sometimes forgot Dick was a doctor. Having completed her medical studies here at Sydney University, she held the role of Honorary Physician to the College.

A chair was soon found, and I watched with interest as Miss Dickinson assessed and then expertly bound his ankle. As a teacher, I might be required to administer first aid to my students, and it couldn't hurt to start learning now.

'Not feeling faint, are you?'

'No, Miss Dickinson.' Freddy looked mortified. Inwardly I chuckled, knowing Dick's fondness for dispensing *sal volatile* from her little glass vial.

'You'll need to stay off it for a few days, but after that you should be back to normal.'

'Thank you, Miss Dickinson. Much appreciated.'

'Why, hello, Miss Taylor,' Freddy said, appearing only now to have noticed me. 'How are you? Enjoying the match, I hope. It wasn't my best effort, but I'll do better next week, so long as this ankle holds up.'

'Fine thank you, Mr Parker,' I said, trying not to blush.

Freddy was a resident at St Paul's, the Anglican college, and the one closest to our own. We had met twice before through Freddy's older sister, a fellow resident in her final year. With his blond hair, blue eyes and elegant cheekbones, Freddy Parker was undoubtedly the most handsome young man I had ever seen. I blushed even more deeply, trying not to make eye contact in case he guessed my thoughts.

Beside me, Miss Dickinson had returned her attention to the match, and although I couldn't understand exactly what she was saying, it sounded encouraging. I followed her gaze and, for the next thirty seconds, tried to follow her lead.

'Miss Taylor?'

I looked back and saw Freddy gesturing me over.

'Are you all right? Shall I fetch another chair so you can elevate your foot?'

He waved away my offer with a smile, then lowered his voice so that I had to lean in close. 'Why was Dick asking if I felt faint back there? I know she's awfully tough herself, but I hope I don't give the appearance of some kind of a man-mouse.'

I chuckled. '*Sal volatile* is her favourite remedy,' I whispered. 'I don't think she gets much opportunity to practise serious medicine, so you would have been doing her a favour if you'd been faint.'

'That makes me feel much better, thank you, Miss Taylor. Maybe you should be the nurse, or rather the doctor here.'

I laughed again, but became suddenly self-conscious. To my relief, Miss Dickinson was thoroughly engrossed in the rugby, as was everyone else within earshot.

For the next few minutes, Freddy continued to engage me in conversation, asking about my interests, my plans for the weekend and so forth. At first, I told myself it was only because he was stuck in his chair until the end of the match and needed help from his teammates to get back to college. But after a while, even I had to concede he appeared genuinely interested in talking to me. And, an even more disturbing thought, that he was quite possibly interested in me from a romantic standpoint. Heavens! Suddenly the idea of going back to Sacred Heart, with its strict regimen of rules and routine, sounded very appealing.

Little by little, my rational thoughts began to tame and then finally overpower my emotions. *You're not here for romance, Lillian Taylor*, I reminded myself. *You're not here to find a husband. You're here to get your degree and set yourself up for the future.*

The more I repeated these things in my head, the easier it was to stop myself from smiling and giggling. On the other hand, it also meant losing track of whatever Freddy was talking about.

'So what do you say, Miss Taylor? Shall we meet there next Saturday afternoon?'

'Excuse me? Meet where?' I looked at him in dismay.

'The Nicholson Museum, of course. We were both just saying how we like going there on rainy days to – you know – ponder over who created all those treasures or what the world was like before Man roamed the earth.' His smile was utterly disarming, and I could feel my defences crumbling.

'Actually,' I stammered. 'I think I've seen enough of the university's antiquities and natural history specimens to last me till the end of my degree. I'm more of a reader really. You know, the type that hides away for hours at a time and barely remembers to eat.' I could hear myself blathering like a fool, but I was determined to bring this romance to an end before it could even begin. 'And to tell you the truth, it bothers me that all those specimens were taken from wherever they were originally found, maybe even stolen from their original owners, in some cases, and now they're just paraded on display for public enjoyment and no one gives a fig about who they belonged to in the first place.'

In the midst of my ranting, it dawned on me that I was no longer speaking about the museum's collection, of which I was genuinely quite fond, but about 'The Drover's Wife'.

'Well, I don't know if that's the case, exactly,' Freddy said, looking at me with new eyes. 'Some of my friends are studying archaeology and they definitely give a fig about the countries where these artefacts come from. They just want to preserve these precious things for the future and share them with a like-minded audience.'

'I'm sure that's what they tell themselves, but I've heard stories from the olden days about rich people hosting Egyptian mummy parties where they would take turns unwrapping the mummies just so they could compete for the little amulets and other trinkets which would fall out as they went along. Where's the preservation in that, I ask you? And apparently that's where the idea for the children's party game of Pass the Parcel first started.' From the expression on Freddy's face, I could see that I had said enough. More than enough.

'Anyway, I'd better be getting back. I've got some study to finish this afternoon. I hope your ankle mends quickly, Mr Parker.' And on that sour note, without even excusing myself from Miss Dickinson, I slunk away in disgrace and returned to college alone.

Chapter 6

Women's Higher Sphere

I was not the only one coming of age this year. With my own twenty-first birthday having taken place during the summer break, and with minimal fanfare, some eight months earlier, this year also marked the twenty-first anniversary of The Women's College, my adopted home since leaving Sacred Heart.

Our forthcoming performance of an allegorical mask, here in the university grounds later this month, was to publicly honour this important occasion. Conceived by Miss Macdonald, it was to be staged in the Elizabethan fashion as a series of tableaux with poetry, music, song and dance, and included specially commissioned verses by Mr Christopher Brennan and Mr John Le Gay Brereton. Complementing the lineup of charismatic female figures drawn from past and present would be an orchestra and chorus, together with the dancers like myself.

We were in the middle of rehearsal, and I stifled a yawn and waited in position as Mary Queen of Scots blessed herself before the saintly figure of Joan of Arc, then bided my time as Florence Nightingale locked eyes with Madame Curie. I nodded approvingly as the Sibyl gestured towards Griselda – perfectly on cue – and smiled as Helen of Troy stepped forward, golden tresses cascading behind her as she dazzled our imaginary audience with her beauty.

And now, my turn. With only the slightest gasp of nervousness, I followed the other dancing maidens skipping down the grassy alleys towards the stage as we came together to perform the immemorial circle dance. It started well enough, but within seconds of what should by now have been a tightly choreographed routine, I knew something had gone wrong. I glanced around in despair as girls paired off haphazardly, either forgetting their steps or, in the case of one couple demonstrating the latest Ragtime style, intentionally ignoring them.

'Girls, ladies, please. We must carry on with the rehearsal!' Miss Macdonald was not amused. Ordinarily quite tolerant of her female charges and inclined to find such skylarking rather droll, no doubt the pressure of staging this pageant to an expected audience of more than five hundred was weighing heavily on our principal. I cast an apologetic glance towards noted artist and college friend Miss Thea Proctor, who was playing the part of Madame de Pompadour and had sensibly withdrawn herself to one side.

'I see it now,' proclaimed an elaborately robed figure to my right, invoking Medea's gift of prophecy. 'I predict ... the performance will be a fiasco.' Having already broken character, she began giggling uncontrollably.

'Shush, she'll hear you,' I warned.

Despite this being my final year at the university, I had not completely abandoned the rule of obedience instilled during my time at the convent, and – at least publicly – did not presume to defy authority. Shivering in the cold August wind that typified Trinity term, I tugged at my fleshings. These requisite sheer fabric tights threatened to fall at any moment, exposing my gooseflesh-stippled legs. I shivered again, powerless to stop my teeth from chattering.

Our cast comprised mostly students, current and alumni, together with members of the wider university community, all under the direction of Miss Macdonald, who – though still somewhat green in the face – had already managed to get our rehearsal back on track in the calm and capable manner for which she was known.

As we again came together for the circle dance, this time according to the script, I noticed an unofficial audience had assembled from amongst passers-by, mostly young male students. Was it my imagination, or had our singing suddenly become sweeter, our dancing more graceful?

I resisted the urge to check if any of the young men were directing their admiration towards me and concentrated on my routine. With less than three hundred female students and more than four times as many males, there was no shortage of romantic attention for Women's College residents, both for girls who actively sought such notice and those, like me, who did not.

When the rehearsal finally ended, I set off towards the college at a brisk pace.

'Wait up, Lillian,' a voice called out from behind. 'I want to ask you something.' It was Clara May. She looked determined and clearly had something on her mind.

'Come into town this evening,' she said, putting her arm through mine and matching my stride. 'There's an important debate at my club, Women's Higher Sphere.'

'I'm afraid I can't – I'm having supper with my friend Hilda.' I was relieved to have a legitimate excuse not to join her.

Clara May looked vexed. 'Where are you meeting her?'

'The Australia Hotel. She's there with her mother for a few days before their ship sails to England.'

'Well, that's perfect,' exclaimed Clara May. 'My sister's staying at The Australia Hotel this whole week too, along with her bigwig husband. Your friend can join us. We'll have an early supper, just us girls, and then go to the meeting together.'

'Thank you, but—'

'But nothing, Lillian, it's all arranged. In any case, it was Miss Macdonald who suggested I ask you. She said it would do you good to get out for the evening, and that you'd most certainly find the debate interesting.'

I hesitated. Although sceptical about whether the suggestion really had originated from our principal or whether Miss Macdonald had merely chosen not to disagree, I was curious as to why Clara May had singled me out. This studious but unpopular Science undergraduate always had an ulterior motive. Perhaps she saw me as soft clay crying out to be formed? Or – already kiln set – as a fellow agitator for women's rights?

'I'll meet you downstairs at five o'clock. Don't be late.' She waggled her index finger in my face. My opportunity to decline had evidently passed.

Back in my study-bedroom, warming up in front of the gas fire, I gazed around with satisfaction. After nothing but shared dormitories at Sacred Heart, I valued the privacy and comfort of my own room. Adorning its deep green walls, I'd hung a few treasured sketches and watercolours, received as gifts, or purchased from my allowance under Mr O'Loughlin's bequest. The sturdy bookshelves above my fireplace were packed tightly with novels, both classic and popular. I felt a rush of gratitude for my rolltop desk and even for the simple washbasin tucked neatly in the cupboard.

My gratitude also extended to the rest of the college; to our common room, dining room, visitor's room and library, all handsomely furnished as an expression of what our principal described as 'gracious surroundings', and in her view a necessary part of a liberal education. Miss Macdonald and Miss Dickinson each had their own quarters, as did the five women on staff who produced wholesome meals for us each day (even if not to the standard of the French nuns) and returned my washing neatly ironed and folded each week. Though I was undoubtedly glad to be free of such chores – now that I was no longer an object of charity – I also felt guilty. Aside from a few innocent questions about my family when I first arrived, and respectful silence thereafter, no one asked details of how my fees were paid; if anything, I was envied for having independent financial means.

'Aha!' I exclaimed aloud.

Could *that* be why Clara May had asked me to the debate tonight? Perhaps she saw me as a new independent female prototype? She wouldn't know that without the generosity of my late benefactor, my only means of being here would have been as a servant.

With my front side restored to warmth, I turned my back to the fire and looked outside. Brocade curtains framed a cloudless sky, its penetrating blue hue denying the winter chill. And while the nearby tennis courts themselves held little temptation for me, I found comfort in the sound of balls being thwacked and girls having fun.

~

As the clock chimed five, I went downstairs to where Clara May was already waiting, dressed simply – as was I – in a high-necked blouse and long belted skirt, with coat, scarf and hat in hand. The college was quieter than usual for this time of day, with several girls still languishing in bed, suffering the after-effects of the smallpox vaccination Miss Macdonald had procured for us following the recent outbreak.

After a brisk walk and then the tram ride to Castlereagh Street, I knocked on the door of Hilda's suite at The Australia Hotel and begged for her understanding. Before long, we were all enjoying a delicious meal in the hotel's grand dining room, The Emerald Room. As I sat beneath a canopy of Italian marble columns, chandeliers and intricately decorated ceilings, the surrounding fountains and greenery reminded me of my first visit to Mr Quong Tart's Tea Rooms with Hilda years earlier. Clara May's sister, who proved herself more approachable and infinitely less outspoken than her younger sibling, graciously insisted on charging our entire meal to her husband's suite and giving us money for another cab fare back to the college after the debate. My glass of champagne had left me feeling relaxed and talkative. Hilda also seemed to be enjoying our girlish chatter, along with a second helping from the dessert trolley. Perhaps even Clara May was not so bad when one got to know her.

The only thing that detracted from our supper had been when I caught sight of Freddy Parker across the room. Looking as handsome as ever, he was sitting at a table with Miranda, another girl from college, together with an older couple – most likely his parents, or hers. I had heard that she and Freddy had started seeing each other, but this looked more serious than I had supposed. When Hilda noticed my faraway expression and asked if anything was amiss, I pretended I had been testing my long-distance vision and was relieved to report that, despite my considerable hours of study, spectacles were not yet on the cards.

~

'Well,' said Clara May, as we wove through a sea of dark bowlers and top hats in Martin Place, 'you've seen my brother-in-law in his best possible light.'

Hilda looked confused. 'But we didn't meet him.'

'Exactly,' said Clara May.

Hilda turned to me for explanation.

'She's just being funny.' I looked pointedly at Clara May. 'And somewhat unkind.'

Undaunted by my tacit reprimand, Clara May charged ahead.

While I skipped to keep up with her long purposeful strides, Hilda refused to be rushed. She kept stopping unexpectedly whenever something caught her eye: an artfully arranged shop window or an elegantly attired woman showcasing the latest look from Paris.

The debate was just getting started when we arrived at Challis House. Crammed in like sardines in the overheated salon, Hilda made little attempt to disguise a yawn as her eyes wandered around the room, perhaps keeping an eye out for anyone she knew. Guessing that Clara May would be sure to question us on the way home, I tried to compensate for Hilda's lack of attentiveness by concentrating closely. The women speaking were all so certain of themselves and their opinions, and yet they were in complete opposition to each other – admittedly, the point of any debate. The affirmative side proclaimed that a woman's higher sphere was and always would be in the home, while the negative side argued with equal passion that a woman's ultimate sphere should extend beyond the home, as it did for men, in the performance of public work. Both sides gave compelling examples of well-known women to prove their case. I was left less sure of my position than when the debate began.

Amid the echo of shrill voices and applause, we emerged from the building back onto Martin Place. The wind from earlier had died down and the night had become surprisingly mild. A full moon lit up the sky.

Clara May pointed to the long queue for hansom cabs. 'Let's not bother trying to get back to college now. Let's go back to your hotel, Hilda. We can discuss the debate.'

There was little point arguing.

Before the waiter had even taken our order – coffee for Clara May, together with an expensive bottle of Perrier-Jouet champagne, this time courtesy of Hilda's account – Clara May launched her assault. After dismissing the arguments of those on the side of tradition and conservatism, some of which I had conceded as valid, she summarised the arguments of the negative team, elaborating and embellishing with great enthusiasm. I recognised most of Clara May's reasoning and turns of phrase from articles I too had read in *The Woman's Signal*, *Punch* and other feminist literature freely available in our common room.

I nodded and smiled in all the right places and felt faintly relieved when Clara May directed her attention to Hilda.

'So, Hilda, where do you think a woman's higher sphere lies? In the home or in the wider world?' Clara May sat tall in her chair, her chin thrust forward in challenge.

My best friend smiled innocently, oblivious to danger as the waiter topped up her glass. 'Well ... both, of course!'

Good answer, Hilda, I thought to myself. *Let's hope we can leave it at that.*

Clara May looked surprised. 'So, you agree women should hold roles outside the home in public life?'

'I do,' said Hilda, nodding. 'First and foremost, a woman should do everything in her power to be a good wife and make a good home for her husband.'

My own smile faded as I began to see where this might lead.

'Next,' continued Hilda, 'she should be a good mother and role model to her children, making sure they are always presentable, teaching them good manners and encouraging them to develop as many accomplishments as possible. Especially the girls.'

Clara May bristled. 'But what about a woman's work outside the home? You said you believed in that.'

'I do,' repeated Hilda ingenuously. 'It's something all women should aspire to. Even if she's not from an important family herself, a woman who has married well can enjoy the benefits of her husband's public standing. Apart from hosting afternoon teas and dinner parties in her own home, any woman should endeavour to take her place in greater society, attending all the important events – spring races, charity bazaars, functions at Admiralty House and Victoria Barracks, even garden parties at Government House.' Buoyed by alcohol, Hilda appeared greatly pleased with the eloquence of her speech.

Oh dear, I thought. It was probably something Lady Fitzwilliam had told her.

'Weren't you listening to a single word said at the debate?' said Clara May.

Less certain now, Hilda glanced at me for inspiration. 'It was very hot inside. I could hardly think at all.'

Clara May's eyes flashed and her tone was dismissive. 'I can see why you didn't bother attending university.'

'That's enough, Clara May. You're being rude.' I should have stepped in sooner. Schoolgirl taunts and insults echoed in my ears. Why was it that some people thought they had the right to criticise others just because they looked – or thought – differently to themselves?

'Not at all,' said Hilda, laughing as if Clara May's words had all been in jest. 'Clara May's right. Even if I had been offered a place at the university, I wouldn't have taken it.'

Impressed by Hilda's social skills even if not her ambitions, I felt better about not having come to her aid more quickly. I would soon have my own chance to demonstrate bravery. Sure enough, Clara May hardly drew breath before beginning her onslaught.

'Please tell me you were paying attention, Lillian,' she began. 'Surely you don't see yourself married, stuck at home with a brood of children, playing second fiddle to your husband while he's out making his name in the world.'

'No, I do not,' I replied, speaking truthfully.

'Hmmph,' our inquisitor breathed, relishing this moment of apparent vindication. Clara May turned her arched brows back towards Hilda, who merely fluttered her eyelashes and smiled.

Distracted by their mutual battle, neither girl noticed my own troubled expression. Despite its pleasant beginning, the evening had unsettled me. Even though I did not see myself as ever getting married or having children, it was not because I didn't think these things were worth having – quite the opposite – but that deep down, I knew they were not meant for someone like me.

As Clara May continued to lecture us, unaware she had lost half her audience, I again asked myself which side of the debate I stood for. If I approached my studies with diligence (as I always had) and if I intended to pursue my chosen profession of teaching for the remainder of my adult life (as I did), did that not that mean I had already chosen my sphere? Yet to say that I wanted to devote myself to the performance of public work in the world at large seemed so presumptuous, so self-important. A claim of that magnitude was reserved for women like our principal. Without ever defying the rules of society, Miss Macdonald had always stood up for her beliefs, gaining universal respect while achieving her own aims. Even when she first came to the colony, she had apparently managed to sidestep the usual labels of bluestocking, man-hater or worse; labels often thrown at women with far less radical agendas than her own. No one could deny that our principal – who had travelled to the other side of the world in pursuit of her ideals – had given all of herself as living proof of the legitimacy of her cause: higher education for women to the benefit of all society. Against her shining example, I had no such calling. Teaching was simply the obvious path for a woman like me who needed to support herself and loved to read; if I could share my favourite pastime with others, so much the better, yet one could hardly call this public service or a vocation.

As if she had read my mind, Clara May was now talking about Principal Macdonald. 'Did you know that when she was first appointed to lead our college, she was the highest salaried woman in all New South Wales? Can you imagine – a Scotchwoman of just thirty-two years earning five hundred pounds? More than any other woman in the colony!'

'How on earth did you find that out?' I asked, shaking my head both at Miss Macdonald's achievement and Clara May's nerve in sharing it.

Unlike my high-minded companion, I realised, I felt myself unqualified to fight for women's rights. Cowardly though it was, I would leave that task to more capable women than me. And although women's equality was by no means complete, at least things were better than ever before.

One had only to look at my own life to see the truth of this. Despite my humble origins, the doors of education had been opened wide to me, both at school and university. Very soon – degree in hand, and with good fortune on my side – I expected to find a respectable position as a teacher, most likely even in a private school. Thereafter, provided I did not marry, I had the right to work and build up my own wealth, modest though it would be, and to own property. I could choose to take an interest in public matters, casting my vote as I saw fit in both state and federal elections. Perhaps one day – when women were more ready to support each other, as Miss Macdonald was always encouraging us to do – a woman might even be voted in to lead this country.

~

Later that night I woke from a dream – part nightmare, part fantasy – with my heart thumping in my chest. I had dreamed that, rather than taking the hansom cab back to college, Clara May made us take the tram and walk instead. Just as we reached the edge of University Park, needing only to cross the wide expanse of lawn that led to college, an ill-timed cluster of clouds formed, obscuring the moon and plunging us into darkness.

'Blame the City Council,' said Clara May, in answer to my protestations about missing curfew and the fact of her sister having given us the money for the cab fare. 'It's their fault for refusing to light the streetlamps during a full moon.'

Navigating towards the distant lights of the college, we picked our way through the grass, stumbling from time to time over uneven ground or the occasional fallen branch. All at once, the air closed in around me as I was shoved to the ground. Half-winded and sprawled on all fours, the darkness was overwhelming. A scream cut through the night.

'Give it to me,' said a man's low voice, raspy and threatening.

I buried my face into the cold, damp ground, instinctively covering my head. Suddenly a dark figure stood above me, smelling of rum and cheap tobacco, like the men who spilled out of the public bars around Circular Quay. Rough hands grabbed at my coat, pushing me onto my back. I started kicking but flinched at the cold earth against my stockinged legs and stopped short. Mad with fear, I grasped wildly for the hem of my skirt and yanked it down to cover myself. *Help!* I tried in vain to cry out, my voice frozen and useless.

I heard another man's voice in the distance. All at once, my attacker's hands loosened their brutal grip, then let go completely. More shouting and yelling, then the sound of a nearby struggle. As the clouds parted slightly, I saw my assailant break away and run back towards Newtown Road. The other man dashed towards me, gallantly helping me to my feet.

It was Freddy Parker. My hero.

'We have to get you back to college,' Freddy urged, putting his arms around me in way that felt both protective and exciting. 'He might still be around. Though with the knock I gave him, by Jove, he'd be a bloody fool to come back for more.' The errant moon, having let us down earlier, now rallied in support and lit up the sky, guiding us to safety.

'But what are you doing here?' I asked breathlessly, every bit the damsel in distress. 'How did you know I needed help?'

'I've never forgotten you, Lillian. I'll always care for you,' he crooned. 'But it's too late now. I'm going to marry Miranda.'

Chapter 7

The Perils of Youth

Some weeks later, on the morning after the official staging of our mask, Miranda announced her engagement to Freddy Parker. Was I right in discerning a flicker of disappointment on Miss Macdonald's face when Miranda had burst into the common room to share her news? More likely, the disappointment was mine alone, although I knew full well I was more upset than I had any right to be. I stepped forward to congratulate Miranda and to join the other girls who had all swarmed around to admire her diamond ring.

That night, too agitated to sleep, I got out of bed and turned on the oil lamp. Wrapped in my flannel dressing gown, I went to my desk in search of Hilda's letter from yesterday. I missed my friend. It was postmarked from Fremantle, their last stop before Ceylon. By now, Hilda's steamship may have reached the Suez Canal on its way to London. She and her mother had again planned to stay at the Ritz, before continuing onto Paris and then Italy.

Despite having only just embarked upon her second grand tour of Europe, Hilda's letter had indicated there was not likely to be a third.

Lady Fitzwilliam was confident of helping her make a suitable match on their return home. My friend admitted she was more than ready for this next phase of life to begin.

'There are only so many churches, galleries and operas you can see, before they all blur into one,' she wrote. 'Not to mention that I've already played enough quoits and cribbage on this leg of the voyage to last me a lifetime. It's time for this *Mademoiselle* to become a *Madame, tout de suite* ...' I read over her words again and chuckled to myself.

I'd sent Hilda my reply earlier today, almost immediately after hearing Miranda's news. Choosing to say nothing about this to Hilda, I'd simply reassured my friend that any man would be lucky to have her as his wife. I'd also enclosed a clipping from today's *Herald* affirming the success of last night's pageant, along with the accompanying photograph. Sadly, I was hidden from view by a large pillar.

I put away Hilda's letter for now and thought about Miss Macdonald's speech from the prior evening, in which she had explained the moral behind our mask: not simply as thanksgiving for 'the perils of youth safely past', but also to symbolically depict the college's values, ideals and hopes. In contrast to the Sibyl, for example – the wise woman to whom present, past and future were all unveiled – dancing maidens like me apparently signified womanhood unburdened, plastic, our futures unknown. With her usual winning combination of passion and diplomacy, Principal Macdonald had argued that instead of directing all efforts to the emotions and practical arts – as has too often been the case in women's education – rigorously training a woman's reason and will is more beneficial, not only to the individual in question, but to the world at large.

Although I supposed some might still regard her message as controversial, our principal had long drummed this idea into us girls, reminding us to use our education and every opportunity to train our minds and not content ourselves with simply learning how to sing or paint, or how to keep house for that matter. Her message was something

I had tried to live by during my years at college and from which I drew comfort for the future. I was not blind to the attractions of handsome young men like Freddy Parker – far from it – but I had reached the inevitable conclusion that I had to choose between marriage and independence. Marriage carried the tantalising promise of love, family and security. Yet experience had shown me that all this could be taken away in the space of a single day, in the devastating breath of a single hot wind. Principal Macdonald had eschewed the traditional marital path and had undoubtedly found fulfilment in her work and the companionship of Miss Dickinson and her students. I hoped I could do the same.

If Miss Macdonald's example was not enough in itself (and leaving aside the tragedy of my own mother's life), I needed only to look to Henry Lawson's mother to see that marriage and motherhood held a woman back from carving out her own achievements. It was only after leaving her husband and impoverished life in the bush that Louisa Lawson found success in Sydney, became the Mother of Suffrage, and launched her influential journal with its all-female staff. Even now, in her sixties, and almost a decade after ceasing to publish *The Dawn,* her own poetry and stories continued to appear in print. I rifled through my desk drawer to locate one of my favourite clippings from an interview with her published in the paper.

> Why, a woman can't bear a child without it being received into the hands of a male doctor. It is baptised by a fat old male parson; a girl goes through life obeying laws made by men; and if she breaks them, a male magistrate sends her to a gaol where a male warder handles her and looks in her cell at night to see she's all right. If she gets so far as to be hanged, a male hangman puts the rope round her neck; she is buried by a male gravedigger; and she goes to a Heaven ruled over by a male God or a hell managed by a male devil. Isn't it a wonder men didn't make the devil a woman?

Accurate though this was, Mrs Lawson's bald-faced audacity always left me open-mouthed. I cast my mind back to that letter I had once written to Henry Lawson. With the benefit of hindsight and several years' exposure to more progressive ways of thinking here at The Women's College, perhaps I could have handled things differently? Perhaps I should even have directed my letter to his mother and asked her advice instead – as a self-professed feminist, no less. Now, when I looked at 'The Drover's Wife', Lawson's omission of my name, along with that of Esther and Mother, struck me not as mere oversight, but as a deliberate choice on the writer's part, one that reflected the masculine society in which we lived. Nor was my family's story the only time the writer had made this same choice. Over the years I'd come across other poems and stories by Henry Lawson with titles like 'The Free Selector's Daughter', 'The Shanty-Keeper's Wife' and even 'Brighten's Sister-in-Law'. It was acceptable to write about a woman, it seemed, so long as she was clearly attached to a man. Try as I might, the closest I ever came to finding any poems ending in the word 'husband' or 'son' were the ones that ended in 'mate', which was hardly the same thing.

More awake than ever, I returned to bed and reached for my book, *The Getting of Wisdom*. Henry Handel Richardson's second novel was set in an exclusive Presbyterian girls' boarding school in Melbourne in the 1880s, and it had me hooked from the very first page. Although its young protagonist, Laura, could be positively wicked at times – especially in bending the truth – there was so much about her experiences to which I could relate. Packed to the brim with realistic detail and acutely felt emotion, it was hard to imagine this story having been written by anyone other than the adult version of the clever but wayward heroine herself – let alone a man. I was not alone in suspecting 'Mr Richardson' had adopted a *nom de plume* and that hiding somewhere in the wings was instead a sharp-witted authoress.

Laura's schoolgirl flights of fancy were the perfect antidote to my present state of mind. Nodding and chuckling as I followed the words into an artfully constructed world, more appealing than the one in which I lived, I lasted but a few more pages before turning off the lamp and letting myself drift gently off to sleep.

Chapter 8
Under the Canopy

It seemed I was destined to spend my whole life within or close to the safe, predictable confines of a schoolhouse. Though Ravenswood was undoubtedly one of Sydney's more exclusive independent girls' schools, it lacked the gracious architecture and sheer scale of Sacred Heart, along with its majestic harbour views, but the local community was kind and welcoming and the natural surroundings equally so. The suburb of Gordon was a charming mélange of weatherboard cottages and substantial homes, of rural living and modern comforts, of unsealed roads and tended gardens, all laid out under dazzling blue skies and encircled by great tracts of original forest.

I had been very fortunate to gain my position here, almost two years earlier and not long after the war had started, teaching English and French, mostly to the older girls who were preparing to sit for their Intermediate and Leaving Certificates. After graduating from the university and completing my training at the Teachers' College, my appointment had followed a recommendation from Principal Macdonald to her friend and fellow university academic, Miss Isabel Fidler, whose sister, Mabel, had started the school. Now in its sixteenth year and steadily growing, it was one of the few privately owned schools in New South Wales to have achieved formal registration, and it boasted strong academic results. In fact, Ravenswood girls had earned the university's Fairfax Prize for the past three years running.

Nevertheless, I had my doubts as to how many of those presently doing their Leaving Certificates would ultimately go on to university study or a career. While most families in this growing middle-class area of Sydney's Upper North Shore wanted their daughters to be well educated, the expectation was that after a few years enjoying the social scene they would marry and have children, redirecting their knowledge and newfound insights towards raising the next generation.

Mustering the authority of every one of my twenty-four years, I faced my class of fifth-formers.

'Yes, Olive. What is your question?' With her hand raised high and a desperate expression on her face, I was hoping my student had a vital insight to share with the class on *Macbeth* but, as it turned out, all she wanted was permission to go to the bathroom.

'If you can hold on five more minutes, class is nearly finished,' I said, brightening at the idea myself. 'Does anyone else have anything to say about what we've read so far? How about you, Stella?'

'Why did Shakespeare have to make it all so complicated?' Stella whined. 'Your French lessons are easier to understand than this.'

'I'll remind you of that next time you're struggling with your imperatives, Stella.' My tone was firm, but I allowed myself to smile.

Although I might never have children of my own, I tried to think of myself as a mother cat in the classroom. My job was both to nurture and discipline my little kittens, no matter how adorable their mews or how sharp their claws.

'Can anyone answer Stella's question? Yes, Cecilia, go ahead.'

'Well, it's like poetry, isn't it?' Cecilia began, her expression earnest.

'The language adds to its dramatic meaning. It's like unravelling a puzzle.'

'Exactly, Cecilia, well said!' Although I tried not to show favouritism, girls like Cecilia were the reason I enjoyed teaching. 'Of course, another explanation is that Shakespeare was writing in Elizabethan English, which can make it harder to understand, even though much of it is still in use today. In fact, Shakespeare contributed more than a thousand words to the English language. It's quite a legacy for a man who died three hundred years ago, isn't it?' I paused, giving them time to digest what I had said. 'In our next lesson, girls, we will be meeting Lady Macbeth for the first time.'

At the back of the classroom, I saw Harriette throw her head sideways and mouth three words to her neighbour. 'That's right, Harriette, Lady Macbeth does make an unusual sounding plea to the spirits when she says "unsex me here".' The class erupted into predictable titters. 'But not for the reason you may be expecting,' I added, hoping this sounded suitably mysterious to whet their appetites. 'In the meantime, girls, I'll leave you with another line from Lady Macbeth in that same scene. I'd like you to go home this afternoon and see if you can show some "milk of human kindness" to your families.' I glanced up at the clock. 'Off you go then, class is dismissed.'

I smiled ruefully at Harriette's little performance. I should have anticipated that Lady Macbeth's words might cause a distraction. Hopefully none of the parents would make a complaint about inappropriate subject matter. I suspected I had subconsciously chosen *Macbeth* because of its themes: the question of whether Macbeth, who saw himself as a mere 'poor player' in someone else's script, was predestined to damnation. That and the fact it was the shortest of Shakespeare's tragedies.

As the last students filed out of my classroom, I packed away my books and prepared to go home. Two dark plaits suddenly appeared around the corner of the door.

I grinned. 'Hello, Mavis. Ready to go home?'

'Yes, Miss Taylor,' Mavis replied automatically before contradicting herself. 'Nessie has invited me home to see her new puppy. Could you tell Mother, please?'

'Does Nessie's mother know you're coming?'

Mavis paused and another pair of plaits appeared from behind the doorway. 'I'm sure she won't mind,' said Nessie in her most convincing voice.

'And I'm sure that's true, Nessie. But, just to be certain, I'll ask your mother myself. Hats and gloves, girls. Let's go.'

We left the school grounds and headed past the train station towards Nessie's house.

'Shall we practise our verb conjugations while we walk?' I suggested, only half in jest. Just then, I noticed a young man struggling up from the platform with crutches, one suit trouser leg pinned up halfway. Torn between rushing over to help and giving the returned soldier his privacy, my eyes widened when Nessie broke into song.

'It's a long way to Turramurra
It's a long way to go
It's a long way to Turramurra
To the sweetest girl I know
Goodbye to Killara, farewell Pymble Hill
It's a long, long way to Turramurra
But my heart's there still.'

'What's that you're singing?' I asked.

'I wrote it myself.' Nessie's cheeks flushed with pride. 'All our boys are singing it, but I came up with a new chorus especially for Tom. I put it in my last letter and told him he can sing it whenever he's missing home and thinking of Betsy.'

'What a lovely thought.' My heart gave another sharp tug. Nessie's older brother was fighting in the 18th Battalion on the Western Front. Tom's sweetheart, Betsy, who lived in nearby Turramurra (and not

Tipperary), was with the VADs – the Voluntary Aid Detachments – and, according to Nessie, had faithfully promised to wait for his return.

After exchanging pleasantries with Nessie's mother and cuddling the puppy – a sweet little terrier with remarkably sharp teeth – I walked back towards the house on Greengate Road, Killara, where I lived with Mavis, her twin brother, George, younger sister, Nora, and their mother, Isabel. With Mavis's father having resolved to join the 2nd Division of the Australian Imperial Force, and set to depart for training in Liverpool, Mrs Edwards had gladly accepted me as a boarder when I had first come to Ravenswood almost two years earlier. Like Nessie's brother, Mr Edwards was also in the 18th Battalion.

Mistakenly, I had at first presumed I was there to offset the cost of running the household but, after learning that Mr Edwards's rank meant that his pay was not dissimilar from what he'd earned as a civilian, it soon became clear that my true purpose was to provide Mrs Edwards with company, along with another pair of hands to help with their three children. Only five years my senior, Mrs Edwards was always friendly and yet she was such a chatterbox, and – truth be told – a gossipmonger, that I kept to my room as much as I could without seeming impolite. As a companion, I must have been a disappointment. Even so, the house was rarely quiet as Mrs Edwards lived to entertain, presiding over monthly 'At Homes' and endless cups of tea, listening to the gramophone, playing whist or euchre in the front room, and hosting tennis mornings on the full-size court out back.

I slowed down at the top of one of Gordon's gentler inclines, removing my hat and pushing up my sleeves to feel the sun on my arms. It was a mild September day, the temperature somewhere in the middle seventies, that perfect point of balance when it was neither warm nor cool, and the air felt like an extension of my own skin. A light spring breeze blew in gentle, caressing gusts, carrying with it the faint scent of wildflowers, an elusive suggestion of honey, spice and citrus. Cream flowering turpentine and gossamer wattle added feathery softness to the eucalyptus canopy which loosely framed our streets. I breathed deeply, grateful to be living in this beautiful Sydney shire known as *Ku-ring-gai*. It had been named, I was told, for the local Aboriginal tribe who had once walked these lands. And yet it was the very absence of dark-skinned faces in the places I had lived since leaving my family home that would sometimes prompt me to think of Old Mary and wonder what had happened to her after I left.

Drawn to the past, as always, I had welcomed the opportunity as a newcomer to discover more about the local history from some of the older residents. Waiting at the Ravenswood school gate to meet their granddaughters of an afternoon or catching sight of me from their front gardens as I passed, they had ample time and an endless supply of stories to share, especially for someone who cared to listen, as I did.

Timber getters, I learned, had been among the first white men to come to this once inaccessible region. Spurred by the demand for building supplies for a growing colony, they seized on vast swathes of tall bluegum forests, together with turpentine, ironbark and blackbutt. Next to follow were the orchardists. Last of all came the railway, completed not long before I was born, and which marked the turning point in luring new residents to Sydney's 'healthy highlands district', as it was then known. I enjoyed hearing of how neighbours came together in those early days – doctors, judges, politicians, retailers and wool merchants, among others – to improve communal services through political lobbying and the establishment of local Progress Associations. Already surrounded by tremendous bush reserves in every direction, they had planted yet more trees, expressing the wish that new streets would one day become well-shaded avenues.

More than ever, the endless plains of red earth and the sparse mulga bush of my family home seemed like a distant dream. What would my mother have made of this place? What might Father have said? If viewed through the eyes of an outsider, I suspected many would observe these grand homes and oversized allotments with resentment, likely condemning its inhabitants' motivations as elitist. Yet I couldn't help but admire the way these early settlers had united to create their very own Australian Arcadia; one to which I had unexpectedly been given the key.

I took the short cut through the dairy on Bruce Avenue and emerged onto our street just in time to catch sight of Mrs Edwards's horse and trap heading in the opposite direction. Mingling uncomfortably with my relief was a simultaneous pang of guilt.

Closing the heavy iron gates behind me, I took the key from my purse and approached the house, which had been built in the typical style, with lace brickwork, terracotta tiles and fine timber detailing. A rough-edged stone wall and well-clipped hedges separated the property from the street, while colourful hibiscus and other spring blooms decorated the path towards the verandah and front entrance. Sunshine filtered through the greenery, creating warm yellow light. A perfect day to be outside.

I fairly ran down the long, wood-panelled hallway, brushing against Axminster carpets, potted kentia palms and aspidistra in my eagerness to get upstairs to my bedroom and dispose of my hat and gloves for the day. I located my book and took a moment to admire my growing collection of pictures funded from my modest teaching salary. In the kitchen, I gulped down a tall glass of water and grabbed a handful of biscuits from the ten-pound Arnott's tin, then headed straight to the verandah, lowering myself into the large rattan armchair with an unsuppressed groan of pleasure.

The Sydney Morning Herald lay open on the small table beside me, its pages flickering in the breeze. I pictured Mrs Edwards sitting here earlier today. Aside from her husband's letters and the latest women's magazines, this daily paper was all she read. To my mind, the newspaper bore only bad news these days and was better left unseen.

I thought back to when it all began in the winter of 1914. Within days of the first declaration of war in Europe, Australia had pledged a force of twenty thousand men, and voluntary recruitment for the AIF began immediately. All around the country, men had enlisted in droves, keen to prove themselves and take their part in history. For some, the pay was a welcome bonus. No one wanted to miss out. Not even the events of Anzac Day could stop them; in its wake the tide of patriotism swelled higher than ever. Who would have imagined that less than two years after the first contingent had sailed from Albany, more than a quarter of a million men would enlist? Almost one in every three of suitable age.

Slowly things had changed. Battle after battle, loss after loss, the horror of muddy trench warfare all along the Western Front took its toll and support for the war finally began to waver. New troops were needed faster than they were enlisting. Physical standards and age restrictions were loosened so more could join. Recruitment committees popped up in every town and shire as young men were pressured into volunteering with emotional calls for help from soldiers at the front along with advertising posters and slogans designed to shame. And now conscription was the word on everyone's lips.

Intending to refold the paper without reading it, I cast a furtive glance at the casualty list, hoping not to see the surnames of any families in our school community. Unlike most women my age who had a brother or cousin or even a husband in service, I had no one left to lose. It was one of the few consolations of being alone.

Yesterday's list of casualties had been the 211th such list, representing nearly nine hundred Australians and New Zealanders out of action – the majority wounded. I only hoped these men's wounds would not be mortal but sufficiently grave to keep them out of battle for good. Looking at their names was bad enough. It was even worse when there were photos.

Against my own better judgement, I ran my finger down the list of men from New South Wales killed in action and stopped short at a SGT F. R. Parker, Waverley (prev. rep. wounded). The young heroic face of Freddy Parker – star rugby player and still the occasional hero of my dreams – flashed before me. Could this Sergeant be him? Had Freddy and

Miranda bought a house in Waverley after getting married? A tightness in my chest said they had. I pictured Miranda, the carefree girl I knew at college, and felt my throat swell to think she might now be a widow. And to think that could have been me! Back then, I'd been jealous of her happiness and questioned my prior action. Not anymore. Now all I felt was a distressing rush of both shame and relief.

I pushed away these ugly thoughts, along with the offending newspaper, and made a silent pledge to never again look at such lists. Instead, I gripped hold of my book, as yet unopened. Above me, dense white clouds travelled slowly across the sky, a sea of royal blue, like continents forming and reforming into an ever-changing world map. If only countries could co-exist peacefully like this, without consequence or damage.

The actual world map, as it stood today, was often the object of scrutiny from my students. During French lessons, they would ask me to pinpoint towns and villages named in battle – small, obscure localities no one had ever heard of before, but which would now be forever etched into our history books. France, and the language of its people – once made dear to me by *les sœurs françaises* at Sacred Heart – had become tainted by thoughts of mud, blood, death and despair.

Parroting the language of newspapers and of their parents, many girls spoke of 'our friend England', 'brave Belgium' and 'poor little Serbia', reducing complex international politics to the familiar setting of schoolyard friends and enemies, victims and bullies.

Occasionally one of them would ask me why Australia had to take part in a war so far away, in unquestioning deference to England. Yet I, of all people, understood what it meant to yearn for one's mother and to want to please her, despite the cost.

The comforting firmness of my book still clasped between my thumb and forefingers gradually drew me from my reverie. It was CJ Dennis's charming new verse novel, *The Songs of a Sentimental Bloke.* I skipped past Henry Lawson's preface to the chapter titled 'Romeo and Juliet' – an infinitely funnier and less tragic rendition than Shakespeare's original. For the next little while, at least, I could gratefully surrender my thoughts to Bill and Doreen's touching romance.

A good hour later, I looked up and smiled knowingly as the two gates at the end of the carriage drive swung open with a clatter, flattening the shrubs on either side. Young George strolled in, singing out his usual blithe apology. Behind him, the hourglass figure of Mrs Edwards rose from her seat in the pony trap, waving with delight as she caught sight of me on the verandah.

'Why, Lillian, there you are!' Mrs Edwards turned back to remonstrate with her son. 'Say "Good Afternoon" to Miss Taylor, George – where are your manners? And why can't you ever be more careful with those gates?'

I bid a silent adieu to my peaceful evening and hurried over to help. 'Hello, Isabel, how was your afternoon?' Keen to encourage intimacy, Mrs Edwards had long insisted on first names.

'Wonderful, thank you!' Her pretty face was flushed. 'Such a glorious day, isn't it? Nora doesn't like to be shut up inside here all alone on a day like this. She likes to go out visiting, don't you?' she added, patting her toddler's dimpled leg as she handed her over.

Little Nora's demeanour suggested otherwise. Observing her forlorn expression and the desperate way in which she was sucking on her thumb, I surmised that Mrs Edwards's last comment had probably been directed at me. 'I hope you weren't waiting for me to get home before you went out, Isabel. I walked Mavis over to Nessie's house after school. I thought you wouldn't mind, today being Friday, after all.'

'How sweet of you – thank you! Although you missed an interesting afternoon at Mrs Lloyd's. She was telling us all about her new neighbours.' Mrs Edwards's blue eyes sparkled in a way that only fresh gossip could inspire.

Before she could elaborate, Nora started to cry. Mrs Edwards took the infant back into her arms, murmuring words of love and stroking her fine blond curls. 'Such a glorious day, isn't it?' she repeated. 'I do love this time of year before the heat sets in.' A faraway look came over her face and her hand began to flutter as she pulled at Nora's powder pink bloomers. 'But all this lovely sunshine makes me think of Frank. I hate to think what the coming winter will be like for him and his men.'

I nodded gently, meeting Mrs Edwards's eyes, now shiny with tears. For a second, I thought of telling her about Freddy Parker then immediately dismissed the idea. It would only upset her. Perhaps I'd been mistaken anyway.

'George, stop that at once!' Mrs Edwards shook her head in dismay.

George, who had evidently forgotten his obligations to the horse, was now aiming his slingshot at an unsuspecting pair of sulphur-crested cockatoos perched in a nearby tree. 'Murderous Huns,' he mouthed with a sneer, lining up the hapless birds in his sights.

'I'd better get this one inside and see to our supper,' Mrs Edwards said, as little Nora began to cry in earnest. 'I need to be up early tomorrow to prepare for the cake sale. We all need to do our bit.'

'Yes, of course. We all need to do our bit.' I refrained from sighing aloud as I pictured the endless knitting that awaited us once the children were in bed, tonight and every evening, then felt ashamed when I instead pictured the soldiers to whom our socks and other comforts would be sent. 'Let me help with the baking,' I offered, resigned to losing my morning now also. 'I'll just keep an eye on George and then we'll both come in.'

As Mrs Edwards disappeared inside with little Nora's arms wrapped around her neck, the whining sound of her stay laces were an audible reminder of the price of beauty. Smiling wryly, I thought of Louisa Lawson's old article in *The Dawn*.

With one eye trained on George, I settled back into the armchair and continued reading until the gates clattered open a second time. Mavis skipped up the pathway, hat askew, one glove missing and breathless from her run home.

'I want my own puppy,' she panted. 'I'm going inside right now to convince Mummy.'

'Wait for me,' bellowed George. 'I want a puppy too.' Having thankfully relinquished his slingshot and finished tending to the horse, he raced after his sister through the front door.

I breathed a sigh of relief. Quiet at last. By now, the clouds had all but disappeared and the brilliant blue sky of day was fading into soft sweeps of pink and yellow. I heard a motor car in the distance and traced the sound of the lamplighter making his way down the street. Beyond the darkening hedge, the familiar outline of silvery-coloured eucalypts reached towards each other like old friends.

'So life mooches on,' I mused, a gentle smile playing on my lips as I pictured Bill and Doreen sitting beside me in this poetic suburban scene. With the trees nodding sagely in agreement and night finally falling, I went inside to join the others.

Chapter 9
Aunt Gertrude

Later that week, I joined Hilda and her husband for Sunday lunch at the Wentworth. As the first to arrive, I was surprised to see four place settings laid out on our table. Everything soon became clear when Cecil introduced me to his new lawyer, a Mr Patrick Polding, and held my glance with a meaningful smile. It was not the first time they had tried to help find me a mate. And although there were still days when I questioned my position on marriage and family, today was not proving to be one of them.

'Would you be so kind as to pass the salt, Miss Taylor?'

'Certainly,' I replied, trying not to stare at the spinach stuck between his teeth. I judged him to be in his mid-thirties, at least ten years older than myself, with a receding hairline and soft pudgy hands that looked as if they had seen little physical labour.

'Thank you, Miss Taylor, very kind.' He accepted the silver salt shaker with a slight nod of his head then all but tipped its contents over his plate. 'You would think their chef would have learned how to season food properly, wouldn't you? But that's Australia for you, isn't it?'

Cecil, who I presumed would be paying for today's lunch, looked up sharply from his own meal but said nothing.

'What kind of law do you practice, Mr Polding?' I asked, both to change the subject, and to offer him a chance to reveal another side of himself. There must have been some reason why Cecil, or more likely Hilda, had suggested putting the two of us together.

But instead of answering me right away, he turned to Cecil and smiled broadly, as if amused by my question. 'It's difficult to explain simply, Miss Taylor. It concerns trusts and company law and other such matters, which I fear you'll find uninteresting.'

Hilda noticed my expression and hastily cut in. 'No need for you to simplify anything on Lillian's account, Mr Polding. She's by far the cleverest woman I know.'

'Quite so,' echoed Cecil. 'I believe I mentioned Miss Taylor teaches at an exclusive girls' school in the North Shore.'

Mr Polding turned to me. 'And did you go to university, Miss Taylor?'

'I did.'

'And now you teach ...?'

'French and English.'

'Splendid. I was afraid you were going to say Science or Mathematics.'

'Oh no, Mr Polding. I leave those kinds of subjects to greater minds than my own.'

Hilda choked on her fish, while Cecil hid his smirk behind a napkin.

'I only meant that French and English would remain useful throughout one's life – as a wife and mother, that is.'

'Of course,' I agreed, beginning to enjoy myself.

'So then, I imagine you are looking forward to the next chapter in your life.'

I sat back in my chair and feigned confusion.

'When you can stop teaching and start a family, I mean.'

'I'm sorry if I said anything to mislead you, Mr Polding, but I have no plans to stop teaching. I value my independence too much, you see.'

Mr Polding smiled uncertainly. While Cecil called the waiter to ask for more wine, I followed Hilda to the ladies' powder room.

'Sorry, Lill. I had no idea he was such a bore.'

'That's all right, I hope I wasn't rude. It's just that I've met his type before.'

'Is there any other?' Hilda winked at me in the mirror.

'Touché,' I laughed. 'Your Cecil isn't too bad, though.'

'Then we must find you another Cecil.'

As I rolled my eyes, I saw Hilda press her hands gently against her stomach and turn side-on to the mirror.

'Did the meal not agree with you? Do you feel unwell?'

She smiled mysteriously and cocked her eyebrows until I finally caught on.

'You're expecting!'

Hilda grinned. 'Four months along – I'm slightly offended you didn't notice.'

'I'm so happy for you,' I cried, embracing her warmly. 'Congratulations. A little brother or sister for Annie! You'll have your hands full now.'

'Nothing I haven't wished for,' sighed Hilda, looking delighted. 'And thank goodness for Nanny – I don't know what I'd do without her!'

'Nanny' was how Hilda referred to the young Irishwoman added to their household staff at the time of Annie's birth and was most certainly not in reference to her mother, Lady Fitzwilliam. Hilda had never wanted the so-called 'life of independence' that I was presently living. Then again, her wealth afforded her more independence than most other women with a family.

Cheered by Hilda's news, I maintained good humour with Mr Polding for the remainder of our meal. Afterwards, he insisted on walking me back to Town Hall station. Near the entrance, I saw two middle-aged women scrutinising the incoming crowd. One of them stepped forward into the path of an unsuspecting young man and thrust a white feather into his hands, raising her voice so everyone could hear.

'Don't be a shirker, this country needs you!'

Her companion stepped forward next. 'Every able-bodied young Australian should enlist – no more cowards or cold-footers!'

'Infernal, self-righteous meddlers,' Mr Polding hissed and, taking my elbow, strode past them before they could do the same to him.

Pointing to the large clock, I bid Mr Polding a good day and took my leave, hoping never to see him again. I reached the platform just as the conductor was blowing his whistle.

The train pulled out and I pictured the two women outside the station. Fuelled by their own losses, or by an impenetrable sense of moral certainty – what made them do it, I wondered? I hoped no one had given poor Freddy Parker a white feather or pressured him to volunteer. If he really was the same Sergeant Parker I had spotted in the newspaper, I only hoped he hadn't left any children behind as well as a wife.

In next month's referendum I would do my utmost to ensure other young men still had the same choice by voting against the government's proposal. Despite earlier assurances, Prime Minister Hughes was determined to alter the Defence Act so men could be conscripted, not just to fight on Australian soil – as the Act already allowed – but overseas too.

For months, the whole country had raged against itself in an unwinnable moral battle. Parliament, the mainstream press, conservatives, the Protestant churches – and thus most of the people I lived amongst – all supported conscription.

One of my students had even brought in a pro-conscription poem by Henry Lawson. It was from *The Bulletin*, and in it he doggedly repeated, 'it *has* to be!' He'd had the gall to suggest young men draw inspiration from his own example of discipline, assuring them that war would 'make men of weeds'. Coming from a man who, to my knowledge, had never fought on any battlefield, and was more likely to be found in a public bar than anywhere else, Lawson's flagrant hypocrisy made my blood boil.

If my brothers had still been alive today, they too would be facing this prospect of conscription. Then again, thinking back to their eagerness to leave home, they probably would have been among the first to enlist.

On the other side of the argument – against conscription – joining me and my fellow pacifists and those who believed in constitutional freedom, were the farmers, unions and red-raggers, the Irish and Catholics, led by Melbourne's Cardinal Mannix.

In my conversations with school mothers and grandmothers, some had confessed to feeling hopelessly conflicted. To help their boys already on the front, and honour those they had lost, new men needed to join. But for others, compassion outweighed their own burden and they vowed never to send another woman's husband or son to his death.

So, while our Prime Minister and all too many of my neighbours saw only patriots on one side and cowards and conchies on the other, I saw it differently. No one should be made to join up and give their lives to this war. Yet when so many men had already done so, I couldn't help returning to a question that had plagued me since that day of the fire: what made one human being more deserving of life than another?

I shook my head sadly and glanced around the carriage, keen for a distraction. Seated in the adjacent carriage row, a husband and wife were noisily reading *The Sun*. After a minor argument over her intention to go back into town the following day for the Ball & Welch Spring Show of Modes and his interest in the new Chevrolet motor car, they turned their attention to the theatre guide. At the mention of a new Henry Lawson play, I looked over and scowled. But when the couple disembarked at Chatswood, still squabbling and leaving their paper behind, I snatched it up for a closer look.

The play, which was to premiere at the Theatre Royal at the end of the month, was called *While the Billy Boils*, borrowing its title from the same collection of stories in which 'The Drover's Wife' first appeared.

Although based on Lawson's most famous stories, it had been written by a Mr Beaumont Smith, who was also the co-producer. Henry Lawson, who – for some inexplicable reason – was presently living on an irrigation farm in Yanco, had written an open letter to Mr Smith explaining the background of some of his characters drawn from what the newspaper called 'his book of life'. My heart started racing and my throat went dry. I had been waiting for this moment for years – ever since my fact-finding mission back at school with Mrs Spicer. Finally, here was Henry Lawson's opportunity to come clean and acknowledge my mother as his original source of inspiration.

Though desperate to read ahead, I forced myself not to race through Lawson's letter as he explained that Mrs Joe Wilson was – 'in face and figure' – a portrait of his wife (as he 'idealised' her then), while the early version of Mr Joe Wilson was based on his uncle by marriage, Job Falconer, of Laheys Creek near Dubbo, and 'very much alive'. I paused at Lawson's description of the Falconers as 'a great droving family', but when I read his next sentence, my blood went cold.

'Aunt Gertrude Falconer,' he wrote, 'was also "The Drover's Wife".'

Liar! I nearly shouted out loud. First a hypocrite and now a liar too. Or else so befuddled with beer that fact and fiction had become one in his mind.

Quivering with rage, I read through to the end. I found a second reference to this same Aunt Gertrude, whom 'Doc. Wild', his eccentric bush doctor character, had once nursed through a fever, but nowhere was there any mention of Mother or our family.

As I sat there, Mother McKenna's words suddenly came back to me like a bad dream. What had she said that day in the classroom? Something about how many bush people would likely see themselves in his stories and characters, but that didn't mean it was true. And when I'd pointed out my brothers' names and other duplications of circumstance, she'd dismissed them as a string of coincidences. What if Mother McKenna had been right all along? Where would that leave me now?

No, said another voice from deep inside me. *No, no, no.* Twenty-four years had passed since Lawson had written that story – my whole life. Why wait till now to reveal his inspiration? Henry Lawson had been writing for money his entire adult life. If there was a quid in it for him, or even a few measly bob, my guess was that he would say whatever needed to be said. Maybe this letter was a publicity stunt designed to drum up interest in the new play? This Mr Beaumont Smith must have paid him more than a few pretty pennies to take his old stories and present them on the stage as something new. I bet Lawson simply wanted to keep his latest milch cow well-fed.

And on the topic of letters, it wasn't completely far-fetched to think that Lawson might have received my schoolgirl letter after all and had been secretly concocting an alternative explanation ever since.

Aunt Gertrude, the drover's wife ... I refused to believe it.

Henry Lawson could put it in as many open letters to the newspaper as he liked, he could shout it from the rafters, for all I cared, because my mother was the original drover's wife and nothing he could ever do or say could convince me otherwise.

A world-renowned storyteller he might be, but he was also a story thief.

PART TWO

1920–1922

So at last the end has found me – (end of all the human push)
And again in silence round me come my Children of the Bush! —
Listen, who are young, and let them – if I in late and bitter days
Wrote some reckless lines – forget them – there is little there to praise.
I was human, very human, and if in the days misspent
I have injured man or woman, it was done without intent.
If at times I blundered blindly – bitter heart and aching brow —
If I wrote a line unkindly – I am sorry for it now.

Henry Lawson, 'The Last Review' (1904)

Chapter 10

Castles in the Air

Sunshine streamed into the room, stealing in through gaps between the velvet folds of curtain. Shadows danced and played at the edges of my slumber, enticing me to wake. I opened my eyes slowly, then closed them with a slow smile. Holidays, at last. For a few precious moments I drifted free of conscious thought, gradually bringing my mind into focus as I recalled my plans for the day. A long walk this morning, followed by a visit from Hilda.

Rolling onto my back, I yawned luxuriously and stretched my sleep-stiffened limbs. Though the days were still warm, I adored these cool autumn mornings, especially when I could lie in bed and savour the comforting embrace of flannel sheets and a heavy quilt. What would it feel like, I wondered, to wake up next to someone else? Sharing a bed with Esther as a child had been one thing, but to feel a grown man's body lying beside me would be something else entirely.

I heard movement downstairs in the kitchen and remembered Jean was taking the girls into town today for some shopping, probably trying for an early start.

A year had passed since I'd left the Edwards family, a few months after the war had ended. Honoured with a Military Cross, Major Frank Edwards had been welcomed home as a local hero, his wife doting on him with more care and affection than even a new bride. Little Nora soon overcame her reserve towards the tall, strange man now living in her house and became a Daddy's girl, while the twins vied equally for his attention. I was happy for them. And if jealous thoughts occasionally inserted themselves into my head, springing up like weeds in an otherwise tidy garden bed, I yanked them up before they could take hold.

Since then, I had been boarding with Mrs Jean Campbell, whose two daughters were also students at Ravenswood. Her own husband had not been as fortunate as Major Edwards. Lieutenant Campbell had been killed in the final weeks of the war, and the cruel irony of knowing how close he came to avoiding his fate could be read in the premature stoop of his wife's shoulders and in the rareness of her smiles, which even when they came never seemed to reach her eyes.

The Campbell household was not as affluent as that of the Edwards, and Mr Campbell's loss was felt almost as sharply on an economic front as on the personal. As an accomplished seamstress and embroiderer, long accustomed to making clothes for herself and her girls, Jean had begun taking orders for special occasion dresses from within the school community to supplement her war widow pension and my own modest contribution as her boarder. Even so, it seemed likely that the girls would be switching to the local public school next year and that a second boarder would need to be found. I helped wherever I could, buying little treats for the girls and assisting with chores to lighten their mother's load. With that thought, I threw back the bedcovers with one final yawn and dragged myself over to the basin to wash my face.

An hour later, having split the tasks between us, I put away the ironing board and admired the neatly folded pile of laundry my efforts had yielded. I glanced over at Jean, who was just bringing down the last of her husband's old clothing to donate to the poor. I caught her eye and held her gaze until she nodded. For although I'd told Jean little of my childhood, or of my own losses, our broken hearts reached out to each other and spoke in a way that words and voices could not.

I left Jean to lock up and stepped out for my walk, satisfied I had now earned this time to myself. Even before I had reached the street, I could smell the sweet orange perfume of the murraya, still flowering profusely after last week's heavy rain. I stopped to snap off a twig laden with creamy white blossoms, bringing it to my nose and inhaling deeply.

A flash of colour sailed past my ear. I turned just in time to see the long green tail of a parrot flying low under the trees into some nearby foliage, a male king parrot, unmistakable for its striking red head and breast. Perched beside him was his green-breasted lady friend.

I had no formal knowledge of birds but had learned to identify most of the parrots that frequented our neighbourhood. King parrots were easy to spot with their telltale red and green plumage, while red and blue feathers meant a crimson rosella. The eastern rosella, in turn, could be recognised by its vivid colours and white cheek patches, and the appropriately named rainbow lorikeet by its bright blue head. Then there were the larger species, who flew high over the streets in great noisy flocks – white sulphur-crested cockatoos, yellow-tailed black cockatoos, rosy-breasted galahs and the grey gang-gang. Their loud, screeching calls and large claws struck fear into the hearts of the uninitiated – freshly landed immigrants especially – who found their cries menacing, more suited to a Gothic nightmare than a suburban landscape.

I had recently witnessed this attitude when Miss Mordern, our new Science teacher, joined me on one of my local rambles. When we happened to walk under a tree in which several cockatoos were perched, the fifty-something Englishwoman had lifted her skirts and all but sprinted ahead in her haste to put distance between herself and the birds.

'What's the problem?' I'd asked when I finally caught up to her.

'Have you seen their claws?' Miss Mordern visibly cringed as she cast a nervous glance behind us. 'And those sharp beaks? Imagine what they could do to human flesh and skin!'

'But they've no interest in hurting us,' I laughed. 'They're just having their dinner up there. And they're so attractive, don't you think? Just look at that yellow crest.'

'A wolf in sheep's clothing, I say. And a rather evil-looking sheep at that.'

'Why, Miss Mordern, I would have thought you of all people would appreciate our parrots? As a scientist, I mean.'

'I do appreciate them, Miss Taylor. But I also prefer them preserved, stuffed and safely behind glass.'

She had then spent the rest of our walk trying to convince me of the superiority of the melodious songbirds and other dainty-winged creatures she knew in her youth, back home in Suffolk.

Turning eastward to walk into the morning sun, I smiled to see how greatly the streetscape had altered since last weekend. While the native gums and other trees were evergreen, maintaining their customary muted green foliage all year, autumn was the time when all the deciduous trees would come to my notice, those planted and propagated by human hands; the introduced species, or exotics, as Miss Mordern referred to them. Equally foreign, they hailed from another hemisphere and were now required to follow the earth's seasons in reverse, a consequence that was seemingly less difficult for the gardens to accept than for the gardeners themselves. Spring blooms in September, instead of March? Bare branches in June? Preposterous! To people like Miss Mordern, it was almost as affronting as a Christmas Day that now had to be celebrated under sweltering skies instead of snowflakes.

While I sympathised with Miss Mordern's homesickness, I had less patience for her inability to notice the beauty of her adopted home. Our eucalypts, for instance. Although not deciduous in respect to their leaves, from time to time one could see them shedding their bark instead, presumably casting it aside to make way for new growth, much like the long, shrivelled snake skins my brothers used to find under our house. It began simply enough. Cracks would appear in the tree's outer layer. Little by little, the bark would peel away. Finally, I would see it dropped on the ground in great sheets and strips, forming messy piles at the gum's base. Having shed its skin completely, the tree would emerge, silvery and majestic, almost as if it were born anew. If only I could do the same.

'Miss Taylor,' came a small voice from nearby.

I spun around. There was no one to be seen.

'Up here,' came the voice.

Looking down at me from the fork of the tree was Rosemary Hepburn, the younger sister of one of my students.

'Are you stuck? Do you need help?'

Without pausing to reply, she shimmied down the trunk, her auburn hair glittering in the sunshine like freshly polished copper.

'Hello, Rosie. I see you're fond of climbing.' It reminded of my own tree-climbing days. I was half-tempted to hitch up my skirt and join her.

Rosemary grinned. 'Sometimes I stay up there for hours. But I forgot to bring a book this morning, and I haven't had my breakfast yet.'

'Oh dear,' I said, feigning dismay. 'You'd better get back home then, hadn't you? Quick smart! Your mother might be worried.'

'No, Miss Taylor, she says the fairies will look after me, so long as I don't do anything to upset them.'

'Wise advice indeed. So, there are fairies in all the gardens around here, are there?'

Rosemary nodded seriously. 'They live in the gum trees. You can't see them because they change the colour of their clothes to blend in with the tree trunks. See, this one is quite orange. Like my hair. But that one over there – in front of our house – is almost white.'

'How lovely,' I said, stroking the cool, curved surface of the trunk.

'Your fairies have chosen well. Any of these smooth-textured gums would make a great place to live, not to mention their being good to climb.' Whether pale and ghost-like, rusty-toned and weathered, or dappled like a horse's flank, each variation held its own charm for me.

'Scribbly gums are my favourite,' said Rosemary.

'Mine too,' I conceded. Scribbly gums had always fascinated me. Carved into their silvery-white exteriors was line after line of mysterious script, calling out from the bark like an ancient form of calligraphy, a secret language only trees could speak. When I had suggested this to Miss Morden, she had quickly dismissed my romantic interpretation, explaining that the markings were simply a byproduct of the resident moths who lay their eggs between the layers of old and new bark.

'That's my mum,' Rosemary groaned as a woman's voice called from across the road. 'I have to go.'

'Never mind,' I said, brushing dirt from her dress before she darted off. 'I'll put in a good word for you with the fairies.'

Still smiling over the irrepressible imagination of children, I turned onto Macintosh Street. As I crunched my way through a trail of fallen leaves, the first of the season, I congratulated myself on my new footwear. Drawing inspiration from the school's athletics uniform, my white canvas sand shoes were more comfortable than even my practical black boots. Although I steered clear of ladies' tennis or any kind of competitive sport, I enjoyed being active. Just as we were always telling our girls at school, *Mens sana in corpore sano* – a healthy mind in a healthy body.

I could only be so progressive with fashion, though. I chuckled, thinking of the tongue in cheek article I'd read about 'trouseritis', an apparently painful but recurrent epidemic afflicting only women. Sufferers of this dreaded disease could expect to be rendered ungraceful, unattractive and ugly. Henry Lawson had also felt entitled to poke fun at the drover's wife for donning her husband's moleskins in an emergency. I was all but ready to buy myself a pair of trousers, or at least a divided skirt, just to put him and all these other silly men in their place.

I approached the Waterhouse home and paused to appreciate the many camellias already in bloom. With muddy boots and secateurs in hand, Mr Waterhouse came to the gate to greet me. We had known each other since my student days at the Teachers' College at Blackfriars, where Gowrie Waterhouse – a decade my senior – was then Master of Modern Languages. Mr Waterhouse had moved to Gordon around that time, preceding my own arrival to the area by a year, and he now lived in a beautiful Georgian Colonial Revival home named *Eryldene*, after his wife's birthplace in Scotland.

'*Bonjour*, Miss Taylor. How are you today?'

'Very well, thank you, Mr Waterhouse. You'll be pleased to know my French students are coming along brilliantly, thanks to your latest textbooks. Hello, boys,' I added after spotting young Douglas and Gordon, each bearing a large net and evidently chasing butterflies. 'I was just admiring your camellias. What was it you called them last time? The aristocrat among plants?'

'Indeed they are.' He appeared pleased I had remembered. A man of many talents, Mr Waterhouse was often consulted for his discerning opinions on garden design.

Following my gaze as it travelled around the garden before finally coming to rest on the deep pink blooms adorning one long hedge, his blue eyes twinkled. 'The sasanquas are a joy, aren't they? Hard to believe they cultivate them in Japan for practical rather than decorative purposes.' Ever the teacher, he delivered a short but fascinating explanation of how the glossy green leaves were made into tea and how an exceptionally rich oil could be extracted from the seeds.

'It's certainly one way to enjoy them longer,' he said with mock sorrow. 'By next week, most of these flowers will be gone.'

'Such a shame,' I said, nodding sympathetically. I too had watched their sudden fall each year. All at once, these early-blooming sasanquas would shatter from their stems, leaving a magnificent trail of petals on either side of the long hedge. While I shared Mr Waterhouse's regret, I took comfort in knowing their present beauty would not be lost so much as transformed, at least for a time. As I anticipated this forthcoming scene, I couldn't help but picture myself as a white-veiled bride treading gracefully over this soft pink carpet, bending down to grasp some of the candy-coloured petals, before throwing them into the air. Behind me – and completing this romantic fantasy – would be a carriage drawn by four snow-white horses and decorated with bells and ribbons.

Grinning foolishly to myself, I waved goodbye and carried on my way. Sometimes, I let my feet forge their own path through the streets and surrounding bushland, occasionally finding myself far from home and with an outlook I had never seen before. Other days, I manipulated my route to include some of the area's most gracious homes and its handful of truly fine estates – sprawling mansions with picturesque gardens, complete with orchard, vegetable plot, hen house, dairy and stables. Nowadays, many also bore the addition of a purpose-built garage to house a motor car.

Most of the grand properties I passed were named after places 'back home' in England or Scotland, like Rochester or Aberdour. Others displayed an aptly chosen Aboriginal word, as was the case with the house I was just approaching, *Carinya* – meaning 'happy home'. Along with our shire, many of the local street and suburb names sprang from Aboriginal dialect. I had learned that *Wahroonga* meant 'our home' and that *Warrawee* was an invitation to 'stop here', while *Turramurra* signified 'big hill' and *Killara* translated as 'always here'. As I pronounced these Indigenous names to myself, I noticed how my facial muscles had to move differently than when I spoke English, or French, for that matter, which was arguably all about the lips. Although I would have welcomed the opportunity to learn more of Australia's mother tongue, or rather tongues, I feared that door might have closed already. What hope could there be for any of these Aboriginal languages to survive into the future when already so many of its speakers had not?

I reached the bridge and shivered as a strong wind blew across the gully, gusty and surprisingly cold. As always, when I looked across to Killarney Castle, I thought of my mother. Arguably better suited to another time and place than to our growing middle-class suburb, it had been built for an Irish gentleman sharing my surname, Mr Thomas Taylor, whose memories of County Kerry's lakes of Killarney had taken flight in its 100-acre site. The castle was made entirely of sandstone, hand-hewn from the quarry in which it sat, and was built over three levels, with a slate roof, battlements and its own circular tower. Surrounded by extensive gardens and a small orchard, a bridge to the second level gave the impression of a real moat like something from a fairytale. I half expected to see a drawbridge being lowered to admit my entrance.

The reason Killarney Castle always made me think of Mother had nothing to do with the owner's surname and everything to do with Henry Lawson. 'As a girl,' he wrote of the drover's wife, 'she built the usual castles in the air; but all her girlish hopes and aspirations have long been dead. She finds all the excitement and recreation she needs in the *Young Ladies' Journal*, and Heaven help her! takes a pleasure in the fashion plates.' I hated those two sentences! What gave Henry Lawson the right to declare her dreams dead or patronise her pastimes? What gave anyone that right?

~

'When are you going to get married and have some children of your own?'

The wind from earlier in the day had died down completely and golden sunshine enveloped the garden. Fat white clouds hung in the air, soft and lusciously plump like spun sugar. Under the speckled shade of the Chinese elm, I had set a small round table for afternoon tea. Hilda and I were seated on a mismatched pair of bentwood chairs, and Hilda was playing with a tablecloth I had sewn and embroidered myself under Jean Campbell's encouraging eye.

Comfortably settled into their waterfront estate in Point Piper, not far from Sacred Heart, Hilda was now the proud mother of not one but two delightfully chubby little girls, on whom she lavished all her attention and as many cream buns as the little poppets desired. Although she had left her daughters at home with their nanny today, it had not prevented her from talking about them incessantly and it was endearing to see how much joy and confidence my friend had gained from motherhood.

But eventually Hilda had drawn breath and turned to me with this all too familiar question, 'Come on, Lill, don't you think it's time?'

I laughed and gave my usual reply. 'I'm surrounded by children all day long. At the end of the day, I'm glad for some peace and quiet.' Even to my ears, my excuses were wearing thin.

'That's not what I meant, and you know it.' Hilda sniffed. 'We used to pity the nuns – you remember – for being shut off from the world, with only each other and us silly young girls for company. How is that any different to what you're doing here in the suburbs – hiding away under the canopy – far from town and all the different people you could meet?' She looked directly into my eyes, placing particular emphasis on the word 'people'.

Still smiling, I refilled our cups from the large teapot. 'I'm not hiding away. There are plenty of people here. And I like the trees – sometimes they make better company than a friend who says too much, even with the best of intentions.'

'I'm serious! Don't you ever see yourself getting married one day?'

My thoughts flew back to the image of the pink-petalled carpet, but I shook my head and assumed an impassive expression.

'I hate to say it, Lill, but if you're not careful, you'll be left on the shelf for good.'

'Fine by me. There are plenty of books on all my shelves.'

'You're impossible, Lill.' Hilda groaned. '*Impossible*,' she repeated in French. 'You know, Patrick Polding apparently asked after you just the other day when Cecil saw him in chambers.'

'Mr Polding? Surely, he's not still a bachelor after all this time? I'm shocked – he was quite the catch, I thought.'

'Yes, yes, I know he was tedious, but there are other men out there whom you might genuinely like. If only you gave them half a chance.'

'Can we change the subject please? What lovely weather we're having!'

Hilda sighed. 'We're getting older, Lill. You don't want to be here forever, do you?'

'I know we're getting older. I can see it when I look in the mirror.' I struck a pose and smoothed an imaginary wrinkle on my face.

'Can I give you some advice, all jokes aside?' She took hold of my hand and tapped it against my temple. 'Maybe you should step out of that head of yours and let yourself have more fun.'

As if on cue, the unmistakable warble of a kookaburra rang out, a low chuckle rising to a shrieking human-like laugh that soon had us in stitches.

'Since we're talking about having fun, shall we go to the pictures? You do have picture theatres all the way out here, don't you?' I affected an air of wounded indignation and Hilda poked out her tongue.

'We most certainly do. More than one, in fact. The latest Douglas Fairbanks feature is showing at Roseville.'

'Perfect,' said Hilda, mopping up the last of the crumbs from her plate and washing them down with a final gulp of tea.

Chapter 11

Treading the Inky Way

After rinsing the dishes and returning the table and chairs to their rightful places, we headed to the street where Hilda's new motor car was parked. A young couple was just going by, pushing a large pram in front of them. While Hilda stopped to admire the sleeping baby and say a few encouraging words to the mother, the baby's father seemed much more interested in admiring Hilda's vehicle, the latest model Studebaker Touring Car imported from America.

'Take a seat, my dear.'

I looked at her doubtfully. Apart from the previous Christmas, when I had consented to a very short ride in Cecil's Rolls-Royce, I had no experience with cars. 'Why don't we take the train to Roseville? It's only a couple of stops.'

'Don't you trust me to drive?' asked Hilda, cranking the car with deliberate fanfare.

As we bumped down the macadam surface of Gordon Road, narrowly avoiding potholes and sections where the stone and tar had almost worn away, I soon had cause to question Hilda's self-assured claims. Even so,

I had to admit it was an exciting way to reach one's destination. Raising our voices above the sound of the motor, our conversation returned to the safer territory of Hilda's girls and their latest escapades, before moving onto recent social events and the last of the peace celebrations. Always one to fall for a handsome face, Hilda was counting the days until next month's arrival of the young Prince of Wales, when she hoped to be presented to the future sovereign at one of the many receptions or balls to be held in his honour.

'It's good of him to come all this way to thank us.' Hilda's face was lit up like those of the senior girls at school when they mooned about at lunchtime, discussing their favourite film stars.

'Australia lost a lot of men,' I said. 'That kind of sacrifice deserves to be acknowledged.'

'I know. But don't forget Prince Edward fought too. He could have been killed, like anyone else.'

'Perhaps not quite like anyone else, Hilda.'

'I can't believe it's been more than a year since the war ended. Two whole summers have passed since then. Do you still remember the day?'

'Of course,' I murmured. We both became silent, lost in our memories.

I could never forget the day when the end of the war was finally announced; the eleventh day of the eleventh month, 1918. Following rumours of Germany's capitulation, it was Monday evening when news of the Armistice was officially received. I was in my room when the unlikely sound of cheering suddenly erupted from the parlour, where Mrs Edwards had been entertaining. By the time I came downstairs to investigate, the front door was open and her friends were all running out to the street. People everywhere were shaking hands, hugging and crying. 'It's over!' Mrs Edwards had shouted, tears rolling down her face as she pulled me into a tight embrace. I heard a train horn in the distance, sustained and jubilant. While I had volunteered to stay home with the children, Mrs

Edwards had gone out with her friends, celebrating until the early hours of the morning.

A public holiday was called the next day. With the schools all closed, children took part in parades or romped mad with joy through the streets. Perversely, only the examinations for the Leaving Certificate students were to carry on 'vide timetable', by edict of the Department of Public Instruction. I thus found myself escorting six querulous girls into town and witnessing the celebrations firsthand.

And what a spectacle we met! Pouring in by train, tram and ferry, euphoric crowds filled the city. Flags were waved, confetti flew through the air, and an effigy of the Kaiser was ceremonially hanged and burned. Accompanying this chaotic scene was an ear-shattering cacophony of sound. Church bells pealed and brass bands played, punctuated by the noisy din of rattles and shrill whistles from within the crowd. The only semblance of order, however fleeting, had been when the people came together to sing 'God Save the King' and 'Rule Brittania'.

Thrust into this wild landscape, my Ravenswood girls immediately forgot their initial insult over having to take their examinations and exchanged wide-eyed looks as they followed me, clinging tightly to each other to avoid being separated by the crushing hordes surrounding us. Though the atmosphere was one of pure elation, and the girls were clearly infected by the revellers' exuberance, I was focused on keeping them safe and could scarcely enjoy the experience myself. It was not until many hours later, alone in my room, that the announcement really sunk in. The war was finally over. Peace, at long last.

'No wonder picture theatres are so popular,' said Hilda, bringing me back to the present as Traynor's Picture Palace came into sight. 'So much better than reading a book.'

'Why do you say that?' I asked, pointing to a side street where she could park the car.

'Because from the moment someone steps into a dark theatre, their troubles disappear. You just settle into your seat, listen to the piano and wait for the screen to come to life.'

'True,' I agreed. 'But I would say "easier" and not "better" than a book. As I tell my girls, a reward is only satisfying if you've earned it.' I breathed a quiet sigh of relief as Hilda switched off the engine, then I checked my wristwatch. The feature would be starting at any minute.

'I nearly forgot,' said Hilda, reaching behind my seat. 'These are for you.'

After thanking Hilda, I made a random selection from the large tin of sweets and was soon savouring the familiar buttery sweetness of caramel.

Hilda rifled through the tin until she found what she was looking for. 'You must try a Violet Crumble. They're absolutely delicious!' She unwrapped the foil-wrapped sweet and, to my surprise, popped it straight into my mouth.

After the Spanish flu pandemic reached our shores early last year, carried across the sea by troops returning from Europe, everyone was still being cautious about sharing food. In Sydney alone, despite the widespread use of masks and the closing of many schools and public venues, thousands of people had succumbed to pneumonic influenza throughout the year until the virus had finally run its course. Like millions of others, I had lined up for my Commonwealth Serum Laboratories vaccination and had been among the lucky ones not to be infected.

'*Alors*?' Hilda was looking at me, impatiently waiting for my judgement.

'*Délicieux*,' I agreed, as I bit through the chocolate casing. Sweet shards of golden honeycomb shattered in my mouth. 'You're right.'

Hilda beamed with satisfaction.

Dusk was falling when we drove back to Gordon. Amidst theatrical cries of *au revoir* and kisses on both cheeks, I embraced my friend, and then waved until the Studebaker finally disappeared around the corner, on its way to the punt at Milsons Point and from there across the harbour. Walking back to the house, I could feel myself still smiling. Hilda's visits always had this effect on me.

As I bit into another honeycomb from the tin she had insisted I keep, I knew she was right. Not just about the Violet Crumbles, of course. My dear, sweet-toothed friend was right about something much more important. I did need to stop thinking so much. I did need to let myself have more fun. It was time to start tasting everything life had to offer, while I still could.

~

'Mail for you.' Jean handed me a letter on her way out the door.

'Thank you!' I saw the Bowral postmark and grinned.

I had barely seen Hilda since her last visit in the autumn. Cecil's family, like her own, were graziers and wool merchants. In recent months, with her husband busy travelling the country, Hilda and the girls had been staying with her mother at the Fitzwilliams' magnificent estate in the Southern Highlands.

When I opened the envelope, a small newspaper clipping from *The Sydney Stock and Station Journal* fluttered out. Hilda had circled a notice titled, 'PENSION FOR HENRY LAWSON'. I frowned but read on. 'On the recommendation of the central committee of the Commonwealth Literary Fund the Governor-General has granted a pension of £52 a year to Henry Lawson, the well-known Australian author.'

Thoroughly perplexed, I skimmed Hilda's letter for an explanation and found it in her concluding paragraph. 'I was thinking of that Henry Lawson story we once read at school,' she wrote, 'and how sure you were that he had based it on your family. Maybe you should make a copyright claim and apply for a share of his new pension as a royalty?!'

I gulped. Although I knew Hilda was only joking about the pension, I was astonished that after all these years she still remembered my reaction to Lawson's story. In hindsight, I regretted not having confided in Hilda back then. She might have found a way to make me feel better about the whole sorry affair and saved me from carrying the burden of my hurt alone for all this time.

After reading Lawson's open letter to the newspaper a few years earlier, in advance of Beaumont Smith's successful play of *While the Billy Boils*, I had again toyed with the idea of sending him another letter or even confronting him at its Theatre Royal premiere. However, once the play was advertised for sale, including a full list of cast members and their roles, I was dismayed to discover the drover's wife was not among them. I went back to the article containing Lawson's open letter, which I had saved, and saw there had been no need for him to offer any explanation for his character of the drover's wife. His 'Aunt Gertrude' claim, I felt sure, had been nothing more than hot air or a guilty conscience. Sure enough, Henry Lawson did not attend the Sydney premiere, nor its Melbourne opening night some weeks later. I recalled the producer having made some excuse on Lawson's behalf for his non-attendance. And despite the play's glowing reviews, which saw it tour the country for a further year or two, including talk of a future film adaptation, I too had stayed away.

Since then, by chance, I had also learned that the reason Henry Lawson had been living at an irrigation farm in the Leeton Shire at that time was because the State Government had given him a paid contract to attract new farmer settlers to the area by writing about Yanco and the Murrumbidgee Irrigation Scheme, whether as articles or verse. 'The Government Irrigation Poet', one journalist had dubbed him. Given Lawson's diminished writing output and continued drinking problem, I doubted whether they had got their money's worth.

It now occurred to me that, in all likelihood, this new government pension would go towards Lawson's beer consumption and little else. What was the average cost of a pint of beer these days? Sixpence? A shilling? At a mere £52 per year, that translated to only twenty pints of beer a week – a pint-sized pension, if ever there was one!

If my logic was harsh and my judgement unkind, it was only because the man receiving this pension was Henry Lawson. Alcoholism was a serious affliction. For anyone else, I would have had far more sympathy.

I stood up from the kitchen table, where I had been reading Hilda's letter, and headed towards my room to add her unwitting contribution to my collection of Lawson-related clippings, which had been growing despite my desire to the contrary. Sometimes it felt like the more I tried to avoid him, the closer he got. Whether it was seeing his verses and stories printed in a journal, or a new book advertised to which he had contributed, or his campaigning against foreshore development in our local newspaper, or even his testimonials for cough syrup and a rheumatism cure, it seemed in place of my family, who had disappeared without a trace, Henry Lawson was always there.

~

Just a few days later, amongst a handful of other short obituaries in *The Sydney Morning Herald*, I saw that Louisa Lawson had died. 'After a long and painful illness, Mrs Louisa Lawson died on Thursday. Mrs Lawson was a writer of considerable literary merit and was the mother of Henry Lawson.' Together with the lump forming in my throat, I felt a vicarious surge of pride that Mrs Lawson's personal achievements had been awarded priority over and above her role as Henry's mother. Thursday would have been the 12th of August. I must have missed the original notices last weekend.

I went out to the rubbish heap to look for Saturday's paper and found instead a brief report of her funeral on the front page of the latest *Evening News*. After an eight-month illness, the funeral of the late 72-year-old Mrs Lawson had apparently taken place last Saturday at Rookwood Cemetery. Although this announcement mentioned her famous son up front, it also acknowledged Mrs Lawson's magazine, noting she was the first woman to employ female compositors, along with her role in establishing female suffrage in our state. But even though it stated that her funeral had been largely attended by relatives, including many nephews and nieces, there was no mention of Henry having been among them.

What possible excuse could any son have for not attending his own mother's funeral? My guess was that he was either at the pub or having one of his long 'hospital' stays.

Buried beneath my indignation towards Henry Lawson's treatment of his mother was my own kernel of shame, rotting deep within its accumulated husk of denial. In all those weeks after the fire, when I had been forced to live under the same roof as my aunt, did I ever ask what became of their bodies? Not once. I'd been too afraid of her answer, and of what might be left of them to find. Nor did I ever broach the topic with Mr O'Loughlin afterwards, although it struck me that providing my mother and siblings, or for that matter my father too, with a proper Christian burial, would have been exactly the kind of thing he would have done. As always, fear had kept me silent.

I shook my head again, this time placating myself with the thought that a child's fear and failure could not be compared to that of a grown man. And by that I meant both my father and Henry Lawson.

I thought back to some of Louisa Lawson's editorials in *The Dawn* in which she had campaigned for the Divorce Extension Bill and warned women against tying their fates to the fortune of a drunkard. In defiance of the usual maternal strings of attachment, I wondered whether she had taken her own advice and had learned to keep her son at arm's length to avoid being dragged down into his alcohol-fuelled quagmire.

All week I kept an eye out for further mentions in the paper. In the women's pages of Sunday's *Sun* I found the longest one yet: six long paragraphs under the heading 'Women's Champion'. It was a glowing tribute which hailed Louisa Lawson as 'one of the most remarkable women New South Wales has produced'. As well as crediting her with giving Henry Lawson his 'genius', it commended her own writing and noted a similarity of thought and expression between her verses and those of her son. It concluded with a surprising reference to her invention and patenting of an improved buckle and strap for mailbags, a venture which had previously escaped my notice.

How, I wondered, had a man raised by a woman of such strength of character and diversity of achievement come to write about an equally strong woman like my mother, only to dismiss her as nothing but a 'drover's wife'? Would Henry Lawson have dared, I wondered, to define his own mother by her husband's career? Henry's late father had been a Norwegian sailor who had landed on Australia's shores in search of gold, and Louisa had willingly left him to begin her own career; the mere idea was laughable. Louisa Lawson had evidently been many things in her life, but she was neither a gold-digger, nor a gold-digger's wife.

Chapter 12

'Hashes ter hashes, dus ter dus'

4th September 1922

'Morning, Miss Taylor!'

'Good morning, Wilson,' I said, greeting our gardener and odd jobs man with a smile as I entered the school gate.

'Not much of a start to the spring, is it?' he mumbled, hammer in hand, and seemingly oblivious to the fact that the three silver nails pinched between his lips made him difficult to understand.

'That's true,' I agreed. It had been cloudy and unsettled for days, leaving me feeling similarly out of sorts. As it was, I had spent most of the weekend in bed fighting off a cold.

'Shame about Henry Lawson, eh?'

I stopped short. 'I'm sorry. Did you say Henry Lawson – the writer?'

'You haven't heard, then? Poor sod died on Saturday.'

'Dead?' I grabbed hold of the gate post to steady myself.

'That's right,' he said, finally removing the nails from his mouth. 'Had some kind of seizure on Friday and died the next morning, peaceful like, in his sleep. I always think that's the best way to go, don't you?'

I nodded weakly.

'They're talking about a Commonwealth funeral. Like what they'd do for a politician or someone like that. He was only fifty-five, you know, a year younger than me. You have yourself a good day, Miss Taylor.'

'You too, Wilson,' I murmured.

I had read of Lawson's paralytic seizure a year earlier and the many tributes he'd received in hospital, including dozens of letters from children – quite different, I presumed, from the one I had sent him.

Inside the school building, I tracked down a newspaper and paged through it until I found the funeral notice from Wood Coffill Limited on page 7:

> The funeral of the late HENRY LAWSON will leave St. Andrew's Cathedral, THIS (Monday) AFTERNOON, after service, commencing at 2.15 o'clock for Waverley Cemetery. Motor funeral.

On the next page was a photograph and accompanying article announcing his death. Feeling strangely breathless, I scanned through it quickly, soon confirming Wilson's earlier suggestion of a state funeral. The article concluded with a quote from the Prime Minister, who was expected to attend the service, describing Lawson as 'the poet of Australia, the minstrel of the people'.

A moment later, I was knocking on the door of our Headmistress.

'Good morning, Miss Fidler. Would it be possible for me to leave early today? My only class this afternoon is Third Form English and the girls can easily carry on with their poetry assignment.'

She looked up from her desk. 'Certainly, Miss Taylor. I hope nothing is amiss?'

'Not at all, Miss Fidler. Just something I need to do today. A family errand of sorts.'

I registered the curiosity on her face and was grateful when she dismissed me with nothing other than a reminder to arrange another teacher to stand in for me.

For the rest of the day, each of my lessons seemed to drag on forever, until I was finally alone on the train. This time I read the newspaper article from beginning to end, lingering over the details of Lawson's early family life on the goldfields as the eldest of four children. His father, Peter Larsen (later anglicised to Lawson), was described as a Norwegian sailor turned 'gold seeker, bush farmer and builder', hardworking and educated, while his late mother, born Louisa Albury, was acknowledged as 'a remarkable woman, with many graces of character, destined to take a conspicuous and honourable part in public affairs in the years to come.'

'Let's hope it continues so,' I muttered under my breath. Though pleased to see this acknowledgement, I had my doubts about whether Louisa Lawson would be remembered by our anti-feminist society for much longer. While *her* passing had been a quiet affair, with not even Henry attending the funeral, *his* death had evidently captured the attention of the entire country, culminating in today's public ceremony. Perhaps, I mused, it was really for Louisa's sake that I was going to her son's funeral today.

As I read of the impoverished circumstances that accompanied Henry Lawson's birth (in a tent, of all places) and of his many years of struggle to gain an education and employment while battling exceptional shyness and even a degree of deafness, I felt a tiny trickle of compassion. Some of the details struck me as familiar. Then I remembered having come across snippets of his childhood memories in a newspaper that day at Sacred Heart while I had been polishing the silverware. Somewhere amongst my keepsakes would be that crumpled page from *The Freeman's Journal*. It was all the things I'd foolishly believed we had in common as young children that had prompted me write that letter to him in the first place.

Milsons Point Station was fast approaching, and I gathered my things and prepared to disembark. As I looked out the window towards the bustling ferry wharf and tried to imagine the new North Shore bridge to be built over the harbour, my strange experience from a few weeks earlier came back in a sudden rush. I had been looking out the train window at North Sydney when I saw a man resembling Henry Lawson. He was tall but gaunt and frail, with the same heavy moustache for which Lawson was known. His hat and clothing were old-fashioned in style, and he walked with the aid of a cane. Scampering at his feet were two or three young children, bare-footed and inadequately dressed for the cold, followed by a younger man, more smartly attired, who was carrying a camera and tripod. Both he and his entourage were gone in an instant. But even so, I was sure it had been him.

Henry Lawson and his endlessly long shadow had been following me for too long. It was time to lay him to rest.

~

Instead of joining the foreseeable mass of spectators in the city, where I would likely be relegated to standing outside St Andrew's Cathedral for the duration of the service, I opted to go straight to Waverley Cemetery to await the procession from there. Along the way, I passed scores of waiting children on the side of the road.

I paused at the spiked metal entrance gate, suddenly wary of crossing its threshold. Yet, save for the huddled presence of a few nervous-looking groundskeepers, the cemetery was remarkably quiet. I was early. I wandered down through the vast grounds until all I could see was the dark mirrored sweep of the Pacific Ocean before me and the Norfolk Island Pines bordering either side. With sea and land conspiring to enclose this space, the cemetery formed its own townscape, complete with roads, paths and a smattering of minor buildings. A town for the dead.

The sky itself was attired for this nationwide day of mourning; heavy black clouds had drawn across it, threatening to burst at any moment. Only the cool white of Italian Carrara marble stood out against the darkness. Strewn across the sloping landscape, soaring pillars and stone-carved angels rose from the earth like ghostly figures. And although the cemetery's clifftop setting was beautiful, it was almost too beautiful. Must death and the promise of an afterlife always be glorified?

I chose a quiet position for myself halfway up the northern ridge and at a discreet distance from the gravesite, where a large crowd was slowly gathering.

Little by little, the funeral cortege came into view. With mounted police leading the way, the motor hearse entered the cemetery gates, ushered in by the awaiting Police Band. A string of cars followed, each one disgorging yet another group of sombrely dressed mourners who joined the last stragglers arriving on foot.

At the sight of Henry Lawson's purple-draped coffin, I felt my breath catch. In an instant, the questions which had been biding their time in the back of my mind all day suddenly thrust themselves before me. What happens to a story after its storyteller has died? What happens to its cast of characters when they are finally set free?

Scarcely knowing whether to laugh or cry, I listened to the Police Band play and followed the dead man's passage from hearse to burial site, quelling my emotions with a careful study of the flowers adorning his coffin – a traditional yet patriotic arrangement of lilies, wattle, gumleaves and fern. A child's shrill voice cried out somewhere below and I glimpsed a perambulator being rocked back and forth with increasing urgency. Beside the pram, a little boy with blond curls and a sailor suit tugged at his mother's hand and stared glumly out to sea.

As the Archdeacon began his service, the crowd rippled once or twice more, then settled into place, forming a steady flotilla of women's hats against the rough swell of the ocean. Seagulls screamed and played by the cliff's edge. I strained to hear the clergyman's address, but from where I stood it was impossible to catch more than a word or two at a time, and I turned my attention to the mourners instead.

If such things could be judged from outward appearances alone, it was a motley crew of gatherers. From those whose suits and topcoats were custom-made by the finest tailors in London to those whose items of dress, and sadly also their state of health, had clearly seen better days. Hoping for a glimpse of the Prime Minister in the row of dignitaries closest to the grave, I craned forward, raising my heels and coming up on my toes, when suddenly the moist earth beneath me gave way and I stumbled down the hill, gathering speed in my effort not to fall, only to topple straight into the unsuspecting gentleman standing in my path.

Struggling to regain my balance, I looked up with a start. The man, who had kept his balance, tipped his hat to his head and placed his other hand under my elbow, refusing to let go until I was steady on my feet.

'How do you do?' he asked. Though he was laughing at me, I could see it was not meant unkindly.

I shuffled back to my original position, feeling myself blush as I apologised for my uncustomary clumsiness.

'Careful now, Miss, wouldn't want you to take another tumble. The ground's more even where I'm standing if you'd like to move down. I've a bonzer view from here.'

I assured my rescuer I was perfectly fine where I was. 'I was just trying to see if Mr Hughes was here.'

'No sign of our Little Digger,' he pronounced, still squinting as he turned back to face me. 'I heard he went to the cathedral service in town, but it doesn't look like old Billie's made it this far. No shortage of other bigwigs though.'

I nodded and smiled politely, clasping my hands as I cast a glance his way. He was not much older than me, simply but neatly attired. Silently vowing not to disgrace myself a second time, I dug the heels of my new shoes into the soft turf and returned my gaze to the funeral proceedings. His next question caught me off guard.

'I take it you're a fan of Mr Lawson, then. What's your favourite poem? Or maybe you're like me, and you prefer his stories.' He smiled encouragingly and made little attempt to lower his voice.

As the warmth of another blush crept up from my chest, I stifled the urge to hide my face. Was this stranger really trying to pursue a conversation in the middle of a public funeral?

The man had again turned his back on the service and now faced me directly. He was evidently very tall because, even though he was standing on lower ground, I still had to look up to see into his eyes, and which I now saw were a rich shade of hazel, like warm caramel slowly darkening in the pan.

'I'm not sure how I feel about Henry Lawson anymore,' I said, without thinking. 'I've spent a long time trying to avoid reading his work.' I had not intended to give such an honest response and could see that he was taken by surprise.

'Roy Armstrong,' he said, offering his hand.

'Lillian Taylor,' I replied and shook it.

Without waiting for an invitation, he bridged the small remaining gap between us and stood next to me. 'Just in case you're inclined to take another tumble,' he grinned.

Though my heart thumped louder than usual in my chest, I told myself I was still recovering from the shock of my near accident and focused my attention back to the funeral, trying to imagine what the Archdeacon might be saying about the newly christened poet laureate of Australia. No doubt there would be no mention of his habitual drunkenness, of his erstwhile court appearances to answer charges of neglect or violence toward his wife, or of the impoverished circumstances of his death. I thought about what I might say about the writer if I had been the person tasked with giving his eulogy today.

'I hope they're going to make full mention of his late mother's hand in his career,' Mr Armstrong whispered loudly into my ear, ducking slightly to avoid speaking over the brim of my hat. 'Louisa Lawson, Mother of Suffrage, and all that. She was the one who got him writing in the first place. Published all his early collections, too. My own mum used to subscribe to her magazine when I was just a lad.'

I nodded. Inwardly I smiled to hear a man acknowledge these facts, which I knew only too well.

'What a woman,' Mr Armstrong continued, whistling air through his teeth in appreciation. 'I heard Henry described her as the hardest businessman he ever met – meant as a compliment, I hope. It's a shame she isn't here to see this. Then again, maybe she's watching all this from afar,' he added, winking as he gestured towards the sky.

'Perhaps she is, Mr Armstrong. Perhaps she is.'

My new acquaintance now turned his attention to the bowed heads closest to the grave, inviting me to join his speculations as to who was who.

'That must be the family,' he reasoned, narrowing his eyes to indicate where he meant for me to look. 'Wonder what his kids think of all this? A state funeral for a father whose fame or verses never did much for any of them, especially once the alcohol had a hold of him.'

I contemplated the indistinct figure of the woman who was Lawson's wife, or rather his former wife. Beside her stood a young man and woman, the poet's children, I supposed. I recalled one of my former students telling me earlier in the year that she had shared her Sydney University graduation ceremony with Henry Lawson's daughter, whom he had always called Barta, and who was now working as a librarian at Mitchell Library; like me, a lover of books and presumably the first in her family to attain such an education.

But although he must have let Barta and every one of them down many times over the years, it was not disappointment I saw in their faces but grief. Lawson's son, I now saw, was rocking back and forth on his heels as if willing himself to stay upright and stared solemnly at the coffin. In contrast, Mrs Lawson, though small in stature, stood tall and erect, as if finally vindicated in her choice of husband.

In this fashion, Mr Armstrong and I continued to watch the service together, taking turns to identify various dignitaries from among the official visitors in the crowd. Mr Armstrong took the lead in picking out all the politicians, along with important personalities from the newspaper, literary and art worlds, many of which he claimed to know through his work as a printer. In turn, I pointed to a few professors whom I recognised from the university, including Jack Brereton, who had co-written our college mask in 1913. Although I still felt self-conscious about its unconventional beginning, I was increasingly enjoying our conversation. Despite Mr Armstrong's uncultivated accent and colourful speech, it was becoming clear to me that intelligence and a refreshing measure of common sense and decency lay behind them.

After a short lull in our exchange, Mr Armstrong cleared his throat and turned to face me. 'So, Miss Taylor, if you're not a fan, can I ask what has brought you to Mr Lawson's funeral?'

I opened my mouth and then closed it again. It was a fair question, but one that I was still trying to answer for myself. Around the cliff's edge, the seagulls squawked and bickered, dipping their wings and hovering effortlessly on invisible pockets of air, while down by the gravesite, the baby had again started crying.

Finally, I shrugged and met his waiting gaze. My tone was quiet and even, bearing the faintest hint of a challenge: 'It's rather a long story.'

'I'm in no rush.' He had the grace to blush.

I swallowed uncomfortably, wishing in that moment that I were the kind of person who thought nothing of telling someone to mind their own business.

All at once I heard the melancholy strains of 'Abide with Me' and looked up to see the Police Band playing.

'The service must be nearly finished,' I whispered in relief. Against all odds, I felt tears spring to my own eyes as I watched Mrs Lawson and Barta crying and comforting each other, along with two other women standing beside them. One elderly lady in particular wept bitterly, and I wondered who she was.

Mr Armstrong nodded, then cleared his throat with another small cough, before speaking in an alarmingly strident voice. 'Hashes ter hashes, dus ter dus.'

'Shush,' I whispered automatically, as if admonishing one of my pupils. I kept my eyes fixed straight ahead as the coffin was lowered into the ground.

'Hashes ter hashes, dus ter dus, an' in hopes of a great an' gelorious rassaraction!'

This time I turned to face him. 'What on earth?'

'I'm quoting Lawson, of course – from "The Bush Undertaker". One of his best sketches, in my humble opinion.' He grinned mischievously. 'No one better than Henry Lawson for capturing the bushman's tongue. You ought to read that one, at least.'

Suddenly comprehending what his garbled speech had meant, I let out an unintended laugh and then hastily assumed a less amused expression.

'Was I too loud? Sorry about that,' he said, not looking in the least apologetic.

'No louder than earlier, Mr Armstrong. Not that it would be my place to say anything.' I gulped. If he had not noticed my own rather inappropriate shushing, I had no intention of revealing this myself.

'Sorry about that,' he said again. 'Didn't hear you. Deaf in one ear, you see.' He pointed at his right side and tapped his ear. 'So, if I'm facing the wrong way from someone or there's too much else going on around the place, I don't always hear.'

A war injury, I presumed. I relaxed my stern countenance and nodded sympathetically.

'Well, looks like it's all over down there.' He gestured towards the crowd dispersing from the gravesite. 'Shall we go down and take a gander at who the wreaths are from? And then, Miss Taylor, I would be honoured to escort you back to the tram.' While this last remark was worded formally, he then winked and added a further request. 'You still need to tell me the rest of your story.'

'What story?'

'The one about you and Henry Lawson, of course. There must be a reason why you've been avoiding reading his work all this time.'

My face grew warm as I searched my mind for a suitable response to put an end to this line of conversation once and for all.

'In fact,' he continued, 'what you said reminded me a lot of Lawson's style of writing – you know, where one story leads to another. It's often just one little word that he'll drop in, gives us the idea there's a whole yarn behind it.'

I was intrigued despite myself.

'Take that story I was quoting from earlier, "The Bush Undertaker". It starts with the old shepherd calling to his dog, "Five Bob". Now a name like that just has to have a good yarn behind it, but Lawson doesn't say another thing about it, just leaves it dangling there. I reckon he was probably just whetting our appetites and saving it up for another sketch.'

As he laughed and slapped his thigh in admiration, I thought of 'Alligator', the loyal and longsuffering snake dog from 'The Drover's Wife'. There was certainly a story behind that name, and perhaps I was the only one who knew it.

By now, Mr Armstrong was waiting for me to speak. When it must have dawned on him I had no intention of doing so, he continued. 'Well, here's hoping you'll tell me your story when you're good and ready, Miss Taylor,' he said, smiling coyly as he offered his arm. 'Shall we?'

Chapter 13
The Alchemist

For the second time in less than a week, I took the southbound train towards Milsons Point – only this time, I was on my way to a rendezvous with a young man who was very much alive. When we parted ways after Lawson's funeral, Mr Armstrong had made it seem perfectly reasonable that we should meet the coming weekend for lunch in North Sydney, where he both lived and worked. He had not even offered to come and pick me up, and I couldn't imagine what had made me agree to see him again. The unlikely circumstances of our meeting, along with what now appeared to be our first date, defied comprehension. And yet I had said yes.

Jean Campbell, whose opinion I had first enlisted, had been circumspect, warning me to be wary of smooth talkers and flirts. But although Mr Armstrong had been very persuasive that day, I never had the sense that he was a Casanova or Lothario type whose only intent was to seduce. Hilda, in contrast, was immediately more encouraging, telling me to follow my instincts and listen to my heart. I wasn't sure if I was entirely ready to listen to my heart just yet, but certainly my gut was telling me that Mr Armstrong was nothing like Mr Polding or indeed any other man I'd ever met.

Walking back to the tram after the funeral service that day, Mr Armstrong had seemed excited to discover we would both be catching the punt over the harbour, together with the North Shore train. As I settled down into the window seat, which he had urged me to claim for myself, I had nearly taken out my book to read – as I usually would – but soon perceived he meant to speak with me the whole way home. Moving with surprising ease from one topic to another as our train passed over the terrace rows and red-tiled rooftops of the lower North Shore, we were nearing Chatswood when I asked where he would be getting off the train.

'Oh, I'm long past my stop,' he said, waving his hand dismissively. 'It's just a nice day to be out and about.'

Though secretly flattered, I raised my eyebrows and pointed at the grey skies outside. Caught out making false excuses, he blushed.

Our journey continued. Billboards flashed past. As we came nearer to where I lived, the land allotments grew bigger and the houses grander.

'Why don't we stop for hot chocolate somewhere?' he asked, covering his earlier embarrassment.

I shook my head but smiled, having glimpsed the same large advertisement for Bournville Cocoa on the corner store we had just passed. The man was incorrigible; he had an answer for everything.

In the end, he had insisted on going all the way on to Gordon with me, all but pouting when I refused to let him walk me home. After shaking hands on the platform, he made an athletic dash for the train going back the other way, though not before extracting my promise to meet him at the North Sydney clock tower the following Sunday at midday. With one last wave and a disarming smile he was gone.

It had all happened in the blink of an eye. I had committed myself that day before I knew it. Now, as the train pulled out of the station, my stomach tightened. Only one more stop before North Sydney. I could still change my mind.

Catching sight of my reflection in the glass, I pinched the skin under my cheekbones to bring colour to my face. I removed my hat and brushed away a few loose strands of hair, checking that the pins were secure before putting it back on.

The clock chimed twelve as I approached the North Sydney Post Office. Mr Armstrong was there waiting, grinning broadly as he came forward to meet me.

'Miss Taylor, thank God you came!' As we shook hands, he began apologising. 'Sorry I didn't pick you up myself. I wanted to, believe you me, but I was worried it might scare you off. I figured you'd be more comfortable meeting me under your own steam – no pun intended!' He laughed easily, gesturing towards the station.

Yet again the man had an answer for everything, I thought to myself as I accepted his arm and quickened my step to match his long stride.

By the time we sat down on the shaded balcony of the hotel dining room, my nerves had all but disappeared. I was reminded of how oddly comfortable I felt in his presence. Still conscious of the pleasant sensation of his woollen jacket against the inside of my wrist from during our walk, I glanced around to see if anyone was looking at us. As a teacher, I was used to being noticed wherever I went.

From our small table near the balustrade, our view skimmed over rooftops and onto the harbour below, which glistened and sparkled like a Ceylon sapphire and was the same intense shade of cornflower blue. The food and drinks brought to us by the publican's high-spirited wife were simple but good, and if we occasionally ran out of things to say, it was easy enough to pass comment on something happening at the water's edge or just to sit back and watch the boats going by on this perfect spring day.

I had to stop myself from smiling when he spoke of Monday's funeral almost nostalgically, as if we had been introduced by mutual friends at the spring races and not met at a cemetery. And when he talked enthusiastically of the constant stream of tributes to Lawson which had appeared in the newspaper since then, some of which I had also seen, I found myself picturing the writer's grieving family and feeling less resentful about this public outpouring than I might have done only a week ago. I even felt pity over Mr Armstrong's description of the humble list of effects comprising Lawson's last will and testament. These apparently included a tin matchbox to be given to his ever-loyal publisher, Mr George Robertson, a pipe to Mr Phil Harris, two packets of tobacco to Mr Roderick Quinn, a pair of spectacles to Mr Tom Mutch and his last pencil to the Mitchell Library.

To my surprise, Mr Armstrong wanted to hear all about my work as a teacher, reaffirming my suspicion that he was nothing like Mr Polding. He listened attentively to my description of a typical school day and laughed and laughed as I gave examples of the various kinds of girlish mischief my students could get up to. Not usually prone to exaggeration, I found myself deliberately making my anecdotes as amusing as possible, simply to see him smile.

While avoiding the intimacy of sustained eye contact, I stole furtive glances at my luncheon companion. Objectively speaking, he was very handsome. Hilda would certainly think so. Clean-shaven features and a strong nose and jaw were set off by an abundance of brownish-blond hair that was darker near his scalp and lighter at the ends, as if bleached by the sun. Its tones and texture reminded me of our fine local sandstone.

Not long into our meal, I became aware of something. Whenever I spoke, he would turn away from the harbour, seeming to look back into the dining room, then lean forward across the table to where I sat opposite. Sometimes he would cup his hand to one ear or ask me to repeat myself. I decided to broach the subject directly.

'Was your hearing damaged during active service, Mr Armstrong?'

'No, it's not from the war. I'm no digger – just the opposite, I'm afraid.' He shifted uncomfortably in his seat and I regretted my question.

'Ear infection,' he said bluntly, the beginnings of an apology hanging in the air. 'From when I was a child. Left me completely deaf on this side.

It's not really that much of a problem for me, but a bung ear is enough to keep a man out of service. I did try to enlist.' He looked at me intently, trying to gauge my reaction. 'I was so angry when they rejected me. Thought I was missing out on a big adventure. What a bloody fool!'

Taken aback by his sudden fury, I spoke soothingly. 'Whatever the reason, it turned out for the best, didn't it?'

'Not for my brother, it didn't.' Pain washed across his face, swiftly replacing the anger from a moment earlier. 'A year younger than me, he was, but already married. With a beaut little baby boy of his own. He always had to do everything before me – that was Reggie, you know – I just didn't think he'd die before me, too.'

I listened with sympathy to the rest of his brother's sad story. Then, before I could second-guess myself, I began telling him about my own family; about the fire, about being sent away to boarding school, even about the five windows of the chapel at Sacred Heart. When I got to the part where my father died, he took my hand.

'Oh Lillian,' he said finally. 'May I call you Lillian? And you must call me Roy.'

I nodded, blinking away the tears that had first appeared while he had been speaking of his brother, then sprung forth in earnest as soon as I began my own story and perceived the sympathy mirrored in his face.

'We're a fine pair, aren't we? A couple of survivors, I'd say.' He let go of my hand and pulled out a handkerchief, sliding it across the table towards me.

I wiped my eyes and mustered a faint smile. 'What happened to your brother's family, Roy?'

His expression lightened. 'My brother's wife, Helen, she's doing all right now. She and the little fellow went to live with her sister and family, over on the east side of town. I visit as often as I can. And every year I keep paying her Reggie's share of the profits from the business. In fact, I was there last Monday, just before Lawson's funeral.'

'And the baby?' I asked, thinking of my own baby sister, Eadie. Twenty-two years on, she would forever remain an infant. Like Reggie and other soldiers fallen in battle, none of my siblings would ever grow older than they had been that last day.

'Little Charlie?' Roy's eyes lit up. 'He's eight now – as happy as Larry most of the time – and looks just like my brother. I'm his godfather, you know. So, between me and his other uncle, he doesn't miss his dad – or at least, he doesn't seem to.'

He paused. 'Sometimes, I wonder about how Reggie died. I never talked to my parents about it. They were heartbroken, of course. I'm sure that's why my dad's poor old ticker gave out – not even a year later. Mum held on for a bit after Dad during the war, and then we lost her with the flu epidemic, gone within days. I think it was grief, more than anything. Anyway, what can you do?' he sighed. 'All the telegram said was that Reggie was shot during battle and died of his injuries. I just pray it was quick, that's all.'

Roy sighed again and raised his beer glass. 'I hope you don't mind me having a drink. I know there are plenty of wowsers who'd say otherwise but I don't think one or two ever hurt anyone. We've all got to take our comfort where we can, don't you think?'

Before I could reply, he slammed down his glass with a loud thud. 'Not that I've got a problem, mind you, not like poor old Henry Lawson. It's only deafness we have in common, don't you worry.'

My ears pricked at this mention of Lawson's deafness but, for Roy's sake, I left it at that. 'Go ahead, there's nothing wrong with drinking in moderation. And I understand what you said about your brother. I don't know *how* my family died, either.'

'You said it was a bushfire?' He sat back in his seat, affording me space to answer in my own time.

'Yes,' I said, nodding bitterly as I twisted the handkerchief still in my hands. 'But I don't understand why they *all* had to die. Or even how. I imagine all sorts of terrible scenarios – trees exploding into flames and falling on them as they tried to run, the tin roof heating up and catching alight, our little house burning down around them. Did they suffocate? Or did they burn to death? Were they already dead by the time my brother and uncle got there to fight the fire? And if they were, why didn't the two of them just turn around, when they saw it was too late, and ride back to safety?' I looked away, across the water. 'Were they together in the end or did they die alone?'

Roy grimaced and clasped my hand a second time. 'No one ever told you what happened?'

'No one told me anything. But I never asked, either. And now, of course, it's too late.'

'Come on,' said Roy, pushing back his chair and standing. 'I want to show you something.'

We walked along the harbour's edge in silence, letting the fresh air and sunshine work their natural magic, then headed uphill. Interspersed between the worker's cottages were a few shops and small factories.

Pausing briefly on one corner to catch our breath, Roy gestured towards a row of terrace houses. 'I seem to recall him living up there for a while – Lawson, that is – with his longsuffering landlady, Mrs Byers. She had quite the reputation around here for taking in stray cats and dogs.' He grinned impishly. 'Sorry, shouldn't speak ill of the dead, I know.'

'Is that what this walking tour of North Sydney was all about?' I was disappointed.

'Heavens no, that was only by the by. What I want to show you is just down here.'

I followed him a short distance until we reached a two-storey stone building.

'Welcome to the family business,' Roy said, now pulling a key from his jacket. 'The workshop is this way, and the print factory is out the back. I live upstairs in the flat – well, more of a bedsitter, really.'

I hesitated briefly before entering, crinkling my nose at the overpowering smell of turpentine and something else I did not recognise – sweet and slightly fruity.

Roy laughed knowingly. 'Gum of arabic. You get used to it after a while.'

On first impression, the large room appeared dirty. Its once white walls were hidden under layers of printed sheets and every available surface was covered by equipment and other paraphernalia. But on closer inspection, I began to perceive an underlying order to the arrangement of all these objects. Along one wall, three sloping desks were positioned to catch the light coming through the windows, with a tall stool – like those in a bank – placed in front of each desk. Bales of paper were neatly stacked on one side, sorted according to size, while a row of metal drums lined the other wall. In the far corner, an open bookshelf held polished slabs of pale stone, along with wooden crates filled with little pots of liquid and powder, crayons, sponges and other supplies. I counted half a dozen ink-stained long coats hanging neatly on pegs.

Although Roy had told me he was a printer, I had imagined him working in a large factory. I'd pictured him standing on his feet for hours on end to operate a heavy printing press, like some kind of giant assembly line. But despite the imposing scale of some of the machinery here, this place was nothing like that.

'What do you think?'

'It reminds me of the art studio at the convent.' I heard the reverence in my voice. 'Some of the girls were given extra lessons in fine arts – not just drawing and painting, but also lettering, illumination and so on.'

'You too?' Roy looked hopeful.

'No, not me.' I looked around the room a second time, my eyes lingering over some well-worn tools, and imagined the many years of use it would have taken for them to be marked in this way. I breathed deeply, momentarily forgetting the strange odours as I took the time to appreciate the atmosphere of this special place. In contrast to the delicate feminine spirituality of the art studio at Sacred Heart, Roy's workshop had an undeniably masculine energy. Yet both light-filled chambers vibrated equally with the hum of creative activity, of talent and flair realised through craft and technique, brought to life on paper and canvas. Fingers, tools, practice and patience. A powerful alchemy.

'It was my father's workshop,' said Roy. 'He wanted to pass it onto his sons when he retired. But now there's only me.' He paused. 'Reggie and I worked here together. Both did our Leaving Certificates then came here right after school to learn the trade. Dad insisted on paying us the same as the other apprentices – which wasn't much, let me tell you.'

I nodded, barely suppressing a grin to think my own starting salary might have exceeded his.

'My father was a top-notch lithographer, you see. Most people in this trade have just one or two things they can do really well, but Dad could do everything – blending colours, stipple screens, lettering, even the fine work. We learned all the technical skills here with him and had to practise our lettering over and over – different scripts, different brushes – until he was satisfied with what we'd done. Then in the evenings, we'd go to the Sydney Art School to learn to draw.'

'Still life? Landscape?' I was fascinated.

'Yes, we did a bit of that too, but mostly we learned how to draw the human figure – hands, faces, the whole kit and caboodle. Sometimes the models they brought in even had to pose nude – it was art school, after all.' Roy cleared his throat.

'So, you're an artist, then?' I asked in my best schoolteacher voice, determined to go on as if nothing unusual had been said.

'No, not me. Even Dad had to give up on that idea pretty soon. But when Reggie started the following year, it was obvious who the real artist was in our family.'

I nodded appreciatively.

'Reggie was amazing, could have had tickets on himself but he shrugged it off like it was nothing at all. Even Ashton, who ran the art school, thought he had a real talent. He encouraged Reggie to paint full-time, but he just kept on working here with Dad and me. He'd do his own art on the side. Wasn't long before he met Helen, then soon after that, they had little Charlie, and life was sweet. Only when the war came, and I got rejected, Reggie insisted on enlisting himself – said at least one of us should see what it was all about. Four months later, and that was that.'

Roy glanced around at the walls. 'In Dad's time, we did a bit of everything, as you can see. Lots of commercial work – advertising posters, stationery, calendars and other kinds of offset printing. Plenty of recruitment posters during the war, of course.

'Then, after Reggie died, some of his artist friends got us to do their printing work. Word got around town and now that's mostly what we do. Etchings, mezzotints, lithographs, a few silkscreens. The artists come here to do the intaglio work – the engraving, that is – and then supervise the printing. Just small runs, all signed and numbered. Keeps me busy, anyhow.' He shrugged and led me over to one of the desks, unlocking the top drawer with a small key on a chain. 'Reggie's tools. I don't let anyone else use them.'

I was touched that Roy wanted me to see these cherished reminders of his brother, and bent down to examine the brushes, magnifying glass and other instruments more closely.

'You can pick them up,' said Roy. 'Those were his best brushes – the sable, the camelhair. His stippling pens, his hand rest ... boy, did Dad tell us off if our hands ever touched the board during practice!' He chortled at the memory, then grew quiet once more. 'Do you think we leave something of ourselves behind in our favourite things?'

'I suppose we do,' I agreed, humbled by his continued willingness to reveal his innermost thoughts. I had not expected any man to make himself so vulnerable.

Roy closed the drawer and turned to me with an expectant look. 'What do you say now? We've both shared more stories than either of us probably ever expected to, but you still haven't told me what you've got against Henry Lawson.'

I frowned. 'You'll probably laugh.'

'I promise I won't. I'm not really the joking sort anyway – or haven't you noticed?' The corners of his mouth began to quiver with an expression that was anything but serious. Then, registering my beseeching expression, he apologised immediately. 'I'm sorry, Lillian. I was just trying to lighten things up. Please tell me.'

I swallowed, then stood tall, squaring my shoulders. 'Do you know Lawson's story "The Drover's Wife"?'

'My word, I do. One of his best. Everyone says so.'

'Well,' I began haltingly, 'I'm fairly certain Henry Lawson wrote that story about my family.' I paused as if standing on the edge of a great precipice, then blurted out the remainder of my speech in one long breath. 'I think my mother must have been the inspiration for the drover's wife, and that I was the baby she was holding. I won't trouble you with all the details but, suffice to say, everything fits.'

I waited, eyes to the ground, bracing myself for his reaction.

'Why not?' he mused, his tone thoughtful. 'His stories always were more about observation than imagination. No reason why he couldn't have been observing your family on one of his travels.'

Roy's easy pronouncement left me stunned, more lost for words than if he had responded with understandable scepticism or even ridicule. I felt strangely elated but also tired and empty, as if I had been holding onto something very tightly and was only now letting go.

'Would you like to come upstairs for a cup of tea? I could probably find some biscuits too. Reckon I've got an old copy of "The Drover's Wife" up there somewhere.'

My heart skipped a beat and I felt myself colour. I had never been anywhere near a gentleman's private apartments. And certainly not on my own. 'No, thank you. I should probably be getting home.'

Evidently perceiving the cause of my discomfort, Roy hastily retracted his invitation. 'At least let me drive you,' he implored. 'I could meet your landlady, Mrs Campbell, and we can make plans for next weekend.'

'I didn't know you had a motor car.'

A guilty flush travelled up his neck. 'I was wondering when you'd catch me out.' He turned his head to the side, raking long fingers through his sandy hair. 'You remember I told you I was over in the East last Monday to see my nephew. Well, it's possible I might have had my car with me when we met at the funeral afterwards.'

'But you went straight for the tram back to the city, and then we took the punt and the train home together. You didn't say anything about a motor car.'

'Well, I couldn't let you out of my sight, could I? Not without getting you to agree to seeing me again.' He shrugged sheepishly.

I didn't know whether to be charmed or outraged. 'Roy Armstrong, you are a sweet talker,' I said, finally allowing his boyish smile to win me over for good as I followed him to the car.

Chapter 14
Letting Go

'All right, all right, I'll try,' I sighed.

Roy was nothing if not persistent. Just a few weeks after our first date, I yielded to his suggestion that he teach me how to drive. We chose a warm Sunday afternoon and agreed to combine my maiden voyage with an outing to the zoo at Mosman. To my astonishment, our courtship was now official, and Roy had been given a resounding nod of approval, both from Jean Campbell, who promptly withdrew her original warning, and Hilda, who could not have been more welcoming during our visit the prior weekend. Pulling me aside at the earliest opportunity, she had been lavish in her praise of both Roy's looks and temperament.

'He's clearly swept you off your feet,' Hilda exclaimed. 'But best of all, you've let him!'

Since our lunch that day in North Sydney, and later in Roy's studio, neither of us had raised the subject of Henry Lawson or 'The Drover's Wife', but when I set my picnic basket down on the back seat of his motor car, I spied a small book with the author's name on the spine. Though its cover was different to that of the edition I had snatched from my teacher's desk at Sacred Heart at age sixteen, its title page bore the same vignette by Frank Mahony, depicting the story's closing scene.

Already nervous about my ability to master the skill of driving, my stomach tightened further as I wondered what questions Roy might ask now that he had had time to consider my claims regarding Lawson's story, but thankfully the car's incessant rattling, together with the wind whooshing around us in the open-top, made it almost impossible to speak. I kept my eyes on the road and a firm grip on my new crinoline straw hat. When we were close to our destination, Roy pulled over to the side of the road and stepped out of the car.

'Your turn,' he said, opening my door with a flourish.

I looked at the formal gardens and grand mansions surrounding us. 'What if I crash?'

'She'll be right, Lill – don't you worry.'

'If you say so.' I wriggled sideways into the driver's seat and eyed the controls dubiously. Now that we were no longer moving, the sun burned down on my bare forearms and the air was heavy and oppressive.

With almost infuriating patience, Roy went over his long list of instructions – how to read the instrument panel, when to use the indicators, first gear for this, second gear for that – making me repeat them back to him again and again, until I thought my head would burst.

'Now, let's start. Nice and easy. Release the handbrake and put your foot down on the clutch.'

'Release the handbrake?'

'That's it. She's apples, you'll see.'

'Just let go? Just like that.'

'You got it.'

'You want me to let go? Now?'

'Struth, Lill. If you don't let go, we're not going anywhere.'

In the end, we did not go anywhere, or at least not while I was at the wheel. Chuckling with bemusement, Roy took over and drove directly to the zoo, assuring me I would do better on the return journey home.

'Not a bad outlook, is it?' he asked after paying our entrance fee and entering the grounds. 'Almost makes me jealous of the animals.'

'It's a long way from the plains of Africa or the jungles of Asia.' I laughed. 'But I bet today's weather might make some of them feel even more at home than usual.'

If Waverley Cemetery was the most spectacularly set graveyard in the world, I was sure Taronga could justly be described as its most beautiful zoo. Clinging to a steep, gum-scented incline on the edge of Sydney Harbour, it offered spacious enclosures to its menagerie of residents matched with grandstand water views.

Seen from this privileged height, the harbour displayed itself in all its glory, revealing the furthermost reaches of its perimeter, like the ragged edges of an oyster shell. Inlets, bays and beaches contrasted with headlands, promontories and peninsulas jutting sharply out to sea.

With Roy carrying our heavy picnic basket and blanket, we ambled down the hill, weaving our way through the zoo grounds, arm in arm. After catching the end of the seal show, chortling at the childish antics of the monkeys and admiring the exotic birds in their oversized aviaries, we lingered at the elephant temple, sharing in the excitement as a fresh load of children was hoisted up onto the Indian elephant.

'Old Jessie's been doing this job for almost forty years. I still remember my first time, long before the zoo was moved out here. You never know, maybe one day we'll bring our kids for a ride here too, don't you think?' Roy winked at me.

I looked at him mutely. Although his delivery had been entirely playful, I had the distinct feeling he was only half in jest. I managed to find my voice and suggested it was time to eat.

We sat down under the half-hearted shade of a straggling gum tree. While I unpacked the sandwiches, Roy poured lemonade from a rubber-sealed glass bottle, licking the drops that fell onto his overly eager hands.

'I had another read of your story last night, Lill. You know the one I mean.'

I put my sandwich down and made of a show of trying to find a more comfortable position for myself on the uneven ground, carefully arranging the flimsy georgette folds of my dress to cover my legs. The humidity was making my hat droop even more than the milliner intended, which had the benefit of hiding much of my face from view.

Roy carried on undeterred. 'What was it Lawson wrote to upset you so much? I reckon your mother comes across as a real hero – an Aussie bush heroine. Don't you think?'

I swallowed uncomfortably and looked away.

'Penny for your thoughts.'

'Do you really believe me?' I said at last, peering up at Roy from beneath my hat. 'It's all right if you don't. We don't ever have to talk about it again.'

'Course I do. If you say it's the story of your family, then that's good enough for me.'

Buoyed by his unquestioning acceptance, but knowing it was given without foundation, I insisted on returning to the details of my story to let him judge for himself. Roy listened attentively while I presented my evidence: my father away droving, forever absent ... my mother home alone with the four children, I myself just a baby at that time ... my two brothers, Jacky and Tommy, just as they were named in the story ... the ill-disguised twist on the name of our dog, Alligator ... together with various other details of our household and life in the bush which came together to prove my case.

'Blimey,' said Roy with a sniff. 'No wonder you were convinced. So, it was the shock of reading about your family that upset you from the start? And the fact that no one believed you?'

I nodded. 'It was like finding them and losing them a second time.' Tears sprang to my eyes, and now that I'd begun talking, I found I couldn't stop. 'Sometimes I wonder what was real and what wasn't. What parts of the story I truly remember for myself and what parts I've just taken as fact, because I read them so many times, because that's what Lawson wrote. Then I get mad all over again because he knew things about my family that I didn't.'

'Like what, for instance?'

'Like all the terrible things my mother had to face out there alone. I knew about most of them, because I was there too, living through it all firsthand, but there are other things I never knew about – like her losing a child before I was born, or like my father sometimes "forgetting" that he was married ... to infer that he must have been carrying on with other women when he was away from us – what an offensive thing to suggest!' My voice shook with anger. 'I just don't think she would have wanted me or anyone else to know about any of those things. It's too private.'

'Then what makes you think she told him?' Roy asked softly. 'What makes you think she told him any of it?'

With a sudden gasp I saw what Roy was getting at. Seeping through the familiar layers of bitterness in my mind was the beginnings of a new idea. Mother would never have told a stranger such intimate things about her life. Never. This singular and yet obvious realisation struck me with such force that I almost cried out.

I buried my head in my hands.

Roy's voice was tender. 'Don't be embarrassed. You were just a girl when you read that story. Of course you held onto every detail you could find. Anyone would. I was the same with my brother's telegram.'

'But how could he speak for her like that? She would have hated that.' I looked up in anguish.

'I know what you're saying, I do. But maybe it wasn't like that. Maybe you should just think of Henry Lawson as a storyteller, doing the best he could.'

'A story peddler, you mean? No different to any common hawker selling his wares from door to door. And second-hand wares, at that!'

A dark cloud passed overhead, momentarily obscuring the sun and plunging us into shadow. My jaw remained clenched as Roy continued.

'Honestly, Lill, there's no point in holding on. You have to let it go. And don't forget, he was practically stone-deaf.'

'I suppose you'd like me to forgive him because he was drunk at the time, too.'

'Think about it, Lill. He would have had Buckley's chance of hearing much of whatever your mother told him, if in fact she told him anything. He was a writer, after all – he probably just started with a few solid facts then went from there.'

I thought about all the books I had read and loved over the years, conceding that many of my favourite authors must also have sought inspiration from the lives of others. That what began as a germ of an idea, a mere seed, required careful cultivation under the writer's watchful eye – and pen – before coming to life on the page.

'Look,' he said, shrugging his shoulders. 'I'm not trying to defend the man; I just think you can't ignore the fact of his deafness. I witnessed it myself.' He paused.

'Go on.'

'You remember I showed you that house near my place where Lawson used to stay,' he said. 'As it happens, he lived in North Sydney on and off for years. I used to see him on the street sometimes, in his old battered felt hat, struggling up Blues Point Road with his cane. On his way back from the pub, I'd wager. Once I even saw him in a billycart being pushed by a young lad who said he'd been paid sixpence to get him home.'

I felt my eyes narrowing in judgement, followed by an unexpected spark of compassion for the frail old man I had glimpsed from the train in August.

'One evening after work – just a couple of years ago, it would have been – I spotted him down at Dind's Hotel, drinking with his mates. "Harry", they called him. You could see they were a real tight bunch.'

Roy's expression became thoughtful. 'You always hear Lawson was the shy type, standoffish even. And I could see he was a bit awkward – highly strung, you might say – but he seemed very happy to be with those mates.' He paused, chuckling. 'He had such a strange laugh, I remember. Seemed to suck the air right in and then choke on it. More of a snort than a laugh. Anyway, Lill, the thing is, it was obvious to me that he really couldn't hear much of what was being said. He was trying hard not to let on, but he didn't fool me.'

'What makes you say that?'

'Well, I could tell from how he was reacting to the conversation – like he wanted to be a part of it but just kept missing the punchline. He was faking it, clear as day. I ought to know, I do the same myself sometimes.'

I made a silent promise to speak more clearly to Roy from now on and keep to his good hearing side whenever possible.

'He had such sad, dark eyes. Pitiful. Like a dog who'd been kicked by its master and didn't know where to turn. It's kind of ironic to think he wrote about all those bush heroes. I know he spent a good bit of time in the bush, living like a swaggie, but to look at the man – especially as crook as he was by then – you'd swear he wouldn't last a day. Not that I would either, mind you, never been further inland than the Blue Mountains!' Roy laughed good-naturedly. 'He sure as heck didn't come across like a typical bush bloke. He was really quite girlish, if I'm perfectly honest.'

Although I had little interest in the question of Lawson's effeminacy, Roy's argument about his deafness had finally struck a chord. I recalled a few recent newspaper articles having mentioned it also. 'So, do you think his hearing difficulties would have affected him back then too? He was around twenty-five when he wrote "The Drover's Wife".'

'Hard to say for sure. I know he had an infection as a lad, same as me, but whereas I still have my good ear, I think his hearing just got worse over time. No wonder he was always drinking – probably made him feel better about life. And if he was drunk, it didn't really matter if what he said didn't make sense. Poor old codger.'

Despite everything, I registered another small pang of sympathy at this unexpected window into Lawson's everyday life.

'Still, no need to feel sorry for him, it's probably what made him such a good storyteller. Like they say, when you lose one sense, you gain another. Look at all the fine description in his writing – in just a few short lines, he can make you feel like you're there yourself. I reckon he must have been a bonzer lipreader too.'

'What do you mean?'

'Well, everyone talks about how the bush is the heart of Australia and how Henry Lawson is the voice of the bush. And maybe he is. But you ought to look closely at how he spells the words – the bush lingo, I mean. He just writes the dialogue the way it's spoken, the way he sees it on people's lips.'

'The way he saw it, you mean. Past tense.' I flashed the briefest of smiles.

Roy winked, then directed his gaze at the horizon as he began reciting from memory.

'Arter all ... nothin' matters now, Brummy ...
you uster say as how it'ud be all right termorrer ...
well termorrer's come fur you now, Brummy –
it ain't come fur me yet, but it's a-comin.'

He grinned at me. 'Not bad for a city swell, eh?'

And it was true. He'd pronounced Lawson's spelling perfectly and given the words their full bush accent. I clapped my hands.

'Oh yes,' I said, '"hashes ter hashes, dus ter dus", and all that – I see what you're doing. I suppose you could pass for a swagman. Or, at the very least, a bush larrikin.'

Unlike most people I knew, Roy appeared to delight in keeping his own Australian accent as broad as possible. No plummy pronunciations or gliding vowels for him.

'Glad you approve.' He grinned. 'But what I'd really like to know is whether I've helped you feel any better about all this?'

'I think you have,' I answered, genuinely flabbergasted by the truth of my reply.

'So, what now?'

I looked away from Roy and towards the harbour, my thoughts crashing against each other like waves against the shore. What now? That was the real question, one that only I could answer. Like that day in Roy's studio, I felt lighter, no longer weighed down by the past. At the same time, I was conscious of feeling exposed, suddenly more vulnerable than ever before. Like the shell-bound sea creatures in the harbour rock pools below, I was starting to see that the brittle carapace I had been living within had been of my own creation. The moment had come to reveal my true form to the world.

'Maybe it's time I took the story back for myself,' I pondered aloud, while my eyes followed the smooth glide of a seagull in the distance.

'Too right, Lill. Lawson's dead and his version of the truth can go with him. Cheers to that,' Roy said, thrusting a glass into my hand and clinking it with his own.

'Cheers to that,' I echoed. 'I'm only sorry we haven't got a real drink for our toast.'

Roy laughed heartily at that. We drank from our lemonade in companionable silence. The lump in my throat from earlier was now all but gone.

'Maybe we can also take this story in a different direction? A more romantic one, I was thinking.' Roy raised his eyebrows hopefully.

'I think we already have,' I said, jumping to my feet and brushing the crumbs from my dress. 'Time to go, wouldn't you say? I'm ready for my first drive.'

~

By November, the following month, my driving was coming along so well that I had progressed from back streets to main roads. Not once during today's drive into town had Roy needed to remind me about keeping enough distance between Tin Lizzie, as he called his Model T Ford, and any nearby horse-drawn vehicles. Even my gear changes were getting less clunky.

'I don't know what all those men have been complaining about in their letters to the National Roads Association,' said Roy, after I stuttered to a stop on Prince Albert Road near St Mary's Cathedral. 'A lady driver can be every bit as good as a man.'

'Are you being sarcastic?'

'Not a bit,' he winked, as he helped me out of the car.

'Was my driving making you nervous? Is that why you're sweating?'

'Not a bit,' he repeated, now laughing. 'It's this humidity, is all. It's killing me.' He pulled out his handkerchief to wipe his brow.

It was hot, but I still wasn't sure he was being entirely truthful with me.

'Right then, now that's behind us, are you ready for the next part?'

'I think so.'

'That doesn't sound very confident. Come on, Lill. What's the worst that can happen? You have to take a chance. Look at me – I had every intention of placing that bet on King Ingoda yesterday, and then it completely slipped my mind. I could've made a fortune.' Roy was still smarting after missing out on yesterday's Melbourne Cup winner, although I suspected the main reason he had kept mentioning it during our drive was to distract me from the task ahead.

We had both taken the afternoon off work in order to visit the General Registry. It had been Roy's idea that we go there and try to track down any records of my parents and of my own birth. Even though any documents in my parents' possession would have been destroyed in the fire, it was still possible that some of this information had previously made its way to official registers. And although the thought of delving into the past and reopening old wounds had kept me awake for the better part of the night, I was touched that he had cared enough to suggest it and I had allowed him to convince me that it was worth a try.

'Everyone wants to know where they come from,' he'd reasoned. 'It's only natural.'

I turned to him now. 'Yes, Roy, I'm ready. Let's do it. Are you happy now?'

'That's my girl,' he beamed, holding my hand as we walked uphill towards Chancery Square. 'Who knows? You might find out you're related to a king!'

'You mean like King Ingoda?'

'Oh, now that's cruel, Lill. Don't kick a man while he's down.'

~

Half an hour later, we walked out empty-handed. I had been careful not to build up my hopes, and Roy appeared almost more distraught than me.

'I'm so sorry, Lill. I really thought we'd find something in there.'

'It's all right; it's not your fault.'

'I can't believe they couldn't help you with any of it. No record of your parents' marriage. No record of either of their births, or even their deaths, for goodness' sake. And nothing at all about you.'

'It probably didn't help that I couldn't even give them Mother's maiden name.' I gave a small shrug.

'I know. But even so, I thought at the very least they'd be able to find your birth record, especially since the clerk explained how they'd done that reconciliation with Church records some years back.'

'I don't think either of my parents had much time for the Church.' I shrugged again. I had a funny feeling that Mother had been a spiritualist at some point. 'Did you see that awkward expression on his face when he talked about the Legitimation Act of 1902? About how even if my parents hadn't been married at the time of my birth, once the Act came in, they could have still registered my birth and had it certified in retrospect?'

'I know,' Roy groaned. 'Until you pointed out that they had both died by then anyway. Stupid man, I could have wrung his neck for not paying attention.'

'It doesn't matter. I'm glad we went. You were right, it was worth a try.'

'You're okay, then?'

I nodded. 'It's almost as if I never existed.'

'Oh, Lill, don't say that.' He looked shocked.

'I mean it in a good way. As a fresh chance. Like wiping the slate clean and starting over again.' I was still trying to convince myself as well as Roy.

'That's true,' he said, squeezing my hands. 'I like that idea.'

'And anyway, I know my own birthday. I've never forgotten that, at least. What else could any piece of paper have given me?'

'You mean apart from proving a direct link to royalty then?' Roy gingerly returned my smile. 'At least things are done properly these days with official notification forms, and not just with a spit and a handshake or a "he said, she said" approach. Let's keep that in mind next time we need to register any kind of important life event, you know – births … deaths … marriages.'

I pretended not to notice the obvious emphasis Roy had placed on this last word or his accompanying mischievous expression. He had dropped several such hints in recent weeks, leaving me alternately breathless with excitement or overcome with terror.

'At least it's not so hot anymore,' I said, changing topics. A cool change was blowing in from the south-east and already the temperature had dropped.

'Here she comes,' said Roy, sniffing at the air. 'The Southerly Buster, right on time.'

I fanned my skirts, letting the air circulate. 'The nuns used to say it was a godsend. A true blessing from God.'

'It is a godsend on a stinking hot day like today, all right. The only trouble is that it always sets off my hay fever,' said Roy, eyeing the leaves and specks of wattle that were already billowing through the air.

'Cry-baby,' I teased, then clucked sympathetically as he blew into his handkerchief. 'This town never could hold the heat.'

'Good old Sydney, she's not as stubborn as some.' Roy winked then opened the car door, waiting for me to get in.

'In that case, you can drive us back instead. This lady driver "stubbornly" refuses to subject herself to further criticism.' Feigning a haughty expression, I walked around to the passenger side and let myself in the car. I still remembered Mrs Spicer's wise advice, given years earlier in the Sacred Heart boiler room, to never to let a man tell me what to do. Although Roy had only been teasing, I was determined to keep him on his toes.

'Yes, ma'am,' he shot back, together with an exaggerated salute. 'Hold onto your hat.'

With both of us now smiling, Roy steered us back to the punt at Dawes Point. As we crossed the harbour, the wind continued to pick up.

'Shouldn't we put the top up?' I asked, once we were back on the road. 'I think I just felt a drop of rain.'

'Nonsense, she'll be right.' He pulled his own cap down tight over his ears and accelerated while I watched the sky turned to slate. Whipping up suddenly, gale-force winds began battering our vehicle from all sides.

Sure enough, those first tentative drops of rain were soon replaced by a steady stream not even Roy's optimism could deny. Apologising for his own stubbornness, he pulled over to the side of the road in front of a park. While Roy struggled to raise and secure the fabric hood on his own, I reluctantly did as he asked and stayed in the car, sheltering under the picnic blanket I found still in the back seat from our visit to the zoo. Even with the canvas top now in place, rain continued to blow through the open sides into the cabin. We would soon be drenched. Peering out from beneath the blanket, I saw Roy still outside the car, holding – of all things – a large potato.

'What are you doing? We need to get out of here,' I shouted over the rain.

'Wiping it over the windscreen. Stops the glass from fogging up. Here,' he yelled, thrusting the potato – now in halves – into my hands, 'you do inside, I'll start the crank.'

'But where did the potato come from?' I wiped the freshly cut edge back and forth across the glass, getting wetter with each passing minute and feeling increasingly foolish.

'I always keep a spud and sharp knife in the car. Hope for the best but be ready for the worst, that's my motto.'

I groaned in mock protest then stopped short when I heard him make a loud roar of pain.

'That blasted crank! I think it's broken something this time.' Roy held up his hand, gingerly checking fingers and thumb for movement.

I pushed open the heavy door and jumped out of the car, hardly noticing my new hat now lying crushed on the ground. I took Roy's hand, doing my best to examine him despite the rain that was making everything slippery and hard to see. Although my own meagre experience of first aid was limited to what I'd learned in the Ravenswood playground, it seemed likely that two of his fingers were sprained, possibly broken. Before I could think about offering to turn the crank myself and drive us home, the raindrops turned to hail, bouncing off the road and grass, and clattering against the car's bonnet.

'Take cover,' shouted Roy, leading me back inside the car.

We huddled together, half-pressed against the steering wheel, as a barrage of icy pellets rained upon us, entering from one side at an angle. Roy put his arms around me and held the blanket over our heads. The smell of wet wool filled my nostrils.

'You're saturated,' he said in dismay. 'What a fiasco, I'm so sorry.'

'You're saturated too. And injured. Anyway, it's not your fault.' I began to giggle.

'But you're covered in gooseflesh – just feel your arms.' As he ran his hand over my bare skin, I gave an audible gasp and my stomach cartwheeled.

'May I kiss you, Lill?' Roy asked abruptly, his voice deep with longing.

My stomach flipped again. Thunder echoed in the background and though I'd not yet seen any lightning, I felt a frisson of excitement shoot through my body as if even the air were electric. Timidly I lifted my face towards him in the dim light. He hesitated a moment, and then slowly brought his lips to mine.

The kiss went on for what seemed like hours. Trembling and breathless with desire, I felt like a swooning heroine in a romantic novel. I could even imagine the exact wording to describe such a scene: *If she were to catch a fever and die after today's storm, it might almost have been worth it for this fierce moment of passion.*

'There's something else I wanted to ask you.'

Roy's lips were warm against my throat, his words a velvet whisper. In my present state, I felt like I might agree to anything. This must be how women got themselves into trouble.

'Yes?' I waited, hardly daring to breathe.

'But I'm not sure if I should ask you now, not after what happened today.'

'Why not?' I stiffened, suddenly afraid that Roy might see me differently now. For all I knew, my parents may never have been married. I might well be illegitimate. Roy had never struck me as the kind of person to cast judgement, but then again, I'd only known him a short while.

'I really wanted it to go well today, Lill, but I only made things worse.'

'Just ask your question, Roy.'

'I was really hoping that if we found your records, it might give you the confidence to take the next step. Together, I mean.' He paused to catch his breath. 'Oh, blow it, Lill. A man's got to take a chance, hasn't he? I'm going to do it anyway.'

And before I could even process what he'd just said, he drew me towards him and whispered in my ear. 'Lillian Taylor, will you do me the honour of marrying me?'

Throwing my arms around his neck, I broke into peals of laughter.

'Lillian?'

I felt Roy's confusion and held onto him as he flinched and tried to pull away. 'I'm so sorry, Roy. I misunderstood. I thought you were having second thoughts about me just now. I wasn't laughing at you.' I pressed my face into his chest, surprised to find myself close to tears as I tried to catch up with what was happening.

'What, then?' He sounded miserable.

Though the squall continued outside and though I had not stopped shaking, more powerful now were the thoughts thrashing against each other in my mind. I searched for the right words. 'I never expected that I would ever be married.'

Roy leaped in immediately. 'Is it too soon? I've jumped the gun, haven't I?'

I shook my head.

'It's your career, isn't it? You're not ready to give up teaching? I know you probably won't be allowed to continue working at the school once we're married, but I promise you I'm not one of those old-fashioned men who expect a woman to hide her intelligence. I hope I've shown you that already.'

'No, I know, it's not that.' I shook my head, more in wonder at my own good fortune than anything else. Roy was almost too good to be true.

But now that I had finally met a man who made me happy and wanted to share his life with me, was I brave enough to go through with it? Could I really let myself love someone unreservedly, without second-guessing what might go wrong?

Beside me, Roy kept on talking, clutching at other possible reasons and ready to refute them all.

'Stop, Roy. That's enough now. Please, let me speak.'

He gave a dejected sigh and finally became silent. Yet he continued to stroke my wet hair with more tenderness than I had ever thought possible.

'As I said, I never thought I would ever be married. I never imagined meeting you.' I put my hands around his jaw and drew him towards me in a long, deep kiss. 'And I definitely never imagined a proposal scene like this. But yes – yes, I will marry you, Roy Armstrong. Yes, yes, yes!'

Chapter 15

Something Old, Something New

In place of a soft pink carpet of camellia petals, I stepped out on my wedding day onto a lawn scattered with homemade confetti, holding a bouquet of mauve-blue hydrangeas.

At first, I had thought we might marry the following autumn, secretly wishing to be the fairytale bride I had imagined at Mr Waterhouse's sasanqua hedge. I had also told Roy I wanted to give Ravenswood at least a full term's notice.

'Why wait?' he'd argued. 'Let's get hitched as soon as the school year is over. They can find themselves a new teacher over the summer.'

'It's too soon. I know ours has been a whirlwind romance, but we'll have only known each other a few months by then.'

Roy had waved away this and all my other objections. 'Some couples get married after weeks not months. Anyway, when something's right, you know it's right.'

And because I too had known that it was right, despite my nerves and continued protestations, here I was in the Edwards' beautiful garden, already married in a private ceremony earlier that morning, and now the centre of attention of a smiling crowd of well-wishers.

Isabel Edwards, who had kindly insisted on hosting our wedding breakfast, had been disappointed over our decision not to invite guests to the church service. She did, however, succeed in securing my promise to be a traditional bride in another – and in her mind, at least – equally essential sense. *Something old, something new, something borrowed, something blue* ... so went the old English rhyme.

We began with *something blue*. Along with Isabel's crystalline blue eyes, that fairly glittered with excitement as our wedding arrangements came together, we settled on a loose bouquet of blue hydrangeas. Next came *something new*, with Jean Campbell gladly putting her exquisite sewing skills to use in creating my silk wedding dress from scratch. Not to be outdone, Roy proudly presented me with a seed pearl necklace inherited from his mother as both his bridal gift and as *something old*.

Finding the right *something borrowed* had, however, proved elusive. Isabel had pleaded with me to choose a piece from her vast collection of jewellery and fashionable accessories, but everything was too elaborate, or else valuable, for my taste. I was relieved when Hilda had volunteered the loan of her own wedding veil, originally imported from Ireland and made of distinctive Carrickmacross lace.

My borrowed Irish lace was undeniably beautiful, and this morning in the church, looking out through the sheer layers of my veil and seeing Roy's adoring gaze, I had felt beautiful too – perhaps for the first time in my life. Though others had described me this way before, I had never felt it to be true. This was how it felt to be loved, then. This was what I had finally dared to hope for.

When our brief service drew to its conclusion and the time came to exchange vows, my old fears had risen to the surface so that for a few seconds I could hardly breathe. Then Roy took my hand and began speaking, I heard my own voice answer his ... and then it was done. Married, just like that.

Floating on a cloud of champagne, with all the doubts and decisions of the past few weeks behind me, I felt as light as the bubbles dancing their way to the top of my glass. As my gaze travelled serenely across the garden, I took a leisurely sip from my gold-rimmed crystal coupe and smiled to myself. In addition to the small inventory of friends, colleagues and Roy's family on our guest list, I could see our hostess had rounded out these numbers with some of her own friends, simultaneously lifting the fashion bar. As the perennial party-giver, Isabel was as predictable as she was generous. In my present mellow state, I felt nothing but gratitude.

I spotted Hilda resting on one of the garden benches. Behind her, on the tennis court, Cecil was running after their two little girls. For once, Nanny was nowhere to be seen and I could hear their laughter from here. When I'd shared the happy news of our engagement with my best friend, she'd already been quite advanced into her confinement with her third child but had no intention of missing out on celebrating our nuptials. I waited till I could catch Hilda's eye then raised my glass in a silent toast.

'You cut your hair!' said one of my colleagues with a tone of accusation.

I raked my fingers through my newly cropped hair. 'I'm still getting used to it.'

'I think she looks smashing,' said Isabel, who sported a similar cut herself.

After the long plaits of my schoolgirl years and more than a decade of wearing my hair up, I found my dark bob strangely liberating. My own natural waves appeared to find it equally liberating, springing into place after each wash as if to demonstrate they too were glad put all those years of discipline behind them.

'I think she looks smashing too, Mrs Edwards. Absolutely bonzer,' said Roy, putting his arm around me as he joined our conversation. 'My bride scrubs up a treat, don't you think?'

I bit my lip and suppressed a laugh. 'Don't mind Mr Armstrong,' I told the circle of women surrounding us. 'He likes to provoke a reaction.'

'Indeed, he does. And now Mr Armstrong would like to introduce Mrs Armstrong to some of their other guests. Ladies, please excuse us.' With his usual disarming smile, Roy whisked me away from the tittering constellation of women and steered me towards another part of the garden, where several unfamiliar faces looked expectantly in our direction.

Since our engagement, everything had happened so quickly and there had been no time to meet all the individual characters and networks of people that mattered in each other's lives. Apart from Hilda and her family, it was only Jean Campbell and Mr and Mrs Edwards to whom Roy had been formally introduced. Today had been my first chance to present him to a handful of my old friends from The Women's College as well as my fellow faculty members, including Miss Fidler, Ravenswood's foundress, the unfortunately named Miss Slack, Miss Fidler's first assistant, and a smattering of other teachers whose company I enjoyed. Far from being intimidated by any of these educated and, at times, overly opinionated women, Roy had succeeded in charming them all. Showing great interest in their respective subject areas, he had engaged in a long and spirited discussion with our Art mistress, who gladly accepted Roy's invitation to tour his printing studio.

I pasted a confident smile on my face as we now approached this group of guests unknown to me. It was my turn to meet those people whom Roy had invited to share in today's celebration. These included one or two employees and several mates from the trade, as well as what was left of his own family. Because both Roy's parents had passed away shortly after the war and most of his extended family lived outside Sydney, the family in attendance was limited to an elderly pair of spinster aunts and a single cousin – and, most importantly, his brother Reggie's widow, Helen, and young son, Charlie.

'My sister-in-law's a lovely lady,' whispered Roy as we approached, 'but she could honestly talk the leg off an iron pot. Don't say I didn't warn you.'

'Didn't warn her about what, Roy?' Helen asked, shaking my hand with genuine warmth, and leaning in to kiss my cheek.

'I was just warning Lillian about Charlie. And now look what the little rascal has in his hands!' I turned to look, but with these words, Roy had picked up his young nephew, and now threw him over his shoulder and tickled him until he begged for mercy. Finally, he placed the squealing child back on the ground before me, and the boy eased open his clenched hand to reveal a small brown lizard.

'Uncle Roy!' protested Charlie happily. 'Now he's lost his tail.'

'He certainly has. Poor chap – he's going to look pretty darn silly going through life without a tail. I hope you're sorry.'

Charlie rose to the bait. 'That's not right, Uncle Roy. Lizards drop their tails all the time. He'll grow another one.'

'What about you, then? If we give your tail a bit of a chop, will it grow back too?' Roy turned to me. 'Aunty Lillian, will you go into the kitchen and fetch me a nice big pair of shears, please?'

While Helen smiled benevolently as Charlie and his uncle continued their usual horseplay, I considered my newly acquired title. Overnight, I had become an aunt. For a moment, my thoughts flashed on my own brothers and sisters and of the children they might have had, but I pushed the image away and took another sip of champagne instead.

'Will you be sorry to stop teaching?' asked Helen.

'Yes and no,' I said, having pondered this same question myself in recent weeks since reluctantly handing in my notice. 'I'm sure I'll miss some of my pupils, as well as the camaraderie between us teachers, but not every child is a willing student, and some days are better than others.'

Although I still harboured some misgivings about giving up my hard-won independence to become a married woman, I had felt decidedly better after receiving a warm letter of congratulations from my former principal at The Women's College, Miss Macdonald. She herself had resigned from her post in 1919 and was now back in Scotland, and her congratulations were unhesitating and full-hearted – I no longer felt like I had let her and her aspirational vision of womanhood down.

'The school head, Miss Fidler, was just telling me how sorry she is to lose her. Though, as I told Miss Fidler, not as sorry as I would have been.' Slightly out of breath from all their romping around, Roy now had Charlie sitting comfortably on his shoulders where he could create no further mischief.

Helen laughed. 'I'm sure you'll soon be able to put all that knowledge and teaching skill to use with your own children, Lillian.'

I tried to conceal my surprise at Helen's innocent assumption. Aside from his stray comment about taking them to see Jessie the elephant at the zoo, Roy and I had not yet talked about having children. I sensed that he was giving me time to get used to the idea. Just as I had never thought I would get married, I'd never thought having children would be in my future. Admittedly, I had sometimes wondered what it would be like to nurture my own child instead of someone else's, but I had never expressed the thought aloud, not even to Hilda.

'You must give me some tips,' Helen continued, apparently unaware of the effect of her words. 'I don't think my Charlie would ever open a book unless I forced him. He's always off digging up the garden looking for creepy-crawlies and injuring himself in the process.'

I gratefully latched onto this and began making suggestions for suitable reading to tempt an eight-year-old boy.

The tinkling sound of a bell interrupted our conversation, followed by a short announcement from Isabel who was standing on the back terrace. I saw Hilda stand up from the bench and make her way over, all the while smiling at me as if she had a great secret. Sure enough, Hilda had a surprise for us in the drawing room.

I followed Roy inside, the rest of our party following, and we found chairs set out in rows. A young woman stood waiting by the piano – an up-and-coming soprano whom I recognised from a concert I'd attended with Hilda earlier in the year. She was to perform for us. I turned to Hilda in amazement, overwhelmed with gratitude. The soprano was dressed in the same stunning costume in which she had performed during that previous evening in town. She curtsied prettily towards us, then clasped her hands in front of her and nodded to the pianist.

Throughout the short recital, I listened with delight while Roy sat by my side, his posture deliberately erect and attentive. It was a familiar repertoire, designed to please a broad audience. It culminated in a short but achingly moving aria from Puccini's latest opera. My fluency in French allowed me to comprehend some of the Italian lyrics. *O mio babbino caro* … oh my dear father. I felt my breath catch in my throat. *Oh, my dear Mother – would that you too could have been here today*, I thought. As the singer's voice soared higher and higher, my heart soared with it, and I was transported to a world where pain was coloured by beauty and thus made more bearable.

At the end of the performance, I rose swiftly to my feet to show my appreciation. I was conscious of Roy gazing at me. I smiled at him and stopped clapping for a moment to squeeze his hand. This was my husband. I was Lillian Armstrong now. Mrs Lillian Armstrong. *This man is my family now*, I told myself with a sudden surge of joy. *Whatever happens after this, I am not alone anymore.*

~

We packed our cases into the trunk of Roy's car. With due care for his hand, which had only just healed since that day of the rainstorm, Roy started the crank. Amidst cheers of congratulations and a few sentimental tears, we waved goodbye.

A train was pulling out of Gordon station as we drove past, plumes of smoke rising to the sky like the smudged ink of a copperplate writing exercise. No more schoolhouses or academic gowns for me, no more lesson plans and papers to mark, no more blackboards or crocodile lines of girls. Or at least, as Helen had suggested, not until we had children of our own ...

I shook my head with a toss. No need to think of any of that today. *One step at a time* – that was what I had been telling myself in recent weeks whenever I felt anxious. My other unexpected source of courage had become the Ravenswood school motto. In the same way as others might recite the Lord's Prayer, I had begun repeating it to myself every morning and evening, becoming more convinced of its truth with each passing day: *Semper ad meliora* – always towards better things.

Chapter 16
Semper Ad Meliora

We were off, and on our way to the seaside suburb of Narrabeen, where Roy had rented a holiday cottage for the week leading into Christmas. As we drove, Roy began whistling, random notes at first, and then eventually landing upon the melody from that final Puccini aria.

'I thought we'd never get out of there. Some people can really talk, can't they?'

I raised my eyebrows, then looked down at my new wristlet watch, a farewell gift from the teachers and students. 'It's only just past two – still early. Besides, you're not exactly the strong, silent type yourself, you know.'

'You don't say?' he asked, chuckling.

The sun glinted off the glass watch dial, and I closed my eyes. 'I must have had too much champagne. I feel a little giddy.' Roy welcomed my confession with another loud chuckle. Having previously rolled up his shirt sleeves, he now removed his collar also. 'We can go for a swim when we get there. That'll wake you up.'

I laughed self-consciously. 'No swim for me today. But a walk on the beach would be nice.'

My new swimming costume was far more revealing than the blue-and-white striped knickerbockers we had worn as girls. I wasn't sure how I felt about anyone seeing me wearing it, Roy included. And although I had learned how to swim in the harbour pool beneath Sacred Heart, I was by no means a strong swimmer, and I knew the currents here could sometimes be dangerous.

I relaxed in the passenger seat, protected from the sun by my finely trimmed cloche hat and with a gentle breeze to keep me cool. I looked down and admired the elegant lines of my going away outfit, another product of Mrs Campbell's sewing room. My wedding jewellery, gown and Hilda's veil had been safely hung away in my old bedroom at the Edwards' home, along with many of the plans I had made when I was living there and which I was now ready to leave behind. Back then, I had told myself an independent life was all I needed. I'd convinced myself that I was showing strength by choosing to be alone.

But Roy had shown me it required even greater strength not to be alone – to choose to love and to risk whatever might follow. This morning, Roy had again promised he would always stand by me and that our life together would be a happy one. 'You've had more than enough losses for one lifetime, Lill,' he'd told me. 'Strictly plain sailing, from now on.'

'What are you thinking about, Mrs Armstrong?'

'I was thinking about how wonderful it will be to have our own house.'

A fortnight earlier, we had put a deposit on a piece of land in Gordon. Every day since then, I had stood in front of the sunny, north to rear plot and pictured our new home.

'I was Charlie's age when I first went to Sacred Heart. In all those years since, I've only ever lived in a school dormitory, or a college, or a room in someone else's house.'

Roy put his hand on my leg. 'I'm sorry we're going to have to live in my drab old bachelor flat for the time being, but as soon as the house is finished, you can set everything up just the way you like it.'

With North Shore real estate prices rising every year, Roy had been keen to give up his rooms over the studio and buy into the area right away. A reliable builder had been found and plans would soon be underway to start work on our own brick bungalow, to be built in the Californian style. Roy had assured me that he would not mind commuting to the workshop each day and sounded very enthusiastic about becoming a landlord. Once he found a tenant for his flat, as he explained, the rental income could go towards our new mortgage. More than anything though, he was committed to the idea of creating a dream home for me in the neighbourhood I had grown to love.

As we followed the ups and downs of the winding bush-fringed road that led to Sydney's northern beaches, the flat line of the Pacific Ocean suddenly reared up before us. Although I'd travelled this same road before, I never failed to be struck anew by this first sight of the sea, an unbroken plane of blue on the horizon.

'Don't you think the water looks strange from here? As if the ocean is higher than the land, higher than the treetops even.'

'Just an illusion,' said Roy, matter of fact. 'It's all about distance and perspective.'

'Did you learn that in art school?'

He nodded. 'Any object will look different depending on where you're standing and how close you are to it.'

I considered Roy's explanation, wondering whether it could be extended beyond objects. People, places, thoughts and especially memories could all appear altered according to where the viewer was positioned. Looking back, I was beginning to understand that while I may not have had any control over the events of my childhood, I could still choose how I experienced them today. Henry Lawson and 'The Drover's Wife' had provided one way of seeing my life, a view I had not always liked. But finally, with Roy's help, I had come to understand this was not the only way of seeing it. From now on, it was up to me.

After one last descent, we reached flat ground. Turning away from the lake, we passed paddocks, streets of unfenced fibro cottages and the cheerful sprawl of the campground. Filling the air was the unmistakable salt smell of the sea. While some of the cottages and holiday rentals were little more than shacks, with corrugated iron roofs that looked as if they might blow off in the next big storm, I was glad to see that the small brick and stucco house Roy had found for us was neat and tidy. On each side of the freshly painted front door stood a large pot of scarlet poinsettia. Although two lengths of wire were all that separated the property from its neighbours, pink oleander bushes softened their ugliness and a great clump of strelitzia filled one corner of the garden, greeting us with half a dozen of its aptly named bird of paradise flowers. Roy eased the vehicle onto the nature strip and parked in the meagre patch of shade.

'What do you think?' He opened my car door and waited nervously for my reaction.

'It's perfect, Roy. Shall we go in?'

'Don't you want to have a quick look at the beach?' Pointing to a side path, Roy seemed hardly able to contain his excitement, no less frisky than young Charlie. For a moment, I imagined Roy with a son of his own.

'Let's just put the bags inside and get changed first. I promise I'll be quick,' I added, reminded of the last day of term when the girls were always at their most impatient and difficult to control.

We emerged from the back door of the house a few minutes later, Roy in his swimming trunks and me in a simple cotton dress, both of us barefoot. We took each other's hand and ran together through the little backyard that spilled directly onto the dunes. Sparse vegetation quickly petered out, giving way to masses of soft yellow sand, warm beneath my feet.

'I'm sinking!' I laughed, as I tried in vain to keep up with Roy's eager stride up the dune.

While the afternoon sun was hot on my back, a cool breeze blew off the ocean, confounding my senses. Finally, we reached the hard-packed sand further down the beach, where it was easier to walk. Still holding hands, we sprinted together towards the water's edge until it became clear to me that Roy was pulling me along and not slowing down. I dug my heels into the sand.

'Hey, mister, stop that!' I laughingly protested. 'I told you I'm not swimming today.' I leaned over and grabbed a fistful of damp sand, lobbing it at his chest.

Grinning from ear to ear, Roy bent down and scooped up two large handfuls of his own, pausing only to determine whether he needed my permission to retaliate. With his eyebrows still raised in question, Roy's expression transformed to one of shock as my next blow hit my husband square in the face.

'That's it!' he spluttered. 'All bets are off.'

With Roy giving chase, I ran along the water's edge, darting haphazardly from side to side to avoid the sand he threw at me. Laughing and out of breath, I finally allowed myself to be caught in his embrace and we fell onto the beach together.

'You're covered in sand.' Tenderly he wiped sand from my cheeks before leaning in to kiss me, his lips scratchy but soft.

'Not as much as you!' I returned the kiss then pushed him away. 'Go on, have your swim then. I'll wait here.'

Planting one last sandy kiss on my lips, Roy dutifully pulled himself to his feet. I watched him walk out into the water. Once he was waist-deep, he turned back to me with a longing gaze and a smile, then he plunged headfirst under the next wave.

I held my breath for a moment, then relaxed as he came straight up again, throwing his head back to shake the wet hair from his eyes. He began to swim further out to sea with strong, effortless strokes.

I wriggled back a few feet to where the sand was dry, settling myself into a comfortable position from which to take in the scene. The floating blue expanse I had seen during our drive was, in reality, anchored by a long stretch of yellow shore, flanked by distant headlands and the lagoon at one end. Seen up close from here at the water's edge, the unbroken line of the sea dissolved into movement. Wave after wave folded in on itself or broke into white lace-like foam, reminding me of all that champagne I'd drunk, while its inky blue hue, which had then appeared uniform in colour, was anything but monotonous. Thrusting and diving amongst the shooting spray, seagulls dipped their wings, calling out to each other as they scoured the water for their next meal.

At one end of the beach, further out than I liked to think about, a band of young men gripped long surfboards, occasionally rising to their feet, then riding the waves for a few impossible seconds before being somersaulted back into the heaving swell. *Madness*, I thought, turning away.

Closer by, the sounds of children carried over the roar of the ocean. Splashing and cavorting at the surf's frothy edge, they shrieked and shouted with glee, while the timid ones ran back towards the safety of their parents. Other children crouched in the wet sand with their buckets and spades, carving moats and building sandcastles, only to have them washed away by a big wave or trampled by a spiteful sibling.

I saw Roy emerging from the water then make a beeline towards me on the beach. 'I come bearing gifts.' He stood before me with an assortment of seaweed hanging from his arms like tinsel. 'Don't be shy, my love, look what treasures I've got for you.'

I smirked. 'It's too early for Christmas. And I much prefer your mother's pearls, anyway.'

In reply, Roy draped a long, wet strand of olive-coloured beads around my neck. I instinctively recoiled. I had expected the trailing seaweed to feel slimy or at least to smell like the rotting algae that would wash up on shore below the convent after a storm, but when I rolled one of the little sea-grapes between my fingers and brought it to my nose, I was pleasantly surprised. Fresh and clean, it was curiously appealing. I almost considered biting into one of the beads, until I realised that I was suddenly getting very wet.

'Roy – you forgot your towel!' Roy had let the rest of the seaweed fall to the sand, and was now putting his arms around my waist and dripping water all over me.

'So I did,' he agreed, showing no signs of letting me go.

The front of my dress was soaked. I gave an exaggerated sigh of resignation, turned and led the way back up the beach and over the dunes towards the house.

We washed our feet in the large bucket at the back door before going inside, though we need not have bothered. Despite apparent efforts to keep the place clean, a sprinkling of sand clung stubbornly to the floor and every other surface. Roy, too, still had sand sticking to his skin and was dusted all over with a fine white layer of salt.

'I'm dry now,' he said, drawing me close. 'See? Safe to touch.'

His skin felt cool, like the ocean, while his mouth was warm and yielding. I tasted salt on his lips. As we stood and kissed, I felt him slowly shifting us towards the bedroom. This was it, then.

A thrill of anticipation rippled through me, and I swallowed nervously.

Roy must have sensed the change. He paused, stroking my hair and spoke softly. 'Are you all right, love? Are you scared?'

'I'm fine. I just want to freshen up a little.' Despite my words, there was no mistaking the tremble in my voice.

He twisted the shining new wedding band on my ring finger and brought my hand to his lips. 'I love you, Lill. I don't ever want to hurt you.'

I nodded. With Roy's pledge still ringing in my ears, I disappeared into the bedroom, closing the door behind me. It was the first time he had said that he loved me, the first time anyone had used this word to describe their feelings towards me. Not even Mother had spoken this way to any of us children. Love was shown in actions and not words. At least until now.

My case lay open on the bed. Inside was the paper-wrapped parcel containing my nightgown, another gift from Jean Campbell. Having never expected this day to come, I had amassed no glory box of household linens over the years, no wedding trousseau. After brushing the knots from my hair, I washed myself with water from the large white pitcher on the dresser. I laid my cotton dress over the back of a chair to dry, and then opened the parcel. Slipping the peach-coloured silk gown over my head, I caught sight of my reflection in the mirror and blushed. I had never worn anything like this before. *Princess for a day*, I mused. Wasn't that what every bride wanted? The fairytale wedding was ever enticing and not even I was immune to its call.

I went over to the door and opened it. Roy was waiting outside and gazed at me with palpable desire.

'You're so beautiful,' he murmured.

His hands reached towards me, slow circular caresses that began at the nape of my neck. Humming in my ears was the vibration from Roy's fingertips now grazing against my scalp. His fingers trailed down my shoulders and over my breasts.

'You're so beautiful,' he said again, his voice thick with arousal. 'I wish I could draw you like this so you can see how I see you.' He knelt before me, running his hands from my waist to my hips and bringing me towards him. 'I'd put you on a model's throne – a cutdown table, like we used at Ashton's – so I would be looking up at you like this.'

My thighs quivered as he kissed them through the smooth silken fabric. Struggling to catch my breath, I spoke as calmly as I could, while issuing a gentle remonstration. 'I'm not one of Norman Lindsay's painted nymphs, Roy. I'm not some illusory angel on a pedestal. I want you to see me as I am.'

'I see you, Lill – believe me, I do.'

With this, I led my husband to the bed. As our arms and legs entwined, his face so close to my own that I could see nothing but his eyes, a snatched line of poetry came into my head, '*so let us melt …*' and then all words were gone.

Afterwards, lying in his arms, as dusk fell and the room became dark, I saw that Roy had been making love to me all afternoon on the beach, long before I'd realised it. Knowingly or not, he had used the warmth of the sun and sand to prepare me for the heat that lay within his body. He had given me an open sky to see the possibilities that awaited us and the roar of the ocean to foreshadow our pleasure. This unlikely prince, my larrikin husband, appeared so simple, so straightforward, and yet his sensibilities were refined in a way that could not be taught. His wisdom was of a different kind.

Despite what I had told Roy, I had been frightened of this moment, this act of consummation. After the short-lived innocence of childhood, all those years of schoolgirl whispers and dog-eared chapters in poorly written novels had left their mark, followed by complete conspiratorial silence from all the married women I knew. Only today, at the wedding breakfast, had a few of the ladies looked at me meaningfully when asking where we would be taking our honeymoon. Yet they were all wrong. This union, this melding of bodies and souls, was perfectly natural, perfectly right. I wanted to be here with Roy. I wanted this; I wanted him. Why had no one told me that?

The rest of our week passed by in a blur of happy days. Every morning, we rose early to catch the golden sunrise and walk along the beach, then went back to eat breakfast and while away the rest of the morning as we pleased. In the afternoons, we'd set out exploring, taking a different direction each day – south towards the rock pools at Long Reef, northwards to an isolated little beach hidden by steep towering bluffs, or inland, to follow the crisscrossing streets to reach the lake, where Roy tried his hand at fishing and I fed the ducks. One day, we caught the green and yellow tram along the coast road as far as Manly and ate ice creams by the pier; revelling in the holiday atmosphere, we sat under the shade of a great pine, entertained by the spectacle of the ferries and all those who boarded them. Finally, to celebrate our last evening, we drove to the Collaroy picture theatre and held hands in the dark, feasting afterwards on a greasy supper of fish and chips.

In the same way as the great ocean that stretched before us, I found every day was different and yet the same. Drifting off to sleep in Roy's arms each night, and waking in the same way each morning, I felt myself falling into a peaceful rhythm as unfailing as the tides.

Something was changing within me. Roy felt it too. He claimed I had been hibernating, lying dormant like a tightly closed bud, waiting to burst into life. Or, as I reflected, like a gum tree sloughing off sheets of bark to be revealed all silvery and new. 'Perhaps you've awakened Sleeping Beauty,' I told my husband, pulling him towards me in a long sensuous kiss.

With my wedding night trepidations now behind me, and that first moment of pain already forgotten, I found myself looking forward to our lovemaking each day, impatient to feel Roy's hands moving over my bare skin, for our bodies to rise and fall together like two instruments joined in harmony. Intuitively, I sensed even greater pleasure was yet to come.

When it was time to leave, Roy was doleful. 'I wish we could buy this place for ourselves,' he bemoaned. 'One day all these little shacks will be worth a fortune.'

'One thing at a time, darling. We've only just put the deposit on our own home. You sound like an banker or real estate agent with all this talk.' Smiling indulgently, I covered his face in little kisses.

'Maybe if I hadn't gone into the family business, I might have been,' he joked, lapping up my attention as we laughed together.

And even though I too was sad to see this week come to an end, I was also ready to go back. It was time to celebrate our first Christmas and make a start on our married life together. With the car all packed and the cottage locked up and waiting for its next guests, we walked out together to the beach one last time. *Semper ad meliora*, with a long stick I traced the letters into the sand for anyone to see. Always towards better things.

Chapter 17

Henry

It took scarcely more than a month for me to fall pregnant. Any doubts I had about becoming a mother were eclipsed by the extraordinary fact there was new life quickening inside me.

'You little beauty!' Roy roared, sweeping me off my feet and spinning me round.

'Careful now,' I laughed. 'Don't get too excited.'

He set me back down with a look of panic.

'You're not disappointed we won't have more time together with just the two us? I expect I'll be busy once the baby's born. You might not be first in the family pecking order.'

'I never was,' Roy winked, putting his arms around me.

The months of my pregnancy flew by with surprising speed. At first, I hardly knew what to do with myself while Roy was at work. Without the Monday to Friday demands of my teaching job and with only our small flat to keep clean, I was left with more idle hours than I had ever known. But since not even I wanted to curl up on the sofa and read all day long, more productive activities soon suggested themselves. I made regular trips to Gordon to check on the building progress of our new home, followed by visits to Grace Bros, Beard Watson & Co and other stores to choose fittings and finishes. I familiarised myself with Roy's print studio and business. Best of all, by way of a personal introduction to Sydney's art world, I assisted with client deliveries and accompanied Roy to the many exhibitions put on by the various art societies, both conservative and progressive.

My own modest assortment of watercolours and framed European reproductions had soon been absorbed into Roy's extensive collection. Together with his brother's drawings and paintings, our walls were covered in artists' proof editions of etchings and lithographs he'd printed and even a few original paintings gifted by the artists themselves in appreciation of my husband's meticulous work and perpetual good humour.

Towards the end of my confinement, as my stomach ballooned and I needed more rest, I thought of all the hardships my mother had endured and felt guilty about Roy's tender ministrations and gifts: the flowers, choice pieces of fruit, or boxes of Personality chocolates; the extravagant new pram from David Jones; and the reassurance of a safe hospital birth. Mother had had none of these luxuries, yet I could not recall ever hearing her make a single complaint. Now that I was on the cusp of motherhood myself, there were so many questions I would have liked to have asked her.

'Maybe I wasn't part of a family for long enough to know how to have one of my own,' I blurted one evening after needing help to untie my shoelaces. 'What if I'm not cut out for this?'

'We'll work it out together,' Roy assured me, gently cupping my belly and waiting to feel a kick.

Hilda was equally dismissive of my fears. 'Fiddlesticks! You were a teacher for eight years. And look how good you are with my girls,' she whispered, pointing to her youngest daughter asleep on my lap.

Although I was still afraid – sometimes terrified – of what it would mean to bring another human being into life and with it the danger of losing them, I was also desperate to meet the child whose first fluttering movements had triggered a more powerful surge of love than I'd ever imagined possible.

Two days after my anticipated due date, I felt the first contractions. We drove to the Sanitarium at Wahroonga, Roy gripping the steering wheel so hard his knuckles turned white. I grunted with pain as my stomach hardened.

It was dark when Roy was finally allowed into the room.

I felt his lips against my forehead and smiled a wan smile.

'What happened?' I asked, on seeing the blood-flecked handkerchief in his hand.

'Never mind that, just a nosebleed. The sister said I'm not the first expectant father to get one. But look at what you've gone and done, my darling. Hello, little fellow.' He bent down to kiss me, then whispered something in my ear.

Exhausted from my labour and bedazzled by the baby boy nestled between us, I blinked at Roy's suggestion.

'Henry? Why would you want to call him Henry?'

'Whatever grudges you might still hold against the man, Lill, you can't deny we have Henry Lawson to thank for bringing us together. Without him, there'd be no baby. There'd be no us.' Roy put out his finger, and we both watched in awe as the little pink hand closed around it, a perfect fist of tiny fingers.

'I suppose you're right.'

'I'm always right,' he said, eyes twinkling.

'Hardly.' I was too tired, and much to sore, to laugh.

And so, we named our son Henry. Henry Evan Armstrong. I had asserted the right to choose his middle name: Evan was in memory of my late benefactor, Mr O'Loughlin.

'Thank goodness,' said the sister when I told her our decision. 'We've had that many Archies and Bridgets these past months, ever since they started on the new Sydney Harbour Bridge. It's a relief to have a nice ordinary name like Henry.'

~

Motherhood. Nothing I had seen or done, nothing I had been told, could have prepared me. Yes, there was the pain of the birth itself and the sleeplessness of the early months. But beyond that I discovered an unexpected and sensuous pleasure in having a baby – from the indescribable feeling of his soft warm body against my skin to the sensation of his hungry little mouth drawing down on my breast with a need that only I could fulfil.

Henry was a placid infant, healthy and surprisingly easy to care for. Accustomed to taking charge of a classroom, I learned instead to take my cue from him: feeding him when he was hungry, putting him to sleep when he appeared tired and playing with him in between. Our house in Gordon had been completed just in time for the birth, allowing the two of us to go straight from hospital to the purple-red bricked bungalow, still smelling of fresh paint. A brand-new home for our brand-new family.

~

One afternoon, Roy came home from work and found me reading to Henry in his crib.

'He's a bit young for that, isn't he?' he chuckled.

'Never too young to learn.'

I had been unpacking the last of the boxes and stacking books onto the tall oak bookshelf delivered that morning when Henry had woken prematurely from his nap. It seemed only natural to try reading him back to sleep.

'Sorry to say, love, but whatever it was, I think he found it a bit boring.'

'Shush, he'll wake up again.' I tiptoed out of the room, pulling Roy with me.

Roy took the book and began reading.

'I love a sunburnt country,
A land of sweeping plains,
Of ragged mountain ranges
Of droughts and flooding rains.'

'No Henry Lawson just yet, then?' he teased.

I rolled my eyes. 'You know I love this poem. Remember I told you Dorothea Mackellar grew up near Sacred Heart?'

In fact, Mackellar had written this poem, 'Core of my Heart', when she was just nineteen years old. It had touched the heart of our equally young nation. Her words had offered *Australians* – as we were just beginning to think of ourselves – a new way of seeing our country's particular beauty, recasting its faults and dangers as something to celebrate, despite or indeed because of their very harshness. She had also challenged the prevailing belief that England – with its 'green and shaded lanes', 'ordered woods and gardens' and 'soft, dim skies' – would always remain 'Home', a kind of heaven on earth, while the 'brown' barren colonies of Australia represented its opposite. As someone who knew firsthand what kind of fiery hell the dry landscape could become, Mackellar's words had been a salve against the blistering wounds of my own heart, inspiring me to draw comfort from nature's strength and to find dignity in my sorrow.

'Fair enough. I know,' said Roy. He paused, scratching his head. Then he turned and looked at me strangely. 'Do you reckon your father knew how to read and write? Do you think maybe that's why he never answered your letters?'

Roy's question stopped me in my tracks. 'I'm not sure.'

Although I had no doubt about Mother's literacy, I could not recall ever seeing my father with a book, or even, for that matter, pen or pencil. The thought had never occurred to me and yet it made perfect sense.

'Even so,' I argued. 'Even if he couldn't write to me himself, he still could have found a way to come and see me between droves. I waited for him at Sacred Heart for two whole years. But he never came. I'm sure Mr O'Loughlin would have given him time off if he'd asked. There's no excuse for abandoning a child like he did.'

'Didn't you ever think he might have been ashamed to come and see you?'

'What do you mean? Why would he have been ashamed?' I knew all about shame – my own shame – but this idea was foreign.

'I can think of plenty of reasons. I know he was away working when that fire came through, but don't you think he would still have felt guilty for not being there when you needed him? For leaving his wife and family with no one to turn to except his own brother, and then losing everyone in one fell swoop.'

'Everyone but me, you mean.'

'Exactly. And maybe that's why he couldn't face seeing you. Or maybe he wouldn't have known what to say. Maybe your face would have reminded him of your mother. Who knows? You, of all people, Lill, should know that grief has its own set of rules. Rational thinking doesn't come into it.'

And even though I would never know if any of these explanations were true, their very possibility gave me permission to forgive my father, who – along with Henry Lawson – had borne the brunt of what I now was beginning to see as the misplaced anger of a child incapable of thinking beyond herself.

~

For our first wedding anniversary, along with a bouquet of blue hydrangeas, Roy presented me with a thick leatherbound album for all the photographs we had been taking of Henry and of ourselves holding him. *Our Family*, its cover proclaimed in shiny gilt lettering I recognised as his.

'Paper!' I exclaimed. 'It's beautiful. Thank you, darling. I'll treasure it always.'

In return, I gave him *A Book for Kids* by CJ Dennis, dedicated to 'all good children over four and under four-and-eighty', and which I hoped he would find suitably entertaining to want to read aloud to Henry.

'You little ripper,' he laughed, flipping through the pages and winking at our son. He landed on a page at random and read: 'Tri -, Tri-anti-wonti, Tri-anti-wontigongalope!'

A week later, at Christmas, waiting beneath our fragrant but gangly pine tree, was a second album from Roy.

'I was thinking,' he said, looking both nervous and pleased with himself, 'since you haven't got any of your own childhood photographs as such, you might like to make another scrapbook using Lawson's story as a starting point. I know our visit to the General Registry didn't turn out as planned – although you did say yes afterwards! – but maybe one day we can drive out there and try to track down your old home, or what's left of it, find out if there's anyone still around who might have known your mum or dad, take some photos of the area, at the very least. And in the meantime, I know you've got a few articles and other bits and bobs gathering dust in a drawer somewhere, so I thought you could paste them all in here instead. When Henry's old enough, you can explain where his name comes from and use the album to tell your family story.'

I tore open the wrapping and read the gilt lettering. This album announced *The Drover's Wife* as its title and me as its author. Tears sprang to my eyes at Roy's deliberate arrangement of words, and I felt a surge of love and gratitude. Since Roy first helped light the spark of sympathy in me towards Henry Lawson, I had been keeping an eye out for any new and interesting biographical material about the writer, by way of my own unofficial obituary. Perhaps even as a kind of olive branch. In the months after Lawson's funeral, numerous letters and articles had appeared in the newspaper, some of which I had saved and added to my file. Roy, who had subscriptions to a broader range of journals, had passed on others more recently.

In addition to public thanks from Lawson's sister and former wife, there had been tributes from friends, and one tribute had stood out to me in particular. It was from Mary Gilmore, well-known editor at the *Australian Worker*. Mrs Gilmore, who had apparently known Lawson since he was a young man of twenty-one, declared him very much like his mother, Louisa – in appearance, yes, but also in temperament. Both of them, she said, had been subject to moods and depression.

Intrigued by her assessment, I'd also shown it to Roy, interested to hear his opinion.

'Apples never do fall far from the tree,' he'd said. 'Poor Louisa, poor Henry.'

PART THREE

1939–1947

You build, and build as children build,
Admittedly in vain,
A tower of cards, or dominoes,
To topple down again,
No matter what the first may be,
In numbers or in rank,
The last card is a rotten card,
Last domino a blank.

Henry Lawson, 'The Year Fifteen' (1915), *The Bulletin*

Chapter 18

A Phony War

In September of 1939, when Germany invaded Poland and Britain declared war on its old enemy, I found myself washing dishes in the sink with such force that I chipped two cups from my favourite tea set. Not only because I was shocked by this catastrophic turn of events, but because I was angry at myself for having let down my guard.

Throughout the preceding years, while most of my fellow Australians were watching Europe with ever-increasing apprehension, and a handful of others went as far as taking political action, I had been steadfastly ignoring my own growing sense of foreboding. And now, like a pot of potatoes left alone on the stove, it was ready to boil over and make a mess.

When Roy listened to news broadcasts on the radio at night, I'd lingered over tucking the children into bed or had read a book in another room instead. Just as at the pictures, when the newsreels showed images of the civil war in Spain, or Japan's invasion of Manchuria, or even Signor Mussolini or Herr Hitler and their goose-stepping armies, I'd simply closed my eyes and waited for the feature to begin.

So, on that Sunday evening, having reluctantly let the children stay up for the Prime Minister's radio broadcast, I really didn't want to hear what he had to say to the nation. When Menzies began his solemn speech with the inevitable declaration that Australia too was now at war, I registered the news somewhere deep in the pit of my stomach.

Hadn't we all been promised that the Great War would be the one to end all wars? Setting aside the Prime Minister's grandiose language and familiar haughty tone, I tried to comprehend his explanation of how this crisis point had been reached and what he claimed was now required of all Australians to support the mother country.

Beside me, twelve-year-old Margery appeared unconcerned, and lay sprawled across the red-stained jarrah floorboards, pasting clippings from the fashion pages into a scrapbook. In contrast to his sister, Henry was listening closely, his adolescent features alight with curiosity and interest. Roy and I exchanged uneasy glances. *He's just a boy,* I told myself. *Not even sixteen. It will be over soon.*

~

A few months later, when people were no longer calling it a phony war, and when Germany began invading one country after another, I consoled myself with the knowledge it was all happening a long way from Australia. In any case, I would never let Henry volunteer and this country would never agree to conscription. The last war had proven that.

A year passed by, then a second year. Tens of thousands of Australian troops were now in the Middle East, fighting for the Empire. But although the news was full of Blitzkrieg in Europe or the threat of yellow peril from Japan, our daily rhythms of life remained mostly unchanged. From time to time, something would happen to make my jaw tighten – like the AIF marches in every capital city, answering the call to arms from young men ready to 'give it a go, mate', or the day the minimum joining age was reduced to nineteen – but I told myself our sensible, fact-obsessed boy would never be so foolish.

~

In October 1941, during his final year of school, Henry turned eighteen. Tall, slim, and naturally athletic like his father, his once sandy hair had darkened, and his thoughtful countenance was set off by high cheekbones and a permanent half-smile. Though he himself seldom noticed their attention, I had seen the way Margery's friends were starting to whisper and blush whenever he came into the room.

For me, Henry was still the same little boy as he had always been. From the moment he began speaking, I'd been fascinated to observe his thought processes and interests. Apart from nature, especially insects, it had been building blocks and any kind of large machinery that got him excited. But while Roy took credit for our son's height, at the top end of the growth charts, he insisted his early signs of cleverness were all owing to me. Though happy in his own company, capable of great focus and an adult-like concentration that he would direct towards his investigations, he had also been adept at making friends. From the time he was old enough to join his little mates in the street, he would disappear for hours at a time, returning only to gulp down a quick slice of bread and jam or safely deposit some treasure. Sometimes I'd hear them playing marbles outside our house, where the road was at its flattest, or riding their billycarts down the hill at breakneck speed. Other days, they climbed trees and tore off paperbark sheets to scribble secret code messages I'd find under Henry's bed. But most of the time, I'd had no idea what he was up to.

Margery, on the other hand, was cut from an altogether different cloth. With her clouded grey-green eyes, soft pink skin and flaxen wisps of hair, she was a beautiful newborn. But although I'd been filled with the same intense rush of love as with Henry, I'd also felt a measure of uneasiness. It may have started with Margery's colic, which had made feeding and settling her more challenging than with Henry, or even earlier, during my pregnancy, which I had not enjoyed this time around. Whether it was having to go through the whole summer heavily pregnant, spending my days running after Henry or simply the fact that I was older, I could not say. Perhaps it was true that girls were more complicated – in this case, even before they were born. 'Just wait till you've got one of your own, Miss Taylor,' the Ravenswood school mothers had prophesied years earlier, sounding like a Greek chorus. 'They might behave themselves here with you but they're different at home. You'll see.' While I had said nothing to Roy and tried my best to ignore such feelings, even then I had sometimes asked myself whether I was equipped to give our daughter all she needed.

Later, as a little girl, forever craving the limelight, Margery had wanted my eyes on her at all times, and always on her terms. As much as I had tried to make housework seem like a game – singing nursery rhymes while pegging washing on the line or sitting her up on the bench to stir the cake batter – she resisted my efforts. The days when I most missed my old life as a teacher, along with my pay cheque, had been the ones spent sipping endless cups of imaginary tea with Margery's dolls, followed by daisy-chain making exercises and the futile hunt for four-leaf clovers.

Now, at fourteen, Margery was more beautiful than ever. She was also tall for her age and slim to the point of skinniness – this, despite my concerted efforts to the contrary. Her hair had remained lighter than her brother's, and while both had hazel-coloured eyes, Henry's were flecked with gold, like mine, while Margery's could appear almost green.

The hardest part about having a daughter was that it made me miss my own mother even more. There were so many things I would have liked to have asked her over the years. I so wished she could have met Margery, as well as Henry, and seen for herself how her only grandchildren had turned out. I still remembered feeling that Esther was Mother's favourite child, superior to me in every way. Hopefully Margery did not feel the same about me and Henry. Hilda said it was only natural to have more in common with one child than with another, but in all the years I had observed her with her three girls, not once had I ever seen her play favourites.

Yet as difficult as Margery could be, I could always console myself with the knowledge that nothing could ever take her from us. And if that meant I was sometimes overly judgemental, in comparison to how I was with Henry, who could blame me? After all, safely seeing a son through a war was not a battle Hilda would ever need to face.

On the morning of Henry's eighteenth birthday, by chance a Saturday, I baked and iced his favourite sponge cake, making my own silent wish as he blew out the candles. Later, after a roast dinner with all the trimmings, I pretended to look the other way as Roy handed out bottles of beer to Henry and a few of his mates who had arrived unannounced for their own celebration.

The next day, Roy proposed a trip to the beach, our first for the coming summer season. But Henry, having assumed the driver's seat, instead veered left towards Bayview and the bush-fringed waterway of Pittwater. As we clambered over the familiar foreshore terrain, shoes in hand, I watched a flock of silver gulls fly over in loose formation, cutting through the sky. I filled my lungs with the fresh estuarine air and tried to ignore the newly installed barbed-wire fencing, along with the handful of pyramid-shaped concrete blocks jutting out from the water, which Henry said were intended to stop Japanese tanks.

'Let's try Taronga for our next outing,' I suggested afterwards in the car. Although ever since the death of Jessie the elephant, not even a trip to the zoo felt the same anymore.

~

'But you've always loved coming into town with me to look at the David Jones Christmas windows,' I protested, as Margery and I boarded the train at Gordon, on our way into town.

'I don't see why we had to go today though. Barbara invited me to the beach.'

'But we always go on the first day of your school holidays. It's our tradition.'

Margery's face was sullen, and I was reminded of the tantrums she used to throw as a toddler. At least this was quieter.

'I love your outfit, sweetheart,' I said, trying desperately to put her in a better mood. 'Your wardrobe is better than mine, you know!'

'They're just hand-me-downs,' she mumbled.

Although I knew this latest complaint was just for show, and that Margery adored the clothes passed onto her from Hilda's three girls, which were better-designed and more expensive than anything we could afford, I took the bait anyway.

'I do think you could show more gratitude, Margery. When I think of everything you and Henry have, compared to what I had, it upsets me to see you take it all for granted.' Even as I said it, I wished I hadn't. Sure enough, Margery rose to the challenge, and what should have been the start of a lovely mother–daughter outing was fast heading into ruin.

'Yes, Mum,' began Margery in a mock-obedient voice and manner. 'I know, I know. You grew up in a tiny little house and had to share a room. And your mother was very strict, and you and your sister had to help with chores every single day, except on Sundays when she would take you for a walk.'

I couldn't help myself. The tears came to my eyes before I could stop them. Not only because of the disparaging way she was speaking about my family and our home, but because I'd been too ashamed to admit to her just how primitive our living circumstances had been. As for my years at Sacred Heart, sometimes I had the impression Margery wished she could go to boarding school herself. She seemed to imagine it would be like a giant slumber party, only with nuns to supervise them, not parents.

Margery saw my tears, and to her credit, appeared contrite. 'Sorry, Mum. I'm just sick of you always comparing my life to yours.'

'That's all right, darling,' I sniffed, trying to sound cheerful. 'I know you didn't mean it. Let's just have a nice time today, shall we?'

By mutual silent agreement, we both stopped talking and looked out the window. Despite the Depression, and now the war, the North Shore had continued its steady pace of development. Along with blocks of flats, which increased in number the closer we got to town, many of the houses flashing past were single-storey Californian bungalows, like ours. Others reflected newer architectural styles, from respectable English Tudor and ornamental Art Deco through to glamorous Spanish Mission designs from America. There were even a few modernist prototypes, including homes built to resemble the iconic P. and O. Line ships, complete with flat rooflines, curved walls and porthole-like windows. Occasionally, Roy liked to dream about us taking a sea voyage on one of these passenger liners. After the war, of course. Yet even aside from other obvious obstacles like Roy's work or Margery's schooling, I had little desire to ever leave Australia. Home was where I felt safe. Why risk losing what I had only just attained?

Although the children knew a little about my childhood and about my being sent to Sacred Heart, they had both shown a remarkable lack of curiosity about exactly how I came to be an orphan. It had been enough to tell them little fragments at a time. They behaved as if they thought my life had only started with theirs, which was probably for the best. It wasn't as though I ever wanted them to share the burden of my sorrows. Far from it.

At first, they had been too young to hear the whole truth about how and when the rest of my family had died, and how part of me wished I had died in that fire with them. I didn't want them to go off to school in the morning, afraid their mother could have a fatal accident while they were gone, or that their father might succumb to a sudden illness at work and never come home again.

Now that they were 'old enough' to hear my story – the version made famous by Henry Lawson, the painful details of what I could remember, and the complicated mix of feelings Lawson's story brought out in me – I wasn't sure if I was ready to share it. I had never forgotten my humiliation in the classroom that day when everyone had laughed at my claim. What if my own children did the same? After all these years, I was still looking for actual proof that he had met my family.

Nearly eighteen years had passed since Roy had presented me with that second leather album, dedicated to my mother and family, by way of Henry Lawson and 'The Drover's Wife'. Throughout that time, while Lawson's legend grew ever larger, I had continued to add to my substitute family album, albeit with ever dwindling expectations.

Among my earliest scrapbook entries was the clipping I'd saved with Lawson's open letter in 1916, in which he'd claimed his Aunt Gertrude was the original drover's wife. Beside this, I'd deliberately left a blank page, hoping to fill it with another clipping proving this untrue. I thought I'd struck gold in 1924, when I had come across a small notice saying that Henry Lawson's sister, a Mrs Gertrude O'Connor (presumably named after her aunt), was gathering material for a biography. Perhaps by chance, I hoped, she might have been privy to certain details of her brother's travels and heard anecdotes of people he had met along the way? But the proposed biography never materialised. Instead, I merely gained a disturbing insight into the circumstances of their shared upbringing.

Mrs O'Connor, who was ten years younger than her brother, had apparently only recently learned to write, having sustained a childhood accident which had profoundly affected her sight, hearing and speech. As a young mother myself at that time, I was slightly horrified to read that the incident – a hot water fountain burn – occurred when fifteen-year-old Henry had been left solely in charge by their mother, Louisa, whose health she tactfully described as 'delicate'. Together with Mary Gilmore's earlier remarks, a new picture was beginning to form in my mind of mother and son as two sides of the same coin, spinning wildly between brilliance and despair. Poor Mrs O'Connor appeared to bear no grudges, deferring to her brother's 'genius' while confirming Louisa as the source of his inspiration and early writing achievements.

My next glimmer of hope came in 1930, when an autobiography containing memories of Lawson's childhood was 'found'. I was disappointed and then bemused to discover these extracts were the very same ones I'd first read about in 1908, while polishing the silver at Sacred Heart. I didn't bother writing to the Australian Fellowship of Writers or the *Herald* to correct their error.

Although Lawson's poetry and stories continued to be reprinted in publications of every shape and form, overshadowing these were the many different tributes to the man himself, written and otherwise. There was now at least one Henry Lawson society, whose members recited his works at their meetings and made annual pilgrimages to his gravesite. His former wife, Bertha Lawson, still played a visible role in public events and usually appeared under the title of Mrs Henry Lawson or 'widow', despite their marriage having ended some twenty years before his demise. Still, who could blame her? Given Lawson's track record in child maintenance payments, his name was probably worth more to her in death than in life.

There was an obelisk in Grenfell, to mark Lawson's birthplace, a public park named in his honour, and, most impressive of all, a major statue by the late George Lambert, erected in 1931 on a grassy green knoll of the Domain not far from the Art Gallery. It was a bronze study of the man, complete with 'swaggy' and sheepdog. While its official unveiling by the Governor had attracted several thousand attendees, I'd not been among them.

Unlike before, when as a young woman I had deliberately avoided Henry Lawson, seeing red at every mention of his name, his grip on me had weakened. Was it because starting a new family with Roy had made the loss of my original one more bearable? That I was too busy living life off the pages to still feel the wound of my absence in print?

Among scores of articles, there had also been that book, *Henry Lawson by his mates*, which was an assortment of recollections from Lawson's friends, assembled by his daughter, and given to me by Roy for my birthday one year. Although I'd faithfully read through the impressions and memories of each of its contributors, not one of them had provided the evidence I needed to substantiate my claim.

Of all my scrapbook entries, perhaps my favourite was a tribute by Dora Wilcox, a New Zealand poetess, who wrote, 'There is a story which I do not think Henry Lawson ever surpassed. It is that of "The Drover's Wife". It is very simple but it has the essential quality of greatness.' And while I did not agree with everything in her critique, it was satisfying to tell myself that my family might have sparked such apparent greatness in him. I could feel proud that Mother's life story was recognised as the pinnacle of Lawson's literary achievement even while she remained invisible herself.

I looked up and saw the bridge up ahead. Margery's face had softened, and I squeezed her hand.

'I don't suppose you remember much about the day we all came here for the official opening of the Sydney Harbour Bridge? It would have been just before your fifth birthday,' I calculated, recalling how Premier Jack Lang, Henry Lawson's brother-in-law, had presided over the ceremony.

Margery shook her head, but her expression suggested interest.

'Dad was taking photos and you kept asking why Henry was our "bridge baby" and not you. And then Dad had to put you on his shoulders to keep you safe from the crowds, but also to keep them safe from you! Do you remember that dance you used to do? Ta-ra-ra-boom-de-ay, ta-ra-ra-boom-de-ay,' I sang the tune softly, and pictured Margery in her red velvet party dress, dancing in haphazard circles, oblivious to the impact of her sharp little elbows and high-kicking feet.

'Ta-ra-ra-boom-de-ay, ta-ra-ra-boom-de-ay,' Margery echoed, smiling despite herself.

'And meanwhile, your brother was regaling us with facts and figures about the bridge from the special newspaper supplement. How much it weighed, how many rivets it contained, how it would expand and shrink in different weather conditions.'

Margery smirked. 'That sounds like Henry.'

'And every time he'd remind us it was "the biggest single span steel arch bridge in the world", his cute little lisp would come out.'

This time she laughed.

'But then, when he started talking about thermal expansion, we got so distracted that no one noticed you climbing down from Dad's shoulders and disappearing into the crowd.'

'Did I?'

'Don't act so shocked. You were always running away at that age. Don't you remember how you'd go out through the window or drag a chair to the front door and sneak out while I was doing the washing? I'm sure our neighbours must have thought I was negligent, the number of times I had to go out on the street calling for you. Our little escape artist, is what you were.'

Margery looked impressed with herself, and I was reminded of Roy. Although he'd put on a stern face and waved the wooden spoon around back then, we both knew he'd been in awe of our daughter's ingenuity.

Despite minor disagreements, usually over differences in our approach to parenting, especially when it came to 'Daddy's Princess', our marriage had remained the greatest comfort of my life. Occasionally though, Roy's endless optimism and child-like enthusiasm would push me into the opposite corner where it felt like I needed to be the sensible adult. A tiresome naysayer. And perhaps I was. At times I heard myself speaking to the children and wished I could be more like him, but years of convent school discipline and the example of Mother's strictness dictated otherwise.

I often wondered how Margery and I could be so different. Roy felt I expected too much of her. Perhaps he was right. Yet Margery had always been good at twisting her father round her little finger, while taking me for granted. It was a bitter pill for me to swallow.

Both our children were lucky, so damned lucky, not just because of their privileges, for living in a happy bubble which not even the Depression – nor, as yet, the war – had penetrated, but for the fact that they were not growing up alone. Even if Margery had been too young to remember much of that day in March 1932, she could always rely on us to fill in the rest.

The train clattered over the bridge, and my thoughts returned to its construction. Although remarkable from a technical viewpoint, and not unattractive in a modern way, there was no doubt that it dominated the harbour with its overtly masculine display of strength. Perhaps that was why I'd been so taken by Grace Cossington Smith's painting depicting the bridge under construction, and which we had first seen during one of Ethel Anderson's modernist art exhibitions in her Turramurra home. For me, her painting perfectly captured the spirit of that strange and liminal timespan when the two arches had not yet joined, a moment ripe with promise and possibility, but also fraught with danger. Almost, I mused, like an expectant woman poised to give birth.

Even though I gathered Miss Smith had her family's approval and monetary support, I still admired her courage in pursuing her passion in preference to a more conventional feminine path. How sweet the taste of success, then, to be publicly recognised for her art. And yet, there was always a cost as a woman. Would holding a paintbrush and easel, I wondered, make up for not holding a child?

'Time to get off, Mum.' Margery nudged me, and I felt myself grin, both resigned to and content with my own choice in that respect.

'Now isn't this fun, darling? Father Christmas, here we come.'

~

The next day was cause for family celebration when Henry, who had now officially finished his schooling, collected the Form VI subject prizes for both Mechanics and Manual Hobbies. Although he would not receive his examination results until January, he was expected to graduate with First Class Honours in Mathematics and Mechanics, assuring him a place in engineering at Sydney University, perhaps even a bursary. Sitting beside me at the Sydney Grammar School prize-giving ceremony, Roy was beside himself with pride when Henry shook hands with the Governor, knowing his boy would be the first of the Armstrong family to attain a university education (other than myself, of course). While I shared his rush of pride, my overwhelming emotion was relief. The tightness in my jaw eased slightly. My little boy would be safely occupied at university and could come to no harm as a student.

Despite this, the year ended on a note of disaster, both public and private. First came the discovery of an unimaginable naval tragedy, with the loss of the HMAS *Sydney* and its crew of 645 men. Next, after months of prolonged tension, came the simultaneous Japanese attack on the American naval base at Pearl Harbour and on Allied forces in other Pacific locations. America declared immediate war on Japan, and Australia swiftly followed suit. Not even the broad accent of our new Prime Minister, John Curtin, could soften the impact of his broadcast to the nation. Suddenly the war in Europe no longer seemed so far away, and panic spread through the country like a rampaging bushfire.

The final blow came when Roy's nephew, Charlie, enlisted in the RAAF. At twenty-seven, Charlie was entrenched in a promising research career at the Council for Scientific and Industrial Research. Able-bodied and still single, there had always been a chance he might one day be called up for military training or to join the militia in defending Australian territory if enlistments fell short. But with the threat of war now approaching our own shores, Charlie felt compelled to take a more decisive stance. Other men he knew had already joined the RAAF, including one who had lost his life in North Africa. Silencing all arguments, Charlie insisted he must follow his conscience and felt his father would have expected the same.

Charlie's mother, Helen, had remarried around the time Margery was born. John was a returned soldier, who had fought with Roy's brother, Reggie, in Egypt as his officer in command, a connection which had helped him win Helen's affections, as well as making it easier for Roy to accept him. Also fortunate was the success of John's career as a patent attorney, which meant Helen had no longer needed the annual dividend from Roy's business. Although Roy had consented to this change with some reluctance, I knew he was ultimately relieved to be free of this self-imposed financial obligation, especially once the Depression began.

John was a decent man, but even though Charlie had soon come to love his stepfather and adapt to his new home in affluent Mosman, he continued to regard Roy as a father figure. Having watched him grow into a respectful and thoughtful young man, I was equally attached to Charlie and looked forward to his regular visits, as did the children. Henry liked to follow his older cousin on bushwalks, identifying plant species or scrabbling in the dirt to search for a particular type of ant. Margery was devoted in her own way – during Charlie's last visit, she had helped herself to my lipstick and rouge and greeted him at the door, batting her eyelashes as if she were Colleen Moore or one of the other screen stars she idolised.

I was stunned when Charlie told us of his decision, and afraid to picture him in the air force. Although certain of his expertise in a laboratory setting, I could scarcely imagine absent-minded Charlie flying a plane or performing other critical roles on an aircraft: observer, navigator, or – God forbid – an air gunner or bomber. I thought back to my youth when aeroplanes had first taken to the sky. Then, I'd been inspired by the promise of freedom within their bird-like metal frames. Now I saw death traps for doe-eyed young men.

Over a gloomy Christmas dinner our extended family came together to raise a toast to Charlie's good health and a rapid end to the war. As I joined Helen in accepting a second glass of sherry, we locked eyes, both holding onto the knowledge that, for at least the next eight weeks, Charlie would be safely ensconced in nearby Bradfield Park for his initial training.

I shuddered to think of the thousands of personnel now passing through the large RAAF station just a few miles away in West Lindfield, on the same site where Henry had once taken part in an international Scout jamboree.

While Charlie explained how Bradfield Park was operating in its present wartime capacity, I watched with alarm to see Henry hanging on his every word. With its own depot, hospital, chapel, canteen and even post office, and a dozen different courses on offer, up to three thousand servicemen could be trained at any given time. Although the station and its graduates were held in high esteem, to me it sounded like nothing more than a factory production line, churning out widgets – all decked out in the same overalls, berets and marching boots.

I had spotted some of these airmen during their periods of leave, while heading towards the comfort canteen built for them on the highway or else attending church services or playing tennis with local families.

'Perhaps you'll be allowed to visit us?' I asked as we walked Charlie out to the car.

'We might not even recognise him by then,' said Roy, doing his best to lighten the mood. 'After all that military training, he'll have grown muscles on his muscles.'

'Too right,' agreed our son, clapping his hands with approval.

~

In January 1942, in the wake of Charlie's departure, I faced a dubious milestone of my own.

'Happy birthday, sweetheart,' whispered Roy in my ear on the morning of my fiftieth birthday.

So, this is how it feels to live half a century, I mused, still half asleep and feeling hot and disoriented. How odd to think that my earliest childhood memories now belonged to the distant past, to the Victorian era of the late nineteenth century. I still recalled the fanfare of Federation and had lost count of the multitude of changes I'd seen in my lifetime, for better or worse.

'I feel old,' I told Roy.

'You feel good to me,' he replied huskily, running his hands under my nightgown, and kissing my neck.

As I half-heartedly responded to Roy's advances, my dream slowly came back to me. I had been sitting in the audience somewhere, a university lecture hall or a theatre, listening to a man quoting Henry Lawson. Or maybe, I thought with a start, it was Lawson himself.

'And is it our fate,' he had thundered, 'to wake too late to the truth that we have been blind, with a foreign foe at our harbour gate and a blazing drought behind!'

With its talk of foreign foes and droughts, the poem was uncannily prescient. Last year had been officially named Sydney's driest in over fifty years. Like my own fading spirits, gardens everywhere were growing dry and withered.

'I just want to turn back the clock, Roy. To go back to how things were when the children were little.'

'Don't think you're the first person to feel like that, love,' he said, stroking my cheek. 'And you won't be the last. Whether we like it or not, time will keep on ticking.'

I curled into the crook of Roy's arm, resting my head on his chest.

'Now that's enough doom and gloom for one day, Mrs Armstrong. If we can keep ourselves busy for the next few minutes, I think you'll find the kids will have your birthday breakfast waiting for us in the kitchen.'

~

A month later, not even halfway through Charlie's training, there was an accident. As luck would have it – whether good or bad, it was hard to say – Charlie lost two of his fingers in a drill exercise gone wrong. He was never willing to tell us exactly what had happened and, for once, not even Roy was tempted to tease the details out of him. As swiftly as he had entered the air force, the would-be cadet was made to exit, his short-lived military career brought to a decisive end by a medical discharge.

While the men of our family commiserated and understood Charlie's embarrassment, Helen and I breathed easy once he returned to his post at the CSIR's Division of Economic Entomology in Canberra, studying plant and pest diseases.

One of Charlie's colleagues, by coincidence, was Doug Waterhouse, second eldest son of Gowrie Waterhouse. I still recalled a bare-kneed Doug chasing butterflies as a boy and was glad he'd found his way into a suitably appropriate career path – and one to make his parents proud. As for my former teacher himself, Professor Waterhouse continued to inspire me, not only through his distinguished university career. In recent years, I'd seen his passion for camellias extend to the establishment of a specialist nursery (together with another of his sons), the publication of a stunningly illustrated book and even to Sydney's first exhibition of camellias – held at Macquarie Galleries, no less.

~

Amidst the aftermath of Pearl Harbour, the fall of Singapore and the bombing of Darwin and Broome, American soldiers began pouring into the country. In Sydney, their arrival coincided with the first heavy rainfalls in what seemed like forever. While most of our friends and neighbours welcomed these American servicemen with open arms, I was more wary.

'We need the Yanks,' said Roy. 'Britain's got too much on her own plate to worry about us now. Churchill said he would protect us. Everyone was so sure Singapore would never fall. Now look where we are. Thank Christ Curtin insisted on bringing our own troops back. We've got to look after ourselves.'

My eyes narrowed. 'Don't you think that if we'd minded our own business in the first place and let Britain fight its own wars, none of this would be happening here?'

'The world doesn't work that way, sweetheart. You can't put your head in the sand.'

'And what about the midget submarines, Mum?' said Henry, closing ranks against me as he joined our argument. 'Jap subs – here in Sydney Harbour! Look how close they came. What would've happened if we didn't have enough men here, including the Americans, to protect our borders?'

'But that's exactly what I'm trying to say. All these armies, all these men, it's like bees to a honeypot. We're practically begging the Japanese to attack us. We might as well put up a sign.'

'How can you say that?' My normally even-tempered son looked at me with outrage.

'It's not that simple, Lill,' Roy agreed, taking my hand.

'Well, it should be,' I muttered, tears pricking the back of my eyes as I left the room.

~

Thankfully, in a parallel world at university, far away from battlefronts, POWs and concentration camps, Henry had settled into his engineering studies. Surrounded by like-minded souls and with access to all kinds of machinery and tools, he was – as Roy had predicted – as happy as a pig in clover. I clung feverishly to the hope he would be safe there. Surely, they would never conscript students like Henry. Surely the country needed bright young minds like his for when the war was over.

Even so, Roy was keeping a close eye on the changing announcements in the newspaper each week. The printing industry – other than newspapers themselves, of course – was now categorised as non-essential. How did they put it? *Industries in which production may be allowed to decline substantially without injury to the war effort or which comprise substantial relatively non-essential sections.* Along with paper shortages, Roy had recently lost two valued staff members, reallocated by the Manpower authorities to work in higher priority businesses – one to munitions and the other to steel manufacturing. 'At least they're not sending them to be corset makers,' he'd shrugged, referencing an earlier regulatory anomaly.

The status of young men like Henry remained hotly contested. Many university students already belonged to militia units or were subject to compulsory training, although the army did try to minimise such interruptions during semester. At Sydney University, students in reserved faculties were still being granted exemption from military service to continue their studies: those in their final or penultimate year of studies for certain courses, as well as all students enrolled in medicine, dentistry, agricultural or veterinary science and – most crucially for our son – engineering. As a bursary recipient and scholar of merit, Henry's position was as secure as I could hope for.

But my hopes felt short-lived when new age limits were announced for the militia, now known as the Citizen Military Forces. Now all men between eighteen and thirty-five, as well as single men aged up to forty-five, had to join the CMF. Prime Minister Curtin, once opposed to conscription, was even fighting to overcome resistance from his own party to extend the geographic boundaries in which these CMF conscripts could fight. I could hardly believe it. The unthinkable was finally happening. Conscription would soon be a reality. Against their will, and against any standard of morality, young Australian men could be sent overseas to meet their death. While Henry might still be protected for now, how long would that last?

It was around that time I noticed Roy and Henry having private conversations. I'd catch them standing together at the far end of the garden, earnest expressions on their faces, or suddenly stop talking when I entered the room. I observed the way our son sat on the edge of his seat during Curtin's stirring speeches, no less passionate than an evangelist minister. And at night, in his room, when Henry should have been studying or sleeping, I'd hear him listening quietly to Tokyo Radio on his dual-wave receiver. Beside his bed lay the twin volumes of *The Story of ANZAC*, by local man Charles Bean, a well-known war correspondent who had survived more than six months at Gallipoli himself. A dog-eared bookmark tracked my son's progress through these two books – their heaviness was surpassed only by the ever-increasing weight bearing down on my own heart.

Chapter 19

Chocolate Soldiers

One Friday afternoon in September 1942, after a trip into town to buy a new jacket for Henry's nineteenth birthday with my first batch of ration coupons, I took the train back to Roy's workshop so we could drive home together.

Apologising, Roy grabbed his jacket and hat from the stand. Despite having intended to leave early, he still needed to collect several large pictures from the framer's and deliver them to an important client in Wahroonga.

'Of course, you do,' I smiled. 'I don't mind, I'll keep you company.'

An hour later, with the pictures safely loaded into the van, we drove away from Parker's fine arts supply store and wound our way through the old colonial byways of The Rocks. As we passed the tollbooth at the southern end of the Harbour Bridge, ready to begin the long drive towards *Cheddington*, the grand Georgian home belonging to the *Sydney Morning Herald*'s editor, Roy wound up the window and gave a loud sigh.

'I can't make him wait any longer, Lillian. He wants to enlist.'

'What are you talking about?' My stomach lurched. 'Henry? He's still exempt.'

'It bothers him, Lill. That he, or any other student in a reserved faculty, gets an exemption while other young men are expected to fight.'

'I don't give a straw about anyone else. Henry will wait until he's called up and hope to God it never happens.'

'But it probably will happen soon enough, sweetheart. He doesn't want to wait. And I can't blame him.'

'What do you mean, you can't blame him? Do you want him to risk his life? Is that what you're saying?' I could hear myself becoming ever louder, my voice alien and shrill. 'After losing your brother, I would have thought you'd do anything not to risk losing your son.'

Roy blanched as if kicked in the gut. 'Struth, Lill. If I could take his place, I would. They didn't want me then and they sure as hell wouldn't want me now.' He glanced anxiously at me, then back at the road. 'Try to think about it from his point of view. I know you won't agree with me, but I've always felt Henry grew up feeling a bit ashamed. About the last war, I mean. Knowing that his dad didn't fight when most of his mates' dads did.'

'I don't believe that's true. Not for one minute. He should have been grateful his father was still alive. No, Roy,' I repeated, my lips twisting in denial. 'I don't believe he was ever ashamed of you. And I've never been ashamed of you, either – not until this very moment.'

~

That evening there was a terrible row.

'I'm not sure you know what you're saying, Henry,' I began carefully. 'You seem so happy at the university.'

'I am happy there, Mum. And I'll get back to my studies when the time is right. As soon as we've pushed back the Japanese and beaten the Axis powers for good.'

'He's right, Mum. Someone's got to do it. I bet you'll looking dashing in your uniform, Henry.'

'Leave the room please, Margery. This doesn't concern you.' My tone must have been suitably menacing because, for once, my daughter did as I asked. I took a deep breath and smiled at Henry, forcing myself to sound light and breezy.

'Can't you just concentrate on finishing your studies for now? By then, the war might be over, and you can start working.' I saw Henry's defensive expression and tried a different tack. 'Or even if the war is still going by the time you graduate, you'll have other choices by then. Your qualifications would see to that. There are more ways to serve our country than picking up a rifle, especially for young men of your calibre. Even the government thinks so. That's why civil engineering is on the reserved occupations list. Don't you agree, Roy?' Before Roy could answer, I cut him off and changed tack again. 'And if you're still set on joining up after your degree, you could always be deployed in some sort of technical capacity. A non-combat role. Surely that's the better way, Henry.'

I watched his nostrils flare as he took a deep breath. 'Look, Mum, the way I see it, I'm probably going to get called up eventually. And when that happens, I don't want to be stuck in some Australian country town up north on garrison duty or guarding German internees. I want to be part of the action.'

'Please tell me you're not thinking about joining the RAAF. I know most every young man wants to be a pilot these days, but it's far too dangerous. If your plane was hit directly, or were to come down for any reason, you'd never survive. Listen to me please, Henry. Please.' My head was pounding as stars literally flashed before my eyes.

'No, I'm talking about the army, the second AIF,' he replied evenly.

'But why not just wait and see what happens? If things change and you are suddenly drafted, who's to say you'll be stuck in some country town? You might very well be stationed somewhere important, somewhere you can play a valuable role but without being directly on the frontline. You could be in surveillance or signals, or whatever they call it.'

'I don't want to wait to be conscripted. I can't do that, Mum. It's better if I volunteer from the beginning. I know the militia have been holding their own in New Guinea these past few months, but there are still plenty of folk who don't respect the chocos. I refuse to just sit back and wait to be caught in the draft. I don't want anyone saying I shirked my duty.'

'Well, I have no respect for any woman or man who calls someone a chocolate soldier,' I retorted. 'No one has the right to make you risk your life, no one.'

'It's my decision, Mum. Nobody's making me do this. It's about my own self-respect too. What did you expect? Raising your family in a place like this, sending me to a school like Grammar, where I was surrounded by masters talking about honour and duty, and when even our own Prime Minister – who was against conscription for so long himself – can see there's no other option. We've got to defend this country and fight for what we believe in. There's no time for cowards or excuses. It's time to stand up and be counted.'

'You sound like a recruitment poster,' I almost spat the words. 'And what about all those inventions you've been dreaming of all these years? You could forget about all that.'

'I don't see why. I'll be right there in the field. I'll be able to see how things work firsthand – the types of machinery and weapons that soldiers really need to keep them safe. The kinds of innovations that win wars.'

'Like the Owen,' said Roy, foolishly choosing that moment to interject.

Henry nodded vigorously at this mention of the new Australian-designed submachine gun.

I turned to Roy in disgust. 'More efficient killing machines, you mean.'

'That's right, Dad,' said Henry, ignoring my reply. 'But imagine if I could come up with an even better idea and take it to the Army Inventions

Board. I bet they'd be open to getting a soldier's perspective.'

While Roy nodded uneasily, I rubbed my temples, trying to quieten my voice as the leaden shards of our dialogue ricocheted around the room.

'I wouldn't know anything about that, Henry, but neither would you. You're still just a child.'

I could hardly bear to look at him at that moment – my son, so bright and yet utterly naive. Why couldn't Henry see that life in the army would be nothing like Scout camp? That being trained to use a weapon was not the same as tinkering in his backyard tool shed or learning how to operate the engineering equipment at university? He was too busy thinking of facts and figures, and too excited by the physical machinery of war to consider its morality. Why couldn't he see that human lives were at stake, his own included?

'Look, Mum,' said Henry, standing up. 'I know you mean well, but you keep trying to pretend this war isn't happening. I've made up my mind. I would've liked your blessing, but I only need one parent's signature on my enlistment form.'

I could feel him slipping through my fingers. With a dry throat, I clutched at other solutions, anything to delay his decision or stall his deployment. 'What about officer school then? If we make a few more changes here at home, we could afford to send you.' I stood and put out my arm to stop Henry from leaving the room.

'I'm not going to officer school, Mum.' Henry shook his head in frustration. 'Dad's already told me most of the men who I'll be serving with won't be from around here. They probably won't have finished high school, let alone university. If I cared about rank or mixing with the upper classes, then I would've already asked you to send me to officer school or I'd join the RAAF, but I don't. Anyway, look what happened to Charlie.'

'Exactly!' I cried. 'Look what happened to Charlie. He was lucky his injury wasn't more serious, but don't think he didn't learn his lesson. Anything could have happened. There is nothing heroic about dying in a training exercise or on a battlefield, Henry. There is nothing glamorous about war. You're not going to miss out on some big adventure by not enlisting. Can't you see that?'

'I know that, Mum.' He turned to Roy. 'Dad, we've been over all this already. Make her understand, please.'

'Your mother just wants to protect you, son. We both do.' Roy came forward, drawing us together in an awkward embrace.

'Well, someone has to protect this country,' countered Henry, standing rigid and resisting Roy's efforts. 'It's time we drove the Japs back where they came from, once and for all.'

I flinched to hear such rhetoric spouting from my own child's lips. Just as I opened my mouth to respond, I felt Margery's hand on my arm and spun around.

'Can I go to the pictures now?'

My daughter stood before me, dressed and done up more like a beauty contestant than a schoolgirl of fifteen. I glared at her in horror. 'How could you possibly want to go to the pictures at a time like this?'

Margery bit her lip. 'Barbara's waiting outside. We were planning to walk up to the Empire with her sister for the 7.30pm show. What should I tell her?'

Tell her your brother is throwing his life away, I thought as I snapped back a response. 'Off you go then, my girl,' I said, gesturing towards the door. 'No point staying here any longer. Evidently, I have no control over anyone in this family. That much is clear, at least.'

As Margery retreated in quick time, I cast one last glance at Henry and Roy, then fell onto the sofa in despair. 'I don't understand you men,' I cried, covering my face with my hands. 'I don't understand any of you. You've all gone mad. The whole world has gone mad.'

Chapter 20

Milk of Magnesia

The outcome of that night's argument, and of the many others that followed in the ensuing weeks, was inevitable. On a still and sultry October morning, just a few days before his nineteenth birthday, Henry went straight from his linear algebra lecture to the Sydney University Area Office to enquire about signing up. Giddy with excitement, he relayed his experience over dinner that evening. While Roy listened closely to the details of his conversation with Major Oxley and the sequence of events that would now follow before Henry could formally enlist, I could hardly speak.

Pleading a violent headache, I left the table just as the storm, which had been threatening all day, finally broke. Great gusts of wind rattled the windows and whistled down our chimney. Forks of lightning lit up the sky and rain bucketed sideways. I dragged myself onto the bed and let the cannon fire of thunder drown everything out.

As the semester neared its end, Henry grew noticeably impatient. Charging through his first-year examinations, he wasted no time before formally withdrawing from his studies. With the army medical already behind him and no further impediments to his enlistment, he was duly accepted into the Australian army. Private Henry Armstrong was ready to begin his mandatory infantry training at the Bathurst Army Camp.

Roy insisted on a send-off party with Henry's friends, during which I drank far too much gin and had to excuse myself while everyone was still there.

When Henry left home the next morning, dressed in his new slouch hat and khaki uniform, a lump rose in my throat and remained stubbornly in place, no matter how much water I drank. After several days, I took Roy's advice and saw the doctor.

'Dyspepsia,' pronounced Dr Solander even before peering down my throat.

Despite the absence of the usual symptoms of heartburn or indigestion, it was apparently not unknown for stomach acid to rise all the way back up the digestive tract and cause a choking sensation. Not uncommon, he assured me, especially during periods of anxiety, and was something he'd seen in several of his women patients with sons or husbands in service.

As I sipped on my milk of magnesia, I wondered what Henry would think about Bathurst, where he and his fellow recruits would be stationed for the next six months. As the site of Australia's first gold rush, the town had once attracted diggers and prospectors far and wide. How quickly its population and riches must have swelled, spilling over into surrounding districts, like the goldfields of Eurunderee and Gulgong, where Henry Lawson had lived as a boy. Now that same town was playing host to an army. A shiver crawled up my spine as I thought of Henry travelling, at this very moment, over the Blue Mountains and presumably tracing at least part of the same north-west route that led to my birthplace.

Over the years, Roy had occasionally returned to his idea of driving out there to see what we could find, but each time he'd mentioned it, I'd felt breathless and trembly, catapulted back to a day when the sky had rained flakes of ash and I'd found myself all alone. Even if we could, by sheer chance, stumble upon the blackened remains of my childhood home, even assuming there was anything left for me to recognise, wouldn't it only make things worse? I was trying so hard to go forward, going back felt like a mistake. Especially now, when my own son's life was under threat, I couldn't bear to be reminded of who and what I had lost already.

From what I could ascertain, despite Henry's dogged insistence on enlisting voluntarily and his disdain for conscripts, such distinctions between soldiers were less important than before. Throughout the newly defined South West Pacific Area – whether on the Australian mainland, the territory of New Guinea or further afield in Borneo, the Philippines and elsewhere – the various services within the Australian army had joined together to expel the Axis powers from the region. Experienced AIF soldiers, retrieved from the battlefields of Europe and Africa, now served alongside militia men and conscripts, sometimes even in the same unit. Lines were blurring, literally and metaphorically bleeding into each other. Along with the other Allied forces, they all came under the supreme command of General Douglas MacArthur. Certainly, since the big American war chief had taken charge, the threat of Japanese invasion seemed to have lessened, and the strategy had shifted from defence to offence. I took another sip of my chalky milk prescription and grimaced. Forwards, backwards, advance and retreat. Gaining ground or losing ground. It was no better than a schoolyard game of tug o' war.

~

'Come on, Margery, I don't like it any more than you do, but we have to go.'

With the wail of the air-raid siren filling our ears, Margery – who had only just arrived home from school – followed me out of the house and down the street to join the queue forming outside the shelter under

Killarney Castle, the chosen location for our regular neighbourhood drills. I glanced up at the battlement, rubbing my hand over the cold nubbly sandstone of the castle walls as we waited to be let inside.

If Roy had been here, he would have tried to make light of this afternoon's tedious exercise, telling Margery it was time for 'the princess' to visit 'her castle' – a running family joke, which even I had woven into her bedtime stories years earlier, but which I no longer found funny. It pained me to see Mr Taylor's beloved home, his very own 'castle in the air' (as Henry Lawson had summarily dismissed my mother's girlhood dreams), reduced to such a depressing public purpose.

Roy's nickname for Margery had started even before she was born, when I discovered I was pregnant soon after the christening of the new royal baby, Princess Elizabeth. 'Let's hope it's a girl, this time,' he'd declared, cracking open a bottle of pop. 'A little princess of our own.'

Although I too had hoped for a girl and had at first found Roy's comparison adorable, I was less enamoured with it now. There were scant few young women who didn't want to think of themselves, or be treated, as a princess. And yet the older I got, the more I felt like 'Princess' was nothing more than an honorary title, with no real authority behind it.

It didn't help that 'The Drover's Wife' reinforced my fears. Not only did Henry Lawson suggest that the drover – my father – was 'careless' and very likely unfaithful during his time away from home, Lawson also implied such roguish behaviour was perfectly acceptable since 'if he had the means he would take her to the city and keep her there like a princess'. As if the mere possibility of kindness should be enough to satisfy any woman while excusing everything else! At least I could take comfort in knowing that Lawson's slanderous account of 'the husband' could be nothing more than speculation on his part. I also liked to think that my tough as nails Mother would never have tolerated such a gross betrayal from Father in any case.

So, although I knew Roy meant nothing by his nickname for Margery, other than as a symbol of fatherly affection, I wanted more for our daughter than to be someone else's princess.

Putting aside such reflections, I stepped past Warden Bright and entered the shelter. I waited for my eyes to adjust to the relative darkness inside. Despite my moral misgivings, this cavernous space beneath the castle's ground floor was ideally suited for protection, especially now during late summer when its thick sandstone walls provided a welcome respite from the afternoon heat.

I looked around for Margery and saw she had already sat down next to another girl from Ravenswood, leaving me to find my own seat on one of the long timber benches. I squeezed in beside a flustered young mother whose baby must have been roused from sleep and was now out of sorts.

'He's normally very well behaved.'

'I'm sure he is,' I said soothingly.

'He probably wants a feed, but he's not on the bottle so I don't want to do it here.'

'No one minds if he cries, dear. Hopefully they'll let us go home quickly. That's a darling boy you've got there.' I looked away and tried not to think of my own son.

With Henry gone, and our family unit reduced to three, I was still taking stock. I had kept my eyes closed for so long to anything other than my own personal battle to keep Henry out of the war, and was almost startled by what I now saw. Sydney was hard to recognise. Even our sleepy North Shore suburbs had been transformed. Most conspicuous were the emergency services – an all-encompassing suite of measures to protect us against Japanese invasion, like today's air-raid drill or the slit trenches Roy had helped dig at Margery's school.

Even before Henry's departure, we had all grown accustomed to the inconvenience of brownouts and blackouts, but now the eerie display of night-time searchlights crisscrossing the sky felt like a haunting reminder of the lightning storm on the day of his enlistment.

Some members of our community took to these emergency procedures with gusto, thriving on an atmosphere of alarm and energised by a newfound sense of purpose. Delighting in all manner of absurd rumours (how could anyone possibly believe the Japanese could see in the dark?), they covered their windows with fastidious care and made hooded capes of brown hessian so their children would resemble plants from the air. Others, like me, were sceptical about whether such measures were truly necessary, or even effective, if push came to shove.

From starry-eyed young women to time-weathered veterans, it seemed as if everyone I knew had joined some sort of war relief committee. There were so many, I found it impossible to keep track. There were Patriotic Committees, emergency services volunteers and the hardworking women of the Voluntary Aid Detachments, not to mention the Ku-ring-gai Women War Workers and various golf clubs whose members had mobilised into brigades. There were even local citizens guerrilla squads! In our street, women attended invalid cooking classes or opened their homes to soldiers on Rest and Recreation leave. And there was always more money to be raised, whether for soldier comforts, troop entertainment or POW parcels. Our shire alone had raised 1700 pounds for a Tiger Moth aeroplane for the RAAF, with Roy's name joining the list of other subscribers on a document sixteen feet long.

I saw the seat on the other side of Margery was now empty and went over to join her, quietly excusing myself from the young mother whose baby had just fallen back asleep.

'What's happening at school these days, darling? Are you still knitting for the Polish refugee children?'

'Yes,' sighed Margery. 'And sewing for the YWCA.'

'We're having a fete next week, Mrs Armstrong, to raise money,' her classmate added. 'Don't forget to send in any silver paper and toothpaste tubs for recycling.'

'Thank you for the reminder, Hannah. Waste not, want not, as they say!'

'Wish we could do something more exciting than sewing and recycling,' griped my daughter.

'You used to find your school drills entertaining, Margery. A welcome break from class, you told me.' I rubbed her leg to show I was sympathetic despite my teasing.

In the early days, at the sound of the school whistle, she and her friends had gleefully skipped down to the shelters under the old Assembly Hall, dutifully stopping at the sandbagged entrance to check their blazer pockets for the obligatory handkerchief and the rubber device on which they were to bite down in the event of an actual bomb. But eventually she too had grown tired of these interruptions. Typical for a girl of her age, or for anyone really, she judged world events by how they affected her personally. And although Ravenswood had several boarders hailing from the Pacific Islands, Asia and war-torn Europe – girls whose lives had been directly impacted – Margery just kept on moaning about the restrictions war had brought to her life.

'What have you done with your uniform, Margery?' I asked, suddenly noticing she had made a few tweaks to the design of her navy-blue tunic, including its prescribed length. Her blue and gold school tie was also missing. 'Won't you get in trouble for that?'

'Don't worry, Mrs Armstrong, we're friends with the prefects. They won't dob,' Hannah said with a grin.

'Just make sure you're wearing your hat and gloves without fail whenever you go through the gate – you don't want to risk a Wednesday detention,' I warned. With Margery now a student at the same school in which I had once taught, I sometimes found myself in a precarious position of divided loyalties.

In response, my daughter muttered something about 'silly little rules' and 'pettifogging regulations'. I shook my head but said nothing. Margery had not yet learned that life without restriction was not an option. Not even for a so-called Princess.

I let the girls return to their chatter and wondered when Roy would arrive home this evening. While keeping the business going took up most of his time and prevented him from official volunteer roles, he always found other ways to help. Handy with his tools and stronger than some men half his age, he performed odd jobs, chopped wood and tackled heavy garden chores for elderly neighbours and women whose husbands were in service. Roy believed in the power of community spirit, and that times like these brought out the best in people. But despite most volunteers being well-intentioned, I saw others who seemed to derive a perverse pleasure from the war, motivated more by status than by a genuine sense of duty or innate goodness.

I looked up at the touch of a hand on my arm and recognised Mrs Kirby, a former school parent, who had been particularly difficult to please when I had taught her daughter. 'Good afternoon, Miss Taylor, I mean, Mrs Armstrong. Did you hear about the Italian greengrocer in Roseville?'

'I did, Mrs Kirby. Disgraceful, wasn't it?'

She nodded eagerly and sat down beside me. 'You mean about them being fascists?'

'Oh no, Mrs Kirby,' I said, affecting innocence. 'I mean the baseless accusations and inexcusable vandalism inflicted upon that poor family.'

Presumably hoping to find an echo chamber for her own narrow-minded views, Mrs Kirby now looked deflated. A moment later, she scrambled to her feet. 'I think Mrs Morgan is calling me over. I'd best go say hello.'

'See you next time, Mrs Kirby.'

One of the ugliest consequences of these precautionary measures was that they stirred up the racism. At times I felt steeped in it, like a pot of tea turned bitter on the hob. The Japanese had gone from being our ally in the previous war to a so-called murdering race of sub-humans. *Beware the yellow peril!* While such outpourings of hate were predictable, and slightly more excusable in respect of Australia's enemy nations, I'd also witnessed this same paranoia and prejudice closer to home. Like the snake hiding beneath the floorboards in Lawson's story, you never knew when it might rise and strike a blow, as it had with the local Italian family about whom Mrs Kirby had been speaking.

Despite being longstanding community members and the fact that their son, Jacob, had voluntarily joined the AIF, nasty rumours had started about the family's alleged ties to fascism. Before long, someone had set fire to their garage and destroyed their recently purchased truck. Later that same week in the post office, I'd overheard two women gossiping about the incident. While one lady had been relatively circumspect and had shown a measure of sympathy towards the family, the other maintained they only had themselves to blame and should count themselves lucky not to have been interned. In her view, the family should have had more sense than to keep speaking Italian to one another, and who was to say they couldn't have been using the wireless pole in front of their shop to communicate with their fascist friends, right under everyone's noses. When I quietly pointed out the official government investigation had failed to find any evidence of wrongdoing, the woman just smirked at me, saying 'Where there's smoke, there's usually fire'. Then she'd begun cackling at her own spiteful pun.

For these reasons, and despite Roy's urging, I chose to avoid the committees and volunteer activities wherever possible. Apart from the letters and parcels I sent directly to Henry at the training camp and the camouflage nets I worked on every evening – *God forbid anyone's hands should be idle!* – I wanted no part in the social machinery of this war.

As Mrs Kirby scurried away, I saw she was wearing her government-issued silver brooch, in honour of her son who was serving. Unlike many women who proudly displayed theirs in public, I kept mine in the drawer beside my bed where only I could see it. Like new brides fiddling with their wedding rings, I'd watch their hands creep instinctively up to their lapels and see their expression change as they traced over the rising sun emblem of the AIF and the star for each son under arms. No scrap of metal, or anything else the government might offer, could make up for Henry's absence.

~

It was a relief when, after months of waiting for confirmation, Henry finally came home for a week's leave in the winter of 1943.

I proceeded to spoil him. Aided by the ration coupons I'd been saving for just this purpose, I started by cooking all his favourite meals – thick T-bone steaks and chops flashed under the grill, racks of lamb cutlets served on a platter with little paper frills on their ends, whipped potatoes, freshly shelled peas, trifle for dessert and a ready supply of the sweet, plain Arrowroot biscuits he had loved since childhood.

'Thanks, Mum,' Henry gushed, grinning sheepishly at Margery and Roy as I set down dish after dish.

I also sorted through his laundry to find loose hems needing stitching and socks needing darning, barely containing my disappointment when Henry insisted he could now do this for himself.

Already I could see changes. Once long-limbed and almost gangly, he had filled out these past months. His shoulders had broadened, and he walked straight and tall, like a man who knew exactly where he was going. His skin, and even his voice, had darkened and hardened under the harsh extremes of an inland climate.

'Our boy's growing up,' said Roy, skimming his fingers over the shorn ends of Henry's hair and failing to notice my accusatory glare.

On his last day home, all four of us went into town for a stroll in the Botanic Gardens and splurged on high tea at The Australia Hotel. Despite the drab pall that had enveloped our city during the war, I'd never seen so much activity on a Sunday afternoon. It felt like every second man or woman was in uniform. And everywhere I turned, there were American soldiers – basking on park benches in the sun-filled gardens or strutting through the streets in their tight-fitting uniforms, polished shoes and shining medals. They looked and acted more like officers in comparison to their Aussie counterparts. Only the navy men, dressed in their white and blue sailor suits and chewing gum, reminded me of little boys.

Standing out from the Red Cross volunteers and formally attired servicewomen, I counted an alarming number of young women dolled up for a night on the town. Sporting Victory Red lipstick with long lanceolate nails painted to match, pancaked faces and lashes laden with mascara, they teetered on the arms of their male companions, giggling in their Yank-snatcher heels. I wondered what their mothers would think of their behaviour. *Too much time and too much money*, was what everyone said about the American servicemen on leave, quick to cast the blame. That was another thing about war. It made the future too uncertain and encouraged young folk to act on their impulses, living life for today, regardless of the consequences.

As we walked down Martin Place towards the train station, planes roared over on their way back to Richmond and the winter sun faded into night. Skipping ahead in the direction of the flower stalls, all run by women these days, Margery stopped short at the sound of a long wolf whistle then whirled around.

'They've got some nerve, those Yanks,' muttered Roy, grunting approvingly when Henry stepped forward to take his sister's arm.

'Hubba hubba!' slurred a man's voice from somewhere nearby.

Our daughter giggled nervously. 'Thanks Henry, you're a brick,' I heard her say as they walked on ahead of us.

Seen from behind, arm in arm with her brother, sixteen-year-old Margery could easily be mistaken for a young woman out with her sweetheart. Below her knee-length skirt, long shapely legs in patent leather court shoes, albeit sensibly mid-heeled, moved quickly to keep time with her brother's even longer strides. With our son already suffering the consequences of his own youthful impulses, I could only hope Margery would grow to have more sense than some of the girls I'd seen this evening.

Cold sea air blew off the harbour, whooshing towards us once we turned onto George Street. I turned up the collar of my tweed jacket with a shiver, bracing myself for more.

Henry left us the next morning, his army pack crammed full of nuts, biscuits and other comforts. Joining his newly assigned unit, he was to be shipped up to North Queensland for the next stage of training under jungle conditions.

As he clambered into the waiting truck, I gritted my teeth and waved goodbye to our boy a second time, clutching Roy's arm for support. Moments later, having finally cast off the smiling visage I'd maintained so carefully all week, I began to cry.

'Don't worry, love,' said Roy, squeezing me tightly. 'Chances are, they'll put him on garrison duty, nowhere near the frontline.'

I continued to cry.

'There, there, love. He can't go far until he turns twenty anyway. I wouldn't be surprised if he never even gets out of Australia. New Guinea at the furthest. I told you what Curtin said – we'll have to keep fighting off these pesky Japanese raids a little while yet, but he's confident we're not at risk of a full-scale invasion anymore.'

I mustered a faint smile for Roy's sake and refrained from telling him that I was no longer confident about anything.

Chapter 21

Women at War

In exchange for the privilege of motherhood, I had willingly traded both sleep and time to myself and, over the years, I'd all but lost the habit of walking on my own. It was only in recent times that I had rediscovered this pleasure. The rhythm of my feet, the taste of fresh air in my lungs and the feeling of being at one with nature was more effective than any tonic from the pharmacy. Like a salve to my senses, the minty smell of eucalyptus or the honeyed aroma of wattle calmed my turbulent thoughts, while the endearing pose of a lone kookaburra or the jewelled brilliance of a parrot brought a smile to my lips. I'd gaze up at the sky, far above the canopy, and tell myself it was the same sky under which Henry slept. Out here, alone, I could almost believe there was no war.

To keep up this fragile charade, I had to carefully map my routes. I followed one of these today as I exited the house and kept my head down, moving quickly. As always, I avoided the train station and all the people coming and going. I avoided the churches, now displaying Allied flags as a show of their nationalism, no longer content to preach the word of God alone. I had become adept at listening for volunteers as they marched through the streets in groups. Even the VADs – such models of feminine efficiency in their vermillion lipstick and military-style uniforms – made my skin crawl when wearing their anti-gas respirators during drills.

The only positive consequence coming out of this war was that all those positions left vacant by men could now be claimed by my own sex. We could become *women that matter, women at war*, as the cinema newsreels proclaimed. From bus conductresses to ambulance drivers, from polishing planes to operating a tractor, from grease monkeys and mechanics to cooking for hundreds, it was a triumph to witness these capable, mostly younger women in action. At Ravenswood, breaking new ground, Margery told us there were teachers bearing the title of *Mrs*, some of whom had previously taught there before getting married. When Roy had asked whether I might like to do the same, suggesting it might help distract me from worrying over Henry, I'd made some excuse about leaving those jobs for the women who really needed them. What I should have said was that I wanted to be at my post when our son returned.

Every night, as I lay in bed trying to sleep, I would think about the war ending and allow myself to anticipate the joy of Henry's homecoming. I imagined him arriving unannounced, calling our names as he banged on the door. I also imagined him coming home early, whether injured or gravely ill, my mind racing through different scenarios until I found the one I liked. Perhaps, like Charlie, he might lose some fingers or break his leg badly, anything that would prevent him from serving and necessitate his discharge. And if he were not well enough to come home directly, I had a solution for that too. I'd write to the powers that be, calling upon Hilda's family for extra clout, and have him sent to the Lady Gowrie Convalescent Home right here in Gordon, a magnificent Spanish Mission style mansion that had been taken over by the Red Cross and staffed by the Ku-Ring-Gai VADs. Instead of playing host to parties for Sydney's rich and famous, its palm-filled garden and Hollywood style swimming pool had become a practical source of rehabilitation for returned soldiers.

Sometimes, walking up the steep terrain of Rosedale Road, I'd catch sight of a young man, usually an amputee, supported between two women, and would inevitably picture Henry in his place.

Along with my walks, sometimes I turned to music for comfort. I would tune into Opera Lovers Hour, losing myself in the texture of voice and orchestra. Radio plays were occasionally diverting, too, even if lacking the power of live theatre. And I had plenty of time to read every day. Often, when I would first sit down and find my place in a book, my thoughts would be all aflutter, darting hither and thither like finches in a cage. But eventually, the words would work their magic, and I'd feel my whole body begin to relax as my mind became still.

Over the years, my love of the written word had never faltered. Through university, I'd gained familiarity with all the classics of English literature – Shakespeare, Dickens, Thackeray and the other great writers of the Victorian era – along with a smattering of works from France, Russia and America. In contrast to other types of writing, it had always pleased me that so many of the best novels were written by women. As a teacher, I'd taken great delight in introducing some of my girls to the fictional worlds of Jane Austen, George Eliot, the Brontë sisters and other brilliant women whose literary productions had transcended the parlours in which they were written.

I was sorry that I had largely failed in my efforts to share my passion with my own daughter, who preferred films over books. As I waited for the cars to pass so I could cross the street, my mind turned to our most recent conversation on reading.

'Won't you come with me to the lending library, darling? I was thinking of the Crows Nest branch, but we can go into the city if you'd prefer more choice.'

Margery had looked up at me through her sunglasses from the back lawn where she was sunbaking on a towel, doused in coconut oil. 'No thanks, I need to stay out here for another hour at least.'

'Would you like me to borrow something for you? A mystery novel perhaps? Or a romance?' At this point, I was willing to put aside any high and mighty notions of great literature, so long as she would read something.

'No thanks. I might walk up to the shops later and buy a magazine.'

'How about reading *Little Women* again?' Louisa May Alcott's classic coming of age novel had been one of the few novels to have made a strong impression on Margery. However, while I had once aspired to be like Jo March – independent, obstinately antisocial and ready to forego romance for a life among books – Margery's sympathies had always lain with Amy, the youngest sister, consigned to a life of dullness and deprivation (as Margery saw it) until a holiday in France with her rich old aunt changed everything.

'No thanks, I'm too old for that book now. Besides, I've read it before.' Margery had flipped over onto her stomach, signalling an end to our conversation.

'All right, Amy,' I'd teased. 'I'll borrow it for my own sake. I'm not too old to read it again. Don't let yourself get too sunburned.'

It *was* a wonderful feeling to recognise oneself – or one's loved ones – in a book (even if not everything about the character in question was necessarily to one's liking). But thinking back to my own younger years, hardly any of the books I had read were written by Australian authors. Fewer still by Australian women. Fortunately, there had been some exceptions. I was thinking here of the Australian expatriate, Henry Handel Richardson, whose long-suspected feminine identity had eventually been revealed, and of the acid-tongued Miles Franklin who, after travelling the world for many years, had now returned to Australia, where I supposed she would live out the rest of her own 'brilliant career'. Both of them had created memorable young heroines out of step with their contemporaries, from whom I had drawn great comfort and inspiration.

It was a sad fact that most Australian writers had to leave our country, or at least publish abroad, before their worth was recognised. Henry

Lawson had voiced the same complaint, hence his disastrous decision to take his young family to London in 1900. Almost fifty years later, despite a whole generation of gifted Australian novelists, women especially, having risen to prominence – Katharine Susannah Prichard, Dymphna Cusack and Eleanor Dark among them – not much had changed. I simply could not understand why so many people refused to read Australian books or cringed at the mention of familiar settings and events. Why were they so convinced life was superior elsewhere? Why shouldn't Australia presume to possess her own culture, instead of just a favourable climate?

This same problem also existed in the art world, although Roy assured me this was changing. Since Henry's enlistment, our usual gallery outings had lost some of their appeal for me in the same way everything else had. Even so, it was gratifying to see women having claimed a place for themselves on gallery walls, perhaps even more than they had on bookshelves. Along with forerunners like Thea Proctor, Hilda Rix Nicholas and Margaret Preston, undisputed doyenne of Australian art, many of these women artists came from my own generation, like Grace Cossington Smith, Anne Dangar and Alison Rehfisch. Together, they had shown the world that a woman's eye could recognise beauty just as readily as that of a man, and that a woman's hand could take up a paintbrush to capture that beauty, with equal daring and perhaps even greater sensitivity.

My only other source of diversion was far more mundane. By courtesy of the very public mandate of self-denial and sacrifice, housekeeping had become rather challenging for me and most women around the country.

Our usual deliveries of milk, bread and ice still came to the house, though less frequently than before. Since our street had been connected to the sewerage a few years earlier, we were no longer reliant on the weekly nightsoil service, although Roy liked to joke that the 'dunny cart' would be the next thing to be rationed. Basic everyday objects were now expected to last 'longer than shock troops on a battlefield', as again he joked. Putting aside my husband's wisecracks, living with austerity took me back to the Depression years, with the same expectation that all our clothes and household items would be re-used, recycled or repaired. But now, even if one had the money, many things simply weren't available to purchase, especially anything considered a luxury. With ration coupons for tea, sugar, butter and even meat, there was always enough food to put on the table every day, but I was finding it increasingly time-consuming to get it there. Unless one was prepared to take the risk of buying on the black market, shopping for most housewives had become a game of patience, skill and luck. All too often, I'd arrive at my destination to find the shop door closed. Hanging in the window would be the telltale sign: *quota sold for today*. I knew of quite a few women who were turning into serious hoarders over these shortages. Petrol rationing meant that Roy took the train to work most days, while fuel shortages and wood rationing made life at home less comfortable.

Despite tobacco rationing, Roy had taken up smoking around the time of Henry's enlistment. Out of consideration for me, he never smoked in the house, reserving this comfort for when he was outside, where he claimed it kept the mosquitoes at bay. Although I hated how the smell lingered on his clothing and breath, I didn't begrudge his new habit. As a way of coping, it seemed harmless enough. What I didn't like, however, was that he had recently invited Margery to share in this habit, first by teaching her how to roll his cigarettes, and then by sometimes letting her puff along with him. When I questioned whether he thought it a becoming activity for a sixteen-year-old schoolgirl, he told me not to worry, claiming they had their best conversations out there. 'About what?' I'd asked, trying not to feel jealous. And although Roy had assured me it was simply his chance to answer Margery's questions about the war, and anything else she felt like talking about, I couldn't help but wonder if they talked about me as well.

With paper shortages and some of Roy's staff now in the services, his business had shrunk considerably during the war. Like his father before him, Roy was now willing to take on whatever printing work he could get. Longstanding relationships with the city's top advertising agencies and a reputation for quality had resulted in several lucrative government contracts, including those from the War Effort Publicity Board. Sometimes when I was out running errands, I'd look at the recruitment posters and other government-sponsored advertisements at the train station or in shop windows on the highway. I hated the rose-coloured images they presented of military life and resented the implicit accusation cast against those who, like me, still opposed the war. I couldn't help but wonder whether any of this propaganda had been printed in Roy's factory. Surely, he would never have approved such appalling depictions of Japanese soldiers, painting them as sub-human? Irrespective of my suspicions, I never asked, telling myself it was better not to know.

Ever since that day when I felt Roy supported Henry's decision to enlist, an unwelcome space had formed between us, creating a kind of no man's land that neither could cross. Although Roy also appeared conscious of this invisible new divide, we still managed to show our love in other ways, dispensing small kindnesses throughout the day and sharing familiar rituals from which we both drew comfort.

~

'When was the last time you updated your album?' Roy had asked the previous evening after tuning into the first episode of Henry Lawson's new story adaptations on 2GB.

'It's been a while,' I'd conceded. 'I can't quite see the point anymore.'

But this morning, I had retrieved the album from its cupboard and was now looking at the handful of clippings I'd collected in recent years but not yet bothered to paste inside.

The first thing I picked up was a review of last October's stage play from the radical New Theatre League in which Oriel Gray had linked various Lawson stories, though again not the one that mattered to me. As I tossed it into the wastepaper basket, I smiled to see that 'Mrs Henry Lawson' had attended opening night. By coincidence, my next clipping was an advertisement from December for her own new book, titled *My Henry Lawson*. Although I was not sure how much value I would get for the five shillings they were asking, given that her story would be blurred by twenty years of posthumous nostalgia and knowing that Bertha had only met her husband years after he had written 'The Drover's Wife', I put this clipping to one side for now.

Last was a small notice from *The Sydney Morning Herald* dating back to August 1941, announcing that a memorial seat was to be built as a tribute to Louisa Lawson on a site close to her son's statue in the Domain. I'd been so happy to read about it then. Yet now here we were, more than two years later, with no sign of any seat, nor even a word of explanation. Like my mother before me, and like most women throughout the ages, Louisa Lawson was heading down the road to obscurity. Nevertheless, I pasted it into my album, optimistically making a note in pencil on the next page to leave it empty, in case this promised tribute should ever materialise.

The following Sunday evening, after Roy had again tuned into 2GB, he made another suggestion. 'Maybe it's time you shared your album with Margie? You never know, next week's story might be "The Drover's Wife" and you can use it as your cue.'

'I don't think so, not without Henry here too.'

My tone was curt, and my expression equally so, but it was not Roy I was angry with. I was imagining sitting on the sofa with Margery at 7.13pm next Sunday, waiting on tenterhooks to hear if the next story narrated by Lloyd Berrell would be mine. My mother's life told in eight minutes. What could possibly go wrong?

'I'll tell them both together, properly,' I said. 'As soon as Henry gets home.'

Chapter 22

A New Axis

Without Henry and the potent symmetry of two plus two, our family felt unbalanced, almost as if we had lost our centre of gravity. Thankfully, Charlie made a point of staying with us for at least a night whenever he was down from Canberra.

One blustery Friday evening in 1944, with winter fast approaching and my beef stew drying out in the oven, we waited for Charlie to join us at the dinner table. Eventually, he arrived, out of breath and red-faced from the cold.

'Sorry I'm late, Aunt Lillian. I had a longer walk than usual.'

Roy snorted and ruffled Charlie's hair, as if he were still a boy. 'Missed the station again and had to walk all the way back here, did you, mate? Head down in one of your books and got distracted, I'll bet.'

'Not tonight,' said Charlie, hanging his coat on the hook. 'This time I hopped off one stop too early. With the station names all covered over, and everything in darkness, the platform at Killara looked just like Gordon. The train was gone before I discovered where I was.'

'Leave him alone,' I told Roy and handed Charlie a plate as he sat down beside Margery. 'He won't come again if you always give him a hard time.'

'Point taken. Most blokes your age would be too busy courting some lovely young lady to visit their old uncle,' said Roy.

Charlie blushed. 'I think most of the young ladies would prefer to be wined and dined by a Yank than the likes of me. It's hard to compete with orchids and silk stockings.'

'Don't underestimate yourself,' I said. 'Good character always wins out in the end.'

'That and a steady income,' added Roy, winking at Margery.

I rolled my eyes. 'Just ignore your uncle, please. He should have learned by now that flattery and expensive gifts only get a man so far. I'm sure he still thinks it was his charm that won me over, however – and at the risk of inflating his ego – I can assure you charm had little to do with it.'

Roy cupped his hand behind his good ear and winked again. 'I couldn't quite hear what your mother just said, but I'm sure she's right, as always.'

Our conversation ambled comfortably in predictable directions – Margery's studies, Roy's latest projects, the prolonged absence of rain (where it was most needed) and of first-class cricket. Knowing my sensitivity, everyone was careful to speak of anything but the war, though we sometimes found ourselves there anyway.

'You still working on that new mosquito repellent, mate?'

Charlie nodded, waiting to speak until he'd finished swallowing. 'Not me personally, but Doug Waterhouse's work has opened up lots of exciting new research possibilities in the lab. His dimethyl phthalate formulation is really doing the job for our boys.'

I felt Charlie's eyes upon me and nodded, signifying permission to continue.

'Doug's repellent formula has been deployed by all the Allied forces right through the Pacific. It's proving extremely effective under jungle conditions.'

'I gather those malaria mosquitoes are every bit as dangerous as a Japanese enemy soldier,' said Roy. 'And are they still using Atabrine?'

'That's right. They've still got Atabrine to help prevent malaria or to treat it if they do get it, but this new spray is helping them to avoid getting bitten in the first place. The troops have nicknamed it Mary.'

Margery looked intrigued. 'Why? Does it smell like a woman's perfume?'

'Hardly!' Charlie scoffed. 'In fact, there's actually some concern about whether the Japanese can smell it on our troops, even from a distance.' His voice trailed as he saw my anxious expression.

'Not a bad idea, Princess,' said Roy, catching Charlie's eye as he too shifted gears. 'Maybe we should ask the Yanks to donate any black-market perfume bottles to the CSIR, instead of using it to try to further their cause with the ladies. Essential research for the war effort, you know the drill. I can just picture the memo from MacArthur now.'

As the laughter echoed around me, all I could picture was Henry sweltering under the humid conditions of the tropics, weighed down by his pack, boots and weapon, battling mosquitoes and other creepy-crawlies. While the insects themselves might not worry him, Henry had always hated the heat, even as a boy. Much to his disappointment, and as Roy had surmised, his first deployment had been limited to a short stint of coast-watching duty. Since then, Henry's unit had been undergoing rehabilitation, reorganisation and yet more training in the Atherton Tableland of Far North Queensland, where even the winters were warm and muggy. No wonder the army tried to keep their troops in good spirits with plenty of visiting entertainment. Speaking for myself, it would take more than a comedian or an over-rouged singer to make me forget what I was risking as a soldier. No shipment of footballs or shuttlecock racquets could divert my attention from the real contest.

As for Henry, an ill-timed tooth infection some months earlier had denied him his only opportunity for home leave. The infection had been in one of his wisdom teeth – as if the message needed to be any clearer, I thought. Roy suspected Henry's latest phase of training would soon be ending and was preparing me for the likelihood his unit would be dispatched to either New Guinea or to Bougainville to relieve the Americans and help drive the Japanese out of the Pacific for good.

I was still in my housecoat when Charlie took his leave the next morning. He kissed me goodbye and whispered his usual words of reassurance.

'He'll be all right, Aunt Lillian. The Japanese are well and truly on the back foot now. The odds are in Henry's favour. It's nothing like the last war – he'll come home, safe and sound, you'll see.'

I accepted Charlie's sanguine platitudes with a tight smile. What I wanted to tell him was that I had never gambled in all my life, that I needed something more than just good odds to keep my son alive.

~

Apart from Charlie's visits, our family social calendar had dwindled in the year and a half since Henry had been gone. While Roy had plenty of company at work or occasionally joined a mate at the Greengate for a beer, I could hardly remember the last time I'd dropped in to see Jean Campbell or invited another family over.

In any case, Margery, now seventeen, was sociable enough for us all. With scant regard for her upcoming Leaving Certificate examinations, she was out of the house several evenings a week, sometimes even sleeping at a friend's place.

The prior evening, before being picked up for a party, she had deigned to let me see her outfit. Dressed in her favourite turquoise silk, nipped in at the waist, with matching bolero, Margery's green eyes and slender figure were set off to perfection.

'Stunning, simply stunning,' I managed to say, faced with the sharp sting of reality. With her eyebrows plucked into thin slanted lines, a light dusting of powder covering her freckles and a single rose tucked into the delicately pinned curls of her hair, our daughter was anything but a child.

But then this morning, returning home after having spent the night at her friend Barbara's house, we'd fallen into our usual roles. I'd heard her slip in through the back door and make a beeline to her bedroom.

'Come back here, please,' I called after her.

She appeared not to have heard.

'Margery,' I called again, louder this time.

Still no response.

I went to her room and opened the door.

'Mum!' she cried, finally acknowledging my presence. 'Can you please knock before you come in? I could have been getting changed.'

'Good manners go both ways, Margery,' I shot back. 'Clean up your room, will you please? It's a pigsty. And when that's finished, you can come and help me clean the pantry. We've had an infestation of ants.'

She shook her head dismissively.

'Don't give me that look. You're always complaining there's nothing to do around here. So now I'm giving you something to do.'

'But I'm going out on Middle Harbour today with my friends. Hannah's brother got given a new dinghy.'

'Not today you're not. You can stay home with me and pull your weight for once.'

The next look I received was one of pure hatred, and I felt myself shrink. Not for the first time, I wondered whether I was equipped to be the mother Margery needed. The mother I wished to be. Our daughter's upbringing was so different to my experience at Sacred Heart: the comforts of home, the joy of family, the freedoms she took for granted. 'Dull as dishwater' was her constant refrain about how and where we lived. All the same, she seemed to fill her days and nights with remarkable ease – going to the pictures, participating in dance lessons, tennis, church suppers, concerts, ice skating in winter, boating in summer and even occasional weekend outings into town or Luna Park.

I left her room, still fuming. All I had wanted to know was whether she'd had a nice time at the party. How had a perfectly innocent intention devolved into such a venomous scolding?

Although forcing her to stay home with me today was the last thing I needed, I was slightly relieved to have found a good excuse to keep her away from Middle Harbour, now that I knew there was gelignite planted under the Roseville Bridge, close to where her little gang rowed out with their dinghies. It had all been part of a plan, apparently, to prevent the Japanese from getting inland to the North Shore and beyond. While the beaches themselves had been covered in thousands of yards of barbed wire, the fallback strategy – should the Japanese forces ever get through to make a landing – was to blow up the Roseville Bridge. Some people apparently considered this an eminently sensible plan. And I knew others who saw nothing wrong with the fact that their children could look up at the sky and name the various kinds of military planes flying overhead, instead of just different bird species, as we had done as children. But I refused to accept any of it as normal.

Thank heavens Margery had no interest in the war or in joining any of the services when she finished school, unlike many other young women, some of whom were even choosing to go overseas. Admittedly, she had little interest in doing very much at all after school. But while Roy was talking about finding her a role in the business, I had not yet given up on the idea of university. An Arts degree, like my own, might still be in question.

Despite the efforts of some of my feminist contemporaries, it was sadly still the case that too few women went on to further their education and embark on a meaningful career. Even Hilda's daughters, with all the privileges and opportunities available to them, had gone straight from school to marriage in quick time, with barely a year or two as debutantes in between. Already, the two older girls had children of their own, and Hilda had settled into the role of doting grandmother as if she were born to it.

Hilda and all her family had been away from Sydney for more than two years. With the threat of Japanese invasion, they had abandoned their various seaside homes and retreated to their family estate near Bowral. But although it was probably now safe to return, Hilda had decided to see out the remainder of the war there. Almost a hundred miles from where we lived, it was too far for a weekend visit, especially given travelling restrictions and petrol shortages, so we'd had to make do with letters and phone calls instead.

Truth be told, Hilda had repeatedly invited me for an extended stay. But I'd always declined, citing Margery's school commitments as grounds for my refusal. Behind the scenes, Roy had been more difficult to put off. 'Some time away would do you good,' he'd urged. 'Why don't you wait till the school holidays and take Margery with you? I can manage just fine on my own for a couple of weeks.' Eventually though, even Roy came to understand what I was doing.

What if something happened to Henry? Or if he came home unexpectedly on leave? The mere possibility of not being here for the arrival of one of his letters felt to me like a betrayal.

~

Not long after Charlie's last visit, around the time of the Normandy landings and the Allied invasion of German-occupied territory in Europe, Henry's unit was shipped to New Guinea. We weren't allowed to know the exact location or object of his mission. The lump in my throat, which had never quite gone away, felt worse than ever. There was no way of knowing whether he would remain on garrison duties or whether he would finally see the frontline action I suspected him of craving all along. The fact remained that he was far from home; far from my own reach and ability to protect him. Almost as terrifying as the thought of Henry being injured or killed was the threat of capture. Chilling reports of horrific living conditions for Australian POWs kept me awake night after night.

Along with the lump in my throat, my ears had also started hurting, a dull ache that would come and go throughout the day. On the few occasions when I thought to check my temperature, there had been no fever to explain my symptoms. It was therefore unlikely to be an ear infection, as Roy had anxiously suggested when I once mentioned it to him. Poor Roy had always fretted about the children whenever they had suffered ear infections growing up, fearful they too might suffer a permanent hearing loss as he had. Instead, I began to suspect there was a cancer growing deep inside me, marking its own coordinates and advancing into the furthest regions of my body. Unnoticed by my family, I had gradually stopped drinking Dr Solander's chalky mixture at mealtimes. It had never helped anyway.

Around me, I sensed a change in tone, like the wind shifting direction. People started talking differently about the war in the Pacific. While New Guinea had generally been deemed necessary, other locations were more contentious. The Bougainville campaign was especially controversial. Some said there was little point; that it was now just a politician's war and that it was time to bring our troops home. Others spoke of it as a clean-up operation, a necessary part of the overall strategy to defeat Japan. The only thing everyone did agree on was that they wanted the war to be over. News of repatriated POWs shipped back from Europe, accompanied by newsreel images of joyous reunions, left me jealous and ashamed. 'Give me back my little boy,' I whispered softly as I moved through the empty rooms of our house, burning for the opportunity to plead my son's case.

Each day, Roy continued to read the paper from cover to cover.

But although he must have formed an opinion about the Australian Brigades still in Bougainville, he said nothing to me. I was convinced he now regretted any part he'd played in Henry's decision to enlist. In truth, I no longer blamed Roy at all. If anyone was at fault, it was I. What had ever made me dare believe I should be a mother? How could I have presumed to think my children would escape harm? As for Henry, though his dreams of developing the next big military innovation showed no signs of ever coming to fruition, he never admitted his mistake.

And so time passed. Each week, I would draft a letter to Henry, calling forth every ounce of strength and optimism I could possibly muster, hoping desperately to capture this energy within the flimsy folds of paper so that my son might be fortified by each line as he read. Afterwards, I would almost collapse from the effort and would remain quiet and withdrawn for the rest of the day. Henry's replies were far less regular. Sometimes there was nothing for weeks at a time, then suddenly two or even three letters would arrive the same day. They were censored, of course. Place names, regiments and who knew what else; forever erased by a neat sequence of snips that made me picture a body riddled with bullet holes. To avoid the censor's zeal, we'd all learned to keep our letters strictly personal, filled with trivial details to which no one could object.

In contrast to my rambling letters to Henry, to which Roy would add a few cheery lines, his replies were frustratingly short. Nevertheless, they served the purpose of letting us know he was alive. Apart from his wisdom tooth, Henry had mercifully remained in good health thus far – unlike many others, who we heard suffered from dysentery and other tropical ailments. And although brief and censored, they still occasionally provided welcome glimpses into his daily life. In characteristic Aussie fashion, it seemed many of the men went by their nicknames, chosen ironically rather than with any intent to flatter. Captain Kelly, for instance, was re-christened Ned or Nelly Kelly. Likewise, when it was discovered that the Staff Captain was a tram conductor in civilian life, he earned the moniker of Ding Ding, the lads wasting no time in whittling him down to size. According to Henry, blokes with red hair were automatically called Blue, while he himself was alternately known as Professor (because he had gone to a GPS school and university whereas most of the other boys had left school at fourteen) or Shorty. 'Because I'm tall,' Henry added, rather unnecessarily, prompting a laugh even from me.

Folding away one such letter after having re-read it for the third or fourth time that day, I had turned to Roy in bewilderment. 'Surely all this joking around is nothing more than a smoke screen. These young men act as if they're infallible. Who are they really kidding? Do they think that death can't happen to them?'

'Of course, that's what they think, Lill. They've got to think that way. How else could they go to war?'

~

As 1944 approached its end, there was cause for hope. Continued Allied firebombing had left its mark on Japan. The promise of victory hung in the air. But for me, so long as the war continued, all hope felt illusory. I stayed home most days now. Sometimes I hardly bothered to get dressed. Even walking our local streets, the only pastime that had brought me respite, no longer held the same pleasure when confronted by flags at half-mast. Every day, I felt my breathing grow shallower and my appetite reduce. The less I did, the more Roy stepped up to fill the gap. He was a good man, my husband. He did most of the shopping now and even helped to prepare the meals when I had one of my headaches. He was, however, persistent in his plea that I spend more time with Margery – to offer help with schoolwork or to take her on an outing – but whenever I tried to speak to my daughter, it always seemed to end with Margery asking me to leave her room. It was safer to let Roy handle things for now.

But not even I could ignore the letter from Ravenswood's

longstanding headmistress when it arrived in the mail. Prompted by professional courtesy towards me as a former staff member, the purpose of her letter was to forewarn us of the likely results of Margery's Leaving Certificate examinations. Knowing my wish for Margery to attend Sydney University, Miss Crago suggested we prepare ourselves for an alternative course of action for the new year.

'Oh Margie, I can't believe it.' My voice shook. 'Look at what Miss Crago has written about your mathematics. Even your English! If she's right about your results, you'll never get a place now.'

Margery snatched the paper from my hands. 'I never said I wanted to go to university. That was always your idea, not mine.'

'But these kinds of results, Margery. They show you didn't even try.'

'I did try, Mum. How would you know? I'm not smart like Henry.'

'Rubbish! That's nothing but an excuse. Academic achievement is not just about being born intelligent. It's about applying yourself, young lady. You've grown up surrounded by books, but tell me when have you ever shown any interest in reading them? All you want to do is go to the pictures, listen to music and jitterbug with your friends, or whatever you call that stupid dance. If you'd put the same effort into your studies as in setting your hair every Friday night, we wouldn't be having this conversation.'

Margery glowered.

'I'm sorry if you don't like hearing what I have to say, but there it is. This is what happens when all you want to do is go out gallivanting, regardless of the consequences.'

'I like going out and having fun. That's what young people are supposed to do. You just want me to stay home and be miserable like you.' Her tone was scathing.

'Don't be rude, please. I don't want you to be miserable. But I do want you to appreciate what you have, especially given what other people are going through, your own brother included.' I opened my arms in a sweeping gesture. 'You take all this for granted. You live in a beautiful home, in a beautiful neighbourhood, but one which you so evidently find boring. You have your own bedroom, which you rarely bother to tidy. You have hot water, indoor plumbing, a telephone and electricity. You go to a good school, where the teachers genuinely care about you and want you to do well. Tennis lessons, dance lessons, a generous allowance, you have it all.' I paused for breath. 'Let's be honest now, shall we? I think it's fair to say you're free to waltz in and out of here whenever it takes your fancy, with a bicycle at your disposal and a father who's always willing to drive you wherever else you might need to go. Even with all the restrictions this war has brought, Margery, your life is a postcard, and so much easier than mine ever was.'

'Lucky me!' returned Margery, her eyes blazing with indignation. 'I don't take it for granted, Mum, no matter what you think. But things are different now. Why can't you understand that?'

'I understand more than you know. For heaven's sake, Margery, you didn't even bother taking care of the last few pairs of nylons I gave you. And now you go around wearing leg paint instead of your lisle stockings, it's hardly respectable. You think you're all grown up, but your behaviour says otherwise. You talk like an American and you claim to be modern, but that doesn't give you an excuse to be irresponsible.'

'You have no idea, Mum. If you think I'm irresponsible, you should hear what other girls get up to – and not just the "fast" girls, as you would call them. Rosemary's sister goes out dancing with a different Yank every weekend. Her fiancé is in Borneo and not even that stops her. I'm perfectly normal and you're just too old-fashioned to see that.'

'Is it old-fashioned to think that my daughter could have a university education? To choose her own profession. To have a real career. At least until you have a family of your own and, even then – it could be your choice.'

Margery sneered. 'You talk like a feminist and tell me that I should have a profession, but you're not out there working, are you? Even if you didn't want to teach anymore, you could still make yourself useful in other ways during this war – most other women are doing their bit – but you just hide yourself away from everyone and everything.'

I fought the urge to slap her face. 'Have you looked in the newspaper lately at the job listings for women? Without a degree, your options will be very limited, my girl. And what do you think will happen when the men come back? Who do you think the best jobs will go to? Either way, you'll be paid less to do the same work and with fewer opportunities for advancement.'

'I don't want any of those jobs in the newspaper. I want to design clothes. I'm good at it, as you would know if you paid the least bit of attention to how I spend my time when I am home. I'm already sewing outfits for my friends and some of their mothers. And they pay me too.' Angry tears spilled down Margery's face, her long painted lashes now glued together in wet sticky clumps.

'Oh Margery, I don't want to argue with you. I know you have an eye for fashion – heaven knows Mrs Campbell always said you were a talented seamstress – but how do you expect to make a good income from that? Don't you want more for yourself in life?'

'It's not like that, Mum. I do have a plan for the future.'

'Go ahead, I'm waiting.' I tapped my foot impatiently.

'I was thinking that for now, I could just work with Dad and do my dressmaking on the side. But when the war is over, what I'd really like to do is work in films. In fashion and costume design.' Margery swallowed. 'I could even go to Hollywood.'

'Leave your family and go to another country? You would really do that?' I felt myself begin to shake as a renewed surge of heat pulsed through me. 'I think it's time for you to face facts and grow up, my girl. My mother always said it did no one any good to spare the rod – we've obviously indulged you too much. I suggest you forget all about Hollywood. And while you're at it, you can also forget about working for your father. I think you'll find that Manpower will have another job in mind for you. If you won't listen to me, perhaps the Australian Government will teach you what it means to work hard, and for very little return.'

Margery glared at me, her pretty face contorted with loathing.

'Really, Margery. You should be ashamed. And not only because of these examination results. Your brother is out there risking his life for ... for you and me and God knows who else ... while you stand here and think only of yourself.'

'And you think only of Henry,' said Margery in a voice devoid of all emotion and walked out, slamming the door behind her.

Chapter 23
'An Artist's Journey'

When Roy came home that evening, he looked at the letter from Margery's headmistress and gave a wry shrug. Assuming his customary role of family diplomat, he calmed everyone down – first me and later Margery. We made a deal with Margery. If the Leaving Certificate results were as unsatisfactory as Miss Crago had led us to expect, Margery would stay on at school and repeat her examinations next year, trying for a better Leaving Pass. If she did well enough, university might still be on the cards. If not, surely the war would be over by then and the threat of Manpower with it. Margery would be free to pursue the qualification of her choice.

While Roy shared my dismay at the idea of our daughter travelling alone overseas after the war, he was less dismissive of her newly revealed ambitions.

'Perhaps Margie takes after my brother,' he said in bed that night. 'Think of the sketches she makes when she's designing a new dress for herself, or that suit she did for Mrs Goode.'

'She's a talented girl, I know that. And she probably does have your side of the family to thank for her creativity – it didn't come from me, that's for sure.'

Roy chortled. 'On the other hand, if she ever does go into costume design, she could always adopt your maiden name as her professional name and just change the spelling – Margery *Tailor*, "seamstress to the stars" ... has a certain ring to it, doesn't it?'

'Very funny.'

'Sorry, I thought we both could use a laugh. But seriously though, she could always go to art school, like Reggie and me, and work as a commercial artist – in advertising, or fashion magazines or what have you?'

'She's certainly stubborn enough to succeed, if that's what she's made up her mind to do,' I allowed.

'Exactly.' Roy grinned. 'Wonder where she got that from? She's plucky, that's all. A real bobby-dazzler, our girl. I know she might not be following the plans we had for her, but life doesn't always work out according to plan. Does it, love?'

~

After breakfast the next morning, I heard Margery leave. I put on the kettle and set about tidying the kitchen, while Roy read Saturday's *Herald* in the other room.

I loaded the cups and saucers on a tray, balancing the teapot. Roy patted the sofa, inviting me to sit beside him.

As I shuffled forward to pour two cups, I cast an idle glance over his shoulder. And when he turned the page, a headline and accompanying visuals caught my eye. 'An Artist's Journey into Australia's "Lost World"'.

Roy noticed my interest. 'It's a special report on the drought, a three-part instalment – I had no idea the situation was this bad. They're saying it's our worst yet. Seems like the government wanted it kept quiet during the war these past years, so they're only now telling us the real story. It wouldn't have done any good for the Japanese to see signs of weakness, I suppose.'

'The worst drought in Australia's history? That's quite some claim.'

I frowned, sceptical of whether it could be any worse than the great Federation Drought, as that hellish time later came to be known. Years without proper rainfall had created the tinderbox conditions for the raging fire that claimed my family in January 1900.

I looked at the sub-heading, 'Western Inferno: The country in which there are no bushfires. There is nothing to burn.' If only that were true. Bitter experience had taught me that dry grass burned better than fresh vegetation. High temperatures, an absence of humidity and a ruthless wind took care of the rest.

'Fascinating report,' mused Roy, looking up. 'What they did was send one of their top journos, Keith Newman, on a two-week assignment into some of the affected regions and rural communities to give a proper eye-witness report on the drought and the soil erosion that comes with it. Plus, they sent Russell Drysdale along with him to make sketches. Look here, love.'

I knew Russell Drysdale as one of the country's most promising young artists. Curious, I glanced back again, this time focusing on the illustrations not the text. There were six or seven sketches on the page, some of them just simple line drawings, others more detailed, yet they were all rendered with sensitivity and pathos.

Roy scratched at the stubble of his unshaven chin. 'This reminds me of when *The Bulletin* sent Henry Lawson out to the far north-west of the colony all those years ago to tell the city folk how things really were in the bush. Back in the early nineties – but, of course, you know all about that. All the way up the Western train line to Bourke, and from there onto Hungerford, right up on the Queensland border. *Bananaland*, as they used to say.' Roy smirked.

Of course I knew this, so I simply nodded, waiting to see where he was going.

'I'm pretty sure Archibald sent him out there to keep him off the drink, as much as anything else. It was a good thing he went, too – even if he never did stop drinking – because a lot of his best writing came out of that time. Assuming, that is, you're willing to include "The Drover's Wife" in that category,' he added apologetically.

I shrugged, waiting for the familiar smouldering of old resentment to flare in me against the writer who had taken my story ... and was surprised when it did not come. Truth be told, I was numb to almost everything these days. Other than Henry, of course, and last night's latest fight with Margery.

'Your mate Mr Lawson must have been a busy boy that year he met your mum. He also had that literary debate going with Banjo Paterson in *The Bulletin*. On one side there was Banjo, who wrote about the bush like a true romantic. And on the other was Henry, who never let you forget the grim reality. Henry accused Banjo of being a toff, and Banjo said Henry ought to stick to the city because he didn't know how to appreciate anything else. What was it Banjo said to him at the end of that one poem?'

I pursed my lips and supplied the missing quote. 'For the bush will never suit you, and you'll never suit the bush.'

'That's it, Lill. Well done!' Roy slapped his thigh and laughed, nearly spilling his tea. 'Two poets battling it out in verse. Talk about a genius publicity stunt.' He paused, chuckling quietly. 'Funny though, isn't it? Even though their attitudes were like chalk and cheese, we still think of them as our two greatest bush poets. Banjo Paterson, the bard of the bush, and Henry Lawson, the voice of the bush, the poet of Australia ... the minstrel of its people.'

'The man responsible for putting the capital B into the Australian Bush,' I interjected sarcastically.

Roy nodded. 'I guess back then, going into Federation, the country needed writing like that to bring the colonies together and help create a sense of national identity. The unsung heroes of the bush, you know the drill. Come to think of it, we still need that kind of inspiration now too. Probably more than ever.' He paused again, his expression thoughtful. 'Sometimes I wonder what stories we'll be telling ourselves when we come out of this war. What do you reckon, Lill? Heroes of the bush – man against nature – the legend of Anzac – mateship above all ... we still hold true to all that, I guess, but I'm not sure if people will be talking about Mother England for much longer. Time to stand on our own two feet from now on, I say.

'Anyway, love, take a look for yourself,' Roy concluded, draining the last of his tea and handing me the newspaper as he got up. 'If you ask me, I'd say Lawson and Drysdale must have come face-to-face with a lot of the same godforsaken sights on their travels. Never mind that they ended up in slightly different parts of the state, or that more than fifty years stands between them. It'll be interesting, I reckon, to see how people react this time around.'

I settled into a more comfortable position on the sofa and studied each of the sketches. It was clear from the images and their descriptions that both writer and artist had been profoundly affected by the devastation encountered during their assignment.

'Talons of the desert grope in miles of drifting sand,' read the description of a grotesquely formed tree lying on its side, an apparent victim of soil erosion. 'From amongst the rotting carcasses of sheep rise the dry skeletons of trees that died in an agony of thirst,' read another. A cluster of derelict huts gave rise to even more figurative language, like something from a Gothic horror tale. 'The windows of the houses are like black sockets whose eyes have perished with despair.'

In contrast to these poetically worded titles, the caption for the first line drawing read simply. 'A drovers' camp near Deniliquin.'

Drover. It was strange how the word still held such power over me.

Conjuring images of my father, whether from memory or imagination, it belonged to a time in my life that could never be recovered. A time when I still had a family and a home. A time of childish innocence, of naive certainty, before I had discovered how quickly life could be snatched away.

I reached for my reading spectacles and looked at the little drawing more closely. In the background was a covered wagon and pair of horses. Beside them, a man's figure – presumably that of the drover – was bent over, tending to his animals. To one side, a lone tree, bare and thin, was the only vegetation in sight, along with a few heavy lines and patches of shading that might have signified scrub or the movement of sand. A few scattered belongings lay on the ground. In front of this rustic temporary camp, a lone woman dominated the foreground. From beneath the shade of her hat, she faced directly outwards, hands on her hips, as if challenging the artist to cast judgement on this lonely scene. Yet far from reflecting criticism, or judgement of any kind, Drysdale had imbued the scene and its characters with a simple dignity. And so rather than feeling sympathy, as I might have expected, for this woman and her lot, I found myself regarding the drover's wife with quiet admiration.

The drover's wife. There it was again. Already Roy had made the connection between this trip and that of Lawson's, and now here was an echo of the drover's wife from Lawson's story – from my story – transposed into an image. The same yet different. For one thing, the drover himself was present – there in the flesh, this time – no longer absent as in the story. And as in life. Yet what struck me most about this sketch was the way the woman stood apart from her husband and looked straight out at me from there in the drawing; she was just a woman in a landscape – no more, no less – living life the best way she knew how.

Unlike Henry Lawson's idealised version of my mother, there was something even more compelling about Drysdale's version. Though humbly dressed, with nothing separating her from the dry dusty earth but an old pair of sandshoes, this new embodiment of the drover's wife stood her ground and commanded respect.

Lawson's famous story had painted the drover's wife as a kind of hero, a bush heroine. That much was true. However, as much as I had never wanted to acknowledge it, there had always been something pitiful about her character – the sense that no matter how many trials and tribulations she overcame, someone or something else would always have the last laugh. Equally tragic were her attempts to keep an orderly house, to dress the children in their Sunday best and push the old perambulator through the bush, as if she were going to do the block in the city, and to admire the fashion plates of the *Young Ladies' Journal* even as she presumed to teach her children how to read. I'd always hated the way Lawson made it seem like she should feel ashamed of the aspirations she'd held as a young bride – building 'castles in the air', as he called them – only to make her dress up in her husband's clothes, forcing her into being someone other than herself just to scare off passing tramps.

In contrast, this small simple sketch from Russell Drysdale revealed her inherent feminine strength. In my mind, at least, he had allowed the drover's wife to speak for herself.

Chapter 24

Little Boy

'Did you hear me, Lill? I'm heading off to work now.' Roy's voice was muffled by the bathroom door. 'I'm just going to drop in on old Mr Bowen first and make sure his fireplace is still drawing properly, and then I'll go straight from there.'

After murmuring an acknowledgement, I soaked the flannel in the basin, pressing its warmth against my face and inhaling deeply.

'Margery's not feeling well again. I've told her she can stay home from school. Check on her please, love, as soon as you're up and about.'

'All right,' I called back, loud enough for Roy to hear me.

'Maybe you should take her to see Dr Solander this morning? Poor thing looks quite pale.'

'If you think so.'

'Thanks, love. I'll be off then. Try to have a good day, won't you? I'll leave work right away if the announcement comes through. It could be any time now.'

I soaked the cloth a second time and covered my eyes. Margery had been looking unwell in recent weeks. Perhaps, like everyone else, she was simply sick of the war.

I pressed the cloth against my temples and kept up my breathing; 1945 was proving no easier to endure than the last year. From all corners of the globe, world leaders had been falling like flies, worn down by the strain of nearly six years of war and, quite possibly, the weight of their own consciences. First it was Roosevelt, then the macabre sight of Mussolini and his entourage, strung up by Italian partisans like rotting carcasses, and then, just as the German forces finally surrendered, came the news of Hitler's demise.

Early reports were conflicting. The official German news announced he had died a hero's death while fighting off the Allies from his bunker in Berlin. Himmler claimed his Führer had suffered a brain haemorrhage, while another Nazi official indicated suicide. The Soviets had rejected all these explanations, maintaining Hitler had vanished weeks earlier and was being hidden underground. All that mattered to me was that this demented Aryan dictator was finally gone and that the Germans had surrendered.

But even after victory in Europe was declared on the 8th of May, still the leaders kept falling from all ends of the world. Just last month, our own Prime Minister Curtin had died in his sleep, robbed of the opportunity to see the Pacific War reach its end. Even Churchill, though very much alive, had been forced to step down after the recent British election and resign as Prime Minister. The man who had led Britain through war was apparently not to be the one to guide her into peace. Of all the major powers, only Stalin, Kai-shek and Hirohito remained standing. How much longer would they last?

The war was moving swiftly now, almost faster than I dared believe. In the past, my family had accused me of burying my head in the sand, but lately, with Henry's life still hanging in the balance, I wanted to know everything that was happening. I was keeping watch for that one vital development which could bring our son home.

With the Allies having secured victory in Europe, the Axis had finally collapsed, and all eyes had turned to the Pacific. After more than a year of American firebombing, devastating one Japanese city after another and killing hundreds of thousands of civilians, only an unconditional surrender could save Japan from complete annihilation. And now even that seemed too late. America's new president had sent shockwaves throughout the world by unleashing his country's mightiest weapons yet. Under Truman's authority, high-powered atomic bombs had been dropped on the Japanese cities of Hiroshima and Nagasaki only days earlier, with many more yet to follow. 'Prompt and utter destruction', the Big Three had threatened from the Potsdam Conference last month in Germany. Now we all knew what this ultimatum had really meant.

To top it all off, and despite its former pact, the Soviet Union had also just declared war on the Japanese Empire. Within hours of its declaration on Thursday, Russian troops had already entered the territory of Manchuria where things had begun so many years before. Where would it all end? When would it end? How many more lives would be sacrificed before peace was restored?

I caught sight of my reflection in the mirror and grimaced. Those first few threads of silver in my hair from before the war had multiplied tenfold since then, taking over like new recruits advancing through the ranks. Roy said he liked the way they sparkled in the sunshine like tinfoil, but all I saw was a leaden shade of grey. I patted my face dry and tightened the belt of my dressing gown.

When I entered the kitchen, I found Margery at the table, still dressed in her school uniform and surrounded by what appeared to be several days' worth of newspapers. Dry toast and black tea stood before her untouched. Roy was right, she did look pale. She had not been herself for some time.

Miss Crago's original warning about Margery's results had sadly proven accurate, leaving Roy with little choice but to enforce the bargain we'd struck with our daughter back in December. Her subsequent return to school had still sparked a spate of fresh arguments as Margery was made to swallow her pride and resume studies with the girls from the grade below. All through term one and even into the beginning of her second school trimester, Margery had refused to curtail her socialising, and I'd feared this second attempt at doing her Leaving Certificate would be no better than her first.

Surprisingly though, around the time of the VE celebrations in May, there had been a complete about face. Virtually overnight, Margery's attitude became more serious. She started spending more time in her room with her books and correspondingly less time with her friends. Even though her latest school results had not yet shown improvement, I felt her newfound diligence boded well. Roy and I had quietly congratulated ourselves on our decision to hold her back. Perhaps Margery had merely been slow to mature and to accept her responsibilities. As Roy liked to remind me, growing up under the dark cloud of war could not have been easy for her.

'Good morning, sweetheart,' I said, with an effort at brightness. I filled the kettle and placed it on the gas ring with a clang.

Startled by the sound, Margery looked up. I saw tears in her eyes and felt the breath rush from my lungs. I lurched forward to snatch the open newspaper from her hands. 'Is that today's paper? Is it Henry? Let me see!'

'No, Mum, it's not Henry,' Margery said, sniffing loudly. 'It's these atomic bombs they've dropped on Japan. Two thousand times more powerful than any other bomb that's ever been created, that's what it says here. Every day on the radio, we hear them boasting about how clever they are to have discovered this new technology and to have beaten the Nazis to it. How atomic energy will revolutionise industry and modern living – like it's some whopping great secret they're excited to share – but it's awful. Just awful.'

I exhaled slowly and rubbed my chest, my heart still beating frantically. Every morning, Roy performed his self-appointed special duty on behalf of us all when he checked the newspaper, running his finger down the Army List of Casualties in the *Herald* – once, twice, a third time – making 100 per cent sure Henry's name was not on it. Bypassing the list of soldiers abroad, Roy would home in on the second grouping, for those men serving in Australia and the Islands. The various lists and categories alone were enough to trigger my nightmares: *killed in action ... died of illness ... previously reported dangerously ill ... accidentally drowned ... wounded in action ... accidentally wounded.* There were so many ways for a soldier to meet, or to prolong, his death. If nothing else, the army was committed to reporting on each of these events with military precision.

I listened as Margery continued her rant, uncharacteristically passionate about world affairs.

'I don't give a fig how many stinking Japanese tanks or factories we destroy. And I couldn't care less how many of their soldiers are killed in this war – they can all bite the dust as far as I'm concerned, if it means bringing our boys home safely – but these atomic bombs change everything. Why the heck would anyone want to create something like that?'

'Who knows?' I replied, choosing to ignore my daughter's salty language. 'So long as men are on this earth, they will always be competing to make the most powerful weapons. Tools, machinery, guns – to some men, it's all the same thing. They can't seem to help themselves, it's in their nature.'

I'd never forgotten Henry's unbridled enthusiasm for the Owen machine gun early in the war and shuddered to think of his reaction to this latest technical innovation. Though it pained me to admit, I knew he'd be fascinated to hear that science had found a way to split the uranium atom to release such a concentrated form of energy.

'Yes, but now that they've invented atomic energy, what's to stop another country using it against us next time? Can you imagine if they dropped one of these bombs over London or New York? Or here in Sydney?'

Gone, gone in the blink of an eye, was my first thought, and I felt strangely detached from the notion, until a fresh idea rose to the surface and my thoughts flew back to Henry. What if Japan ultimately refused to capitulate? What if the Americans kept releasing more of these atomic bombs in the Pacific, as they'd said they would? Not just on the islands of Japan, but further south where battles were still being waged – in Borneo or the Solomons, or anywhere else that Australian forces were stationed? The Americans had been trying to drive the Japanese out of the islands for an eternity. What if someone decided this was the most efficient way to finish the job? For a posse of white-haired old men viewing the war from their ivory towers, such an end might appear to justify the means.

'Don't think about it, Margery, you'll only upset yourself. You really don't look well, sweetheart. Is it your time of the month? Have you tried a hot water bottle on your tummy? That always used to help me.'

Margery stiffened and shook her head.

'Or something you ate? It's been going on for weeks now. I suppose it could be your gall bladder. Dad thinks I should take you to Dr Solander.'

'Look at this photograph, Mum. It's the first picture they've released. Think of all the children, all the babies. Burned alive. Incinerated. *Seared to death*, that one headline said.'

I recoiled, trying desperately not to think of my mother and siblings. 'Surely, they're not showing any of that?'

'Not yet, they're not. This just shows the explosion. It's enormous! This is the second bomb from Thursday – the one over Nagasaki. They say even the flash of the blast is blinding. The American aircrew have to wear special sunglasses to protect their eyes. And afterwards, all the boiling radioactive particles just pour out all over the place, but you can't see what's happening because everything's just covered in dust and smoke for miles, and then it rises into the sky like a giant cloud – more than twenty thousand feet high, they say. Imagine being inside that. This picture was taken three minutes after they dropped the bomb. Look at it, Mum.'

Margery thrust the newspaper at me. She was right. It did look like a cloud – a giant, mushroom-shaped cloud. It reminded of the red dust storms I knew as a child, and I could well imagine the ash and grit and God knew what else trapped within its raging tides.

I took a step back and closed my eyes. Since news of the first atomic bomb had hit last Tuesday, Roy and I had spoken of little else. Like many others, my husband was convinced this shocking new weapon would bring an immediate end to the Pacific War. Our own newly elected Prime Minister had been less optimistic at first. Even after the first bomb, Prime Minister Chifley had predicted the war would continue another twelve months, though after the second, even larger bomb on Nagasaki and Russia's declaration of war, he too had changed his tune. I pressed my fingers against my temples and breathed heavily. How could I possibly bear waiting for Henry for another year? If it was all going to end soon anyway, why not bring the men home now – before any more of them died?

'I don't understand how the Allies can use something like this when they aren't even allowed to use poison gas,' Margery continued. 'Tokyo is calling it a crime against humanity, and I agree.'

'So do I, Margery, so do I.'

My daughter's outrage was entirely understandable, yet I had rarely known her to express such empathy towards others, let alone the Japanese.

'Your father says the main reason we haven't used poison gas in this war is less about an international agreement to ban its use than about the fact that it was never terribly efficient anyway. Now that they've found a weapon that can kill and destroy on a grand scale, I don't suppose they'll let the opportunity go by. Even if they do have to go back and change the rules to make it legal.'

According to Roy, President Truman was already planning to

reconvene Congress to consider a revision of the United Nations' Charter, in light of the possibilities of an atomic age.

'But how can that be fair?' Margery's face was pinched in fury.

'It's not fair, Margery. None of it is fair.'

'Dad says now that Russia has declared war against Japan, they'll have to give up and surrender unconditionally.'

'I hope so, I really do.'

If these new weapons didn't bring an end to the war, nothing would. Yet how could peace be built on such fragile foundations? Like rotten wood hammered into quicksand, I feared nothing good or lasting could come of this.

We had all been relieved when, by Saturday, the first clear signs had appeared that Japan might be ready to concede defeat. 'Japanese Government Seeks Peace – Ultimatum Accepted with Reservation', proclaimed the *Herald*'s front page. And although Japan's conditional surrender had triggered celebrations throughout the country all weekend, with thousands of boisterous young people gathering in Kings Cross and the city, I shared our Prime Minister's opinion that such celebrations were pre-emptive. Nothing was definite until it really was definite. The original Declaration from Potsdam had been crystal clear; no reservations, no deviations, no alternatives. If Japan could not come to terms with putting the fate of her emperor, as well as the nation, into the hands of her victors, then what? My worst fear was that they might choose to carry on fighting to the end.

'Barbara's mother says the Vatican have called the atomic bomb a death instrument that will cast a sinister shadow over the future of humanity,' said Margery.

'Surely it's done that already.'

Where was their Christian mercy, I wondered, when they made the decision to play God? I also wondered about the researchers and technicians who'd worked for years to perfect the bomb for Hiroshima –

educated, intelligent men of science and engineering. Men like Henry and Charlie. What did they tell themselves when they went to sleep at night?

'But Barbara's dad says it's the hope of the future. He says we'll all be using atomic energy soon at home and that everyone's standard of living will be better for it.'

I pinched the bridge of my nose and shrugged. 'I don't think there's anything wrong with our standard of living as it is – at least, not once the war is behind us and rationing stops. The more people have, the more they want.'

Margery avoided my glance and continued reading to herself. Unable to stop myself, I took a closer look at the photograph. A dark column of smoke rose from its base, transforming into a graceful cloud of white billowing up to the sky. It hardly looked real, more like something from the Bible – all fire and brimstone, heaven and hell. Impossible to imagine all that coming from a single B-29 bomber plane.

Roy had told me the aircraft commander who had dropped the first bomb on Hiroshima had been allowed to name the plane after his mother, Enola Gay, stencilled in large capital letters beneath the cockpit. No doubt he intended this as a good luck charm or a mark of respect for the woman who raised him, but to me, it seemed more a curse than an honour. What a horrific legacy for any mother, to have played a part in this air massacre.

This war needed to end. *I* needed it to end. But why did it have to be like this?

Dabbing angrily at my eyes with the collar of my dressing gown, I took today's newspaper from Margery and lay it down on the table, scanning the other headlines: 'Allies Lay Down Five Conditions'. There it was in black-and-white. The Japanese had received their answer. And now the whole world would have to have to wait and see how the emperor reacted. I flipped over the paper with a decisive gesture, grateful to see nothing more frightening than the tight-set columns of the classifieds.

'Come on now, darling,' I said firmly. 'We're not helping anyone by dwelling on all this. I'll make an appointment for you to see Dr Solander this afternoon. And if you're going to be home from school today, you may as well do some studying while you're at it. Try and get some more of that toast into yourself first, though. I'll make you another cup of tea to help wash it down.'

Margery regarded me morosely, clearly unconvinced. Yet again she appeared on the verge of tears. I took two cups from the dresser and made a point of setting them down loudly on the bench. A few moments later came the sound of a key turning in the front door. I was surprised to see Roy walking down the hallway towards us.

'I thought you said you were going straight to work from Mr Bowen's place – did you forget something?'

Roy started to speak but then abruptly pivoted on his feet, swinging his gaze towards Margery, whose cheeks were now streaked with a telltale silvery trail of tears. Choosing not to acknowledge her father's unexpected presence, Margery kept her eyes down, as if even the simple act of refolding a handkerchief required all her attention.

I clicked my tongue and forced my lips into a smile. 'The kettle's just about to boil. Would you like a cup? I suppose you're running late, as it is.'

Roy's face was strangely mottled. He opened his mouth as if to answer then leaned forward to grasp hold of a chair, slowly lowering himself onto it and pulling at his collar.

'Roy, what is it? Are you sick?'

He looked at me blankly. His eyes darted back towards Margery, who was still crying softly, and he grabbed her arm. 'Did you hear me out there, Margie? Did you hear me talking to the postman?' The voice that came out was strangled and hoarse.

I raised my hand to silence Margery, who had finally looked up, evidently confused by his question.

'What do you mean, Roy?' I asked, my own voice now sharp with worry. 'I thought you'd gone. What were you talking to him about? What's the matter with you?'

It suddenly hit me. 'The war's over – isn't it?' I gasped. 'Japan's finally surrendered! Have they just made the announcement? Oh my God, I can't believe it.' Blood charged through my veins, singing in my ears. I felt weak and dizzy with relief.

'No, sweetheart, it's not that,' Roy whispered.

'What then? They haven't dropped another bomb on Japan, have they? Not already?'

Roy sat silent and dazed before us, seemingly rendered speechless by whatever news he had just been told. Only his hands were trembling, as if gripped by cold or fear. Half-crumpled within them, I saw a slip of pink paper.

Pink. Like a telegram. Like a telegram from the army.

My mind whirred, clicking furiously through a thousand explanations like a camera shutter set to maximum speed. A deafening sound came from within as heartbeats rained against my chest like bullets, ready to explode.

'What does it say, Roy? Is it a telegram about Henry? Has he been injured?'

Roy opened his mouth, but this time no words came out at all. His voice broke into a high-pitched cry of anguish. He bent over the table and began to sob uncontrollably, like a little boy.

As my legs finally gave out from under me, I caught a fleeting glance of Margery's green eyes widening in understanding and the corners of the kitchen blurring into a cloud of gathering steam. The last sound I heard before everything went dark was the shrill high-pitched whistle of the kettle coming to the boil.

Chapter 25

It's Over

When I opened my eyes, I was laid out on the sofa. Roy was crouched awkwardly beside me, a glass of water in one hand, pink slip of paper in the other. Slowly the room came into focus, details sharpening as I looked warily from left to right.

A soft keening sound broke the silence.

'Hush now, sweetheart,' I heard Roy say, as he pressed a moist palm against my cheek. 'We've lost our Henry – our darling boy is gone.'

Still the keening persisted, rising to an unearthly crescendo until I could no longer hear Roy's voice.

Little by little, it dawned on me that this ghastly cry was coming from my own lips. Gratefully, I surrendered myself to its will, gliding like a bird from one note to the next, flying further and further into the light. Roy's hands were sliding across my face, now slick with tears. It was becoming harder to breathe, my mouth opening and closing in ragged gasps. Faster and faster came the sound of moaning until my head was spinning free of all thought and the room went dark once more.

~

This time, when I opened my eyes, I covered Roy's mouth before he could speak and took the telegram. Tears streamed as the typed words blurred and swayed in my vision, bleeding into each other on the pink slip of paper. I read the short message over and over, grasping for meaning. *Urgent Telegram ... deeply regret to inform you ... the death of your son Private Henry Evan Armstrong ... 3rd August 1945 ... after being wounded in action on 24th July 1945 ... profound sympathy ...* The same desperate phrases leaped out at me every time but made no sense. The telegram was saying Henry had died ten days ago. How could that be? How could I not have known if my own son were dead? And if he had been wounded in action earlier – on July 24th, as they claimed – then should his name not have appeared on the newspaper casualties list before now? There was no information about our son's injuries, about how or why he died, or even where. Excruciating waves of pain ripped through my chest, leaving me breathless yet again. What had they done to my little boy? Where was he now, all alone out there?

Overcome by the thought of his lifeless body, I let out another agonising cry before finally allowing Roy to guide me to the bedroom.

Later, I heard Dr Solander's strident voice and felt the sting of a needle in my arm. I slept.

~

Two days later, on August 15th, came the announcement everyone had been waiting for – the one I had mistakenly thought had already occurred. Japan had finally surrendered. The war was officially over.

I'd been lying in bed, legs to my chest, eyes closed but awake, when I heard Margery and Roy talking loudly in the other room. The radio clicked on with an ugly crackle. The theme from Elgar's military march faded out into the formal voice of the presenter, followed by the working-class accent of Ben Chifley. He spoke for a few minutes, his speech slow and steady, with a slight whistling sound that hinted at a childhood lisp but may just have been static.

Though I'd not been able to hear the finer details of the announcement itself, by the time Roy came in, I knew what he was going to say.

Too late, I thought, as Roy entered the bedroom and told me the news. It didn't matter anymore. My little boy was gone.

Henry was dead. Killed. Our son was dead now. Though I repeated the words over and over, like a broken record, I could not believe them to be true. If I waited patiently enough, it might all have been a dream, no more real than a nightmare. I might yet wake.

Roy had stopped talking and was taking off his shoes to lie with me on the bed. He placed his head beside mine on the pillow, and I moved over to make room. I felt the weight of his long limbs enfolding me from behind and allowed myself to disappear into his embrace as we quietly wept together. All at once, we heard children's voices in the distance. Shrieks of glee and laughter carried up from the valley as they ran down Rosedale Road.

'They must have been let out early,' Roy murmured, holding me tight. 'The rest of today and tomorrow will be a public holiday.'

'Yes.' Across the country, peace celebrations and church services had been planned for days, waiting only for this announcement.

A knock at the door. Margery crept in and sat tentatively at the foot of our bed.

'Why couldn't Japan have surrendered last month?' she asked, her voice catching. 'Then America would never have dropped those horrible bombs and Henry would still be alive. Poor Henry,' she cried. 'It isn't fair.'

I reached for her hand and stroked it mechanically. For once, Margery and I were on the same wavelength.

After a time, Roy and Margery both left the room, and I heard the radio turn back on. A live ABC broadcast from somewhere in the city, most likely Martin Place. In the background, crowds of people cheered and shouted for joy, just as they had after the last war, when I had steered my sixth-formers through the hordes of happy revellers to reach the building where their Leaving Certificate examinations were being held.

Drawn to the radio, I dragged myself off the bed and into the living room. As I sank down into the seat next to Roy and listened to the broadcast, I was reminded of a young woman I'd once met while visiting a friend in hospital who had lost her baby after an unusually protracted first labour. Ordered by her doctor to stay in hospital for a few days to recover, this grief-stricken young woman was made to share a ward with my friend and two other ladies – now mothers – whose babies were wheeled in and out at all hours of the day and night. Forced to look upon each perfect downy-haired infant as it passed her bed and to hear their heartbreaking little cries and gurgles, she confessed it felt like torture; all she wanted was to hear the voice of her own little girl, whose tiny form she had barely glimpsed before it was whisked away. If that were not punishment enough, she also had to suffer the indignity of letting the sister manually express her breastmilk every few hours, to help women whose milk had not yet come in, only to fall victim to mastitis herself on the day she was to go home – the day we met. Listening to the sounds of joy and frivolity coming from the radio, I finally understood how she must have felt.

I recognised the radio presenter's charismatic voice as that of Talbot Duckmanton, a former pilot and war correspondent. Caught up by the spirit of the day, he took obvious delight in describing the gay scene unfolding around him. Shouting and screaming, whirring their gas alarm rattlers in the air, crammed onto the footboards of trams and spilling out from vehicles of all kinds ... the crowd was quite literally mad with excitement, as he laughingly summed it up for his listeners. Someone had hung an effigy of Adolf Hitler, just as they had with the Kaiser almost thirty years earlier, and people were booing and kicking, while others danced the hokey-pokey. Girls with cheeks painted V for Victory smiled and waved. Over the noise of the crowd, I heard the roar of a Mosquito plane doing steep turns around the GPO.

'It's indecent,' I murmured, unaware I had spoken aloud until the others looked at me in surprise. 'Tens of thousands of Australian men have died. We should all be in mourning not having a public street party.'

'I understand, love, you know I do,' said Roy, chewing his lip. 'But think of the families whose boys are coming home. Folk have suffered through this war in all kinds of ways. They want to celebrate the end of that. It's over now. They want to celebrate peace.'

Peace, I thought, *if only*, and sighed audibly. The war in the Pacific might have ended, but today's fragile peace would not last. One day there would be another war. Today's losers would rise from the mire – as Germany had done after the last war – and try their hand again. Australia and its allies might not be so 'lucky' next time. Pandora's box had been opened. The secrets of atomic energy could not be kept forever. Who knew what might happen next?

Roy nudged me, nodding his head towards the radio. 'Good man,' he said, swallowing with difficulty. 'We're not alone in this.'

Mr Duckmanton had shifted gears. Putting aside the boisterous displays of merrymaking in Martin Place for the moment, he invited listeners to reflect on the sadness of the occasion and consider those who had made the supreme sacrifice. He drew attention to the Cenotaph, and the many people stopping to raise their hats before this cherished World War I memorial. My eyes grew misty as I nodded stiffly at Roy, temporarily appeased.

Since the telegram's arrival, Margery had not gone back to school and Roy had told his staff to make do without him. The prospect of a future without Henry was unimaginable. Monday felt like an eternity ago. Nothing would ever be the same. Time would always be divided into before and after. And while today's announcement would bring relief to many, nothing would bring back my little boy.

As the broadcast continued, I saw a faint glimmer in Roy's eyes. Like the vicarious pleasure that mothers so often derived from their children's achievements, or that I myself gained from reading, Roy had always drawn comfort from the happiness of others. He was lucky in that regard, and I did not want to ruin this for him. Though my own life was over, I owed it to Roy and Margery to let theirs go on.

'I'll get dressed,' I said, leaning over to kiss Roy's cheek before I stood.

For the rest of the day, I moved through the house like a machine, going through the familiar futile motions of cooking and cleaning. The next morning, I got up and did it again. And so, it would continue.

~

Weeks passed and spring unfolded in the garden. Inside our house, my family underwent its own transition. One by one, grief pulled us into its merciless grip, then cast us out in different directions like leaves scattered by the wind.

Without relinquishing his watchful gaze over Margery and me, Roy responded by turning outwards, choosing to direct his pain into lessening that of others. More and more horror stories surfaced from the war. Heinous tales of murder, massacre and other atrocities, of unspeakable Japanese cruelty towards the Australian POWs and – at the other extreme – acts of ritual suicide or hara-kiri, almost incomprehensible to a Western mind. From under the cloud of ground zero and the cataclysmic events of Hiroshima and Nagasaki emerged sickening reports of victims and survivors. So too from Europe came grisly eye-witness accounts of suffering, starvation and survival from the Nazi concentration and labour camps and the indescribable horror of the death camps themselves. As the Allies prepared for the coming military tribunals, war criminals everywhere were being rounded up to await trial and execution.

Faced with such large-scale evil, Roy threw himself into forging connections with returned soldiers from our own neighbourhood, doing anything and everything to help smooth their way as they returned to families and old occupations or took up new roles in our rapidly evolving post-war society. In vain, he tried to persuade me to join his quest, hoping to convince me that the best way to stem a loss was to give, and keep on giving, until the empty chasm within me was filled to the brim with someone else's gain. What Roy failed to understand was that I didn't want to feel better.

It was hard to know what Margery felt. After those few days at home, she had returned to school without complaint, though neither I nor Roy had the heart to push her about her studies anymore. Fortunately, the war's end also meant the end of Manpower and the threat of Margery being forced into employment. Let her get through her exams as best she can, I thought. Then see what the future holds for her.

Although she still came to the breakfast table most mornings with red-rimmed eyes and little to say, she was also putting on a brave face – complete with lipstick and freshly set hair – to meet up with her friends every weekend. Margery's closest pal, Barbara, still had several returned soldiers living temporarily in her house, former congregation members whose families had moved out of Sydney during the war, and who were now being restored to good health by the wholesome cooking and Christian care of Barbara's mother, Mrs Blackman. Hardly surprising that these young men had stepped into the role of dance partners for Barbara and her friends. The prospect of Margery grown up and ready to begin dating no longer disturbed me, as it had in the past, when viewed through the filter of Henry's death. Margery and the rest of her generation were right to embrace life while they still could.

With Roy and Margery thus preoccupied, I had time to myself. Time to sit alone with my sadness through the long hours of the day when the house was otherwise empty. I found my own relationship with grief was unexpectedly intimate, almost as if grief had stepped in to take the place of the living being I'd lost. Grief was there when I made the bed every morning and when I turned off the lamp each night. Only in those first moments after waking would it leave me. Then I'd be struck anew with the shock of remembering, and grief would return to my side for the rest of the day, keeping me company. I accepted my new companion with gratitude, like welcoming back an old friend from childhood – which, in many ways, I was.

Sleep, though less predictable, was my other ally. Sometimes it brought instant relief, a temporary refuge for my pain. Other times I was plagued by fearful nightmares from which waking brought no respite.

From time to time, well-intentioned neighbours came to our door. I sat patiently through tasteless cups of tea and thanked them for their cards and casseroles. Charlie visited from Canberra as often as he could, sometimes bringing Helen, who looked equally helpless in the face of our tragedy. The first time he came, I'd watched Margery throw her arms around her cousin and cling to him for comfort, howling like a puppy left alone for the first time. Though I felt my heart splintering in two, I kept my composure. It was Hilda's first visit that saw me sobbing like a little girl as I buried my face in her fox fur jacket, which smelt faintly of camphor.

Not fair, not fair, was what everyone said. As if they somehow expected life should be fair, when I knew perfectly well it never had been.

If I had to name a single silver lining, it was that the painful lump in my throat and aching in my ears that had plagued me since Henry's departure had finally and inexplicably subsided. Perhaps it had simply been eclipsed by the pain in my heart. Or perhaps whatever had been causing it in the first place had now leached out of my body along with my tears. For a time, I'd been convinced it was cancer; my delusional notion that if I were to die, Henry might be allowed to live. Perhaps I'd only been half wrong. Who could say? Perhaps some higher being – whether God or his nemesis – did exist after all and had made a different trade-off, contrary to my wishes, in taking Henry's life over mine.

Chapter 26

Heroes Be Damned

In October, we received a visit from Private Jim Carruthers, a young man who had served in Henry's unit and whose name we recognised from his letters. On returning to Australia and being discharged from the army, he'd written to us immediately, wishing to pay his respects. I baked a teacake in readiness, and Roy put on his best suit, changing his tie twice before settling on a striped regimental design of maroon and blue.

'Holy mackerel!' Jim exclaimed when we opened the door. 'Henry told me his folks lived in a nice neighbourhood, but I never seen anythin' like it! Some of those big estates I passed on my way here from the station look fit for a prince. Your place is really nice too, Mrs Armstrong,' he added quickly.

Roy laughed nervously and waited for my reaction.

'Thank you for coming, Private Carruthers, it's a pleasure to meet you.' I extended my hand in welcome and had it thoroughly shaken.

'Call me Jim,' our guest urged, now pumping Roy's hand with the same vigorous action as he entered the house. 'I'm a civvy now.'

Taking his hat and jacket, which I couldn't help but notice was too short in the sleeves, I led the way into our front room, where morning tea was waiting.

After an initial awkward silence and a brief discussion about the weather, Jim's candour returned and he spoke freely, filling the gaps in our knowledge of what had happened to our son. He began by confirming the battalion's various deployments throughout the prior year, information Henry had not always been permitted to share in his letters. The two had struck up a friendship after meeting in the training camp at the Atherton Tableland. From there they had been shipped out to Lae, New Guinea, where their unit was assigned to defensive duties from mid '44. Earlier this year, in April, they had been transferred to the outer islands of Bougainville in the Northern Solomons.

'*Bougainville.*' I repeated the word to myself, deliberately pronouncing it in the French rather than Australian way. I'd never heard of these exotically named islands before the war and had at first mistakenly pictured a cluster of thorny canopies in pink, purple and red. Only later was I reminded that bougainvillea, the ornamental climber of which I'd been thinking, was native to South America, not the Pacific. I supposed they might have been named after the same person, some French explorer from long ago.

I shook my head, willing myself to concentrate, no matter how great my fear over what I might hear.

According to Jim, other Australian units had been sent to Bougainville from late '44 onwards, months before their arrival. Australia's II Corps had been brought in to free up the American troops there, who were now needed for the Philippines.

'Our job was to mop up after 'em,' said Jim matter-of-factly, as if it were no more onerous a request than mopping up a mud-flecked locker room after a rowdy team of rugby players. He accepted a second slice of cake and added sugar to his tea, stirring energetically.

'It wasn't too bad when we was in the islands. A bit boring, in fact.

Henry was always tryin' to hang around with the sappers to see if he could lend a hand wiv some of their engineering-type jobs. But apart from protecting the airfield, we mostly kept ourselves entertained doing surveillance of some of the other islands still occupied by the Japs. We'd take turns volunteerin' and go out raiding in these American PT boats.'

Jim was reminiscing about this time almost as if it had been a long summer holiday, and I felt a smile creep over my lips. I allowed myself to picture Henry as he was before the war, a boy of fourteen or fifteen, catching fish from a rowboat, lost in a Boys' Own adventure with his mates on nearby Middle Harbour.

'So, it must've been the end of June they finally moved us onto the Bougainville main island. Hardly seems worthwhile, when you think of how quickly it ended after that, but that's war for you. How was anyone to know them atomic bombs were comin'?' He shook his head and took another quick gulp of tea.

'By the time we arrived on the mainland, the 11th Brigade had cleared out and we took responsibility for the Central and Northern sectors of the island. We was all part of the 5th, you know, one of them Jungle Warfare divisions they created specially for the South West Pacific. Smaller, lighter on the ground, not so many heavy weapons or vehicles as a normal infantry division.' Jim paused, waiting until he saw Roy nodding in confirmation. 'So, you see, we'd had plenty of experience living in jungle conditions and done so much flamin' training it was practically comin' out of our ears, but we hadn't come face-to-face with the Japs before then, not in actual combat.'

Jim settled back in his seat, seemingly gathering his thoughts. 'What they needed from us was to contain the Japs in the Bonis Peninsula and patrol towards the Buka Passage. On one side of the peninsula, you had the 8th Battalion, and on the other side, the 27th. The Japs had cut some of our signal wires by then too, so it was a hard slog, you know,' he said, snorting at the memory. 'I reckon a full month went by without any of us gettin' anywhere. We'd lost a few men and plenty more wounded. Thank God we had the kanakas – the Bougainville natives, you know – to lend a hand and guide us forwards. They had a kind of sixth sense for gettin' through the jungle, even in the dark, but it wasn't like that for us,' he said, laughing ruefully.

'One day, we finally got the order to attack. They'd given us some tanks on the ground and even some air support, so we went ahead and attacked this one ridge where the Japs had really dug in. We went at it again the next day too, until we took some heavy fire and had to pull back. Those Japs were ruddy well camouflaged. There was bunkers everywhere. And that was the day Henry got hit.'

I flinched instinctively. So now we knew, our son had been shot that day. Although we had already come to a similar conclusion from the telegram's scant details, it still made no sense to us that Henry had never been officially reported as wounded during the ten-day interval before his death.

'July 24th?' asked Roy in a hoarse voice.

'Yeah, must've been. I know it was a Tuesday. Crikey, that was a day and a half.' He shook his head and sniffed.

'And you say Henry was shot?' Face flushed, Roy sat forward on the edge of his seat.

Jim nodded sadly. 'He didn't think much of it, at first. Wasn't a direct hit, you see. Just a scratch really, on his shoulder.' Jim reached across and tapped his hand down on the back of his left shoulder to indicate the position.

'It was like this, Mr Armstrong, Mrs Armstrong,' he said, looking at each of us in turn. 'A few blokes went down in them attacks. We was all licking our wounds that night. I told him he ought to show the medic, but there were other blokes who were a damned sight worse off than either of us – excuse my language – and he'd said it was nothin', just a scrape. The next mornin', Henry was as right as rain – or as right as you'd expect to be, dossin' down in the jungle like we did. I reckon we was all pretty fired up. It was the first real action most of us had seen. Everyone was talkin' and carryin' on a bit, you know. I don't reckon anyone was thinkin' completely straight.'

Blood whirred in my head, and I fought the urge to cover my ears or run from the room.

'Come to think of it, you might've heard about one of the blokes from the other platoon that day. Frank Partridge? Madder than a cut snake, he was. Those Japs didn't know what hit 'em.'

Roy tilted his head, casting an anxious glance at me while Jim continued.

'You'd never have picked it – quiet young bloke, younger than Henry and me both, I reckon. Cool as a cucumber usually, but he went berserk that day, you couldn't stop 'im. Mind you, the Japs had been doing some bloody awful things going into it, so Partridge wasn't the only one who might've been looking for revenge. He ran straight into the line of fire, wounded 'n' all, and bunged a grenade into one of the Japs' bunkers. Then, when one of 'em kept firing, he grabbed the Bren from the gunner who'd copped it earlier and provided his own cover fire so he could go right on into the bunker himself. I heard he grabbed the Jap by the scruff of his neck and finished 'im off with his hunting knife.'

'I read about him in the paper,' affirmed Roy, casting another sideways glance at me as his voice died down to a whisper. 'A new version of hara-kiri, they called it.'

'Too right. Ripped 'im open like a tin of sardines, is what I heard. Afterwards Partridge came out of the bunker with one of their machine guns – a woodpecker, complete and everything – although even the Japs agree our Owens beat their guns any day. He would've kept going, too, 'cept for the fact he was losing too much blood. I heard the Lieutenant Colonel recommended 'im for a gong, maybe even a VC.'

Bile rose in my throat and I dug my elbow into Roy's ribs. He gave a sharp cough, prompting Jim to move on.

'Sorry, Mrs Armstrong, you probably didn't want to hear any of that. Now where was I?' he asked, smacking a fist against his head and suddenly nodding. 'That week or so after the attack was pretty bad, and we was busy getting ready for another one. Didn't hardly know if I was Martha or Arthur half the time.'

Nauseous and light-headed, I heard Jim's voice as if from a distance. He spoke of depth charges, artillery and mortar shells, ambushes and patrols, flamethrowers, machine gun and rifle fire, calmly rattling off this ferocious catalogue of military tactics as if were nothing but a classroom spelling list.

'So, like I said, Henry was right enough at first. But then after a few days, he started saying he wasn't feeling so good. Bit tired, but jumpy at the same time, like his heart was goin' too fast. Hot and bothered, was how he looked to me. But then again, we was all feeling like that – bloody tropics! His stomach was sore too, and he'd had the runs before that, so he might've had a touch of dysentery. We just thought he needed to sleep it off, so we let him stay back in the tent one day, while the rest of us went on patrol.'

Roy took my hand and squeezed it tightly as Jim continued.

'When we came back that arvo, he'd had a bad turn. He was breathin' fast and that got me worried right away. We got the medic to look at him and then me and O'Dowd and a couple of other blokes carried him on a stretcher back towards the other camp. It was pitch black by then – couldn't have done it without the kanakas helping us. Couldn't hardly even see the ruddy moon, as I recall.

'He slept most of the time that we was carrying 'im, but then he'd wake up and start goin' on about one of his big ideas again, tryin' to explain the theory to me, with all the technical details an' all. It was probably just the fever talkin', but he sounded pretty sure of hisself. Then again, it was always just Greek to me when Henry was prattlin' on about his inventions. We had to sleep two in a hole on Bougainville, you know. He'd give me a right earbashing most nights when I was trying to get to sleep – and that's a fact.'

A strange laugh erupted from my throat. I clapped a hand to my mouth and pressed the fingernails into the soft flesh of my cheek.

'When we got to the other camp where they had the field hospital set up, the Doc picked it right away. Infected wound, he said, from where the bullet clipped him that day. Must've been festering all along. Said he needed penicillin.'

I held my breath, guessing what was coming and dreading it.

'Poor bugger didn't wake up the next mornin'. Septic shock, the Doc called it. Blood poisoning is what they used to say. Knocked off more soldiers in World War I than actual combat, you know, but not so many these days. I just thought the heat had got to him and he was a bit crook, that's all. But I should've known better.' Jim looked at the floor, his white-knuckled hands twisting in his lap. 'Wish I had the chance to do it over and get 'im seen to properly from the start. Fair dinkum, I feel so lousy about it.'

Roy leaned over to where Jim sat and clasped his knee. 'Mrs Armstrong and I are very grateful that Henry had a mate like you, Jim. You mustn't blame yourself.'

I looked at Jim through a film of tears and nodded emphatically.

'Men like that Frank Partridge might make it into the paper, but as far as I'm concerned, you're all heroes. You all deserve medals and a lot more besides.' Roy gave Jim's leg another pat, then took out his handkerchief and blew noisily.

'Heroes be damned, Mr Armstrong, but thanks anyway. Lookin' back, I can't even think why I joined in the first place. Dunno what I expected.' He rubbed his temples with both hands, momentarily silent. 'Once you're there – once you can see this enemy everyone's been talkin' about for so long and you can eyeball them for yourself – you just want to stay alive.

So, you try to keep your wits about you, you follow orders and you look after your mates. Sometimes it works. Sometimes it doesn't.' Jim bit his lip and glanced around the room, his eyes resting on a collection of framed family photographs. He walked over and stopped in front of a picture of Henry in school uniform, proudly clutching his prize medals.

'In the end, I reckon it just comes down to luck,' he said with a heavy sigh. 'I say that if a bullet has your name on it, that's all there is to it.'

'Did Henry think like that too, Jim?' I asked, finally finding my voice. 'Did you boys talk about the possibility of getting shot? About death?' Henry had always been so infuriatingly full of bravado and unwilling to talk to me about all such risks.

'Sometimes we did, Mrs Armstrong, though I reckon it's best to can that kind of talk most of the time. Gets a bit depressing, you know.'

I nodded, resigned to the tight-lipped reticence typical of most men, though admittedly I was often guilty of this myself. I was pleasantly surprised when Jim kept talking.

'Henry didn't believe in fate or anything like that. Reckoned he was far too rational to think that way. He always said if death came for him, he wouldn't feel anything by then anyway so it wouldn't matter.'

It matters to us, I thought. *It will always matter to us.*

'The one thing none of us wanted was to be captured by the Japs. Henry and I talked about that too. It weren't about being yellow or nothin' like that, we just thought it was a helluva way to go. Worse than any bullet.'

Roy blew into his handkerchief and clicked his tongue in sympathy.

'Have you seen some of them poor blokes back from Changi?' Jim continued. 'Or the Burma railway? No word of them for years. Everyone thought they must've been dead – may as well have been. Walking skeletons, some of 'em. Makes my war look like a spring picnic compared to what they went through.'

I shuddered as images of shrunken, emaciated bodies forced

themselves into my head, not only of Australian soldiers and POWs, but also European Jews or others who had been condemned to ghettoes and work camps. I thought of the innocent Japanese victims of the two atomic bombs, and those who, like the people of France, or even Bougainville, had woken up one day to find their homes in occupied territory and their fields turned into battlefields. Across the world, from north to south and east to west, they had all become prisoners of war, each in their own way. And survival, as I knew full well, always came at a price.

Roy stuffed his handkerchief back into his trousers and clapped his hands together, signalling a change of topic. 'So, Jim, what are your plans now?'

'Well, I reckon I'm ready to get married.'

'Married?' asked Roy, blinking rapidly. 'That was quick. You haven't been home for that long, have you?'

Jim grinned. 'It's nothin' like that. I've known Joy since I was a kid. Reckon our mums cooked up the idea of us two getting married while they were still peggin' out our nappies on the clothesline.'

'Well, congratulations to you! Does she know what she's in for now you're all grown up?' Roy sounded enthusiastic, but I could see in his face the effort it cost him.

'Reckon so. She wants me to take her dancin' at the Trocadero tonight. She's got it all sorted for us to go with her sister and her husband. She's even told me what to wear.'

'That's a good sign, Jim,' said Roy, clearing his throat as his breath caught. 'When a woman starts giving orders, it means she's taking you on as her responsibility for life.'

'Leave him alone,' I chided, mustering a tiny smile. 'Joy's a lucky girl to have you and I'm sure she knows it. I hope the two of you will be very happy.'

'Thanks, Mrs Armstrong. She sure can dance.'

I smiled encouragingly as Jim's face took on an endearingly dreamy expression. I liked this plain-speaking young man and did not begrudge him anything, neither his life nor his future marital happiness. Even so, I couldn't help but give voice to what might have been.

'I'm sorry our Henry never had the chance to meet the right girl and get married. That he never knew the love or affection of a woman himself.'

Jim opened his mouth then closed it again, as if he had something to say but had changed his mind. He returned the photograph to the mantlepiece, casting a quick glance at the one beside it. 'Where's your daughter hiding today? Henry mentioned his little sister to me often enough, but she doesn't look so little in this photo.'

'Well spotted,' said Roy. 'That's our Margery – taller than her mother by half a head.'

I nodded. 'Margery's eighteen now, but she's always liked dressing up, as you can see. She stayed at a friend's house last night. I was hoping she'd be back in time to meet you but, as usual, she—'

'Never mind,' said Roy, cutting me off before I could say anything critical. 'Any other plans, apart from getting married?'

'I'm starting a job in two weeks, Mr Armstrong. Then I'm going to put my mind to findin' a place for us to live – they're as rare as hen's teeth these days! Not that I'm complainin', I was lucky to be sent home on the first ship. Bit of a nasty fungal infection,' he added, abruptly squirming in his seat. 'A lot of the other blokes are still stuck in Bougainville guardin' the Japs.'

'Demobilisation's a slow process,' agreed Roy. 'It's good you can get on with your life sooner. I hope they've set you up with a soldier loan.'

Jim blushed again. 'I'm really sorry for your loss, Mr and Mrs Armstrong. I dunno what to say. We was good mates, Henry and me. He was a top bloke, true blue. Did I tell you he used to call me Jungle Jim, like the comic strip? And I called him Flash Gordon, 'cause the same bloke drawed that series too.'

'Really?' Roy chuckled. 'Henry told us his nickname was Professor or Shorty.'

'Yeah, that too. The others called him one of them names, but I liked to call 'im Flash because he came from Gordon.'

'Flash Gordon,' repeated Roy. 'I like that. It always was one of his favourite comics.'

'Well, Flash always said I should come here after the war. That he'd show me his workshop and some of those wacky inventions he was always goin' on about. I told him I was probably too much of a boofhead to understand 'em, but he said he'd give it a try anyway. Reckon I'd like to take a gander now ... if that's all right.'

As Roy led Jim out to the backyard and the small tin shed that would forever remain Henry's workshop, I sat quietly, rehashing our conversation from beginning to end. It was surreal listening to Jim talk about Henry, hearing anecdotes about their experiences together in a place I would never see myself. It hurt to think of him living a soldier's life in a world about which we knew so little – a world I'd wanted no part of. But it comforted me to know he was not alone, and to imagine the banter and affection that accompanied him through at least some of his days in the army. Painful as it was, I also felt a small measure of relief to know how he had died – to know he hadn't suffered too much ... that he might have simply gone to sleep thinking he'd finally come up with the one idea no one else had ever thought of ... that he had figured out the one invention that would earn him immortality.

When they came back inside, and Jim started to take his leave, I handed him his hat and jacket. Then I took a deep breath and asked my final question.

'He's buried at the army cemetery at Soraken with the other Aussies, Mrs Armstrong.' Jim's tone was hushed. 'I was there when the chaplain gave his service.'

'Does everyone have their own grave? What does Henry's look like? Would you say it's a peaceful spot?' Roy's questions came in rapid succession before I could say anything myself.

Jim paused, his eyes flickering up to the ceiling. 'It's quite nice really, I think you'd like it. They must've cut down the trees to clear a good space when they built the cemetery. Of course, there aren't any big gravestones or monuments like you'd see here – just white crosses, set up in rows, nice and neat. The kanakas look after the diggin' and tendin' to the plots, with wheelbarrows and gardening tools and what have you.'

I was struggling to take in so much new information all at once. Until today, I'd pictured Henry having died in the field, or rather jungle, not in some makeshift army hospital. For his burial, in the rose-coloured reality of my dreams, I'd seen my son laid out on a bed of palm leaves, as if asleep, surrounded by colourful orchids and the sound of water rippling from a nearby stream.

'I made sure everythin' was done properly, Mrs Armstrong, I promise you that – even down to 'is meat tags,' Jim added unnecessarily. 'Henry and me often felt a bit sorry for the kanakas, you know. We got on all right together, even got to learn a bit of Pidgin English ourselves from talkin' to 'em. Like I said, we needed 'em as guides and they did a ruddy good job for us too. I reckon that for every American or Australian soldier that was killed or wounded, there were probably ten or twenty Japs who bit the dust. Mind you, half the time, starvation got to 'em before we could. But even so, Henry said that if we counted up all the deaths, the biggest tally of all would probably belong to the Bougainville natives. First they was a German colony, then they was given to the Aussies after that Treaty of Versailles, then the Japs come in during this war and all hell breaks loose – Yanks, Japs, us and them. They was the only ones who knew what they was doing there anyway, the rest of us was all just like fish out of water. Too ruddy hot and wet for me! Pretty bloody depressin' really.'

I shared an appraising glance with Roy. This young man understood more than he gave himself credit for. These island colonies were like pawns on a chessboard.

'Time I headed off, I reckon. Thanks again for the tea and cake. I'll let you know when I'm settled and maybe you can pay me and the missus a visit one day, you never know.'

'You never know,' agreed Roy, shaking his hand warmly. 'Good luck, son.'

~

Before falling asleep that evening, I reflected on Jim's comment about a bullet having someone's name on it – a common enough belief among soldiers – and compared his fatalistic attitude towards death with Henry's more reasoned and pragmatic outlook as a man of science. Although I knew women who consulted their horoscopes in the newspaper every day, reading into each line with scholarly dedication, I was certain the only facts my son would have regarded as being written in the stars would be found in a textbook on astrophysics.

There must have been other soldiers in Henry's unit who had seen things differently. Men who had looked to their faith to sustain them through battle, telling themselves God had a plan. I was under no such illusion. How then, without science or faith of any kind to guide me, could I ever hope to come to terms with my son's death?

Next to me in bed, Roy was snoring gently, one arm circling my waist, as if determined to protect me even in sleep. I curled my fingers around his fist, holding on.

Like Henry, I had never really believed in fate. But as I lay beside my husband, contemplating these questions, I reached a new conclusion. It was this. In the same way that every character in a novel had an arc to fulfil, perhaps the life of every living creature had its own trajectory – as sure as that of the bullet that clipped our son's shoulder. It dawned on me that from the day he was born, Henry had been moving inexorably towards his death, twenty-one years later, marching to a cadence he alone could hear.

Chapter 27

Say Goodbye to Hollywood

One afternoon, not long after Jim's visit and with Henry's birthday looming, we met with the minister from our local Methodist church. I had reluctantly agreed to Roy's suggestion to hold a memorial service for Henry on what should have been his twenty-second birthday. Although conflicted about the church hall as a choice of venue, I conceded it might be slightly more bearable than having the service at home. Jean Campbell and other women who had known Henry since boyhood had already offered to help with refreshments and, throughout our short conversation, the minister had been suitably respectful and restrained in his sympathies. We drove home after the meeting in silence.

Just as Roy was turning into our street, a maroon-coloured Dodge came out, heading towards the city. Although I didn't recognise the car or the uniformed young man driving it, I glimpsed Margery's friend, Barbara, in the passenger seat. I then spotted Margery in the back of the vehicle, sitting beside another young man. Unlike Barbara, who'd been engrossed in conversation and not noticed us, Margery was looking directly out the side window as they made their turn. She reacted instantly, freezing in mid-air like a possum stunned by torchlight. In that moment, which must have lasted only a second or two, but felt much longer, we locked eyes. Written on her face was the same guilty expression I had seen time and again, right back to the days when she was merely a naughty little girl caught in the act of 'borrowing' my jewellery.

'Hmmm,' was all Roy said as we rolled up the driveway and into our garage. But by the time he'd unlocked the back door and put on the kettle, we agreed I should telephone Barbara's mother to see if she knew what the girls were up to on this school day afternoon.

'Ah,' said Mrs Blackman breezily, her chirpy voice echoing down the phone line. 'They'll have been driving Colin to Central Station to say their farewells. Mr Cartwright has been one of my lodgers and now that he's all better, he's going back to his parents' farm up north, towards the Queensland border. I expect he'll be writing to Margery, though. I know he's a fair bit older than her, but he's taken quite a shine to your girl. And she to him, so far as I can tell.'

'Hmmm,' repeated Roy when I relayed this message. 'We'll have a little chat with our Margie this evening when she gets home. Find out what it's all about.'

Over a strong pot of tea and then a stiff whisky, we quietly discussed details for the memorial service – who to invite, who should speak, what we would wear and so forth. All I wanted was that the occasion should reflect the kind of person Henry was, so that his friends would remember him properly, yet achieving this within the parameters of what might be seen as a parish social event seemed an impossible task.

I felt a sudden pang as I thought of the blazer I'd bought for his birthday with my first allocation of ration coupons back in '42. Hardly worn, it was still hanging in the wardrobe, along with the rest of his clothes. Sometimes I liked to be alone in Henry's bedroom, positioning myself at his desk, imagining how he might have felt as he looked around the room. Occasionally, I'd find Roy in there already. Knowing how much this space meant to us both, I had been dreading a request from Margery, half-expecting she might insist on converting this space into a sewing room, as she'd intimated in the past. Margery, however, had been uncharacteristically diffident since Henry's death and had not voiced requests of this or any other kind.

Today though I walked past Henry's door and went straight to Margery's room. I was hoping she might feel up to saying a few words at her brother's service and was looking for something suitable for her to wear. As I approached the large maple wardrobe, my eye was caught by an envelope propped up against the lace pillow on Margery's bed, addressed to 'Mum and Dad'. Tearing open the letter with trembling fingers, I skimmed its contents then rushed out of the room.

'Good God,' thundered Roy as he read the letter. 'What the hell does she think she's doing? She wants to go off with this soldier, this Colin Cartwright, and get married. Is she out of her bloody mind?' A stream of profanities discharged itself from my husband's mouth. 'What kind of man takes a girl from her home without so much as a word to her parents? Just wait till I get my hands on him. I'll kick him from here to next week.'

Margery's letter was a bombshell, worse for the fact that neither of us had seen it coming. Roy was beside himself. But even though I'd never seen him so irate, I knew it was mostly shock making him speak this way. He would soon calm down and look for a way to put things right and make the best of the situation. Such was his nature. My own response was different. I was beyond tears. Beyond profanities. I could barely speak. Hurt and betrayal pulsed through my veins, humming in my ears like an overheated aeroplane engine. But there was nothing left inside me to explode. I was empty. Hollow.

Stumbling around our kitchen like a drunkard, Roy suddenly looked at his wristwatch and leaped forwards, wrenching the car key from its hook on the wall. 'If we hurry, maybe we can still catch them. Mrs

Blackman said Central, didn't she? What train do you think they're on? Get your purse, Lill. Let's go!'

Despite the light-headedness still threatening to overwhelm me, I heard myself speak as if from a distance, my voice cold and sharp like steel. 'I'm not going anywhere, Roy, and neither should you. Margery's made her bed and now she must lie in it.'

At the mention of the word 'bed', Roy's face crumpled. 'But we've got to stop her, Lill. If she really fancies this young man, we can get to know him and talk about it. I just don't see why she has to get married so quickly.'

'Why do you think?' I paused significantly, waiting for his own stammering brain to kick into gear. 'She must have gotten herself into trouble with this boy ... this man. Stupid, stupid girl. Look at the note. It says she didn't know what to do at first but that she's found her own solution. That we don't need to worry about her anymore.' I thrust the letter in his face. 'So that's exactly what I'm going to try to do. Not worry about her. And if you love me, you'll do the same.'

Roy's mouth fell open and he clutched his stomach. 'You think she's gotten herself into trouble? You think she's pregnant?'

'Of course she's pregnant. Why else would she run off like this?' I flinched, already hearing the raft of common insults to which Margery could soon find herself subjected ... *preggers* ... *up the duff* ... it was all so sordid, I couldn't bear it. I couldn't bear any of it.

'It's my fault, Lill. I should have protected her.' Roy paced back and forth, tearing at his hair.

'Don't be stupid, Roy. It's not your fault.' As her mother, the blame for Margery's predicament rested squarely on my shoulders. How could it be otherwise?

Roy sat limply, rubbing his eyes. He looked again at his watch and at the key in his hand, his head swinging back and forth between the door and the letter in front of him. 'I don't think we can catch them today, anyway,' he said slowly, uttering just one word one at a time, as if hoping to alter their outcome. 'I don't even think I have enough petrol to get that far. I could go tomorrow, get a train ticket and follow them up north. What do you think?'

He picked up the letter, biting his lip as he read it a second time. When Roy turned to face me, he suddenly looked like an old man. Even his eyes were different. Dilated in shock and robbed of all colour. Just two black caverns rimmed in gold. A small spot of blood appeared on his lower lip.

'I think that if you go after Margery tomorrow, I may not be here when you return.'

Roy gaped at me in bewilderment, as if hoping his hearing had failed him as it so often did. 'Please sweetheart, be reasonable,' he implored. 'It might all work out. Look here – she says they're going to get married, that they'll live with Colin's family for the time being. She says he's got a job lined up as the farm manager for a neighbouring property, and that his parents are willing to help out till they get on their feet.'

Poor Roy was like a tightly coiled spring. Six solid feet of heart, flesh and muscle contracted and aching to be released, if only he knew which direction to take.

'Can't you see, Roy? It's crystal clear.' I glared at him. '*His* parents. *His* family. She doesn't need us anymore. Margery's made her choice, and now you need to make yours.'

As I left the room, I heard him open the high kitchen cupboard and take down the whisky bottle we had only just put away. Moments later I heard him speaking into the telephone. I listened as my husband struggled to converse naturally, politely commenting on Mrs Blackman's latest fundraising effort and the continued challenge of rationing now that the war was over. After reinforcing his request that Barbara call as soon as she returned home, he lay down the receiver. Next came the sound of a match striking and the smell of cigarette smoke wafting through the house, as strange and unwelcome as the letter on our kitchen table.

I shut the bedroom door behind me and sat down at my dressing table. As a single cry of anguish escaped from my clenched lips, I picked up the large bakelite hairbrush and threw it against the wall. I began to weep, letting the tension ease its way out of my body at last. It was all over now. There was nothing left. Since Henry's death, I thought nothing could ever touch me again. Now this. Outside the window it started to rain, a heavy downpour that flooded the gutters and muffled my sobs.

Head throbbing, throat aching, I finally stopped crying. I opened my mouth and drew in long shuddering breaths. Still gasping, I caught sight of myself through swollen eyes in the three-fold mirror of the dressing table. Peering back at me from the glass, refracted and forlorn, was my reflection. Each angle revealed another pathetic image. A triptych of despair.

If only Margery had come to me earlier. I would still have been furious, what parent wouldn't be? But I would have forgiven her soon enough. Falling pregnant outside of marriage was not a crime, nor should it be, but at her age, how could it be anything but a mistake? Heaven help me, I would have willingly raised that baby as my own, neighbourhood gossip be damned, if only she had asked. Roy too would have consented to such a plan, or any plan that kept us together. Even if Margery had dug in her heels and insisted on marrying him, they could have stayed here. Roy could have brought him into the business and given him a job. If only we'd known.

With a sudden jolt, I recalled Margery's lingering stomach upsets and gasped. That had been months ago, even before Henry's death. I cast my mind back to her endless moods and tearfulness.

I bowed my head in shame. What a terrible mother I'd been not to have noticed what was right in front of me. How utterly neglectful. And how naive and misguided my daughter – to have let it go on all this time without a word to the two people who would have done anything for her.

Who still would, at least in Roy's case.

A flash of fury momentarily eclipsed the self-reproach which had consumed me. Even though I could have forgiven Margery back then, it was too late now. How could Margery do this? To herself, as well as to us? A silly young schoolgirl who had gotten herself pregnant. To a returned soldier, at that. A convalescent, who might be damaged in all kinds of ways Margery could not even fathom. To a man who, according to Mrs Blackman, was much older than herself. A farmer from somewhere up near Queensland. What had she been thinking?

The Margery I knew, the girl I had raised over eighteen challenging but nevertheless wonderful years, had always craved excitement, the allure and glamour of the city. That Margery could barely tolerate living here in the suburbs, much less life in the country. After last year's failed exams and that first blushing confession, hadn't she chattered endlessly about her ambition to pursue a career in costume design? To go to Hollywood, for goodness' sake! Why would she give all that up? The only possible reason I could think of was that my daughter hated living at home so much she was willing to do anything to get away ... to get away from me.

The thought hit me like a deluge. My eyes burned, not only from crying, but also from wrath. Margery's actions were a complete rejection of the values I'd sought to instil in her; a complete rejection of the life she'd been given. And for what? To become a farmer's wife. Was that really the only legacy she wanted to leave behind? Imprisoned by the obligations of motherhood and the relentless tyranny of distance, she would be forever trapped. Lost in the Australian landscape for the rest of her life, like the grandmother she never knew.

Gone, once and for all, were Margery's prospects of a further education. Dashed eternally were her own hopes for a life of fashion and fame. Silly, silly girl. She had no idea what lay before her. As soon as she stepped onto the platform and boarded that train today, she'd have no choice but to leave her dreams behind, along with her cherished movie star scrapbooks and her box of dressmaking patterns. From this day forwards, they were all just 'castles in the air'. Henry Lawson's damned story was coming back to haunt me yet again.

At the thought of Lawson's story, another wave of light-headedness hit me, followed by another wave of remorse. This truly was all my fault. In every possible way. If only I had overcome my own insecurities and had shared my family story with Margery. It might have made a difference. Or else, at the very least, when it all went wrong, she might have trusted me enough to confide in me and let me help her.

Perhaps, if I had told her everything that had happened to me as a girl, every loss I endured, every humiliation I'd suffered, she might finally have understood why I wanted so much for her, why I had always held her to account and pushed her to live up to such high expectations. Hadn't Margery already pointed out my hypocrisy in wanting her to be an independent woman when I was hardly one myself?

And why didn't I share it with her? Was it fear? Insecurity? Because I was scared my daughter would laugh at me like my classmates had once done? Because I was worried she might judge my humble beginnings and forever see me differently? Or because holding back from sharing my story was the one thing I could control in this whole damned war? What a deluded fool I'd been. What had I been thinking? That I could somehow bring Henry back safely just by staying silent?

I was no better than Henry Lawson. No better than any man – or woman – who stole another person's history and kept it for themselves. My story – Mother's story – was Margery's story too. Why hadn't I seen that before it was too late?

There was no one to blame but me. Not only had I been trying to impose some kind of idealised narrative on Margery, I had been keeping my own secrets and manipulating the truth. Margery was right, I was a hypocrite. I was even worse than Henry Lawson. At least he had shared our story with the world.

I heard the clinking of glass. I pictured Roy drinking alone in the kitchen and began sobbing all over again. Poor Roy. He didn't deserve any of this. I should have told both Henry and Margery everything. But now it was all too late.

Outside, the rain had eased slightly, slowing to a patter. Reflected by the mirror, I watched it cascade down the windowpane. Against this shimmering background, my image began to double and waver, edges softening and blurring until I could feel myself disappearing into the silver glass, along with the rain.

Unlike Roy, I had nothing to say to Margery. Nothing left to ask, other than the questions right in front of me, staring back at me from the mirror. Who was that woman captured in the glass? What point was there to her life now? And – the most excruciating question of all – did I still deserve to call myself a mother now that I had lost both my children?

Chapter 28

A Portrait of Friendship

'*Bonjour, ma cherie!*'

I looked up from my book and waved as Hilda bustled towards the table I'd chosen at the far end of the coffee lounge, bringing with her a cloud of expensive-smelling perfume. We embraced and kissed, first one cheek then the other.

'I'm late, I know. *Pardonne-moi*. Have you been waiting long?'

'Not at all,' I lied, reaching for my bookmark. '*Pas du tout*.'

Apart from occasional dialogues with Professor Waterhouse, as my former language master, these token exchanges with Hilda were my only opportunity to speak French, a playful routine carried over from our years at Sacred Heart.

Hilda's cheeks were flushed, and beads of perspiration shone at her temples, but otherwise she looked well. Dressed in an elegant suit of gold-dyed silk with matching gloves and hat, there was no evidence of lingering wartime shortages in Hilda's fashionable ensemble.

I showed her my book, borrowed earlier that morning from our new Gordon library. 'It's Eleanor Dark's latest novel. It's wonderful – like a novel and philosophy book in one – although I do think some of its judgements about the North Shore are a little harsh. Her character, Marty, says we're a pleasant and kindly people but that we avoid thinking at all costs.' Admittedly, I had made similar observations myself on occasion.

'*The Little Company*,' read Hilda and raised her eyebrows. 'Not today, my dear. Today you have anything but little company.' Still breathing heavily but justifiably pleased with her pun, she sat down. Her voice softened. 'How are you, Lill? I've been worried sick about you.'

Hilda and her family had only recently relocated back to Sydney. The last time we had seen each other had been over three months earlier – soon after the news of Henry's death, but before Margery's shock departure.

'I'm all right,' I said, trying to tell myself it was true. 'At least I can always rely on a good book to cheer me up. And I can always rely on you, too.'

'*Toujours*,' affirmed Hilda. 'I'm glad to see you're not wearing black. It's so depressing. Makes everything worse, I think.' She nodded approvingly at my bottle green slub linen suit. 'That colour suits you. I remember my Aunt Bunty insisted on wearing black crepe for years after my uncle died, even though we all knew she was glad to be rid of him and even though Mother repeatedly told her fashion etiquette dictated otherwise by that time. In the end, we suspected wearing her widow's weeds was my aunt's sly way of advertising her availability on the secondary marriage market. And it worked, too.' Catching sight of my nonplussed expression, Hilda stopped short. 'Sorry, Lill. I'm prattling on dreadfully, when all I really want to know is how you've been coping – since Henry, I mean, of course. And now with Margery gone too.' Tears welled in her eyes, and she placed a gloved hand over mine. 'It's too much, Lill. It really is too unfair.'

Interrupted by the sudden intrusion of the waitress, I withdrew my hand and pasted a smile on my face. After a cursory glance at the menu, I ordered fruit cake and coffee, while Hilda opted for sponge cake and Earl Grey tea.

'Just something light,' said Hilda, peeling off her gloves and thrusting her hat and jacket towards the young woman. 'Since I'll be dining out for lunch, too.'

Hilda looked at me anxiously. 'So, tell me, dearest girl. Is it getting any easier yet?'

'A little, I suppose,' I replied, unsure of how to put my feelings into words. 'It's not my own loss that troubles me most. I could bear that, I think, if that were all. It's Henry I grieve for. For everything he'll miss out on. Life has let him down, and I can't help feeling I've let him down too.'

Hilda shook her head emphatically and dabbed at her eyes.

I looked away, determined not to cry. I wondered if I should tell her about the nights Henry came to me in my dreams – an elusive shadowy figure, yet undoubtedly my son. Sometimes he would speak to me, though never with any words I could recall. Try as I might, I could never quite grasp his meaning. Afterwards, I'd wake and feel unsettled for hours; grateful to have felt his presence but distraught to think he was trying to communicate some vital message that I was failing to comprehend.

'I keep finding myself cooking his favourite dishes for dinner,' I confessed instead, shrugging apologetically. 'Yesterday I even baked cookies. It's so stupid. As if that could help anyone.'

'But it does help, Lill. Surely anything that makes you feel better is a good thing. What does Roy say? How's he doing?'

'Roy's been spending a lot of time out back in the workshop. He keeps looking through Henry's sketchbooks and studying his technical models from years ago. He's convinced Henry might have been onto some genuinely good ideas.'

'Clever boy, your Henry. Just like his mother. Smart as a whip.'

'You know, when Henry was little, I sometimes used to worry about what would happen when he grew up and got married ... whether he'd move away to another city ... or whether he'd start doing chores the way his wife asked him to do them, instead of the way I'd shown him. I always had this sense with Henry – not with Margery, ironically enough – that I only had him on borrowed time. Now, of course, I know I was just being selfish. It should never have been about that at all. And I'm just so sorry that he'll never know the love of a woman other than his mother or sister.'

'You've nothing to be sorry for, Lill. And you're right. Men are simple. They can only be loyal to one woman at a time – and some of them can't even do that. I've seen it with my brother, and a lot of my friends, those with grown sons, have said the same. I suppose I'm lucky having only girls. How does that Irish proverb go? *A son's a son till he takes a wife, a daughter is a daughter all her life.* Yes, that's it.'

I winced before I could stop myself.

'Sorry, Lill,' Hilda gasped. 'I don't know what I'm saying today!'

'Never mind. *Ne t'inquiète pas, ma chérie.* Here we are.' I smiled at the waitress with exaggerated politeness as she set down her tray.

Hilda waited before resuming our dialogue. 'I'm so glad I convinced you to meet me. It's good to get out of the house at a time like this.'

'Roy says the same.' I added milk to my coffee and stirred. 'It's been almost three years since Henry left home, so I don't feel his absence in the house anymore as much as I used to. But Margery's only been gone for weeks. The house feels so empty. Unnatural, somehow.'

Hilda put down her cake fork. 'Oh, my dear.'

'I'm sure I'll get used it eventually. In a strange way, it reminds me of when the children were small. Can you remember how it felt when you finally had the opportunity to go somewhere without them? A doctor's appointment, or a special party or something like that. Though I expect you probably had more of those opportunities than me,' I smiled, thinking of the various nurses and governesses who had passed through Hilda's household. 'In my case, I always had to wait for Roy to get home or ask someone to babysit. But then, even though I was excited to be out on my own, I could never quite relax. I always felt like I'd forgotten something. I'd keep looking over my shoulder and waiting for a little hand to grab hold of mine.' I frowned. 'That's how it feels now, only worse.'

'I do remember that feeling,' said Hilda. 'I still get it whenever the grandchildren go home after staying with us for a few days.'

'I know Henry's gone, rationally speaking that is, and I know Margery's gone now too, but I still keep expecting to see them just the same.'

'And what does Margery say? What are her plans?'

'I don't know, Hilda.' I gave a terse sigh. 'We're not speaking. Or writing, for that matter. All her letters are specifically addressed to Roy, not me.' This one simple action on Margery's part had told me everything I needed to know.

'You haven't made it up with her, then?'

'No, I can't. Not yet. They were married a few days after she left Sydney. Apparently, his parents were the only witnesses.'

'Oh, Lill.' Hilda wrung her hands.

'She's expecting a baby, you know. And I dare say it will be born very much sooner than one might wish.'

'Poor little Margery. I rather suspected.'

'Poor Roy. He's doubly heartbroken. He still blames himself for letting Henry enlist, although I stopped holding him responsible a long time ago. Henry was determined to join up, even I saw that in the end. Now he blames himself for not protecting Margery. But, of course, everyone knows it's always the mother who's to blame in these instances. You know Roy, though. He's being strong for my sake, and I know he's promised Margery he'll bring me around eventually.'

'It's not your fault, Lill.'

'You don't think so? You don't think I've been a terrible mother? Because I do. No need to sugarcoat it for my sake, I don't deserve anyone's sympathy.'

'Of course it's not your fault, Lill,' Hilda repeated, looking aghast at my outburst. 'And you're not a terrible mother. How can you even say such a thing? If Margery only knew all the things you went through as a child, it's no wonder you're struggling to cope with this now. And coming on the back of Henry, too. I'm surprised you're still here in one piece, truly I am.'

I felt my shoulders relax ever so slightly. Although I knew Hilda would always take my side in any argument, it felt good to let myself off the hook even just for a moment.

Hilda glanced around at the neighbouring tables and lowered her voice even further. 'Girls have been falling in love and finding themselves pregnant throughout the ages. The same thing could happen in any family. A good many girls, or should I say their parents, opt for a quick wedding. I expect it's the most expedient option if the gentleman in question is prepared to accept his responsibilities. Other girls don't even get the choice and must give up their babies for adoption. I'd hate to think how many young women get sent on a long "holiday" to some distant relative and are forced to come home and pretend nothing happened. Sounds to me like poor Margery took matters into her own hands and tried to find a workable solution. I know it's not the path you wanted for your darling girl, but who's to say what either of us might have done in her position? The world is different now. Young people have so much more freedom these days.'

'Of course,' I said, trying not to bristle. 'I know things have changed, Hilda. Especially since the war. I'm not so naive to think today's young women wouldn't consider pre-marital relations in a different light to our generation, but Margery was still at school, for goodness' sake. She was too young for any of that.'

'And yet she wasn't,' said Hilda, squeezing my hand.

'If she was so ready to be grown up, why couldn't they have used necessary precautions?' I whispered through clenched teeth. 'Roy said the American troops were all issued with sheaths, along with their other army rations. Mr Cartwright – Colin, that's Margery's husband, as I keep needing to remind myself – should've known what to do. I'm sure the Australian soldiers were equally well-equipped in that regard. He's almost ten years Margery's senior. And he grew up on a farm, for goodness' sake, so he knows how these things work. He should have known better, even if Margery did not!'

Hilda blushed. 'I don't know what to tell you, Lill. At least he's done the right thing now. I hope they'll be happy together in the long-term, despite this shaky beginning. And I hope you'll soon find the strength to forgive her – and yourself. Try to look on the bright side.' Hilda must have seen my dubious expression and gave me no chance to interrupt. 'He could have been a Yank, Lill. That would have been much worse, wouldn't it? All those war brides leaving the country these past months, makes you wonder.'

I nodded, but inwardly I wondered if it might have been better if Margery had fallen for an American. Over there, she might have found something closer to her dreams, something more than the loneliness and hardship I feared awaited her.

'You've hardly touched your fruitcake,' chided Hilda. 'No wonder you've kept your figure all these years. You're putting me to shame. They do say old age for a woman means losing one's waistline, hair and teeth, but at least I still have two out of three going for me.'

I gave her a warm smile. 'Your figure suits you perfectly – it's as generous as your spirit. Don't ever apologise for either.'

'That's a very nice way of putting it, thank you. I'll try to remember that next time my dress zipper won't do up.' Hilda's face became uncharacteristically wistful. 'I'm so glad the war is over. Six years was a long time. Sometimes even I found it difficult to be generous-spirited. I'd let myself get caught up in all the hatred. I remember when I first heard the name of Adolf Hitler back in the thirties. It was in a magazine quoting his views on healthy living. Healthy living! When I think of all the despicable things that man did, it makes no sense. Makes me wonder what anyone is capable of. I can't imagine how much you must hate the Germans for starting this war, Lillian. Or the Japanese especially.'

I shrugged. 'I try not to. As much as I hate what happened to Henry, I can't blame an entire nation of people. I remind myself of all the wonderful things created by these enemy nations, who were once our friends, and will be again someday, I hope. Think of the German composers and the music they've given the world. Or think of Japanese art and calligraphy. All countries are capable of both good and evil actions, as much as we try to tell ourselves otherwise. And sometimes an action is both good *and* evil, depending on where you stand.' I concluded my speech by adding sugar to my coffee and stirring vigorously.

Hilda nodded miserably. 'I just don't want to think about another war,' she said. 'Not now, not ever. Remember what they told us back then about the Great War? *The war to end all wars.* And we were all so innocent we believed them.' She snorted angrily. 'I don't think any of us would believe that kind of promise ever again, but I hope it's not in our lifetime. Or that of my children, or my grandchildren.' Hilda sighed, pouring herself another cup of tea. 'And I really don't want to knit another sock for the rest of my life.'

'You never could turn the heels properly, could you?' I said with a sly grin.

'I never could,' Hilda giggled. 'The sisters would be very disappointed in my efforts, although I did try my best.'

'I'm sure you did. I'm sure your family helped countless soldiers and their families in many other ways too. At least you weren't like some women who chose their volunteer activities according to how well the uniform flattered them.'

'Only because most of them didn't make uniforms in my size,' sniffed Hilda, holding out her arms in despair. 'I've spent three days this past week trying to slim down in one of those dreadful sweat boxes at Joh Bjelke-Petersen's, but it's barely made any difference.'

'Never mind,' I said, closing my eyes to the extra cream Hilda had ordered with her cake. 'What are you doing after this? You mentioned lunch.'

Her smile returned. 'I'm meeting my girls at the club, but first we're going to David Jones for our annual Christmas shopping spree. The children have made long lists for Father Christmas so hopefully we can get everything today. It's frustrating that we're still stuck with rationing, but at least the store is finally back to normal trading.'

'Sounds lovely, my dear.' I pictured Hilda and her daughters being greeted by name as they traipsed through our city's most exclusive department store, merrily charging their purchases to Hilda's store account and issuing instructions about gift wrapping and delivery.

'Would you like to join us, Lill? The Christmas windows are probably up by now, and I'm sure the girls would love to see you.'

I felt a sudden pang. This would be the first year I wouldn't be taking Margery into town to see the David Jones Christmas window displays, followed by high tea in their glamorous Lacquer Room restaurant. Even after Henry's enlistment, it had endured as one of our few mother–daughter traditions.

'Thanks for the invitation but I'm going to the National Gallery after this. I'm curious to see if anything looks different since Hal Missingham came in as director.'

'Is it Archibald Prize time already?'

'No, not yet. Not till January. Although Roy thinks it will probably go to William Dargie again this year. If he's right, that will be his third time – near enough to a hat-trick. Not that I'm aware of anyone taking bets on art prize winners just yet.'

Hilda grinned. 'Thanks for the heads up. In that case, I think I'll spare myself the trip. I still can't understand what all the fuss was about with that winning portrait he did a couple of years ago – you know, the one he got taken to court over. Some people take things far too seriously.' Hilda waved her cake fork in the air for emphasis.

I cocked my head. 'You mean William Dobell, I think, and all the palaver over his exaggerated portrait of Joshua Smith?'

'Right you are,' said Hilda, grinning sheepishly as she scooped up her final bite. 'Dobell not Dargie.'

As I struggled to finish my own dry fruit cake, I wondered how many people knew that a portrait of Henry Lawson, as Archibald's former protégé, had set the original wheels in motion for this long-running annual prize. In the past, I had found it rather galling that Lawson's legacy should extend to the art world as well as the literary sphere. But none of that seemed important to me anymore.

I looked up with a start, suddenly aware that Hilda was still talking.

'Perhaps I should ask Mr Dobell to paint my portrait one day. What do you think, Lill? Although I'd hate for him to exaggerate certain of my features.' She tilted back her head and pushed the soft flesh of her chin upwards with a fretful expression.

'You should! You'd have nothing to fear. One of Dobell's strengths is his ability to adapt his style to suit the nature of his subject. I'm sure yours would be a veritable masterpiece.'

Hilda brushed away my compliment but appeared pleased as she peered out the café window, craning her neck towards the millinery shop opposite. 'Would you like to take a turn down the arcade together? Although even The Strand is not quite what it used to be. The whole of Sydney's crying out for a fresh coat of paint.'

'I dare say none of us are quite what we used to be,' I replied mildly. Although the three-storeyed grand arcade, originally built during the Victorian era, had admittedly fallen into a relative state of disrepair since its various changes of ownership, a great many of its boutiques – selling furs, jewellery and other luxury items – remained well outside my household budget. 'I'll just buy some vanilla almonds for Roy on the way out, but I'll gladly look with you.'

We parted ways a short while later at the Pitt Street end of the arcade. Hilda's new Moray hatbox pressed into my ribs as she drew me into a tearful embrace and issued her final words of advice.

'Make it up with Margery, Lill. The longer you wait, the harder it will be.'

'Maybe,' was the best reply I could offer.

Chapter 29

Pool of Reflection

When I opened my eyes and heard the drone of cicadas outside, I knew it was going to be another blistering hot day. The mercury had hovered in the high nineties most of yesterday and today promised more of the same. Despite the cool change that had blown in before dinner, the house had remained hot and stuffy overnight, and sleep had been elusive.

Competing with my grief for Henry was my now constant worry over Margery and the forthcoming birth of her child. There was still no news as to exactly when the baby was expected but from what I could glean it was only a matter of weeks, not months. In the nearly one hundred days since Margery had been gone, she and Roy had continued to write. There was a telephone on Colin's family farm, but perhaps because it shared a party line, allowing others from the local exchange to listen in, they had only spoken a couple of times, and even then, only briefly.

Margery's letters attested to the fact that she was safe and well. Apart from this all-important information, I had no wish to know their contents. If my daughter had wanted to communicate with me, she would have made that clear in her correspondence, but all her letters continued to be addressed to Roy alone. Caught in the middle, Roy claimed Margery and I were equally stubborn. He maintained Margery was waiting for me to make the first move towards reconciliation, but I wasn't sure this was a move I was capable of making any time soon. I wasn't convinced that I deserved to be in Margery's life. Nor was I sure that Margery even wanted me. Maybe she was better off with Colin's family. Maybe Colin's mother could give Margery what I had so clearly failed to give.

Beside me, Roy gave a loud yawn and blinked through heavy lids. 'Don't go yet, love,' he mumbled, reaching for my hand. 'Stay a bit longer.' Early in our marriage, Roy had developed a sixth sense for when I was getting ready to leave the bed of a morning, even without me having moved a single muscle.

Just when I thought he had fallen back to sleep, his low voice cut through the semi-darkness, startling me with a question I'd not yet considered.

'Do you think Margery will have the baby baptised?' he asked. 'Because I wouldn't want to miss out on that.'

I pictured a small country church with Margery and Colin beside a sun-weathered clergyman. I imagined the baby, cocooned in some lacy christening gown handed down from Colin's family, and heard its thin cry of anguish as water was dripped over its head.

'But you don't even believe in God,' I replied testily. 'Nor does Margery, as far as I know.' Colin's family was Methodist, as were we, at least on paper.

'Even so, I'd like to be there. I'd like us both to be there.'

Without answering, I tucked my head into the triangle of Roy's shoulder and used my feet to push down the sheet. As I lay there waiting for a breath of cool air to blow in through the window, it occurred to me that the birth of Margery's baby would at least be officially registered, including the question of its legitimacy, and that this was more than I could say about myself. I mulled over terms for a hypothetical bargain.

If God, or any other force that ruled over our lives, saw fit to bring this baby safely into the world, then maybe, just maybe, I could ask Margery to give me another chance.

'Please just think about it, love,' Roy coaxed, kissing my forehead, before rolling out of the bed. He grunted as his feet touched the floorboards. 'And don't forget the street party this afternoon. I promised we'd be there.'

Today was Australia Day, the 26th of January, marking the anniversary of when the British First Fleet dropped anchor in Port Jackson. Although history was not a subject I had ever taught, I still remembered this and a long list of other notable dates relating to the Empire drilled into us as schoolgirls. I also remembered the controversy at the time of Australia's sesquicentenary in 1938. Members of the Australian Aborigines' League had staged a protest, proclaiming that this date should be recognised as a day of mourning, not of celebration. The League had not been successful in its aim that year, and I could not recall anything further being said about the subject since the war began. As I slowly dragged myself out of bed, summoning the strength to begin my day, nothing could be further from my own mind than the thought of celebrating.

~

At breakfast, Roy looked up from the newspaper, spectacles balanced precariously on the end of his nose as he read out the arrangements for this three-day weekend. It was the first Australia Day since peacetime. Also for the first time, this public holiday would be observed on the same day by every state, in this case Monday, that being the closest working day to today. According to the *Herald*, ice and milk would be delivered as usual, but there would be no bread deliveries from Saturday right through till Tuesday. Grocery shops – apart from those employing only the proprietor or his family – would be closed. Butchers would also be closed from noon today but should still be open this morning. This last point was a fact upon which Roy was relying, given his intention to walk up to the shops and buy four pounds of Mr Billy Barrett's best beef sausages as our contribution to this afternoon's street party.

'Maybe we could go and watch the Regatta on Monday?' Roy asked me.

'We'll see.'

'Or if that doesn't grab you, I was thinking of rounding up a few of the young vets and taking them to the Cricket Ground. New South Wales versus South Australia.'

'Be my guest, you haven't been to the cricket in a long time.'

'And tonight, at eight o'clock,' he announced, again reading from the paper, 'they'll be broadcasting Australia Day messages from General MacArthur from Tokyo, and Mr Attlee from London.'

'Let's hope the party will be over by then. We wouldn't want to miss that.' I rolled my eyes. 'Sorry,' I added when I saw Roy's face fall. 'I didn't mean to be so sarcastic.'

'It's all right, love. I know this past month has been especially hard, what with Christmas and all.'

Christmas had been abysmal. I winced at the memory. Roy and I had gone to Mosman for Christmas dinner with Charlie, Helen and John's extended family, all the while thinking of our empty dining table at home. After that experience, by unspoken agreement, we declined invitations for New Year's Eve.

That evening, as we ate our meal in miserable silence, with the sound of fire-crackers and merrymaking in the distance, all I wanted was to turn back the clock to the previous New Year's Eve so we could start 1945 again and find a way to make it end differently. Knowing Roy's fondness for New Year's resolutions and his irrepressible optimism, I'd had a feeling that when midnight came, he would ask me to forgive Margery and agree to making the trip up north with him in time to meet the baby. Instead, and while it had pained me to disappoint him yet again, I took myself to bed with a headache before nine, leaving him to see in the New Year on his own.

~

At two o'clock, just as the heat was reaching its climax, Roy and I walked to the end of our street for the Australia Day party. In front of the Delaneys' house at Number 29, our neighbours were gathering under the shade of two big trees. The smell of freshly cut grass added a surprising herbaceous aroma to the smoke from the nearby charcoal barbecue. A battery-operated radio played a lively jig at maximum volume, lending a carnival atmosphere to the scene. Two pink-fleshed watermelon halves sat on either side of the radio, into which someone had carved a serrated border like the gaping jaws of a jagged-toothed shark.

Roy set up our folding chairs where no one would trip over them and helped himself to a drink. The men had congregated to one side, near the barbecue, while the women milled together on the other, fussing over plates of food. Mothers whose children were still young were either coaxing suitably sized tidbits into unwilling little mouths or slapping away the cheeky hands of those who had already helped themselves to more than their fair share. Resigned to my fate, I waved goodbye to Roy and took my place among the ladies of the street.

As usual, one topic of conversation dominated all others, that of children. Admittedly, I could still recall my own eagerness to mix with other new mothers when Henry was small. I'd had so many questions and no mother of my own to ask. For some, today's party would provide an opportunity to gain the advice of women more experienced than themselves. For others, it was a chance to boast about their children's achievements and, by association, themselves.

'These savoury scones are delicious, Mrs Anthony. Did you make them?' I asked, hoping to introduce a new subject.

Mrs Anthony looked pleased. 'That was my Cassi, actually. She's top of her class in home economics. Ever since the Pattison family donated the Domestic Science block at Ravenswood, we've been treated to all sorts of delicious meals. I'm ready to hang up my apron for good.'

'Lucky you,' said Mrs Crowther. 'I wish Jenny had taken some of those lessons before she left school. Silly old me said it was a bit of a joke to call it a science, when it was nothing more than just common-sense practical skills handed down from mother to daughter. But then the joke was on me, of course, when she refused to spend any time with me in the kitchen so I could teach her!'

Everyone laughed, even me, although her innocent comment about passing knowledge down the generations had sent heat rushing from my core to my fingertips.

'What's Jenny doing now?' asked Mrs Anthony.

'After her Intermediates, she took those classes in stenography, which she quite enjoyed. She was offered a secretary position afterwards, but then her father said no, didn't he?' Mrs Crowther scowled. 'He felt she shouldn't take a job that another girl might really need, so now I'm stuck with her at home but I'm still doing all the cooking!'

Everyone laughed again, while Mrs Anthony turned to me. 'How about your Margery, Mrs Armstrong, is she a good cook?'

I looked at her uncertainly, fairly confident that everyone was aware of Margery's new living circumstances, even if not the state of our relationship. 'Margery's more like Jenny than your Cassi, I'm afraid. She never showed much interest in learning how to cook either, although she's a much better seamstress than I ever was. But now that she's a married woman and with a baby on the way, I expect she'll become a competent cook soon enough. She'll have to, won't she?'

'I'm sure Margery will be fine.' Mrs Anthony smiled warmly, as if trying to reassure me about more than my daughter's cooking skills.

'Necessity is the best teacher,' added Mrs Crowther with a meaningful nod.

'That's true,' I mumbled, gratefully biting into my scone.

With the conversation having now moved on to tennis, I was relieved that none of the women had tried to press me for more information. No doubt they would talk about Margery, or about Henry, amongst each other when I wasn't here, though probably even then without any ill intent. Talking about each other – gossiping, for want of a better word – was simply something women did. Perhaps it was easier than talking about ourselves.

But although I was grateful for their generous attitude towards Margery, I knew I was unworthy of the same.

Other than this talk of children and the upcoming school year, our conversation was confined to holiday plans and anecdotes, the latest dressmaking patterns and whose turn it was to host morning tea, interspersed with peals of laughter. Although I'd never been overly sociable, before the war I would have enjoyed this chance to relax with our neighbours, but ever since Henry's death, occasions like this left me claustrophobic. Amongst all these mothers, I felt like an imposter. But when a cup of sickly-sweet punch was pressed into my hands, I gave a loud thank you and kept smiling.

Trapped within this feminine circle, I pictured my daughter's lithe young figure now swelling in pregnancy. Anticipating the painful contractions of birth that Margery would soon endure, my stomach contracted instinctively, and I was engulfed by yet another rush of heat.

Nearby, I could hear the men complaining about continuing beer shortages, even while the empty bottles piled up around them. Roy, normally generous, was carefully guarding his own supply, kept cool under a large pile of ice inside our zinc-lined wicker basket, along with the sausages, which he appeared to have forgotten.

As the angle of the sun began to lower, I was gradually losing shade.

Beads of perspiration formed along my hairline and at the small of my back. I craned my head towards our house in the distance. Heat reflected off the surface of the road, playing tricks with my vision.

After an hour or more of standing like this, it had become unbearable. The two chairs we'd brought were only a few yards away in the shade, but I knew sitting there alone would invite unnecessary attention.

'Excuse me,' I said, addressing no one in particular. 'I'll just pop home for a minute and take down the washing. I left our towels on the line.'

It was as good an excuse as any and my apology was met with understanding.

'They'll be baked to a crisp. Just like me,' said Mrs West, grimacing as she inspected her forearms, which had turned a disturbingly deep shade of pink. 'Don't you just hate it when the towels get all dry and crusty?'

'Easily fixed,' said Mrs Aurisch, who could always be relied upon to offer a remedy for every household problem. 'Try putting bicarb in with your wash from the beginning, then a dash of vinegar with the rinse water. Keeps our towels nice and soft.'

'It sure is a hot one today,' panted Mrs Rickward, a newcomer to our street, nursing a chubby toddler on her hip and squinting up at the sky through fashionable sunglasses.

I glanced at Roy, trying in vain to catch his eye. Embroiled in conversation, he remained oblivious to my attempts, and I decided not to spoil his fun. When he eventually came to notice my absence, it would not be difficult to guess where I had gone and why.

~

Back at home, I drank a cool glass of water and looked forward to losing myself in a book for the remainder of the afternoon.

Although the condition of our bath towels had never been my concern, I went outside to take down the washing. The shrill song of cicadas filled the air. High-pitched and constant, it was the sound of thousands of wind-up toys, whirring and buzzing en masse. I scanned the treetops, smiling in sheer admiration at the volume of sound produced by such tiny creatures. Henry had once told me that greengrocers, our most common variety, were louder than almost any other insect on the planet, yet thinking back to the party, I couldn't recall hearing them. Perhaps their chorus had simply been drowned out by that of our street's human residents?

With the sun bearing down mercilessly on our well-situated clothesline, I wet a cloth and draped it around my neck. Days like today made me think of summer weekends when the children were young and still compliant enough for Roy to rally them into the car and head to the beach. They were always much happier after swimming, claiming they felt cool for hours. Once Margery and Henry reached adolescence, they wanted to go to the beach with their friends instead, and then not at all. Somewhere around that time, I remembered the Plumridges moving into the big house two doors down and installing their own pool, the first in our street. After discovering a shared interest in engines, Henry had made friends with Donald, their youngest, and was often invited over for a swim. Three years their junior, and a girl to boot, poor Margery was usually excluded from such invitations. To avoid argument, Henry would sneak out and slip through the gap in our side fence to make a mad dash across our neighbour's yard, before clambering over a second fence to get into Don's back garden.

Now that the Plumridge boys were both grown up, I wondered whether anyone still swam in their pool. Even before Henry's enlistment, Don had joined the RAAF and gone overseas. After an elaborate wedding, he and his bride had just moved into a new home down the line in Wollstonecraft, not far from town where Don would be following in his father's footsteps as a stockbroker.

Everyone in the street had been so impressed with the Plumridges' swimming pool when it first went in. After a long day at Don's place, Henry would saunter in with sunburned shoulders, darkened tan lines where his swimming trunks began and ended, and a huge smile, bubbling with stories about frogs found floating in the pool or the water dragon who had taken up residence. Sometimes, when he'd fail to return by dinner or was needed home earlier, I'd been forced to retrieve him myself. Mrs Plumridge had always offered tea or a glass of sherry, while I tried not to look at the boys cavorting in the pool as if they were sea creatures – jumping, diving and, in Don's case, doing somersaults. I still remembered the sound of their laughter and their games of blind man's buff. I even remembered the pungent smell of the dirty old flannel tied over their eyes, while they lurched from one end of the pool to the other, their voices reverberating in the air.

But even though I could remember all these details, I could no longer picture the swimming pool itself. Would it still look the same? There was only one way to find out. I had no doubt Mrs Plumridge would let me see the pool if I asked, but I also knew this would involve a long and painful conversation about Henry. With everyone occupied at the street party, perhaps I could just slip over and take a quick look. No one need ever know.

Following my impulse, I went straight to that part of our side boundary where the conifer hedge ended, and the smaller shrubs began, and put down my washing basket. The gap in the fence was still there, its three missing palings never replaced. Turning sideways to make myself smaller, I stepped calmly over the low crossbeam, parting the greenery.

As I darted across our neighbour's yard, feeling like a naughty schoolgirl, I heard a sharp bark and jumped. It was Cedric, their three-legged beagle, loping over to greet me. I bent down to pat him.

'Sshh,' I whispered, raising a finger to my lips. 'Don't tell.'

The second fence was harder. I tucked my skirt and petticoat into my underwear and took hold of the railing, hoisting myself over the top and landing with a thud on the other side. I pulled down my skirts and swallowed, glancing guiltily towards the house.

The Plumridges' allotment was a double-sized block. Against the green of the surrounding lawns and garden beds, the pool was like a shining blue canvas, set within an emerald frame. Not so much a painting, as a window to the sky. A narrow sandstone walkway ran along each side, except at the far end, where there was a low wall from which three aged copper spouts protruded, releasing a steady trickle of water. I recalled Henry and Don diving into the pool from this wall and Mrs Plumridge's stern warnings.

From over the fence, muted by the cicadas, I could hear the dog barking again. Cedric was clearly convinced there was an intruder in his midst. As indeed there was, I acknowledged, feeling myself redden. I crept forward through the grass towards the pool. It would certainly be awkward if Mrs Plumridge happened to choose this moment to come home. What on earth would I say?

I peered into the water, marvelling at its mesmerising colour – cornflower blue, like the sapphire ring Roy had given me soon after Margery's birth. Lining the interior was row upon row of blue-fired tiles, two inches square, that gave the pool its hue.

I looked back at the house to reassure myself of no activity from within. Then, very quickly and with no real inkling of what I was doing or why, I removed my skirt and shoes and lowered myself onto the wide ledge of the pool's first step, gasping as my feet hit the water.

Giving myself no time to change my mind, I dropped down to the second step. So much colder than I had expected, especially on a hot day like this. I reached the third and final step and laughed at the chill sensation of water lapping against my skin, higher and higher. Although my heart had remained in constant pain these past months, a magnet for my grief, the rest of my body had become something of an afterthought, almost numb. It was a relief to know I could still feel something after all.

The water was pooling around my thighs now, nearly wetting my underwear, and sending shivers down my spine. The hem of my petticoat had risen to the surface, as if hungry for air, and was floating out around me like a lily pad.

I eased the elastic band over my hips and pushed the sheer fabric down to my knees, lifting one foot, then the other. I threw the sodden loop behind me on the sandstone with a shrug, noticing how the water dripped from its edges, forming a wet patch that grew bigger as I watched, like dark ink spilled onto a page.

Only then did I peer back down into the water, captivated by the sight of my bare legs submerged. Unaccustomed to the sun, they were pale and ghostly. I was like one of those mangrove trees growing in the mudflats of Middle Harbour, with half my trunk underwater and half out. Halfway between this world and another. A liminal state. A place of infinite possibilities.

I took a few deep breaths. I was growing used to the temperature now. At the same time, my body felt altered, energised, even transformed, by its contact with this other medium. Little by little, the cold was seeping into my core. My limbs felt lighter. And although the sun still blazed down from above, I no longer felt its warmth against my skin.

I let out a deep sigh and tilted my head back as far as it would go. Hanging in the sky were a few soft clouds, like smudges of paint from an artist's hand. The air was alive with the deafening sound of the cicadas, vibrating in my ears and drowning out thoughts of anything but this moment. I dropped my hands into the water with a splash, feeling its resistance as I trailed my fingers forward and back, twisting and turning as if performing a dance.

Surrounded by the bleach-like odour of chlorine, I thought of Margery and the tiny baby floating inside her womb. Would they even take her to a hospital to deliver or would she rely on a local midwife? Or even the flying doctor service. What if the baby came early? Or if there was a complication? Suddenly gripped by a bout of shivering over all that could go wrong, Lawson's story came unbidden. I recalled his cold and clear-eyed account of the drover's wife – carrying her own dead child and riding nineteen miles for assistance – and cursed his ghost for interfering once again.

I wiped my eyes, waiting for my teeth to stop chattering. My entire body felt awash with sensation, as if each of my faculties had become heightened to the point of no return. Instinct told me I needed to latch onto something concrete.

I considered the wall at the far end of the pool. How would it feel to plunge in headfirst? To dive down, in one swift graceful motion, like a mermaid from her rocky clifftop into the swirling ocean below.

Instead, I dropped down from the last step until both my feet were touching the bottom. The water was at my breasts now and the white cotton voile of my sleeveless blouse quickly became translucent. Through the sheer film of this outer layer and my equally thin undergarments, I regarded my pale skin, faintly rippled with gooseflesh. Gripping the sandstone edge with one hand, I tipped back my head and neck until the water reached my hair. Cold! I straightened my back and shook my head from side to side, spraying droplets of water like rain. I leaned back a second time, testing the water's buoyancy, the way it seemed to want to hold me, like an invitation.

I pictured Henry and Margery, running in and out of the surf as young children, giggling and laughing hysterically as if they had discovered some great secret.

I came back to the present. When I opened my eyes, the skies unfolded in a brilliant blaze of blue.

Chapter 30

Rollercoaster

Margery's baby was born two weeks after Australia Day, the 10th of February. A boy. A gloriously healthy baby boy.

The news came via a call from Colin's mother, Iris Cartwright, while I was washing up. Roy picked up the receiver within seconds. Once I realised who was on the phone, my breath stopped. I clenched the sponge with both hands until I heard him erupt into joyful laughter and hearty congratulations. Even then, I couldn't move, my hands reddening in the hot water, while I listened to Roy repeating all the details and writing them down. He sounded so proud and earnest, I began to cry.

I did the maths in my head, counting back nine months to the tenth of May. The war in Europe had officially ended two days earlier. The baby must have been conceived around the time of those VE Day celebrations. Perhaps even that day? I wracked my brain, trying to remember what Margery had been doing. Luna Park? Yes, that was it. She and Barbara wanted to be on Sydney Harbour in the heart of all the action. Margery had bragged she was finally ready to brave the rollercoaster, which had surprised me, given her ingrained fear of heights, but I couldn't recall her commenting about it afterwards. Perhaps that was because she had lied to us and gone somewhere else instead? How long had she known this returned soldier before being led down a one-way path to adulthood?

Why had Margery never mentioned Colin's name that week or at any point before her elopement? Had I really been so neglectful, so dismissive and unapproachable, that my own daughter felt she could not talk to me? Yes, was the obvious answer. It was all finally making sense. Margery's behaviour had most definitely changed after those peace celebrations. Looking back, I wanted to kick myself. If I hadn't been so distracted thinking about Henry still at risk in the Pacific, I might have thought more deeply about her odd moods and frequent withdrawals to her bedroom. Whereas I had falsely drawn the conclusion that Margery had finally seen the light, choosing to put her social life to the backburner and apply herself to her studies, she might simply have been taking stock. Perhaps even regretting what had happened? But eventually, as the weeks and months went on, it must have dawned on my poor child that she was pregnant. This, I now suspected, must have been when the lipstick and hair curlers had come back out, while Margery worked hard to convince Colin to do the right thing and marry her. And all that time she had felt compelled to keep it a secret.

Before he put down the receiver, I heard Roy thank Mrs Cartwright for her invitation and promise we'd be in touch.

I lay awake most of the night. My little girl, with a child of her own. Only one month shy of her nineteenth birthday, my daughter had become a mother ... a 'girl-wife', just as Henry Lawson had described. As a whirlwind of competing emotions tumbled through my mind, I took comfort in the list of facts Roy had hastily scrawled on the notebook by the phone. *Baby boy ... 7 pounds, 7 ounces ... straightforward labour no problem ... doctor not needed ... midwife experienced ... hair dark ... good set of lungs ... Francis William Cartwright.*

I pictured his soft dewy skin, tiny fingers and toes, and milky newborn smell. My first grandchild. How extraordinary. With every inch of my being, I wanted nothing more than to hop straight on the train and travel up with there with Roy. To shake Colin's hand and welcome him to our family, to get to know each other during the long drive from the station to their farm. Above all, I wanted to take Margery in my arms and to cradle my grandchild.

But even though my prayers had been answered and Margery and baby Francis were both safe and well, I still could not bring myself to see them. I hadn't forgotten my silent bargain that morning of the Australia Day party. But now that I knew Margery's baby was a boy, and not a girl – as I'd inexplicably been expecting – my anxiety had intensified.

Almost as soon as I'd processed the miraculous fact of the baby's arrival, I had registered that same feeling as when Henry was little and which I'd talked about with Hilda – that nagging sense he was mine on borrowed time. Here was my grandson, this perfect baby boy, conceived under the illusion of enduring peace at the penultimate conclusion of a long and bloody conflict. What chance did he have of growing up without incident, of living out the term of his natural life without being pulled into the next war?

No chance at all, said the voice in my head, *not if the past is anything to go by*. Hadn't this been what I had tried to protect myself from for all those years? To spare myself from further loss under the pretext of living life as an independent woman?

In the morning, I told Roy my decision. He was crushed, as I knew he would be. Apologising for my absurd threats and cruel ultimatum when Margery had first left us, I gave my blessing for him to visit our daughter and her new family as often as he liked. Margery deserved the love and support of at least one of her parents.

I made myself scarce while he spoke to Mrs Cartwright, telling her that while he would be delighted to come as soon as he could arrange it, I had unfortunately been unwell and was not up to the journey.

That week, while Roy prepared for his departure, putting in long hours at work, I kept busy with my own preparations. Margery had asked for her sewing machine, along with various other bits and pieces. To this list I added warm clothing and whatever else I thought she might need that I could cram into the cardboard box. Summer would soon be over.

Although I had made Roy offer to buy them a new pram and bring it up with him on the train, we'd been told it wasn't needed. Mrs Cartwright had already dusted off Colin's old one, along with a wooden crib, and even a highchair for later. I received the same message regarding newborn-sized clothing for the baby. Mrs Cartwright and Margery had everything in hand.

Thought hurt by these implicit rejections, I could not resist contributing to the newborn's layette by purchasing rompers in bigger sizes and various shades of blue. These I carefully wrapped within the folds of Margery's own baby blanket and the embroidered bed linens from Jean Campbell and packed them into a wicker basket.

Over several shopping expeditions I procured a generous supply of Margery's favourite toiletries, which I assumed would now be impossible for her to buy herself, along with magazines for her to look at while nursing the baby. Once the gift hamper was completed to my satisfaction, a pleasing combination of both practical and luxury items, I baked a fruit cake for Mrs Cartwright, hoping its taste had not been spoiled by the many tears fallen into its batter, as I tried to swallow my own jealous thoughts.

I sealed the cardboard box, tying a strip of old cloth to form a handle that Roy would be able to carry on the train, along with the wicker hamper and his own small travelling case. Only then did I allow myself to wonder what Margery would make of my absence. Roy had generously spared me from any comments she might have made during their one phone call since the birth. But who knew what Margery had said about me to Colin or his family? Whether she had gone along with Roy's excuse about me being unwell and protected us both from judgement, or whether she had told the truth, whatever she supposed that to be? It broke my heart to think – or rather, know – that Margery would be hurt by my absence and continued silence. Did she believe I was simply being bloody-minded and judgemental in withholding my forgiveness? Or would Margery open the various packages and understand what I meant them to convey? Would she gain any measure of comfort from these gifts and recognise in them her mother's love, flawed as it was? Would she ever understand that I was punishing myself, more than anyone else, by staying away?

~

The night before Roy left, Charlie came for dinner, bringing his new friend, Peter. The pair had met through their work at the Council for Scientific and Industrial Research in Canberra, where Peter had recently joined Charlie at the CSIR's Division of Economic Entomology (or, as Roy liked to call it, the Division of Bugs and Banking). Following an end of war organisational reshuffle, they were now engaged in the same insecticide research project. Peter did not strike me as a typical scientist. Tall, slim, fair-haired and charming, Margery would have been swooning.

Once introductions were behind us, and while I was occupied with showing Peter some of our paintings, I heard Charlie whispering to Roy: 'For Margery.'

I winced instinctively at the sight of Charlie's missing two fingers as he handed over an envelope. Roy laid the envelope on his palm, assessing its weight.

'Just a card,' explained Charlie, now smiling in my direction, 'plus some photos I found from ages ago, when we all went to Clifton Gardens together. Remember that day?'

Roy nodded wistfully, catching my eye.

'There's a little something extra in there to help with the baby, too,'

Charlie added. 'Best keep it in your jacket pocket, Uncle Roy. Wouldn't want it mislaid.'

'Thanks mate. Very kind of you. I'll make sure she gets it.'

At my urging, Roy had already opened a new bank account in Margery's name – as something that she and Francis could always fall back on, without needing her husband's permission. In addition to its generous opening balance, I was also planning to deposit a little of my own housekeeping money each week. It wasn't much, by way of independence, but it was all I could think of for now.

Over a meal of roast lamb with all the trimmings, Roy and I took turns asking after Peter's family and his new role at the CSIR. Bright and bubbly, Peter was a brilliant conversationalist and before long we were all on first-name terms.

In recent years, Charlie had rarely spoken of his work, and certainly never in detail. Perhaps he was conscious of not divulging confidential information, especially during the war, or perhaps he had presumed Margery and I would find it boring. Peter, in contrast, had no such qualms. With little prompting, he launched into a colourful account of some of their colleagues, adopting different voices to imitate the way they spoke, together with distinctive mannerisms. At one point he used the half-chewed bones from his lamb rack as a prop, carrying on with his skit despite the warning elbow from Charlie. By the time he had shared yet another anecdote proving Charlie had not outgrown his childhood absent-mindedness and, irrespective of lab safety protocols, was as accident prone as ever, Roy was in stitches. Even I allowed myself a wry chuckle or two at Charlie's expense.

'Charlie, mate,' said Roy, wiping away tears of laughter, 'I hate to say it, but hearing you talk about your job and co-workers all these years, I always pictured a bunch of strait-laced scientists – white lab coats, hair plastered down with Brylcreem and eyeglasses as thick as Coca-Cola bottles, but Peter makes it sound like you're working for the Wirth Brothers' Circus.'

Peter flashed a wide smile in Roy's direction, his eyes twinkling under long eyelashes. 'You're onto us now, Roy. Charlie's head of our little department, so that makes him the ringmaster. Between the rest of us performers, we've got jugglers, magicians, trained animals and even a lion tamer if you count Miss Whittleworth at the front desk.'

Everyone laughed, and for a few bittersweet moments, I felt happy.

'So, Charlie – have you met any nice young ladies recently?' Roy almost always asked this question, and I shot Charlie a sympathetic glance.

'Afraid not, Uncle Roy,' Charlie shrugged, giving his usual reply.

'What about you, Peter?' asked Roy, turning towards our guest.

'Afraid not, Uncle Roy,' mimicked Peter.

Roy snorted, almost choking on his laughter, while I laughed out loud. It was a novelty for my husband to encounter someone with an even more wicked sense of humour than his.

'Listen to these two, Lillian. First a circus act and now they're a comedic duo. But seriously, boys – why not? Don't you want to settle down and get married?'

'Let's just say I'm married to my work, Uncle Roy,' Charlie said, demonstrating remarkable patience.

Peter chimed in. 'Me too, Uncle Roy – had the honeymoon just last week.'

'I give up,' said Roy, putting his head in his hands. 'Just remember, the best girls won't wait for you forever.'

Once upon a time, Hilda and everyone else had given me the same advice. In hindsight, I could see their point. Like Roy, I hoped Charlie would soon find the right girl and start a family. He would surely make a wonderful father. But tonight, I had also noticed the way Charlie looked at Peter. It was not unlike the way Roy had looked at me when we first met, how he sometimes looked at me still. I filed away my observation for now.

Our conversation took a darker turn after dinner when Roy asked

Charlie what he thought about the atomic bomb testing in the Pacific. My jaw clenched instinctively. Not content with the damage already wrought by their nuclear weapons on Japan last August, America was intending to test more of them in the Marshall Islands in a few months' time in a remote island locale called Bikini Atoll, conveniently located far away from America. They planned on assembling a mighty armada of one hundred naval ships, just so they could count how many would be destroyed by each blast. To make matters worse, they were even planning to bring in livestock as test subjects, with pigs, goats and rats set to take the place of sailors and other human targets.

Charlie acknowledged his reservations about these experiments to be led by a joint American army–navy taskforce. Although he'd been following the reports, he claimed to know little else apart from what had been printed in the newspaper.

Despite Charlie's reticence, it soon transpired Peter had an American friend, a physicist who had worked as a researcher in Washington during the war. Only later, once his friend had returned to his peacetime university position, did Peter learn he had been involved in the top-secret Manhattan Project.

I had been clearing the table, but now stopped what I was doing, unwilling to stay quiet any longer.

'It makes me sick to my stomach to think that America already possesses a nuclear weapon a thousand times more powerful than what they dropped on Hiroshima. Why even make something like that? Why would anyone want to create the instrument of their own death? I'm sorry, Peter, but hasn't your friend read *Frankenstein*? He and his colleagues are no better.'

'You're not wrong,' said Peter. 'I've thought the same myself. However well-intentioned, I think Oppenheimer might be the world's latest "Modern Prometheus".'

'Frankenstein, the monster?' asked Roy, still stuck on my comment.

'You're saying the scientists are monsters.'

'No, Roy.' I shook my head impatiently. 'Victor Frankenstein was the scientist who created the monster.'

'Oh, I see,' said Roy. 'I never read that book. More of an Agatha Christie man myself.'

Peter looked at me and grinned. Having had my say, and now feeling validated by a fellow reader, I continued my kitchen duties while the others returned to the specifics of the upcoming tests.

Charlie's description of Bikini Atoll gave the impression of an untouched tropical paradise, causing me to think of Bougainville where our son had fought and died. The palm-fringed volcanic islands and coral atolls of the Marshall Islands seemed an incongruously beautiful setting for the ugliness to follow.

From what I could understand, there were to be two bombs. The first, a replica of the one used on Nagasaki, was to be dropped from several hundred feet and had been christened by the Superfortress crew training for the task as the Model T Bomb, since its technology would soon be outmoded. Then why, I might ask, test it now? The second, to be detonated underwater from within the Bikini Lagoon, was predicted to produce an explosion temperature of one hundred million degrees Fahrenheit, winds with a velocity of a thousand miles an hour and waves one hundred feet high. *Pure insanity,* I thought, shaking my head in disgust. I swiped my tea towel over the dishes in the rack, stacking each plate on the kitchen bench with a loud clatter to signal my protest.

Charlie appeared before me in the kitchen doorway. 'How are you, Aunt Lillian? Thanks for having us tonight.'

'My pleasure.' I bit my lip to hold back any tears.

'I'm so sorry. This past year – it must be so difficult for you.'

'Thank you, Charlie, but I'm not the only mother to have lost her son.'

'I know, but all this with Margery too. Nothing's happening the way you would have wished. You just need more time to adapt.' He put his arm around my shoulder. 'That's what I told Margie – in my letter, you know. That she just needs to give you a little more time to get used to things. I was thinking about how, at a biological level, every species needs thousands of years to adapt – more, in some cases – but on a behavioural level, we humans can learn to adapt to almost anything during our lifetime. It's been proven.' He smiled encouragingly.

'Thank you, darling,' I replied, trying not to let my expression betray my reaction. Charlie had always found comfort in science. For him, it was a faith stronger than religion. But although Charlie's simplified explanation of evolution gave me no comfort, I appreciated him trying.

'I never knew Father,' Charlie continued. 'And I was too young to really notice Mother's grief when he died. But losing Henry, even for me, has been a terrific shock. I still catch myself sometimes, especially at work, thinking I must write and tell him about something or other, then I remember he's gone. I can't even imagine how much worse it must be for you and Uncle Roy. And for Margie, too, of course.'

'Did you write to him often?' I asked, smiling through my tears. Henry had idolised his clever older cousin. Theirs would have been a life-long friendship.

'Every couple of months. Not often enough, I think now. Scientific stuff, mostly. It seemed to interest him.'

'Did you keep any of his letters?' I held my breath.

'I wish I had. For some stupid reason, I never thought anything would happen to him. I even promised you it wouldn't.' Charlie shook his head regretfully.

'Not your fault,' I said automatically, squeezing his arm.

Charlie sighed. 'We know a lot about our world and man's place within it, but sometimes I think there's so much more we'll never know.'

I waited.

'Like grief, for instance. I understand the evolutionary purpose of pain as a kind of survival mechanism. But what's the point of emotional pain, I wonder? The kind of grief people have to endure every single day?'

I blinked in surprise. Charlie was becoming more philosophical with age. The war and Henry's death must have impacted him even more than I, and perhaps even he, had realised. One of these days, Peter or I would have to introduce Charlie to some alternative reading genres to those he favoured, so he could see that universal truths about mankind were more likely to be found in fiction than in scientific literature.

I began crafting a suitable response, but was suddenly overcome by a wave of tiredness. 'Thank you for coming tonight, Charlie dear. It means a lot to us both. And I really did enjoy meeting Peter.'

~

The next morning, I drove Roy to the station and returned to an empty house, acknowledging this week would be the first time I was going to be properly alone since our wedding day. Although long accustomed to being on my own in the daytime, it felt different going to sleep by myself in our lopsided double bed, knowing I would wake up the same way.

All week, the weather added to my sense of unease. February was, for me, Sydney's only unpleasant month – a single aberration to an otherwise ideal climate. The air was thick and heavy, like a revoltingly rich pudding served at the end of a dinner party one had to finish for fear of offending one's host. Even rousing myself for my walk required enormous effort, as if climbing a mountain instead of a hilly suburban street.

The house appeared to share my distaste. Floorboards groaned and creaked underfoot. Doors stuck in their hinges or refused to close, and furniture developed a cloudy film. Outside, on the stone path, moss bloomed like a lush carpet. And our front verandah tiles had become so slippery I had to watch my step going to the letterbox each morning.

I kept thinking about how Roy was faring. The weather would be hotter up there, though perhaps less muggy since the farm lay inland. It must have been a long and bumpy ride, enough to trigger one of Roy's sciatica attacks. I hoped he'd been given a comfortable bed – perhaps on a screened verandah – and wondered if he'd be staying with Margery or in the main house with her in-laws. The flies would be a shock to my city slicker husband. Hopefully by now he would have learned to keep his mouth shut and his wisecracks to himself when outside. Maybe Margery would give him a cork hat.

Still smiling at this cartoon-like image, I felt a pang of self-reproach that I'd forgotten to pack the pills for Roy's back pain, a feeling which rapidly mushroomed into an all-encompassing sense of guilt and misgiving about Margery. With one hand pressed ineffectually against my chest, I tried again to tell myself she was better off without me. That Margery had chosen Colin's family over ours. And that I had forfeited the right to be in her life, both as her mother and as grandmother to Francis. I even tried consoling myself with the idea they would be safer living in the country than here in Sydney, where we might find ourselves the victims of some future nuclear test gone wrong. But the more I tried to convince myself I was doing this for her, the less I believed it.

Chapter 31
A New Stamp

'Ready to go?' I asked Charlie, who was down from Canberra for the weekend, travelling alone this time since Peter had work commitments. After a night in Mosman with his mother, he'd spent last evening with us, sleeping in Henry's old room.

'Bye, Uncle Roy, hope you feel better soon,' Charlie called out.

'Bye, mate,' wheezed Roy, still recovering from his latest bout of bronchitis under a pile of blankets. 'And don't forget to tell Pete, all work and no play makes Jack a dull boy.'

'No fear,' grinned Charlie. 'But I'll tell him anyway.'

Six months on, Peter and Charlie were now flatmates. Although Charlie had never come out and said anything directly, I had reached my own conclusions about their relationship, but when I'd tried broaching the subject with Roy, he'd been uncharacteristically prudish, muttering some excuse about just not having met the right girl. Either way, I knew I was not alone in having missed Peter's playful presence and affectionate ways.

'I can't get over how warm it's been,' said Charlie, removing his jacket as we set off towards the station. 'It's freezing in Canberra. We get frost nearly every morning.'

'You've forgotten how mild and beautiful our winters are in Sydney,' I boasted, gesturing at the sky, an attention-seeking blue that defied all reasonable expectations. 'And that one week we always get in August when it's genuinely hot like this.'

'The colour of cobalt,' Charlie agreed, squinting upward.

'So, has Peter succeeded where I failed ... in getting you to read any novels?'

'Afraid not. Although Uncle Roy did lend me a book of Henry Lawson's stories a while ago. I didn't mind them, in fact.'

'Not you, too,' I groaned.

Charlie looked confused. 'I thought you wanted me to read something other than scientific papers. Lawson's stories seemed well observed to me – not flowery, like a lot of others from that era. Short and to the point.'

'I'm not denying he was a skillful writer, Charlie, but surely brevity isn't everything? If I'm enjoying what I'm reading, I like it to go on as long as possible. I'm always sorry when a good book ends.'

Charlie appeared unconvinced. 'Well, I also liked his sense of humour – very dry, even cutting at times.'

'Really? Personally, I think Peter could rival him for sarcasm any day,' I said, only half-joking.

'Like that story where he talks about the rabbit-proof fence between the New South Wales and Queensland borders, with rabbits running up and down both sides. And then he says something about the fence being a source of amusement for the rabbits themselves, along with Pasteur, poison and inoculation.'

'Trust you to home in on the scientific references,' I laughed, despite myself. The story to which Charlie was referring, 'Hungerford', was also one of Roy's favourites. He'd always claimed the irony was so thick you could cut it with a knife. I also knew my husband appreciated Lawson's little gag at his own expense in that story, in making fun of his deafness.

'Uncle Roy did say you weren't much of a fan of Henry Lawson.'

'He said that, did he? Let's just say I'm more of a fan now than I used to be.' I thought back to the day Roy and I first met at Henry Lawson's funeral and our first conversation in which I'd had to admit my reservations about the writer.

Charlie cocked his head.

'I'm glad you liked them, Charlie. If it's got you reading, that's all that matters. But on a different note, and since I have you to myself right now, there is something I've been wanting to ask.'

Charlie glanced at me sideways and pulled at his shirt collar.

'Why did you enlist, back in '41, when your work qualified you for exemption?'

Charlie shook his head. 'I still ask myself the same thing sometimes. I can't really explain it.'

'Something about honouring your father's name, wasn't that what you said?'

Charlie blushed. 'I did, didn't I? Made it harder to argue against, especially for Mother.' He smacked his lips together and exhaled. 'By the time Japan joined the war, so many of our best men were already fighting overseas so I remember thinking it was high time the rest of us stepped up. And I suppose I had a younger man's faith in my own immortality.'

'And why the air force and not army? You've never been one to care about image.'

'No, nothing like that, of course. It was a calculated choice. Even though I convinced myself nothing would happen to me, I suppose I figured at least this way it would be quick and clean if it did.' He waved his hand in the air, his missing fingers conspicuous by their absence. 'Pathetic really, to think I never even got up in the air before that stupid training accident. But in hindsight, it was best thing that could have happened to me.'

‘Thank goodness, yes. If only something similar had happened to Henry.’

‘I’m sorry, Aunt Lillian. I still can’t believe he’s been gone a year. Do you think it’s true what they say about time healing all wounds? Has it gotten any easier?’

‘Yes and no,’ I said, trying to keep the tremor from my voice. ‘The wound may not bleed anymore, at least not noticeably, but it never heals completely. Not in my experience anyway.’ I was thinking not only of Henry, but of my old wounds too.

‘What about Uncle Roy? I know he’s thrown himself into making life easier for some of the veterans living around here. It seems like he’s found a way to make the best of things.’

‘He always does.’ I admired Roy’s indomitable spirit, even if I could not match it.

‘One of my colleagues,’ Charlie began, ‘whose son was also killed in the war, told me it was like permanently losing your spectacles and being forced to make do with someone else’s instead. I found the comparison inadequate, at first, but it stuck with me.’

‘It is like looking at life through a veil,’ I agreed. ‘There are days, or at least moments, when I can still laugh and feel happy, but it’s not the same as before and never lasts for long. It’s something Roy and I are still trying come to terms with. No joy will ever be complete but it’s the best we can expect.’

Roy had once likened our situation to one of those children’s toy batting sets where the rubber ball is attached to a bat with a piece of string or elastic. One could only throw it so far before it snapped back into position.

Charlie nodded sympathetically. ‘What about you and Margie. Isn’t it time you both let bygones be bygones?’

‘Easier said than done, Charlie. It’s complicated between us, even though I have a long list of regrets. Roy likes me to remind me of how I felt as a young girl at Sacred Heart, before my father died. I used to write to him all the time, but he never once replied or came to see me.' I pursed my lips, remembering how certain I'd been that Father was punishing me for having survived the fire and, years later, the rush of relief when Roy convinced me it was very likely the other way around. I hated myself for now doing the same with Margery.

Charlie frowned. 'That must have been terrible. It was hard enough for me growing up without a father but at least I could tell myself he was a war hero. Yours was still alive.'

'Until one day when he wasn't,' I spoke quietly. 'And that was even worse.'

I paused in front of a house where Margery had once played tennis with her friends and sat down on the low sandstone wall, originally built to curve gracefully around a line of conifers defining its front perimeter. In the thirty or more years I'd been making this walk, I had watched these trees grow tall and wide, and the once gracious wall was now bent and bulging like an ill-formed set of teeth. Lichen bloomed silvery-green on its porous surface.

'Watch your trousers,' I said, as Charlie sat beside me.

'He was a drover, your father, wasn't he?'

'That he was.' I nodded wryly. 'I used to wish I could join him on his droves. I thought it sounded so exciting, much better than boarding school with the nuns.'

'Like Chips Rafferty in *The Overlanders*? Pete thought that scene with the crocodiles was the most thrilling thing he'd ever seen. I liked the stampede myself and the footage they shot from the air. Incredible scenery – wouldn't mind going there myself one day.'

'Thrilling maybe, but dangerous too.' I shrugged.

'How did your father die? Was it a stampede or a bad fall? Or a snake bite?'

'Nothing so dramatic, I'm afraid. I was told he died of a fever.'

Charlie's countenance was solemn. 'At least he died doing something worthwhile. It's like what Chips's character said in the film, about when he tried to enlist and got knocked back. The sergeant told him to stick to the cattle because "bullocks are more important than bullets in this war". Droving is an important part of this country's history, isn't it?'

'I suppose so. Someone's got to do it, anyway,' I said, rising to my feet. We walked on in thoughtful silence until a vicious-sounding bark stopped us in our tracks.

'It's all right. He can't get to us,' I told Charlie, who had swivelled round in alarm. I gestured to the spiked metal fence behind us, through which a large Rottweiler was baring its teeth. 'He's just protecting his property. We can't hold that against him.'

'Fair enough,' he agreed. 'And thank goodness for a sturdy fence like that, but I don't know why so many of the other houses have fences just as high. I don't think there are too many burglars or vagrants to worry about around here. Who are they trying to keep out?' he added, with an uncharacteristically mischievous wink in my direction.

I dismissed Charlie's apparent accusation with a wave. 'I'm sure it's the same where your mother lives.'

'In some streets, yes, but the topography is different there. Everyone in Mosman shares a common ambition, you know.'

'Namely?'

'To look upon the sea, of course. And if that means building their houses with the bedrooms downstairs and living room up top or facing right onto their neighbours' yards or roofs just to catch a glimpse of the water, they'll cheerfully look past all those impediments and remind themselves they own a harbour view.'

I gave a small grunt of admiration. Charlie had a point, both about Mosman's understandable obsession and about my fellow residents. While most of them behaved in a 'neighbourly' manner, they certainly did their utmost not to see or hear anything of their neighbours from within their own four walls. Generous land allotments helped make this possible, along with judicious planting of trees and hedges, all coaxed into shape to afford maximum privacy. Our own garden was no different.

'I don't think they're trying to keep anyone out so much as wanting to create a special place that is just theirs,' I said in defence of my community.

'Isn't that the same thing?'

'Not quite,' I said, although inwardly I acknowledged its considerable barriers to entry, economic and otherwise.

'Or maybe they're scared of communists getting in,' Charlie grinned.

We turned into the next street and I noticed another heavily fortified property. Perhaps Charlie was right to poke fun. Apart from keeping intruders out, the downside of having too many walls was that they also kept their occupants cloistered within, out of touch with the rest of the world. Perhaps my cherished neighbourhood had more in common with Sacred Heart than I'd ever considered?

As we neared the steps leading to the train station, the sunshine was laced with the sweet and heavy fragrance of jonquils. Charlie stopped at the foot of the stairs and turned to me.

'I've been thinking about what you said about losing a child.'

I stiffened.

'You know that poem, the one that's inscribed on all the war memorials and that they recite every year at Anzac Day? "For the Fallen" I think it's called.'

My eyes misted as I recited the familiar lines. 'They shall grow not old, as we that are left grow old: Age shall not weary them, nor the years condemn.'

Charlie nodded. 'I know it's supposed to be comforting, but it almost makes it sound as though the dead are better off than the rest of us who are left to slowly wither away – because of sickness and frailty and everything else that comes with old age.'

'It's the price we have to pay for living,' I said softly.

'I've been trying to think about it objectively. Biologically, if you like, from a scientific viewpoint.'

I was not surprised.

'If you think of nature – plant, animal, insect – anything living ... each organism has its own life cycle which it follows to maturity. At that point, the organism is ready to reproduce, and the life cycle begins all over, from one generation to the next. And if an organism can do that, you could say it's fulfilled its potential – its purpose.

'Or think of a single flower,' he continued, gesturing towards the bed of yellow-centred jonquils beside us. 'It begins with someone planting a bulb. Eventually, the bulb shoots and we can see it above the ground. Before long, the leaves start to grow and flower buds appear. One day the flowers open, just like these, and everyone is happy.'

'And then?' I tried not to sound impatient.

'Well, then it's time for the flowers and foliage to die back and for everything to start over again. Provided the soil is well-drained, the bulbs can even just stay in place for the next flowering season.'

'And?'

Charlie shifted his weight. 'What I'm trying to say – probably not very well, I admit – is that I think what makes it so sad when a young person dies is knowing that their lives have ended prematurely – quite literally, before they reach maturity – and before they ever had a chance to fulfil their potential.'

It was hardly a new thought and yet there was both logic and poignancy in the way he had expressed it. I waited before answering, letting the idea wash over me. Perhaps Charlie was right. Perhaps the ultimate purpose of life was to fulfil one's potential, in the same way that an organism completed its prescribed life cycle, or a flower took what it needed from earth and sky to reach its full bloom.

'I see what you're getting at. And thank you for not using any jargon.'

Reassured, Charlie pressed on. 'That's one of the reasons why war is so tragic. All those young men, cut down in their prime, with no regard for the natural order of life.'

I sighed, avoiding his glance.

'Henry's death was a tragedy. No lines of poetry can ever change that fact – you and I both know that. But Aunty Lillian, you mustn't forget Margery is still alive. She's still so young. She's already produced one child so to that end she's fulfilled at least part of her potential, biologically speaking ... but she's still young. She still has so much of life ahead of her and I just can't believe you'd want to miss out on being a part of that life.'

Charlie must have seen me flinch as his speech became more rapid and he reached out to touch me. 'I know I don't have children, I probably never will, so I can't presume to understand what you're going through, but I've known you for most of my life – and I've known Margie for her entire life – and I really don't think the two of you should be apart any longer.'

He was right, of course. Even as he spoke, Charlie was demonstrating his own steady advancement towards maturity. The years were going by, just as they always had and always would, long after I was gone. With a sharp pang, I thought of Henry, who would forever be twenty-one. As for Margery, as Charlie had pointed out in his own clumsy way, she was still young and full of potential. I had already missed her nineteenth birthday. How could I possibly justify missing any more?

I glanced back at the jonquils with an uneasy conscience. Could I honestly say I had given my daughter everything she had needed to reach her own bloom? I paused, waiting for the usual voice in my head to speak up, telling me Margery was better off without me. But for once it was strangely silent.

'Thanks, Charlie. I'll think about what you've said, I promise.'

~

With Charlie's words still ringing in my ears, I left him to board his train to Central and headed to the post office for the first of my errands.

'Two dozen ordinary stamps, please, Mr Banks. Five shillings' worth.'

I waited while our postmaster tore off the required number and handed them over. Just as I was folding the long sheet in half, ready to stow it in my purse, I noticed the image printed on the stamps and raised my brows at the sight of a familiar profile. With that unmistakably grand moustache, together with full eyebrows and a shock of hair combed to the side, it could only be one man – Henry Lawson, yet again! I examined the stamps more closely, angling my head back and forth until my ageing long-sighted eyes gained focus. Beneath the detailed line drawing, which I recognised as the work of Lionel Lindsay, was Henry Lawson's signature, together with the year of his birth and of his death, 1867–1922. As if I could ever forget.

Old Mr Banks must have noticed my agitation. 'Everything all right, Mrs Armstrong? Anything else I can help you with?'

'No thank you, Mr Banks, that will be all. I just hadn't seen these new stamps before.'

'Hadn't you? We've had them since June. They came out in time for Lawson's birthday. It's a good likeness, isn't it? You're too late for first-day covers though, I'm afraid.'

I looked at him blankly.

'If you're a collector, that is,' he clarified, evidently perceiving my confusion.

I shook my head politely. 'I'm not a collector.' *At least, not of stamps*, I added silently.

~

Inside the newsagency, I scanned the display of journals and magazines until I located the title Roy had asked for. As I headed towards the counter, my eye was drawn to a cover. I rarely purchased women's magazines, preferring to read books over the assortment of articles, advertisements and romance serials offered by the *Women's Weekly* and other such periodicals. A gorgeous young woman graced the front of this week's issue, dressed in a red suit. With the model's head tilted to one side and her blond hair pulled back becomingly, I was reminded of Margery. 'New Hair Styles, Page 11' declared the caption.

Taking the magazine from its shelf, I found page 11 and began reading. 'Madonna centre-parting with halo of curls, suits the girl with oval face and regular features.' Yes, that was my girl. 'The back hair is swept with a slight undulating effect across the back and then up, merging in with the top curls. Charming for evening dates.'

Although my darling daughter no longer had any 'evening dates' to look forward to, it was exactly the sort of article she would love to read. Or, at least, she would have. I bought the magazine, thinking Roy could bring it with him next month on his planned second visit to the farm.

~

Errands completed, I headed home, weighed down by my string bag of oranges and my equally heavy thoughts.

As I trudged down Rosedale Road, I paused to admire the wattle in full bloom, a series of brilliant yellow flashes, like bursts of sunlight, scattered across the valley. Each year, their appearance was a welcome reminder to me that spring was just around the corner. Attracted by an especially glorious specimen about fifteen feet high, I came forward to trail my fingers through its powdery soft golden orbs, breathing in the rich floral aroma. Sweet and woody, it smelled like the local honey Roy liked on his toast each morning.

Buoyed by their beauty, I walked with renewed energy, revelling in the balmy winter sunshine. Halfway across the bridge, an unexpected image popped into my mind, of Henry Lawson's flower-laden coffin at Waverley Cemetery. Strewn in amongst the traditional lilies and wildflower bouquets, I recalled the sprays of golden wattle, glowing ethereally against the cloudy sky as if lit from within.

I thought again of the stamps in my purse and took them out for a second look. Row after row of Lawson's copper-toned visage greeted me. His head was turned sideways, sparing the viewer from looking directly into the writer's eyes – famously dark and expressive – but I still felt the burden of his penetrating gaze.

'Now that's enough,' I heard myself saying, almost as if he were an old friend. 'Isn't it time you left me alone? And anyway, having your face on a stamp might seem like a great honour, but think of how many grubby little tongues and fingers you'll be subjected to while you're travelling from one mailbox to the next.' I knew I was being childish, but it made me feel strangely better to finally talk back to the man whom I'd once allowed to speak for me.

Roy had been right, all those years ago, in wanting to name our son Henry and in encouraging me to start that album. Lawson's funeral had undoubtedly led me to Roy. This unprecedented public event had marked the start of the happiest chapters in my life: romance, as fresh and thrilling as in any book I had read; love, marriage and the kind of companionship I had never imagined possible; a beautiful new home and neighbourhood, a million miles away from where my life began; and most of all, our two precious children, Henry and Margery.

I put away the stamps and began my advance up the final hill, wishing I'd left the oranges for another day. Halfway up, I had just stopped to switch hands and wipe the perspiration from my brow when I was startled by a high-pitched young voice.

'Look at this good one!' exclaimed the little girl, clutching a long sheet of paperbark she had stripped from the tree and scrutinising it for flaws.

'A very good one,' I agreed, thinking of another little girl and her older brother who had liked to tear sheets from that same paperbark and write secret messages which neither Roy nor I were allowed to read. Henry's boyhood messages, I could fairly guess, would have been filled with outlandish ideas and top-secret designs for his so-called inventions. Darling boy.

But what about Margery? What secret messages had she been writing back then? What girlish dreams had she held for herself and not wanted to share? With a shudder of remorse, I suddenly thought of how Margery had dared to share them once – her dreams of a costume design career in Hollywood – and saw anew how hurtful it must have been to have them dismissed by her own mother. Instead of recognising her talent and encouraging her ambitions, I had done the opposite. For all my criticism of Henry Lawson, I too had relegated my daughter's dreams to mere 'castles in the air'.

'Bye-bye,' the little girl sang out as she scampered towards the nearest house, slamming the gate behind her.

'Bye-bye,' I echoed, waving longingly at her retreating form.

Chapter 32
The Drover's Wife

It was Roy who had suggested I see the Drysdale paintings.

After having gone on his own the afternoon before, dropping off some prints to the gallery during his first days back at work, he had come home looking like the cat that got the cream. He said only that the exhibition was a knockout, and I should not miss seeing it myself. At breakfast, he had reminded me of Drysdale's sketches in the newspaper more than a year earlier, noting that the artist's present show of oil paintings was directly inspired by his journey into the state's interior, where he'd been sent by the *Herald* to document the cataclysmic effects of the drought.

Instantly, I had pictured the little black-and-white sketch of the drover's wife and wondered whether the artist had chosen to make a larger painting of this subject. Russell Drysdale's simple but capable line drawings, along with their accompanying harrowing descriptions, had captured my imagination back then, none more so than that of the drover's wife standing in front of the makeshift camp. In fact I had torn out and kept that page from the *Herald* that Saturday, and had done the same with the remaining two instalments from its special drought report. I had then folded them neatly together and tucked – though not glued – them into my scrapbook devoted to 'The Drover's Wife', where I could look at them again.

~

I felt a tingle of anticipation as I approached Strathkyle, the block of flats on Bligh Street in which the gallery was located. Macquarie Galleries had been the first commercial gallery to which Roy had introduced me, soon into our courtship, and had remained my favourite. And although Roy had always described them as Sydney's top gallery, he still said it was a miracle they had survived the Depression. Back then, an impromptu visit usually meant finding Basil Burdett languidly playing the spinet in a darkened gallery, with just a few lonely pictures in the front room. After Basil went off to become art critic for the *Herald*, we had watched John Young scrape through the rest of that difficult time largely on his own until he'd finally handed over the reins to a younger generation in 1938. Since then, it had been jointly run by two highly capable women, Treania Smith, herself an artist, and Lucy Swanton, who had a degree in art history. Fortunately, both women had taken an instant liking to Roy and often sent printing business his way.

Roy always said the Misses Smith and Swanton were as different as apples and oranges but that they shared an eye for talent and an uncanny knack for business, putting on shows for established artists, but also those whose work was considered too 'adventurous' by other galleries. From my own observations, the pair were driven not by the desire for profit, of which there was little enough, but by their love of art and unwavering loyalty to their artists.

I pushed open the gallery door and was welcomed by the sweet-citrus fragrance of brown boronia. Aside from the art itself, there was something special about this place that always put me at ease. It may have had something to do with the way the gallery's interior was decorated with a few thoughtfully chosen pieces of furniture – like the red lacquered chinoiserie chairs or the antique chest where the drawings were kept – which gave the idea of how the paintings might appear in one's own home. Or it could have been the attraction of its charismatic directors – Treania and Lucy, as I now knew them – whose passion for art demanded reciprocation. Having been lulled into an appropriately receptive state, and regardless of the artist on show, I would invariably find at least one or two works which called out to me and stayed in my mind long after leaving. Sometimes, though not nearly as often as I might have liked, I'd leave a red sticker in my wake – *Sold!*

Between Roy's business and my own amateurish enthusiasm, buying an artwork had long felt natural to me, yet 'collecting' art remained a surprisingly uncommon pastime in Australia. For most of our friends, even those with sufficient financial means like Hilda, going to an art gallery merely provided them with something *to do*, something *to see*, perhaps even something to *talk about*, but rarely something *to acquire.*

This was where I felt Macquarie Galleries was making good inroads. Roy had declared it a stroke of genius when, during their first year at the helm, Treania and Lucy introduced their now infamous 'Show of Fives' – their annual group show in which every painting was priced at just five guineas. Given the concession this represented to usual selling prices, it was astonishing how many well-known artists were keen to participate, Russell Drysdale included. With plenty of bargains up for grabs, Roy and I had been forced to compete with a new crowd of young collectors to secure our purchases, including a moody little landscape by Alison Rehfisch one year and one of Thea Proctor's ballet drawings the next, chosen in memory of the summer in which Margery had wanted to become a prima ballerina. And as Roy and I well knew, once someone began collecting, they almost never stopped. The pursuit of beauty was highly addictive.

I closed the door behind me with a soft click and bent down to smell the boronia spilling out from an earthenware vase by the entrance. At the other end of the room, with their backs to me, two women were engaged in animated conversation. I recognised Treania's tall and elegant figure, even before she'd turned to greet me. For once, the director's bright red lipstick and infectious giggle were outdone by the elaborate coiffure of her companion, which had been dyed an arresting shade of hydrangea-blue. I gave a discreet wave and entered the first and largest of the three exhibition rooms, thankful to find myself alone.

~

Hanging from the walls were perhaps nine or ten oil paintings. Most of these pictures, painted on canvas or inexpensive Masonite panels, were modest in size – twenty by twenty-four inches, in the main. Yet the images contained within them struck me with the full force of the scorching Australian sun, leaving me dry-mouthed and breathless, as if I too were trapped in that barren landscape.

I stood in the centre of the room, legs trembling, anchored to the spot, like one of the brittle tree skeletons in the paintings. Slowly I eased myself into the nearest chair. Surrounded by the earthen colours of my childhood – red, brown, orange and ochre – I was transported back in time as image after image bombarded me with an inescapable vision of death and loss. Murky shapes distorted by dust. The gruesome remains of livestock defeated by starvation and thirst. Upturned tree trunks with roots exposed, both hideous and vulnerable. Placed among these ruins were a few straggling survivors, human or otherwise. And every one of them lay trapped between a mouldering earth and menacing sky.

Defenceless in the face of such a visual onslaught, I felt myself being pulled into a kind of nightmare state, a sepia-toned world that was at once alien and yet wholly familiar. Heat rose like a furnace in my chest as I broke into a sweat. I fumbled inside my handbag for my pocketbook and fanned myself.

When I closed my eyes, a boy's face flashed before me. At first, I thought it was my brother, looking down at me from the saddle, a half-remembered glimpse from a day I wanted to forget. A moment later, Tommy was gone, and there instead was Henry, feverish and babbling incoherently from an army stretcher. I clamped my hand over my mouth, stifling a cry, and felt a burst of anger towards Roy for telling me to come.

In the background, I dimly made out snippets of Treania's conversation with the blue-haired lady. How pleased she was for Russell Drysdale – Tas, as she referred to him – and the success of this show, which signified a marvellous advance in his artistic development. How Lucy had put on Drysdale's first show at Riddell Gallery in Melbourne years earlier, and therefore how eager they had both been to let him show here when he moved up to Sydney. About how critics were already beginning to speak of him as Australia's most distinctive painter, except for that one newspaper write-up which had unfairly described the works as monotonous.

Gradually restored to my senses by the reassuring normality of their dialogue, I roused myself from the chair and entered the second room. Stark and dramatic images of decay were reinforced by their titles. *Dead Bullock. Eroded Tree Form. Landscape with Dead Horse. Desolation.* I felt another wave of deja vu and wished the artist had included a greater number of gentler subjects in his exhibition. I yearned to see something hopeful. Even so, the critic Treania had mentioned had been wrong – Drysdale's paintings were not monotonous, as he'd claimed, so much as relentless. Unyielding. Endless and overpowering, like the Australian landscape itself.

In one of the bigger pictures, curiously titled *The Walls of China (Gol Gol)*, sand dunes rose like bleached mountains in the backdrop. The sky was a deep angry red, like a gaping wound. A great tree lay upturned on its side in the foreground, its tortured trunk and gnarled branches virtually indistinguishable from its roots. Elsewhere were more of these uprooted tree forms, some resembling animal carcasses: timber and bone stripped bare of flesh. In another picture, two of Drysdale's tree skeletons had assumed anthropomorphic form. Rearing up from the dust on the hind legs of thick, stubby roots, the trees' upper limbs came together, locked in struggle like a pair of boxing kangaroos. Two human figures had been painted into the background, reduced to the status of bystander while the real drama played out before them.

But unlike the surrealistic paintings I'd seen at Contemporary Art Society exhibitions, and of which Drysdale's paintings reminded me, these trees were more than the product of an artist's unconscious imagination. This tragedy, although of mythic proportions, had taken place in the dimensions of the real world, less than five hundred miles from here.

Drysdale was showing us nature at its worst. Nature at war with itself. And in his drought-stricken settings, I recognised the landscape of my past – the same landscape that had sparked the fire which took my family and stoked the fever that stole my father's final breath. I understood the war being fought on these canvases, for I had been suffering its consequences my whole life.

Even so, I could see there was more at stake here than the devastation of the land and its people. Drysdale's paintings revealed another kind of war. That of man's war against himself. Man against man, nation against nation, Axis against Allies.

Reflected in Drysdale's drought-ravaged trees, I couldn't help but see the tortured, emaciated bodies of POWs and Jewish concentration camp victims. In their decayed trunks and torn branches, I saw severed limbs, blown off on the battlefield or amputated afterwards. And in the apocalyptic landscape that held these wounded trees, obscured by an atmosphere thick with deadly particles of dust, like those of Hiroshima and Nagasaki, I saw a vision of the world's future.

~

'Extraordinary, aren't they?' said Treania, who was suddenly standing beside me.

'They certainly are,' I murmured, half-wishing I'd left when I had the chance.

'It's Australia, all right,' she continued, sweeping her arm around the room. 'But not as most of us know it.'

'True.' I had no intention of revealing anything of my own childhood experience.

'He certainly hasn't given us Streeton's blue and gold palette, or a shearing shed full of rowdy young men harvesting *The Golden Fleece*,' said Treania, smiling broadly. 'There's nothing tra-la about any of these works.'

Treania's almost disdainful reference to Arthur Streeton and Tom Roberts did not surprise me, even though most of the country still regarded the plein-air landscapes of the Heidelberg School as the pinnacle of Australia's artistic achievement. In that regard, I supposed it was no different to prevailing attitudes over what constituted good writing, which for many began and ended with the bush poetry of Henry Lawson, Banjo Paterson and a few others from *The Bulletin*. Although I'd been too young to recognise it then, those years leading into Federation had been the last time art and literature collaborated so effectively to build our young nation, and our national taste remained arrested there.

Treania must have noticed my near silence because her voice changed abruptly, becoming uncharacteristically tender. 'I'm so sorry about Henry. I just can't believe it happening like that ... when the war was virtually over.' She took hold of my hand and squeezed it.

'Thank you, Treania.' Evidently Roy had not told her of Margery's news. I scanned the walls, wondering whether to steer our dialogue back to the relatively safer topic of the paintings. Although I genuinely liked Treania, I'd always felt a little intimidated by her superior knowledge and somewhat imperious manner. It didn't help that she stood a good head taller than me, even without her heels.

'Congratulations, anyway,' I said, pasting a smile on my face. 'What an extraordinary show. Mr Drysdale has certainly rammed home his message of what farming communities have had to endure on top of the war – an epic battle of their own.'

Treania nodded. 'He's captured the universality of human experience. We got a glimpse of it in some of his earlier work – you remember the Riverina series – but he's taken his art to an entirely new level with this exhibition. It's truly remarkable. For once, even the critics dare not hide behind their usual assumptions. I'm so sick of the way any art produced in this country is automatically presumed second rate compared to something from England, or America too, for that matter. Tas may have started by imitating the Europeans when he was younger – Cézanne, Modigliani, what have you – but this work is all his own. And it's uniquely Australian.'

I felt the surge of another wave of grief and an accompanying rush of heat as I remembered our family bushwalks to Ku-ring-gai Chase National Park. While the children took daring leaps between rocks or ran ahead and hid in caves, Roy would be on the lookout for Aboriginal engravings. These too, I felt, were a uniquely Australian art form. I thought of asking Treania whether she knew if anything had come of the idea for a new Aboriginal Art room at the National Gallery, including their wonderful bark paintings of Arnhem Land, but she was already gesturing at another painting.

'Did you notice how his representation of the human form is changing?' she asked. 'Tas was always painting these elongated, rather stylised figures, but now his people are becoming much more solid and substantial. Look at Joe here,' she said, indicating the corpulent form of a man in blue dungarees. 'Or at these lovely, rounded contours,' she added, pointing at a nearby portrait of a woman. 'It's all about volume and shape. Like a sculpture. Of course, some people will try to put it down to the influence of the British formalists, like Sutherland or Henry Moore, but I maintain it's entirely his own vision.'

'Substantial,' I echoed. 'Equal to the task demanded by the landscape.'

Treania looked at me with an expression of surprise and approval.

Any further insights were interrupted by the sound of the front door swinging open. Street noise drifted into the gallery. 'Excuse me a moment, will you please? I thought Lucy would be back by now.' She scowled slightly. 'I'd better see who it is.'

~

I resisted the urge to leave and entered the third and final room of the gallery alone. There it was. On a small wall of its own, almost as if it had been waiting for me, hung the one painting I had been hoping to see. From its unassuming beginnings as the little black-and-white newspaper sketch, Drysdale had produced an exceptional painting. When I came forward to read the inscription, I smiled with satisfaction. *The Drover's Wife*. Now even the title confirmed its significance to me. But although she was once again nameless, just as in Lawson's version, I saw nothing to offend me here.

As before, the drover's wife stood alone in the foreground and behind her, at some distance, the drover tended to his horses beside a covered wagon. In the original drawing, I recalled the woman's figure had been quite small, shown in reasonable proportion to the cloth-covered wagon and its large, spoked wheels. By contrast, in this composition, she dominated the painting, occupying almost half the canvas. All other objects that made up the background – the trees, the wagon, even her husband – had been reduced to an incidental narrative. The drover's wife stood alone, in apparent command of the landscape. Not as a separate entity, but very much a part of it.

Her few humble belongings, which had previously lain on the ground by her feet, had instead been gathered into a single suitcase, held lightly at her side. As if she had just arrived at this scene or else was preparing to depart. Judging from the shadows, it may have been late afternoon.

Although the sky was pallid and the few trees thin and spare, the setting was surprisingly tranquil, not marred by the same foreboding atmosphere as in many of the other paintings. The gentle wash of its cloudless grey-green sky and the blushing putty-coloured earth reminded me of an old sepia-toned photograph, the sole enduring record of a forgotten chapter from the past. And just like a photograph, the drover's wife stood poised as though seen through a lens. Not stiff or posed uncomfortably, as with a formal portrait sitting, but simply caught mid-motion – in medias res, so to speak – then fixed in position for all eternity.

I tried to imagine how the scene might have played out. I supposed Drysdale must have taken photographs during his journey, to capture the details his initial sketches could not, and which were needed to inform the artist's final work. Did Drysdale speak with her that day? Or she with him? Or could it be that the drover's wife lived only in the artist's imagination and in this collection of brushstrokes before me? As if to affirm this last thought, my gaze fell upon the signature in the lower-right corner of the picture, where the artist had painted his name in a small but distinct longhand.

With increasing fascination, I returned to the painting itself, searching for clues. As befitted her surroundings, and just as in the sketch, the drover's wife was simply attired. Her dress and shoes had been painted in the same deep brown hue as the horses tethered to the wagon behind her, the colour of richly tanned leather. Against this tawny material, her skin was surprisingly light, almost luminescent, as if coloured by flecks of gold and not only by the sun. Her hat was a darker shade of brown. From beneath its tilted brim, a small face looked steadily out at me. Gently holding me in its gaze.

Set apart and shaped like a pair of dark almonds, her eyes drew me forward. It was not a particularly beautiful face, in the way that women were usually portrayed in art, nor was it plain. Her features were small and regular, her countenance serene. What had she been thinking about in that moment, I wondered? Although her expression gave little away, it was not impassive in the sense of being cool or unemotional, but neither was it vacant. Instead, I had the impression that a world of thoughts and emotions lay hidden beneath this composed exterior.

All at once – and for the first time in years – I heard my mother's voice, brusquely upbraiding us children as she did if ever we complained and reminding us never to burden others with our troubles. Yes, that was it. Here in this painting was a woman equal to the task of living. To the challenge of standing, quite literally, on her own two feet. Not asking for help or sympathy, but inspiring it all the same – just as my mother had done, inspiring Henry Lawson and countless readers for over fifty years.

Still, I wanted to know more. What other secrets lay behind her seemingly modest demeanour? There was something I needed to learn from this bush-woman, this wife of a drover, if only I knew what. And yet, it was her very quality of reticence, of self-possession and dignity, which excited me and made it impossible to turn away.

Enigmatic was the word that finally came to mind as I contemplated her benign expression, triggering an obvious comparison to another famously enigmatic smile from an artist's muse: Leonardo da Vinci's *Mona Lisa.* I remembered a radio program presented by John Young while he still owned the Macquarie Galleries. He and Lloyd Rees had been debating the question of whether there existed any Australian masterpieces in the way the *Mona Lisa* was an undisputed masterpiece of Italian art. Although I couldn't recall their conclusions back then, as I stood here before Drysdale's painting of *The Drover's Wife*, I knew I had my answer.

Curiously, the longer I stared at the drover's wife, the more she seemed to be looking back at me instead, her eyes full of warmth and understanding. Or was it simply my own gaze, thrown back like a reflection?

I tallied up the losses of my life and wondered how they would compare with hers. A tear slid down my cheek as I felt them all afresh.

Suddenly my breath caught in my throat. As the true gift of the painting finally revealed itself to me, my lips instinctively formed a smile.

On one level, the drover's wife was undoubtedly the subject of Drysdale's painting. This was *her* story. Willingly or otherwise, she had resigned herself to being the object of the artist's gaze and of ours. Yes, this was her story – or at least, it began that way. But on another, more fundamental level, I was the one who felt seen today. And so it became my story too.

Lay down your burdens, I could almost hear the words whispered from the canvas, like a verse from the Bible. A feeling of calm rippled through me, and I breathed easily for the first time in what felt like an eternity.

I looked up at the sound of raised voices and the entrance door swinging open and shut. I pulled out my handkerchief and hastily dried my face. As my eyes lingered on the painting, I was struck by another notion. Though small in scale, I now saw that this canvas was large enough to hold my own grief. Large enough to remind me that others saw and felt and suffered as I did but found the strength to carry on. I pictured my mother urging me to pick up my suitcase and get on with it. To keep going, come what may. I imagined her telling me that all life had its seasons, like the cycles of nature. For every fire there is a flood. For every drought there is an end. Beneath even these crumbling soils in Drysdale's paintings lay the seed of future growth.

I retraced my steps back to the gallery entrance. As I cast sideways glances at the walls, I asked myself why so many of the pictures appeared less dark than before. Was it only my imagination that now perceived an underlying quality of permanence behind the painted surfaces of destruction? A sense of resilience and renewal, both from the land itself and the figures which inhabited it? I now had to concede that mixed within these oily layers of suffering was strength and beauty. The kind of noble grace personified by the drover's wife herself. Seen through *her* eyes, they were transformed into something else entirely.

With my head still turned towards the paintings, I exited the front room and collided quite hard with Treania Smith.

'Silly me,' she apologised, graciously accepting responsibility. 'I'd almost forgotten you were here.'

I rubbed my forehead and stammered an apology.

'You must have enjoyed the exhibition to have stayed so long. Which one would you take home if you could?'

I removed my hat and pretended to inspect it for damage as I considered my response. '*The Drover's Wife*', I finally admitted.

'That's my favourite, too. You would have seen it's not for sale, of course. Bonnie Drysdale wanted to hold onto it for herself for the time being,' said Treania, referring to the artist's wife. 'But you never know, she might change her mind. Perhaps once it's made the rounds of all the major exhibitions, she and Tas might consider selling it to you. Though I expect one of the state galleries will make an offer before then. Would you like me to contact Roy if there's any chance?'

'Could you?' My heart contracted. 'Though I expect it would be outside our budget anyway.'

'You don't think he'd agree to spending a couple of hundred guineas on a single picture when your walls are already full?' Treania's tone was playful but her smile was sympathetic. 'I wish I could offer it to you for less, I really do.' Although the gallery was now empty, she lowered her voice. 'Between you and me, when it came to pricing Tas's pictures this time round, Lucy would simply pluck a number from her head and then double it. Heavens! Of course, he's worth every penny, but still.'

I nodded sadly.

'The show was completely sold out almost before the opening, you know. Every newspaperman in the country had seen the sketches in the *Herald* and wanted to get his hands on the paintings. You probably noticed most of them are just on loan.'

'I think I was too busy looking at the works themselves to read many of the labels.'

'Ha,' she laughed. 'It's quite the who's who list in there: Fairfax, Murdoch, among other newspaper bigwigs; an American Army Captain; an Australian Major; a legal silk. The rest of them were snapped up by his friends, family and other longtime supporters. Tas and Bonnie kept back a few of the best works for themselves, like *The Drover's Wife*. But we did let Hal Missingham have *Walls of China* – he was determined to secure at least one important piece for the National Gallery.' Treania's ice-blue eyes sparkled with pride as she mentioned our state gallery's unconventional new director.

Shaking her head as if she still could not quite believe it, she continued. 'That newspaper commission was an absolute godsend for Tas. It's not just his commercial success that's been taken up a notch. He came back from that trip saying he felt like a new man. It triggered something in him which has completely transformed his practice. And to think that it might have gone to another artist except that—'

Treania was stopped mid-sentence by the arrival of her partner, Lucy Swanton, whose petite form was weighed down by the gigantic abstract picture she was dragging through the door.

This time, I seized the opportunity to take my leave.

'Give our regards to Roy,' both women entreated as I went out the door. 'And come back next week for our Sydney artists' group show.'

'It'll give you another chance to see *your* painting, Lillian,' added Treania with a meaningful wink.

~

I emerged onto the street with a rush of sound, discombobulated. All around me, people were going about their business. Cars, trucks and trams whooshed past, setting my nerves on edge after the relative quiet of the gallery. It was another astonishingly warm day for this time of year, and I felt overdressed in my winter coat.

I followed my feet, zigzagging upward through the streets until I reached Hyde Park and the relief of its cooling greenery. Out the other side, I finally came to a standstill in front of Henry's old school. From somewhere behind its dignified sandstone exterior, a bell was ringing. Lunchtime was over. Muffled in the distance, I heard the high-pitched voices of the Form I boys mingling with the seniors' deeper tones. A familiar spasm moved across my chest, and I gripped hold of the heavy iron gate. I pictured Henry, full of promise in his Grammar uniform, and then as I'd last seen him, dressed for the army. I screwed my eyes shut and tried instead to visualise the drover's wife and her suitcase. As the spasm slowly subsided, I began walking. It was time to go home.

By the time I re-entered Hyde Park, my shoulders had softened and I was breathing more easily. To my left, at the periphery of my vision, rose the outlines of the Anzac Memorial and, before it, the Pool of Reflection. I stopped and threw in a coin, whispering a prayer of my own. On my right, the central avenue of Hill's weeping figs stretched all the way down to Macquarie Street and, from there, to Sydney Harbour, where so many of our city's roads all led. Although my feet were aching, it was a good kind of ache, and even my stomach had started to rumble with the promise of appetite.

As I left the park and headed westward through the bustling streets toward Town Hall station, I felt calmer, and clearer in my purpose, than when I had arrived that morning.

Chapter 33

What Are the Odds?

'Sure hits the spot,' Roy groaned blissfully after downing his first mouthful of beer. He sank further into the cane sofa and stretched out his legs onto the ottoman, while ignoring the blanket I'd brought out to prevent him from catching yet another chill.

On Friday evenings, for as long as I could remember, my husband had liked to sit out on our back verandah before dinner, washing away the week's trials and triumphs over an ice-cold ale or two. Tonight, having agreed dinner could wait, I accepted the glass he poured and settled in beside him on the sofa. The sun was just beginning to set, illuminating the golden tips of the gums that towered beyond the high hedge of our backyard. These conifers had grown tall and dense during the years of our marriage, laying down their roots in the same way Roy and I had done.

'Listen,' he said, pointing to the sky.

High up in the eucalyptus canopy, I heard cockatoos feasting and the soft rustle of empty seed husks falling to the ground. A feeling of peace and acceptance washed over me.

For a few minutes, we chatted about Roy's day at work and the gardening jobs he had planned for this weekend. In his usual thoughtful way, he had pushed the ottoman towards the middle so we could share it. I arranged the blanket over us both, then leaned back against the cushion, snuggling closer to Roy. I gave a loud yawn. The beer was making me mellow.

Ready at last, I began telling him about my experience at the gallery, starting with my horror at the sight of Drysdale's drought-stricken landscapes and how I had nearly left the exhibition without seeing the last room. Roy listened intently, interrupting only once or twice to clarify something I had said or to take my hand and kiss it softly. Finally, I told him about *The Drover's Wife* painting and the strength of my reaction.

When I had finished, Roy nodded with satisfaction. He had wanted me to see the exhibition for this very reason, and he'd immediately understood why I would respond to the painting as an echo of Henry Lawson's story, and why I might regard it as a kind of make-believe portrait of my mother. Although he raised his eyebrows at the price Treania had mentioned for the painting, I felt sure I could talk him round, should the artist ever be willing to part with his masterpiece.

'So, do you think Drysdale's painting was directly inspired by Lawson's story?' I asked him.

'It might have been,' he said, scratching his head. 'I'm sure Drysdale would have been familiar with it. I know he came here from England as a young lad – around the time our Henry was born, in the early twenties, I think. Australia's in his blood, all the same. His family have held land here for generations, so I'm sure between that and his schooling, he would have come across all the old stories and bush ballads.'

'Including "The Drover's Wife",' I said, nodding briskly. 'Surely, he knew what he was doing when he gave it the same title. His drawing wasn't called that in the original newspaper description, you know.'

'That doesn't mean much in itself. I remember those drawings in the paper too. Some of them obviously turned out to be studies for larger works, but not all. Once Drysdale got back to Sydney from that trip, he probably just kept turning the images and ideas over in his mind to see where they took him. I reckon what we see in those paintings now is as much about reality as about what went on in his head afterwards.'

Lost in my thoughts, I was only dimly aware of Roy topping up my glass.

'The more I think about it,' he continued, 'the more I reckon Drysdale's version of the drover's wife doesn't have anything to do with Lawson. Or with any woman – or wife – in particular. He's looking at the bigger picture. No pun intended!' Roy chuckled at his joke.

He was probably right. All the human subjects in Drysdale's paintings had a universal quality. Treania had said as much. They may not have been real people, in the sense that Roy and I were real, but they were authentic. They stood for all men and women.

'Here's to *The Drover's Wife*,' said Roy. He raised his glass in the air before taking a long swig. 'It is a good title,' he said, letting out a deep sigh of pleasure. 'Kind of rolls off the tongue, doesn't it? You can ask Mr Drysdale who she is yourself, if you like, and whether he was thinking of Lawson's story when he named it. I could probably get us an introduction. He's a sociable man, you know.'

I shook my head, suddenly shivering in the cool evening air.

'Why not, love? He'd probably invite us along to one of his parties. For a member of Australia's landed gentry, he keeps quite the bohemian circle, the way I hear it. Artists, thespians, creatives of all types. Wouldn't you love to be a fly on the wall?'

Unlike years earlier, when I had written to Henry Lawson, seeking confirmation of my memories and validation of my family story, I didn't need this man to interpret what I had seen today, or how it made me feel. No longer would I second-guess my memories or seek external approval.

'No, thank you,' I said.

'Are you sure?' Roy asked, winking as he opened another bottle of beer. 'Picture this. Copious quantities of alcohol, home-brewed if need be. Jazz music and boogie-woogie dancing. A big pot of stew. Divans on the enclosed verandah in case guests need somewhere to sleep. Come to think of it, his place is just up the hill from Sacred Heart. He's probably been keeping the nuns awake with his loud music. I think he has a couple of young kids, too, so I don't know how that all works.'

Although I had no reason to doubt Roy's account, I found it difficult to reconcile with the seriousness of his paintings. It was also curious to think of Drysdale painting *The Drover's Wife* within such proximity of where I had gone to school forty years earlier.

'What makes you think some of the younger nuns haven't been sneaking into his parties all along?' I asked, assuming my best poker face. 'Just don't tell the Reverend-Mother, she might get jealous.'

Roy laughed. I could see in his eyes how glad he was for this small chance to again trade banter like this.

But when Roy spoke next, his demeanour had shifted, and his tone had grown serious. 'You know Paul Haefliger, the *Herald* critic? He told me the war was one of the main reasons why Drysdale started having all the parties. Paul said that Tas and Bonnie always kept an open house for servicemen on leave in Sydney. That it was their way of helping the soldiers and giving them a place where they could forget the war for a night or two. A proper R&R experience. Apparently, he really wasn't happy to have been refused service. And I know how that feels,' he added pointedly.

'Why was he refused service?'

'On account of his eyesight. Detached retina, or something like that, when he was still at school. That's how Drysdale got started on his career path as an artist, in fact. Paul said he was given drawing lessons back then as therapy for his eye.'

'I didn't know that.'

'Haven't you seen his picture in the paper and those thick eyeglasses he wears? Even after an operation, he's virtually blind in one eye.'

'Really?'

'Anyway, I gather he tried to enlist two or three times. In the end, some doctor told him to paint for his country instead. I don't think he was ever actually named as one of our official war artists, but I reckon he's done his bit now with these paintings, don't you? Good on him, I say.'

I stroked Roy's arm. It pained me to see how much he still suffered for his own hearing disability, which, by keeping him out of the Great War, had perhaps contributed to his brother's decision to enlist instead. Maybe even our son's.

'I don't remember who told me this,' said Roy, squinting slightly as he looked up at the sky. 'It might have been Paul or Treania, or maybe Lucy, but I gather the poor bloke has always been petrified of going blind in the other eye.'

'What a terrifying thought,' I murmured, wondering if Roy harboured a similar fear about his hearing.

'It'd certainly be enough to make a man get on with his painting every day,' he said.

'Or enough to send him to the drink,' I added, pointing to the now empty bottle of beer in his hand. We shared a laugh, and Roy turned his head and kissed me gently on the lips.

As darkness slowly descended on the garden and the cockatoos grew silent, I drained the last few drops of liquid in my own glass and surrendered to another big yawn.

What a strange day it had been. And now this evening too, in its own way. Strange but lovely, all the same. My ever-present grief for Henry and my constant state of remorse over Margery had briefly faded into the background while we had been sitting here.

Instead, like a bird returning to its nest, my thoughts kept circling back to the drover's wife. Not to Lawson's printed version that had plagued my younger self, nor even to Drysdale's gently painted masterpiece that had given me such comfort today. But to the woman who was my mother. Though I knew it was futile, I tried to picture Mother's face, and was not surprised when all I saw was a pair of almond-shaped eyes and a mouth not yet ready to smile.

'What are the odds?' I asked Roy, as we finally went inside for dinner. 'Of having one's life story told by a poet who was all but deaf and one's portrait painted by an artist who only sees the world with one eye.'

~

Roy lay asleep beside me, while I tried to do the same. But every time I closed my eyes, I saw Drysdale's painting and heard my mother's voice. Eventually, I gave up and tiptoed out of bed. Already waiting for me at my desk were the Henry Lawson postage stamps which I had bought just days earlier, after my walk with Charlie. I sat down at the desk before I could talk myself out of it. Pen in hand and blank sheet of paper before me, I started to write.

16 August 1946

Dearest Margery,

I hope this letter finds you all well. As you know, your father is planning to visit again sometime in spring. With your permission, I would dearly love to join him.

I know that I have hurt you deeply – not only since you left home, but before then too.

I'm not sure if I can ever properly explain to you my reasons for staying away these past months, nor can I expect your instant forgiveness – but I am finally ready to try. I can only hope you are ready to listen.

I am ashamed to think little Francis should have two grandmothers still living but only ever know one of them. Wouldn't it be wonderful if we could celebrate his first birthday, or even Christmas, all together?

I have taken the liberty of enclosing a postcard and stamp for your reply.

A single word from you will suffice to indicate your willingness to try to put the past behind us and look to the future. There is, incidentally, a long story behind this stamp and the man whose legacy it honours, as well as the unnamed woman behind it. I hope to share it with you soon.

With best wishes always from your loving mother.

Chapter 34

Core of my Heart

'If I'd known that going to hospital would get you and Margie back together, I'd have done it much sooner,' Roy teased for the third time that morning while we packed the car by torchlight.

'I wish you'd stop saying that. It's not even true. I worked hard to get this invitation, you know. And keep your voice down, you'll wake the neighbours.'

Although Roy had gone ahead with his planned second visit this time last year, in the spring of 1946, this was the first time I was being allowed to join him, albeit to a new location. Margery had been unmoved by the letter I had written to her last August. Even now, the memory stung. When her reply finally did come, it was addressed to Roy and indicated in no uncertain terms that he alone was welcome. Almost equally hurtful, albeit irrationally so, had been Margery's complete lack of interest in discovering the story behind the Henry Lawson stamp which had delivered my attempted reconciliation. As Roy boarded the train on his own, I'd made him promise not to tell her anything about 'The Drover's Wife' or my family history. She would hear the story from me. Or not at all.

From the minute Margery collected him from the train station, Roy went to work, advocating on my behalf. By the end of that visit, our daughter had apparently warmed ever so slightly to the idea of seeing me. Roy suggested that another conciliatory letter might do the trick. And so, I wrote not one but two more letters, each one more apologetic and remorseful than the last. Until finally, Margery relented.

Our reconciliation began slowly, first with the exchange of a few more letters, followed by a series of phone calls, which thankfully became less awkward with time. Margery was punishing me, I knew that. But I also knew how much I had hurt her. And I was willing to give her time to come around. Ever so gently, I began coaxing her to let me come and see her. I was desperate to meet Francis – little Frankie, by then – and to earn back Margery's trust and love. But Margery kept putting me off with one excuse or another; from harvest season to Frankie not sleeping well to Colin's family having friends coming to stay for Christmas and no room for any more guests. I'd also got the sense she wasn't keen for me to meet her mother-in-law, sending me into tailspin of insecurity and shame.

Then suddenly, just days into the new year, Margery announced they would be moving. The neighbouring farm which Colin had been managing had just been sold. At first, we'd both presumed Colin might join his older brother to help work their father's property, perhaps even expand it for the next generation. Instead, he'd accepted an offer to manage another farm belonging to that same man, also growing premium wheat, but located much further inland, not far from the thriving agricultural town of Moree, in the fertile Gwydir Valley. Up till then, they had been living in a tiny cottage built on the senior Cartwrights' land. It didn't sound like much at all to me. Nothing about Margery's new life matched up to her dreams or mine, but I had vowed to keep myself on a tight leash and rarely let myself think such thoughts, let alone express them aloud.

No sooner had they settled into their new farm at Moree than there was another announcement. Margery was pregnant. Again. This time, I should not have been shocked, although for some reason I had presumed she would wait. With the new baby due in early winter, there would be barely sixteen months between them.

It was a lot to take in. My beautiful daughter, twenty years old, living on a farm, now with two children already, and who knew how many more to follow. Margery was more like her grandmother than she would ever know. Perhaps it was true, what they said. Apples never fall far from the tree. Roy had once used this expression about Henry Lawson and his mother, Louisa, but the same might equally be said about the women in my family. How had I managed to roll so far away from this proverbial apple tree? The answer was cruel but simple. Almost everything in my life could be traced back to the horrific bushfire which stole my family while setting me on a new path, all on my own.

I couldn't help feeling that I had failed Margery all over again. Yet I kept reminding myself her life was not mine to live. Margery was writing her own story now, in which she was the protagonist, not me. It was enough if she let me play a supporting role.

With Margery's new baby now on the way, and in keeping with my new part, I suggested she and Frankie might like to come back home to Sydney a couple of weeks before her due date. She could have her baby at Royal North Shore, while I looked after Frankie, and then all three of them could stay with us until she was strong enough to resume her usual duties at the farm. Margery wouldn't hear of such a plan and assured me Moree hospital was more than adequate, but that if I really wanted to make myself useful, we could visit after the baby's birth.

I could barely recognise my once demanding daughter in the pragmatic independent woman she had become since leaving home. And although I felt proud of how much she had matured, I knew I could claim no credit. Or if I could, only in the same way as the fire could claim credit for my academic success or my work as a teacher.

The sound of Roy coughing brought me back into the present. I looked up from behind the car boot. 'Are you all right, darling? Do you want me to drive the first stretch?'

'Stop fussing, woman. I'm fit as a fiddle. You don't even know where you're going.'

'Neither do you,' I scoffed. 'You haven't been to their new place yet either.'

'Let's hope you can read a map then,' Roy shot back. 'Right, in you go, we're off.'

As it turned out, the day Margery went into Moree hospital to have her baby – another boy – was the same day Roy went into hospital here. A bad head cold had turned into bronchitis, then rapidly advanced to pneumonia, not that we knew it at the time. If Dr Solander had given him sufficiently strong antibiotics in the first place, he might have recovered on his own, but after three breathless days, during which he got progressively worse, not better, I panicked and drove him straight to hospital.

I was convinced Roy had contracted tuberculosis and was going to die. I had heard of the benefits of streptomycin and I had also read an article about a Darling Point businessman who had spent nearly £400 importing vials of the drug from America for his wife to be treated at Royal North Shore: I was ready to mortgage our house if needed. To Roy's embarrassment, I reiterated my willingness to pay whatever cost was required to every nurse and doctor we saw that day. Thankfully, within a short space of time, a less serious diagnosis of pneumonia was instead confirmed, and although Roy was still quite ill, the doctors assured me my beloved husband was not knocking on death's door just yet.

Thus, despite his teasing just now, Roy's illness had not been the cause of my reconciliation with Margery. If anything, it had delayed our visit by almost three months while we waited for him to make a full recovery and catch up on overdue orders for the business. Margery had naturally been very concerned about her father when she heard he was in hospital, but by then she'd already given birth and had her own hands full.

I couldn't wait to see her, and to meet little Frankie and now baby Jeffrey too. But equally, I was wracked with anxiety about the reception I might get.

Unused to rising so early, I swallowed a yawn as Roy turned onto the Pacific Highway, heading north. To my right, in the semi-darkness, I caught a glimpse of the library and Gordon Public School, and to my left, the Council Chambers. Apart from our occasional family holidays at the beach or weekends in the Blue Mountains, years earlier, I wasn't used to leaving home myself. I glanced back and gave a tiny wave.

'I saw that,' said Roy, laughing. 'Don't worry. It'll all still be here when we get back.'

I ignored Roy and closed my eyes, thinking of the gifts we had packed and hoping Margery would approve. For baby Jeffrey, it was mostly practical items, along with a few more extravagant outfits in case Margery wanted to show him off to her new friends in the district. For Frankie, I had wooden blocks and a shiny new tricycle. And for Margery, other than a renewed supply of her favourite toiletries, with some specialty maternity products thrown in for good measure, I had chosen dressmaking patterns from the new spring collections by McCall's and Butterick, together with several yards of fabric.

'I wish she didn't live so far away,' I said. 'Seeing as they had to relocate anyway, I wish they'd chosen somewhere closer to Sydney.'

'You do know Colin is a wheat farmer, don't you, Lill? There aren't too many of those in our neighbourhood.'

'Yes, all right, but what made them choose Moree, do you think? I thought it was mostly sheep and cattle out that way.'

'You're right, Moree's been riding the sheep's back for years, same as a lot of other places, and plenty of the earlier graziers got wealthy because of it, but Colin tells me the land is particularly well-suited to wheat farming too. Nice rich black soil and plenty of water. The Moree floodplains are sitting right on top of the world's biggest artesian basin, you know. That's why the town was flooded at the start of last year when they got all that rain.'

'Flooded?' I looked at him in dismay. 'I've been worried about drought conditions and bushfire, but now you tell me there's flooding as well.'

'Don't worry, Lill. Margie and Colin's place is on higher ground. They'll be fine next time it floods. By then, they might have saved up enough to buy their own farm anyway. And you're right. Drought is the bigger worry – God knows Moree and most other parts of the state were suffering for years before it broke last winter. They had another dry spell this year too, but it looks like they've just come out of that with last month's rain. Colin said their wheat crop was wilting for a while there, but that the pastures are recovering quite nicely now.'

'You're hardly inspiring me with confidence about our daughter's safety,' I muttered, rubbing my temples. During our most recent phone call, Roy had asked Margery to put Colin on the phone, and I presumed this to be the source of all his information, although who knew how accurately Roy had understood what he'd been told. Agriculture was hardly a subject with which either of us were familiar, despite my droving roots.

'So, I shouldn't tell you about the grasshopper plague that followed the rains, or the effect of the cold snap on the lambs and freshly shorn sheep, or about how the drought kept the rabbit numbers down for a while.'

'No, Roy, you shouldn't.'

I swallowed another yawn and glanced out the window where the landscape was zipping by, sliding in and out of focus. By now, the busy metropolis of Sydney was long behind us. I sat back and watched the sun rise pink and yellow over the Hawkesbury as we crossed the Peats Ferry Bridge. Soon we were drinking sugared tea by the side of the road, before continuing north up the highway for the first leg of our 400-mile journey.

'It looks different to what I expected,' I admitted to Roy half an hour later, thinking of the large-scale map hanging in my old classroom at Ravenswood. 'I thought we could just follow the coastline before it was time to head inland, but I can't see the ocean at all.'

Roy smirked and tapped the road map spread out on my lap, pointing out the many lakes, inlets and bays that rendered such a route impossible.

'Point taken,' I laughed. 'There's probably a reason I never taught geography.'

My smile faded as we drove past a white picketed cemetery and church. I pictured Henry's grave, as Jim Carruthers had described it, far across the ocean in Bougainville. I took a deep breath, telling myself to instead think of Margery and her boys.

I glanced back at the road map, tracing the towns along our path. Singleton, Muswellbrook, Scone, Gunnedah, Narrabri. Places I'd heard of but never seen before today. Some had Aboriginal-sounding names, like Baan Baa and Pallamallawa, while others had indisputably British origins.

It occurred to me that if one were to draw an invisible line westward from Margery's new farm, it would end up somewhere right between Bourke and Hungerford, where Henry Lawson had made his infamous and only journey 'out back'. And although I had never quite pinpointed the exact location of where my family home once stood, I supposed it to be somewhere on that same dusty track.

I sucked in my breath.

'What is it?' Roy asked, glancing across from behind the wheel.

'It's this map.' I angrily pushed it away. 'When I think of how far I had to go to make a new life for myself in Sydney … and then to think that Margery willingly gave all that up and chose to make her own home not that far from the one I lost.'

'It's not quite the same though, Lill, is it? And there's still a good bit of distance between where you came from and where Margie is now. Her life up here on the farm would be very different to what you remember growing up with.'

I sniffed. 'Those floodplains might be more fertile than where I was raised, but Margery's workload sounds almost as demanding as my mother's would have been.'

'She's got her hands full, that's for sure. But she's not been left on her own, like your mother. Colin's a decent chap. You'll see. He's a man of few words, and I'm pretty sure he hasn't read more than three books in his whole lifetime, so you won't have a lot in common, but he's solid as a rock. And that should count for something.'

'It does.' I nodded grudgingly. 'What do you and Colin talk about when you're together?'

'Not much,' Roy grinned. 'We play darts though. And he's surprisingly musical. We had ourselves a little singalong one night. I'm sure we can do the same here too. Margie said there's an old piano in the new place.'

'That sounds like fun,' I said, grasping onto this image. 'Anything else you remember from your last visit?'

'No beer, that's what. Colin's mother didn't approve of the stuff. She didn't even let Colin keep any at his own place, even after they'd replaced the old cool safe with a kerosene refrigerator. I sure hope Margie's got a beer waiting for me this afternoon.'

'You never mentioned that before.'

I was rather happy to hear this negative report about Margery's mother-in-law. Perhaps the two women hadn't gotten along quite as well as I thought. Perhaps this had even factored into Colin's decision to leave the family farm and take on his new position.

'You did bring the Lawson book to show Margie, didn't you?' Roy asked suddenly, referring to my little green clothbound volume containing 'The Drover's Wife'.

'I did.'

'And the scrapbook album?'

'That too.' The knot in my stomach grew tighter.

I twisted round and reached for the carpet bag behind me, carefully extracting the leather album from between the pair of actual family photo albums from when Margery was a little girl, which I had also brought to show to Colin. Somewhere in the bag was also my newest album with the photos from Roy's two visits to see Margery. Each time he returned home, I had taken the camera film straight to the store for developing and, for weeks afterwards, I'd pored over each photograph with a magnifying glass, as if proof of their continued wellbeing lay within these static black-and-white images.

Although Margery's figure had bounced back quickly after the birth, she already appeared older and somehow altered in her expression. As for baby Jeffrey, he looked nothing like Margery – or Henry, for that matter – neither as a newborn nor at seven months. He was most definitely his own little person. I was itching to see him for myself.

I settled back into my seat and balanced *The Drover's Wife* album on my lap. Roy's gilt lettering on the front was perfectly formed and still gleaming after all these years, his father would have been proud.

Beneath the original title and my name, Roy had recently mounted a photograph of Drysdale's painting which he had taken himself and then hand-coloured. After Drysdale's solo exhibition, *The Drover's Wife* had also been hung in the gallery's next group show, and Roy and I had gone back together to see 'my' painting, as Treania Smith had again referred to it, although by then she'd also confirmed that the artist had no intention of selling. While it lacked the full impact of Drysdale's painting in the flesh, with its Old Master brushwork and rich sepia tones, Roy's photograph was nonetheless captivating. I gazed at the small face under the tilted hat and imagined Mother gazing back at me, willing me on.

I put on my reading spectacles and tremulously turned to the first page, trying to imagine how Margery might respond to my collection.

My quasi-family history began with Henry Lawson's story of the 'The Drover's Wife', clipped from the newspaper. Over the years, I'd seen it reprinted in all manner of publications – from *The Bulletin*, where it had first appeared in 1892, to the *Women's Weekly*, and from *The Sydney Morning Herald* that sailed over our front fence every morning to a Communist Party newspaper someone had once thrust into my hand at Town Hall station. Admiration for Henry Lawson and 'his' story was universal. As I hoped my scrapbook would soon demonstrate to my daughter, it was still regarded as 'the best thing he ever wrote' and 'the most beautiful of all Australian tales', while the drover's wife herself was heralded as 'a symbol of brave womanhood'.

During the twenty-four years in which I'd been keeping my album, the writer's reputation had risen to ever greater heights, attaining a near-legendary status and inspiring a legion of fans and academics determined to keep his legacy alive. In some ways, my album was no different. In seeking to honour my family, and reclaim his story as mine, I had ended up paying homage to the man myself.

'You know what's funny?' I looked over at Roy, raising my voice over the radio which he had just turned on. 'For better or worse, Henry Lawson almost feels like a member of our own family now, too.'

'Why not?' Roy laughed. 'I've heard of stranger things. We did go to his funeral together, let's not forget.'

I turned back to my album and continued looking through its clippings. Along with official admirers, there was no shortage of ordinary people who staked their claim in having known Henry Lawson personally. They came forward at regular intervals to share their anecdotes, especially shopkeepers around North Sydney, where he had lived for so many years. Roy recognised some of these characters himself.

Here, for instance, was an article about Mrs Pearl Johns, whose late husband, Frank, ran the old general store at McMahons Point. She spoke of helping Lawson hide from the police and how her husband was forever having to give him money. Mrs Johns still remembered how every tiny observation or incident, no matter how insignificant, soon made its way into his work. 'Everything that happened sent Mr Lawson off to write a poem or story,' she told the reporter. I grunted knowingly.

Next came Mr Grant who had run the Blues Point Road barber shop for over fifty years. He reminisced about shaving Lawson's chin and trimming his long and gingery droop of a moustache, while the writer regaled Mr Grant's other customers with his stories, often returning several times over the course of the day with some new yarn or incident for their amusement. I shook my head with a snort.

'Do tell,' prompted Roy. 'I could use some entertainment.'

'I'm just reading that interview with Mr Grant, the barber.'

'What was it he said?'

'Not him, the journalist. He makes the point that apart from Mr Grant's barber shop and a few other old haunts, the Australia that Henry Lawson knew and loved no longer exists. That "Arvie Aspinall" isn't waking up to his alarm clock at 4am to go to the factory in Redfern anymore, and that "the drover's wife" now flies to Sydney every year for the holidays!'

'Too right!' laughed Roy. 'I read in the paper there are plans underway for a new aerodrome at Narrabri, which is not that far from Margie's place. We could be there in a couple of hours instead, once that's up and running.'

'Maybe next time,' I said, feeling brave.

Also scattered throughout my album were the few printed mentions about Louisa Lawson, Henry's fearless mother, and one of our country's earliest and most influential feminists. Why was it that the word 'feminist' still had such negative connotations? Even amongst my own sex. What was wrong with an expectation that women should be afforded the same rights as men? And so, while I was looking forward to telling Margery all about Louisa Lawson, I also hadn't forgotten my daughter's spirited accusation towards me on the question of feminism, when she had rightly pointed out that – ever since getting married, at least – I was all talk and no action. Either way, I still felt Henry Lawson owed his mother a debt of acknowledgement that was sorely lacking when he was alive.

'I really hope that history will one day remember Louisa Lawson just as affectionately as it remembers her son,' I said, turning to Roy and patting my album.

'Hear hear,' Roy replied and gestured towards craggy peaks in the distance. 'Getting closer now, Lill. That'll be the Great Dividing Range.'

'It's beautiful,' I sighed. 'Mountains always make me think of refugees, for some reason. All those people who had to flee their country during the war just to stay alive. I'm glad we've given some of them a home here.'

'I'm told some of them make great coffee too, apparently much better than our instant stuff.' Roy winked.

I had now reached that point in my album where Russell Drysdale appeared, starting with his original sketches in the *Herald*. After these came the glowing reviews of his Macquarie Galleries exhibition, where I had first seen the *The Drover's Wife*, rendered anew in oil paints instead of words. Just like its predecessor by Lawson, Drysdale's version had been an instant hit.

In addition to Roy's hand-coloured photograph of the painting on my album's front cover, I'd pasted more photographs inside, including one – sadly out of focus – of me standing in front of it.

'I feel a bit like the drover's wife myself today,' I said, turning to Roy. 'Here she stands, holding her little suitcase in one hand, with her husband and the wagon behind her. And here I am – with my own assortment of bags in the back of the car – making my way down the open road, with you by my side and a thermos of tea at my feet.'

Roy's face lit up. 'A suitcase, you say? I always assumed she was carrying a kerosene tin.'

'I hope you're joking!' I elbowed him sharply and peered more closely. Roy might had have a point. A kerosene tin would not have been out of place for the drover's campsite. 'It's definitely a suitcase,' I said firmly. 'It's clearly allegorical.'

'Whatever you say, love,' said Roy, assuming a saintly expression.

At the end of my album there were still a few blank pages – how and when they would be filled? And by whom? In the context of everything I was about to tell Margery about my childhood, and my tragic experience of losing every member of my family, what would she make of my unofficial archive? What would she say about this hotchpotch of clippings that was simultaneously a reproach and a tribute to Henry Lawson and his tale? And would she look at Drysdale's painting and see what I did?

I put away my album and tilted my head from side to side, stretching my neck in a way that felt both painful and exquisite. Late afternoon sunshine streamed through the car, warm and yielding like butter. These backroads were even bumpier than the highway and I stifled a yawn. Shadows danced across my vision. My eyelids grew heavy.

Despite the many articles I had gathered about Henry Lawson over the years, including the clipping with his one stray reference to his Aunt Gertrude, the one thing missing from my album was the proof I had been searching for all along: some kind of evidence to substantiate my original suspicion, then conviction, that my mother, who had lived and died as a drover's wife, was *the* drover's wife.

But, in truth, it no longer mattered to me as it once had. And after reading some of Lawson's mates' recollections, there was even some confusion in my mind as to whether his all-important trip to Bourke in 1892 had come before or after the story's publishing. Had he met Mother and the rest of my family during this – or some prior – journey? Or had he not? Had the entire heroic tragedy of 'The Drover's Wife' simply been a figment of his – and then my – imagination? Or had it started with some original grain of truth, that swelled and germinated under his watchful eye, just waiting to be passed on and gather meaning over time like any other myth?

'Not long to go now,' said Roy, coughing into his sleeve. 'Should be there in under an hour.'

My eyes blinked open with a start.

Flashes of sunlight bounced around the cabin, the Chevrolet's chrome trim now coruscating like crystals. Apart from a few short stops, including Roy's nap after lunch, we had been driving all day, from sunrise to sunset. We had travelled over highways and roads of every size and surface, and passed through countless towns, some of them so small there was nothing but a dilapidated main street and a post box to distinguish them from the surrounding paddocks.

The great Hawkesbury River of this morning and the knowledge of the nearby ocean were distant memories now, having long given way to the pleasant monotony of farm country, interspersed by great tracts of bush. After a while, it had blurred into one long sweep of brownish green.

It was peaceful out here. I could feel that for myself. But there was also a sense of being forgotten or left behind that seemed to cling to some of these places and which frightened me.

Yet as we got closer to our destination, I could see that Roy was right. This place was nothing like my childhood home. And farm life today was probably very different to the way it had once been. Driving past one seemingly endless paddock, I saw a young farmer on his tractor, faithfully going about his work. In place of the isolation and hopelessness I had expected, I perceived a sense of honest purpose, of respect for the land and what it could provide to those willing to work hard and who could withstand its capricious ways. Stray lines from Dorothea Mackellar's poem came to me. Here was the poet's hot gold hush of noon, here the sweeping plains, here too, as Roy had already warned me, would lie the inevitable challenge of droughts and flooding rains. *Core of my heart, my country!*

'Should be just up this way,' said Roy, suddenly veering left at the sight of a red tin letterbox. A long row of trees flanked one side of the property as a windbreak, both decorative and practical.

I got out of the car to open the gate. This simple gesture came to me automatically and I laughed to myself at this unexpected gift of memory. As we bumped along the narrow dirt road in first gear, watching out for the little stones and bits of gravel flicked up by our tyres, the sky began to glow with the setting sun, plunging the landscape into riotous colour and making everything new. Liquid layers of amber propelled the car forwards while the blood sang in my ears with the high-pitched whir of insects.

Just as the farmhouse came into view, perched at the top of a small ridge, the horizon itself seemed to burst into flames. *Like a picture*, I thought. Beside me, Roy gave a whistle of appreciation.

We wound down our windows and rolled slowly up the gravel drive. Margery walked towards us. Dressed simply in what must have been her housecoat or an apron, she was silhouetted against the sun. *Woman in a Landscape*, an artist might title such a painting. Suddenly, a little boy teetered out from the side of the house, followed by a man wearing boots and a hat, and carrying a baby in his arms. The screen door flapped shut behind them like a thunderclap, breaking the spell under which I had fallen.

When I looked again, Margery was no longer alone. No longer just a woman in the landscape. Instead, standing before me, gathered in a heartbreakingly familiar arrangement of two plus two, was a different image. Here, now, in this one perfect moment, was something I had never dared hope to see again. A family.

Epilogue

We'll live for life and the best it brings till our twilight shadows fall;
My heart grows brave, and the world, my girl, is a good world after all.
Henry Lawson, 'After All' (1896)

I heard Cedric barking at the postman, right on cue, and went outside to collect the mail. In amongst the rest was a letter from Margery, addressed to us both, as they were these days. Smiling to myself, I tore open the envelope.

1 September 1954

Dear Mum and Dad,

First things first – I'm happy to report there's another grandchild on the way! A girl this time – or at least that's what I think, because it feels different to how it was with the boys. Colin thinks it's probably just because I'm that much older, although 27 is hardly ancient. I hope it is a girl, because I could certainly use another pair of hands around this place. And I'm outnumbered as it is! When you come up at the end of the month, could you please bring me some more of that soap I like and whatever else you can think of?

A new baby! My breath caught and I almost cried with delight. I hoped Margery was right and that it was a girl. I loved my two grandsons fiercely, but even now, at seven and eight years of age, they preferred following their father around the farm to spending time with Grandma Armstrong. A girl would be different. I hoped so anyway. Grinning happily to myself, I continued reading.

How are you feeling, Dad? I hope your chest isn't still playing up. You don't want to end up in hospital again like last year. On the other hand, it was the best excuse I've ever had for coming home for a visit. Although you really could have timed your hospital stay better so that your 'Princess Margery' could have called on her Majesty in February when she was in town – wink, wink.

Mum, thanks for sending those magazines and the newspaper clippings from the coronation tour. Didn't she look beautiful? All those ballgowns especially. And that Andamooka opal set they gave her in Adelaide – fit for a Queen! I'm still disappointed I didn't get to see her myself but that's life, as they say. Thanks for the 'wattle yellow' cotton piqué too, that'll make up nicely as a skirt, though it might have to wait until after the baby now.

Born less than a year before our daughter, and hence the excuse behind Roy's nickname, the lovely young woman we'd always thought of as 'Princess' Elizabeth was now our Queen. Her extended visit to Australia in February had been a triumph. Even I had succumbed to a dose of royal fever and had braved tumultuous crowds to watch Elizabeth and her dashing Prince Philip disembark from their royal barge. With even the train and bus timetables having been altered to give the couple right of way, it was no exaggeration to say the entire country had quite literally come to a standstill. During their eight-week royal tour, a staggering three out of four Australians were given the chance to set eyes on our young and beautiful sovereign. Sadly, Margery had not been one of them.

Poor Margie. All those dreams about being a costume designer, and now she had to content herself with the prospect of a pretty new skirt to wear to the next local dance. Still, if that was enough for her, then it was enough for me. In any case, it was no one's business but hers. I had finally learned my lesson, even if I did need the occasional reminding.

Over the past seven years, ever since our reunion, I'd had time to observe Margery with her husband. Although I found Colin to be decent and dependable, just as Roy had promised, I had the sense that Margery wasn't entirely satisfied with her marriage and that she was holding back from telling me something. Perhaps her reticence to make herself vulnerable was a trait she had inherited from me.

If I think of anything else I need before next month, I'll write again. Don't bother bringing any more books for the boys, they haven't read the last lot yet. If anything, you could bring them some of Henry's old tools – at least they'd be put to good use. They are looking forward to another singalong with you and Dad and some more of your campfire yarns, especially Jeffrey. Who would have thought you could switch from making up fairytales and princess stories for me as a little girl to swashbuckler adventure tales to excite my boys? We'll cook up some damper or johnnycakes and make a night of it.

Yours,

Margery

I smiled ruefully about the boys not having read the books I'd brought them. What had I just been telling myself about having learned my lesson? Perhaps I still had a little way to go. I also suspected Roy would not be quite ready to part with Henry's tools just yet.

Now sitting at my desk, I looked up as Roy came in from the garden, smelling faintly of fertiliser. I said nothing to spoil Margery's surprise, and let him read her letter over my shoulder.

'You little beauty,' he roared, pulling my off my chair and spinning me around.

'You never change, Roy Armstrong,' I laughed, growing giddier with each turn.

'Well, aren't you glad about that, Mrs Armstrong?' He set me down and kissed me.

'More than you'll ever know,' I whispered, pressing my cheek against his.

'Our Margie can be a bit sparing with her praise, I'll admit, so for her to comment on your storytelling, the boys must really have been happy with your last effort.'

'I know, I'm quite beside myself. And her describing them as campfire yarns made me think of Henry Lawson. When it comes to imagination, maybe I've finally found something he and I have in common.'

'Something other than a drover's wife, that is.'

I grinned.

While Roy disappeared to get changed out of his dirty gardening clothes, I took out my album. I wanted to bring it with me in a few weeks' time when we visited Margery at their new farm, the one they now owned themselves, along with a new mortgage. Margery's reaction to my album during our first visit to Moree in the spring of 1947 had been what could at best be described as lukewarm. She had been genuinely sympathetic to hear just how impoverished my family's living circumstances had been. She had even shed tears alongside me when I finally shared the tragic details of how they had all died and how lonely my life had been, both by necessity and choice, until I had met her father. Yet my connection to Lawson's story and Drysdale's painting had not touched my daughter in the way I had hoped. I still remembered her exact words that day. 'Look around you, Mum. There's not much time in my day for reading stories or staring at paintings. I'm glad they gave you comfort, you deserve that, but they'll never mean much to me.'

Although far from the reaction I was hoping for, I had eventually made my peace with Margery's point of view. Perhaps it was my fault for leaving it too late. Or perhaps it was her way of punishing me one last time, although I liked to think she would never do that deliberately.

Perhaps, in putting aside her own dreams, Margery had chosen to anchor herself to facts forevermore and to eschew fiction in all its disguises. Or perhaps, as Roy suggested, we were just different.

Nevertheless, I did want to show Margery the latest addition to my album. I was planning to sweeten the experience by combining it with news of my role as a volunteer with the Art Gallery's new membership society, assisting with film nights and other such events. I knew she'd be pleased that I was finally getting out of the house and showing community spirit, even if it wasn't the kind of community that would interest her, and even if I wasn't doing much more than putting out a few chairs and ticking names off a list.

I flicked through my album and stopped at the entry that marked a turning point in the life of *The Drover's Wife* painting and which always left a heavy feeling in my chest. It was a small notice in the paper in January 1953, reporting that the painting had recently been sold. Instead of going to a public collection, as I'd always imagined would happen, it had been sold to a private collector from Adelaide. According to the report, Mr Kym Bonython had procured *The Drover's Wife* directly from the artist, together with two other works.

Knowing that I'd missed my chance, once and for all, I tried telling myself I was not upset. Roy, who had seen my wounded expression, went to see Treania Smith. 'I was rather surprised that Tas parted with those pictures,' Treania had readily admitted to Roy, followed by a rueful giggle. 'He must have needed a little ready money for his recent home renovations.' But when Roy asked about the purchaser, she'd been coy. 'Interesting young man,' she ventured. 'Quite the colourful character.' According to her, Mr Bonython came from a prominent Adelaide family and had been recognised for his distinguished service in the RAAF during the war. 'He's absolutely mad about Jazz,' Treania had concluded. 'Maybe that's why he and Tas got along so well.'

But although *The Drover's Wife* was now in a private collection, its public life was thankfully far from over. Mr Bonython evidently recognised the value of his new painting and was committed to raising its worth even further by loaning it to numerous important exhibitions, where it could attract even wider acclaim.

This led me to the final pages in my scrapbook and which I particularly wanted to show Margery, even at the risk of another lukewarm reaction.

In July of the previous year, just six months after its acquisition, *The Drover's Wife* had been sent on its maiden voyage abroad. Travelling all the way to London to take part in the first official exhibition of contemporary Australian painting, its celebrity tour of Britain was kicked off with a month at Mayfair's New Burlington Galleries. Australian art, according to the newspaper, was finally 'come of age'.

At the joint request of the British Arts Council and the Australian Government, a total of twelve Australian artists were selected for these coronation displays. Not everyone was happy with the final selection. Ten of these artists were presently living in New South Wales, and only two were women. More traditional artists, and even modernists like Margaret Preston and Grace Cossington Smith, were overlooked in favour of younger, more radical painters. No Aboriginal artists were represented. But I was pleased that of the almost sixty works included in the exhibition, no less than ten were allocated to Russell Drysdale. Along with *Walls of China* and other important landscapes was *The Drover's Wife*, small but mighty. My heart swelled to think of how far from home *my* painting (as I would always think of it) had travelled. I tried to imagine what my mother might think of being seen in all these faraway places. And what British audiences would make of her.

After the touring exhibition came the greatest honour of all, with Drysdale's historic inclusion in the XXVII Art Biennale in Venice. This had been in June, just a few months ago, and marked Australia's first ever appearance at this prestigious international event. All the artists who had participated in the earlier coronation displays were supposed to have been hung in Venice as well. But in the end, there was only sufficient space for a mere three artists and sixteen pictures. *The Drover's Wife* was selected to be one of these.

Once again, *The Drover's Wife* had proven its worth. *Her* worth. It was almost enough to make me want to journey to Italy to witness this honour myself. For a few magical moments, I'd imagined Roy and myself in Venice, as if entering the scene of an Arthur Streeton or Canaletto painting – casually stepping into a gondola to experience the splendour of the Grand Canal or stumbling through the crisscross of smaller canals and ancient alleys to emerge onto Saint Mark's Square.

Despite indulging myself in such momentary fantasies, there had been no trip to Italy in June. Nor would there likely ever be. But as I stroked my finger over the cut-out newspaper image of *The Drover's Wife* there in Venice, I smiled softly and sat up taller in my seat.

'You've gone a long way, Mother,' I whispered to myself.

I thought back to the red dirt yard and that two-roomed house where my life began, forever immortalised in Lawson's story, and of my last image of my mother that morning of the fire, Baby Eadie on her hip. Just another woman in a landscape; gone, but not forgotten anymore.

'A very, very long way,' I added.

As I closed my album, I thought about Margery's new baby and the prospect of another grandchild, finally allowing myself to imagine a granddaughter. I could only hope. And this time, unlike with her mother or grandmother or great-grandmother, she could do or be whatever she wanted. No pre-determined narratives of any kind other than the ones of her creation. Which of us might she resemble, in looks or in temperament? What passions would be hers to discover and nurture? What castles in the air would she build, and then find a way to make real?

For my part, and provided I had Margery's blessing, I would start by reading to my granddaughter and talking to her about the importance of stories. Sharing the lessons that it had taken me a lifetime to learn, I would tell her that everyone has a right to tell a story, any story – that in the telling, or the retelling, the story becomes our own. But at the same time, I would remind her that stories are not possessions to hold onto, secrets to keep, knowledge to control, but something to be shared and celebrated – or, if a sad story, to be mourned together. And finally, the most important lesson of all, one that I was still learning for myself. I would tell her that if you don't like how a story ends – how *your* story ends – you can always start a new one.

Author's Note

If I have done my job well, I hope there will be a small part of you that's wondering how much of *The Story Thief* is true. Did Henry Lawson really meet Lillian's family during his 1892 travels to the 'back o'Bourke'? Could Lillian's mother genuinely have been the inspiration behind Lawson's celebrated story of 'The Drover's Wife'?

It was vitally important to me that everything about Lillian's story *could* have happened, hence why I deliberately anchored every aspect of the narrative in fact: in real places, real people and real events. Instead of fictional settings, I sent Lillian to be educated by the nuns at Sacred Heart, then to The Women's College at Sydney University, and finally to a teaching career at Ravenswood in Sydney's North Shore. I also placed Lillian in iconic locales such as the Queen Victoria Building, Taronga Zoo and Narrabeen Beach, not to mention Waverley Cemetery. History is with us today.

Amongst my cast of fictional characters, I sprinkled real-life individuals including Louisa Macdonald, Evelyn Dickinson, Eben Gowrie Waterhouse, Treania Smith and numerous other cameo appearances. Although, by necessity, I invented their dialogue, my research helped guide their characterisations. One notable exception was Mrs Spicer. As the supplier of Lillian's holiday reading material at Sacred Heart and her first source of information about Henry Lawson, she is entirely fictional, but Lawson fans may spot her name (and geranium-watering habits) as coming from another of his best-known characters.

Telling Lillian's story against the backdrop of real historical events proved the most challenging of all these constraints. I am unapologetically a reader and not a historian, nor even a Lawson academic. But in the course of writing this book, I unwittingly became a non-professional version of both of these, and – thanks to the remarkable online resource of Trove – read more newspapers than throughout the entire rest of my life. Between Federation, women's suffrage, two world wars, the Depression and the ongoing battle for recognition by Australia's First Peoples, there was a lot to learn. My – or rather Lillian's – interpretation of these events and social movements is by no means definitive.

The only facts which I knowingly (and somewhat reluctantly) altered 'for the sake of a good yarn' were the timing of Russell Drysdale's Macquarie Galleries exhibition resulting from his *Sydney Morning Herald* drought-reporting assignment (delayed from late 1945 to August 1946), the issuing of the first Henry Lawson postage stamp (brought forward from 1949 to 1946) and a couple of Lawson anecdotes from North Sydney shopkeepers (which did not surface until a few years later). I also suspect Mr Quong Tart's Tea Rooms had closed by 1908. For these changes and any inadvertent errors, I sincerely apologise.

Despite all this, *The Story Thief* is ultimately a work of imagination, which brings me back to my original question. You may be disappointed to learn that Henry Lawson's legendary journey to Bourke and Hungerford took place in the spring of 1892, some months *after* his story of 'The Drover's Wife' was first published in *The Bulletin* on 23 July 1892. Up until then, Lawson had not travelled any further north or west in the then colony of New South Wales than the gold-rush districts in which he was born and raised. Notwithstanding my conscious decision not to specify the exact whereabouts of Lillian's childhood home, this factual timeline suggests Lawson could *not* have observed young baby Lillian and her family *before* writing his sketch, regardless of Lillian's belief to the contrary.

In 1916, in an open letter to playwright Beaumont Smith, Lawson identified the real people behind some of his fictional characters, including his Aunt Gertrude, who he said was also 'the drover's wife'. Lillian, of course, rejects this explanation, and – to the best of my knowledge – this letter is the only time he ever drew this connection. An alternative source of inspiration (and one supported by Lawson's maternal aunts) is an article written by his mother, Louisa Lawson, 'The Australian Bush-Woman', first published in Boston in 1889, together with the stories and anecdotes she would have shared since his childhood, fuelled by the extended periods in which her own husband was away. If true, it could be argued that Henry Lawson really did take another woman's story and retell it as his own (admittedly rather well). Given the central importance of 'The Drover's Wife' to Lawson's literary reputation, and the myriad versions of this story that have followed in the past half-century, it's a fascinating idea – albeit one not new to Lawson academics. Either way, I do think Lawson must have seen himself in the character of Tommy, the 'dirty-legged' little boy who promises his mother he 'won't never go drovin; blarst me if I do!'

For those curious about Russell Drysdale's painting, *The drover's wife* c.1945, I encourage you to see this 'small but mighty' masterpiece for yourself at the National Gallery of Australia, where it has been hung since the gallery's opening in 1982, first as a loan and then gift from Mr and Mrs Benno Schmidt and the American Friends of the National Gallery.

Not surprisingly, many people assume that Drysdale's painting was inspired by Lawson's story. After all, they share the same name and apparent subject matter. Lou Klepac OAM, esteemed art historian and author of the definitive Drysdale monograph, assured me the artist denied this connection. Regardless, it gave me great pleasure to weave these twin works and both their talented creators throughout my narrative.

Lillian's reaction to *The drover's wife* painting gives a fair clue as to my own feelings about Russell Drysdale and his picture. My feelings about Henry Lawson are more nuanced. Like Lillian, who started out angry to see her two brothers (and even the dog) named in Lawson's story, while leaving unnamed all the girls and women of her family, I too have reached a hard-won truce with the writer and an admiration for the extraordinary body of work he produced – despite not all of it being palatable to a contemporary audience and despite his personal flaws. To quote Lawson's friend, Redgum (the penname of John Gilmour Lockley) in *The Sun*, 8 September 1922: 'Henry Lawson had a habit of stumbling. But that is not your affair or mine. Many of us stumble, and do nothing before or after the fall. Henry Lawson dug in hard between times. The result of his digging is with us in black and white.'

With respect to my own research sources, and in keeping with my conviction that the greatest 'truths' can be found in fiction, I began my task by immersing myself in Australian novels written in the periods about which I was writing, or as soon as possible afterwards. This led me to classic Australian authors such as Barbara Baynton, Miles Franklin, Ethel Turner, Henry Handel Richardson, Amy Witting, Katharine Susannah Prichard, George Johnston, Sumner Locke Elliott, Eleanor Dark, Dymphna Cusack, Florence James, Olga Masters, Ruth Park and T.A.G. Hungerford. Supplementing their stories were memoirs and biographies, including works by Albert Facey, Stella Bowen, Robin Dalton, Gwen Kelly, Jill Ker Conway, Anne Summers, Meg Stewart and Drusilla Modjeska.

Also underpinning my novel is a good deal of scholarly writing. In addition to the Lawson sources which Lillian mentions in her album, I was guided by many books, essays and articles including those by John Barnes, Alan Barton, Robyn Burrows, Gregory Bryan, John Kinsella,

Olive Lawson, Christopher Lee, Brian Matthews, Frank Moorhouse, Kay Schaffer and Grantlee Kieza, in addition to *The Henry Lawson Complete Works* (1984), introduced by Brian Kiernan and compiled and edited by Leonard Cronin. In writing about Henry Lawson's deafness, I drew upon articles by Curtis Robbins and Michael Uniacke.

As a devoted art lover and collector, I primarily used my own amateur response to *The drover's wife* painting to inform Lillian's perceptions of Russell Drysdale's work. I am however indebted to a host of valuable books, articles and interviews by Christopher Allen, Kym Bonython, Jean Campbell, Geoffrey Dutton, James Gleeson, Paul Haefliger, Janet Hawley, Lou Klepac, Geoffrey Smith and others. Full details are listed on my website, along with my general non-fiction historical sources, which are too many to be included here.

Finally, I wish to pay tribute to the countless short stories, books, films, songs and other artistic adaptations inspired by 'The Drover's Wife' which comprise the rich tradition of *drover's wives* that I am now honoured to join.

To learn more about the background inspiration and history behind *The Story Thief*, including the chance to read Henry Lawson's original 1892 story of 'The Drover's Wife', I warmly invite you to visit my website, kyrageddes.com.

The People and Places of *The Story Thief*

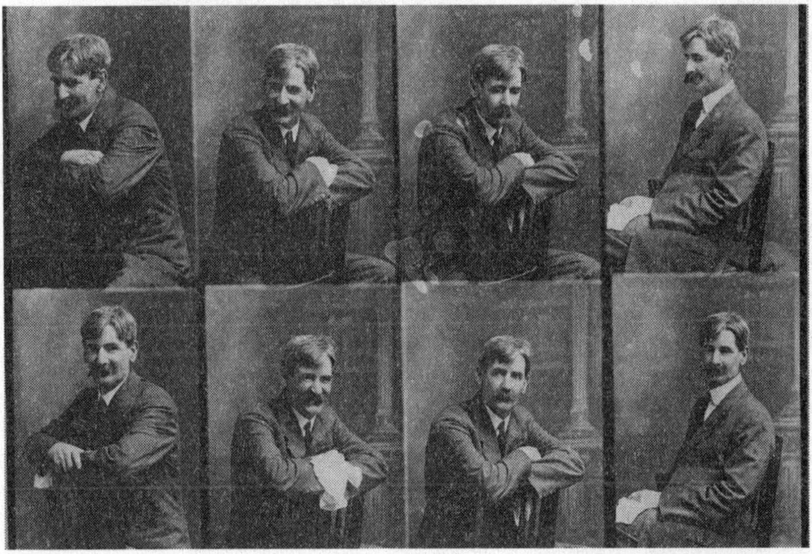

Above: The many moods of Henry Lawson (1867–1922) are captured here – along with his famous moustache and dark, soulful eyes – by William Johnson in 1915 using a 'multiplying camera'.

Right: Henry's mother, Louisa (Albury) Lawson (1848–1920), was known as the 'Mother of Suffrage' in NSW, in recognition of her role in helping secure the right for women to vote. Her ground-breaking magazine, *The Dawn* (1888–1905), was written by women for women. As the hardest businessperson he ever met, Henry called her 'the Chieftain'.

Right: Henry was honoured with his first postage stamp in 1949. Pleasingly, Louisa received the same honour in 1975 during the International Year of Women. (Image credit: Australia Post)

Above: Photographed by *Aussie* editor Phillip Harris in August 1922, just three weeks before his death, Henry Lawson sits in front of his former North Sydney lodging.

Left: Henry Lawson was the first non-official person to be granted a New South Wales state funeral, which took place on September 4th 1922 at Waverley Cemetery. Lillian attends this funeral and meets someone who helps her to take her own story into an exciting new direction. (Photograph taken by Charles W. Lawson, Henry Lawson's older brother.)

Left: Henry Lawson's original story of 'The Drover's Wife' was first published on 23 July 1892 in *The Bulletin*. Lillian first encounters the story at age sixteen and steals the little green and gilt volume of *While the Billy Boils* from her teacher's desk. (Author's own photograph.)

Above: Lillian attends the convent boarding school of Sacred Heart from 1900–1909. Shown here is the school building, as seen from New South Head Road in 1888, and the interior of the chapel, designed by John Horbury Hunt, featuring the five stained glass windows which cast the rainbow at Lillian's feet in Chapter 1. (Images used with permission of the Archives of Kincoppal – Rose Bay School of the Sacred Heart.)

Left: Lillian experiences her first taste of the outside world at age sixteen, in 1908, when she accompanies Hilda and her mother to Mr Quong Tart's Tea Rooms in Sydney's iconic Queen Victoria Building. George Street bustles with the thrum of pedestrians, horse drawn carts and trams. (Image captured 1917, courtesy of City of Sydney Archives.)

Left: After leaving Sacred Heart, Lillian enters the progressive environment of The Women's College at Sydney University in 1910, where she completes her Bachelor of Arts. Avoiding romance at all costs, Lillian draws inspiration from real-life historical figures, Principal Louisa Macdonald and Miss Evelyn Dickinson. (Image courtesy of The Women's College Archives.)

Right: In 1913, aged twenty-one, Lillian is one of the dancing maidens (albeit hidden behind a column!) in a classical mask performance to celebrate the college's coming of age, an anniversary in which she shares. (Image courtesy of The Women's College Archives.)

An Artist's Journey Into Australia's "Lost World"

WESTERN INFERNO

The country in which there are no Bushfires. There is nothing to burn

Worst Drought in Australia's History

Left and below: In late 1944, Russell Drysdale was sent by *The Sydney Morning Herald* on an assignment into the state's drought-afflicted interior. The resulting three-part report included the sketch below of *A drovers' camp near Deniliquin*, which became the study for Drysdale's masterpiece painting of *The drover's wife* c.1945. It remains one of the most-loved works in the collection of the National Gallery of Australia. (Image used with permission from the Estate of Russell Drysdale.)

A drovers' camp near Deniliquin.

All images courtesy of the State Library of New South Wales unless otherwise specified.

Acknowledgements

In writing a novel inspired by Henry Lawson, as one of Australia's greatest storytellers, I would like to begin by paying my respects to this country's first storytellers, including the Darramuragal or Darug people on whose traditional lands this book was written. Equally, in acknowledging the sublime artistic talents of Russell Drysdale in capturing the landscapes and people of outback Australia, I would add my sincere acknowledgement towards our earliest artists.

I am grateful for the generous assistance I received from numerous archivists, individuals and subject specialists, including: Tracy Bradford, School Archivist, Kincoppal – Rose Bay School of the Sacred Heart; Dr Olivia Murphy, Vice Principal, and Kylee Nicholls, Archivist, The Women's College within The University of Sydney; descendants of the extraordinarily talented Professor EG Waterhouse, particularly Michael Waterhouse and Jill Waterhouse, who is also a historian; Bridget Cohen, Lead Archivist and editor of 'The Sydneian', Sydney Grammar School; Leigh Hay, editor of 'The Lawsonian', the newsletter of the Henry Lawson Memorial and Literary Society Inc., which celebrated its centenary in 2023; Nicole Alexander, best-selling historical fiction author, who ensured I had properly interpreted the prevailing weather conditions and other aspects pertaining to Moree; Wendy Sharpe AM, one of Australia's most acclaimed artists, who tirelessly gives back to her community and who cast her expert eye over the chapter set in Roy's lithography studio; Alan R Dodge AM, former Director of the Art Gallery of Western Australia, who was a young curator at the fledgling Australian National Gallery when *The drover's wife* first came into its possession, and who has provided generous professional and personal encouragement; Dr Christopher Allen, art critic and historian, who, along with Alan Dodge, kindly reviewed my chapters in which Lillian engages with Drysdale's work; and Lynne Clarke, daughter of Russell Drysdale, who was a young girl at the time *The drover's wife* was painted, and who made me immeasurably happy by saying that *The Story Thief* excerpts she read, including my description of Macquarie Galleries, left her feeling quite nostalgic.

I also thank Mrs Clarke for granting permission, on behalf of the Estate of Russell Drysdale, to reproduce the image of *The drover's wife* c.1945 in the inside cover design of this book, as well as the 1944 sketch, *A drovers' camp near Deniliquin.* For permission to quote from 'The Drover's Wife' (1980) by Barbara Jefferis (my favourite retelling), I sincerely thank her grandson, Michael Little. The extract from 'My Country' was kindly provided by arrangement with the Licensor, The Estate of Dorothea Mackellar, care of Curtis Brown (Aust) Pty Ltd.

I warmly thank Dr Michelle Hamadache, my then tutor and now Director of Creative Writing at Macquarie University, for first introducing me to 'The Drover's Wife' back in 2014, and to Associate Professor Jane Messer for designing that ENGL304 course. Who would have guessed it would lead to this?

I am grateful to my early readers who variously and bravely endured excerpts and complete drafts of my original manuscript, including: Alison, Brie, Elina, Gabbie, Jilly, Margaret, Shelley and Toni. Special mention goes to my most devoted reader, Andrea Blake, a gifted teacher and writer herself, and to my friend Liane Moriarty, who provided input to an early draft as well as sage counsel throughout my writing journey (even if her own success does set the bar ridiculously high!). I'm also grateful to Laurel Cohn and Philippa Donovan for their thoughtful manuscript assessments, and to the Australian Society of Authors for the opportunity to pitch my novel to my ideal publisher, Affirm Press. The email I received from Affirm's CEO, Martin Hughes, after reading my first fifty pages will undoubtedly endure as one of the top five moments of my life.

Although I maintain that Henry Lawson owed his mother a greater debt of gratitude than that which he acknowledged, thankfully he did appear more aware of his good fortune in his chief editor, JF Archibald, of whom he said, 'I don't believe he could touch a line of prose without improving it'. In this spirit, I would like to sincerely thank my brilliant editors – Kelly Doust (also my publisher extraordinaire), Laura Franks and Anna Thwaites – along with the rest of Affirm's stellar team. I am both proud of and grateful for the book you have helped me write.

Finally, I would like to thank my friends and family for their unerring support and faith in me, despite the many years it has taken to reach this point. To my father, Karl Schnell, by your example, you have taught me how to live a good life; I also thank you for making an exception to your otherwise exclusively non-fiction reading list! To my brother, Marcus, I hope you noticed all the flora and fauna mentions scattered throughout. To my daughter, Lauren, know that your own creative well runs far deeper than mine and that your daily presence helps me miss your *Oma* just that little bit less. To my son, Justin, your insight, sensitivity and humour have brightened our lives since the day you were born. And to my darling husband, Rohan, your love sustains me; together, we walk through life.

Book Club Questions

1. Henry Lawson's story of 'The Drover's Wife' has inspired a rich tradition of drover's wives retellings by other authors and creatives. Why do you think this is?
2. Aside from 'The Drover's Wife', the novel also mentions classic Australian literature from Miles Franklin, Henry Handel Richardson and others. Has *The Story Thief* inspired any interest for you to re/discover these works or do you prefer to read and encourage new Australian authors?
3. What emotions did Lillian experience upon seeing Russell Drysdale's painting of *The drover's wife* and why was she affected in this way? How does that reaction differ from her response to first reading Lawson's story?
4. Were there any particular passages or quotes that stood out to you? Why?
5. Lillian starts out by accusing Henry Lawson of being a story thief, but eventually comes to a different view. What is your opinion on story 'ownership'? Does anyone have the right to tell any story?
6. *The Story Thief* deliberately plays with notions of 'truth versus fiction' by weaving Lillian's fictional story into a factual historical setting, including real people, places and events. What did you enjoy about this aspect of the novel?
7. How did Lillian's childhood traumas shape her choices and subsequent path as an adult? For example, why do you think Lillian reacts so strongly to the prospect of her son choosing to enlist, or to her daughter's departure?
8. There are many types of love: familial, maternal, romantic and platonic, to name a few. Which types of love come more easily to Lillian and why are others so difficult for her?
9. What does the novel have to say about women's changing place in Australian society? Is *The Story Thief* a tribute to Lawson's original story or a feminist rebuttal?
10. We get to experience several pivotal events in Australian history through Lillian's eyes, such as female suffrage and the Great War. Did you learn anything new about them?